To An
B

CW01429817

The Kinnons of Candleriggs

Largs 2004

Jenny Telfer Chaplin

BeWrite Books, UK
www.bewrite.net

Published internationally by BeWrite Books, UK.
32 Bryn Road South, Wigan, Lancashire, WN4 8QR.

British Library Cataloguing in Publication Data. A catalogue record for this book is available from the British Library

ISBN 1-904492-64-9

Also available in eBook format from www.bewrite.net

Digitally produced by BeWrite Books

Cover image: Carole Spencer © 2004

To world-famous novelist Evelyn Hood for her ongoing friendship
and encouragement over the years.

Jenny Chaplin, well known to loyal readers worldwide for her books on Scottish social history and for her articles in the *Scots Magazine* and the *Scottish Banner*, presents her first novel.

Jenny, as a Fellow of the Society of Antiquarians of Scotland, is well qualified to write her historical novels after years of research into and writing about Scottish social history.

She now writes her novels in her centuries old cottage on the Island of Bute under the name Jenny Telfer Chaplin to differentiate between her fiction and non-fiction writing.

Also by Jenny Chaplin:
Non-fiction
From Scotland's Past
A Glasgow Hogmanay
The Puzzle of Parkinson's
One Editor's Life
Alone in a Garden (Poetry Collection)
Thoughts on Writing (Co-authors: Fay Goldie & V. Cuthbert)

Fiction
Tales of a Glasgow Childhood
Childhood Days in Glasgow
Happy Days in Rothesay
We Belonged to Glasgow (An anthology)

Acknowledgements:

Chief Librarian Eddie Monaghan and his staff for their patience, help, and expertise during my many years of research at the Rothesay Public Library on the Scottish Island of Bute.

The
Kinnons of Candleriggs

Part One – The Early Years

Chapter 1

Pearce decided he must talk to his father before Kate 'showed' and greatly daring, Kate had lingered in the hallway outside Pearce's father's study.

She missed Pearce's opening, but his father's bellow was loud and clear: "Damnation man, not again. This is too much. You've already run up gambling debts you can't pay and now you tell me you've got your sister's lady's maid with child. Are there any more?"

"Certainly not, father. What do you take me for?"

"A bloody stupid young fool who doesn't learn from his mistakes. That's what. You should have stayed in Canada out of sight."

After a short silence, Pearce said something Kate didn't catch.

"What's to do now?" Mr Kinnon shouted. "What's to do now? Pay the baggage off. I'll need to do that, I suppose, yet again. Then get her out of this house this very night."

Kate had jumped at a touch on her arm and turned to see Mistress Martha, her face red, staring at her.

Without knocking, Martha pushed Kate ahead of her into the study.

"Damnation, Martha, this is not woman's business."

"She is my maid, father. Of course, it's my business." Martha turned to Kate. "Is this true? Are you with child?"

Kate nodded, thinking she had an ally.

"You'll get no reference from me. The very idea, sneaking around seducing my brother. Father, pay her now. She can collect her things and go."

"I'll not have another life on my conscience," Pearce said quietly. His sister and father stared at him.

"It's a bit late for that," his father said.

"And how will you avoid that?" his sister sneered. "Marry her?"

Pearce stood silent for a moment frowning before he nodded. "Yes."

"Oh, sweet Jesus, Pearce, be sensible," his father said. "That's impossible. I won't have it."

Martha laughed. "I was joking, Pearce. There are no brothers to worry about this time, you know. You're quite safe."

His face scarlet, Pearce shouted, "I was never afraid of the brothers. It was the family that feared the scandal. I will marry Kate."

"Don't I get a say in this?" Kate said, and recoiled when all three shouted: "No."

"For God's sake, Pearce," his father said, "don't let your stubborn pride and pig-headedness back you into this stupidity."

Pearce glared at his father. "My mind's made up. I will marry Kate."

"You haven't asked me yet," Kate protested.

"You will marry me." It was a statement and not a question, but Kate nodded, then said: "Yes."

"You'll not get a penny piece of mine if you do. Neither of you."

Pearce swept Kate out of the room, told her to collect her possessions – such as they were – while he ordered the carriage to take them to the nearby town.

The marriage in the Registry Office in Belfast before they caught the ferry from Larne was not quite what Kate had envisaged, but they were married.

Chapter 2

Kate drew her woollen shawl tightly round her shoulders. She shivered as she watched the dark, forbidding banks of the River Clyde lined with docks and warehouses so different from the green fields of Ireland, drift past on their way to their destination, The Broomielaw. The passage across the Irish Sea from Larne had been anything but smooth. Kate felt she would have been queasy anyway, but the motion of the ship and the smell of unwashed clothes and bodies in steerage had made her morning sickness unbearable.

She looked up at the tall, handsome man beside her. My husband – she savoured the words – my husband.

In his fine woollen suit and Ulster cape he stood head and shoulders above the other men thronging the deck.

Kate's nose wrinkled at the stench from the river blending now with the offensive odour from the steerage passengers.

"Why are we going steerage?" she had asked Pearce, her husband of three days – her husband.

He had brushed the question aside in his cultured accent. "A temporary financial embarrassment, my dear. That's all. Nothing for you to worry about. We'll be back on our feet in no time."

Kate coughed and Pearce glanced down at her. "You are not going to be sick *again*, are you? We're almost there."

Shaking her head Kate said: "No … no, I'm fine." She hoped she would be, if they tied up soon.

The gangway secured, passengers streamed off, but Pearce waited till the rush abated before he turned to Kate. "Right, Kate, we'll go now. Pick up your bundles."

Pearce picked up his two bags and strode down the gangway with Kate stumbling after him clutching her two bundles to her chest.

"Why on earth don't you have proper bags?" Pearce said, but he didn't wait for an answer. "Wait here."

He marched over to a group of men lounging at the entrance to the quay. They watched his approach and Kate saw them eying him up and down obviously appraising his clothes and bearing. Short of them he stopped and snapped his fingers. The men got to their feet and one, touching his forelock, stepped forward.

"Kin we dae somethin fur ye, sur?"

Kate couldn't really understand the dialect but the gesture and the intonation were unmistakable – her husband was gentry.

Pearce said something to the man, indicating his bags.

"Come, Kate." He walked smartly off the dock.

The man picked up Pearce's bags, grinned at Kate, and Kate, with a sigh, heaved her bundles up again and trekked after them. They crossed several streets redolent with ammonia and recent droppings from the many horses. Finally, they stopped on a street with iron rails in the middle. The man put the bags down. Pearce handed him a coin. The man touched his forelock and left them.

Kate wasn't anxious to put her bundles down on the dirty street. She balanced them on Pearce's bags and waited.

"There will be a tram along shortly, Kate," Pearce said. "Until I get established again we have to watch our pennies."

"A tram?" Kate questioned.

"Yes, a tram. A public conveyance that travels on those iron rails drawn by two horses. God, do you know nothing?"

Kate made no reply, waiting in silence as she often had in the past as a lady's maid when the mistress was out of sorts.

Eventually a tram arrived and Kate clambered aboard with her bundles, following Pearce. After what seemed a long journey, Pearce got to his feet.

"We get off here."

On the street as the tram pulled away, Kate looked round and was not impressed, but Pearce turned to her.

"There, across the Glasgow Green. My aunt has her town house there. It's a little early for her to be up and about, but my cousin Calum may be in town. Come, Kate."

The houses across the Green were grand, Kate thought, even grander than Laggan House in Ireland. Could she ever be the lady of such a house?

Pearce walked boldly up to the front door of one of these mansions and pounded the door soundly with the brass knocker.

The pert young housemaid who answered, bobbed a quick courtesy to Pearce: "Oh, Mr Kinnon. The mistress isn't about yet. Was she expecting you?"

"No … not this early. We'll wait."

"Oh, certainly, sir. Please come in. I'll have a fire set in the morning room."

She glanced at Kate as she followed on Pearce's heels into the morning room, but made no comment.

Almost at once a young girl, the tweenie, Kate thought, bustled in and, completely ignored by Pearce, laid and lit the fire.

Chapter 3

As Kate watched the girl at work she could see herself four years ago ...

A recent orphan, lucky to have been taken in by Laggan House she was told, Kate, the tweenie, did all the work that was beneath the dignity of even the lowest housemaid.

Fires had to be cleaned, laid and set, and scuttles replenished before the gentry stirred; water heated and jugs set out ready for the housemaids to carry upstairs; the gentry safely ensconced in the breakfast room, chamber pots to be removed, emptied, and cleaned; breakfast dishes to wash; vegetables to prepare; laundry to be sorted for the laundress. At everyone's beck and call but never to be seen or heard by the upstairs gentry and certainly never to be acknowledged by them if accidentally encountered.

Kate sighed. Had she only been the tweenie for a year? It had seemed an eternity of first up in the morning and last to bed at night with never a moment's rest in between.

The mistress had been outraged that the tweenie would dare touch a book in the library then reluctantly intrigued that a tweenie could actually read or even want to read. When she heard Kate speak, she was even more surprised. The local accent for sure, but more refined and educated than most locals and certainly well beyond what the mistress expected of one of the lower house servants. The refined accent that had caused so much grief for Kate from the other servants as a tweenie was her salvation. The lordly butler himself saw her trained through upstairs maid to parlour-maid where she was actually seen and occasionally even acknowledged by the gentry.

When the lady's maid to the unmarried daughter of the house took ill Kate was unexpectedly elevated to the dizzy heights of lady's maid.

"I really don't know what those duties are," she stammered.

"Nonsense, girl, just do what I tell you and you'll be fine. If I'm not pleased you'll hear all about it," was the reply.

And Kate had heard about it. She'd endured scoldings, deserved and undeserved, but she'd survived. Mistress Martha like her mother was obviously intrigued by Kate's background. Unlike her mother, however, she pursued her interest and in long sessions of Kate brushing her mistress's hair she heard of Kate's mother's death in childbirth when Kate was twelve and of the death of her father, a weaver and lay Baptist preacher when Kate was fourteen.

"Oh, that's why you don't go to Mass with the others," she said, and with that Mistress Martha dropped the subject, her curiosity satisfied.

In the early spring of 1877, Kate had heard from her mistress that her older brother, Pearce, was to return to Ireland and Laggan House. The other servants, when the housekeeper and butler were out of earshot, eagerly filled in the details.

Pearce had been dispatched to the Colonies some six or seven years before in disgrace. Gambling debts he couldn't meet, some said, but others hinted a darker secrets ... a maid seduced and great with child drowning herself in the river and her brothers vowing vengeance.

Kate had laughed. If the latter story was true, why was he returning?

"The girl's brothers sailed to America last autumn," the upstairs maid whispered.

Pearce had arrived, a splendid figure of a man. He had scandalised the housekeeper and cook to their audible disapproval in the servants hall by lounging in his sister's room while Kate brushed Mistress Martha's hair.

"These manners might be all very well in the colonies," they agreed, "but here in Ireland ...?"

At first, Kate was disconcerted by Pearce's stare, but became used to it.

One afternoon off, she met him on the street of the small town near to Laggan House. He doffed his hat to her, just as if she were a lady, and invited her to have afternoon tea with him in the one small teashop the town main street boasted. Embarrassed, she stammered out a refusal, then flattered by his insistence she agreed. In the course of their conversation, she told him that in her limited free time she retreated to a secluded gazebo to read.

Much to her surprise, he began to meet her there and soon they became lovers. In the house, he was cool, formal, and polite, but in their arbour, he was ardent.

When she told him she was pregnant, he was stunned, then furious. Kate could still see his face when she had shouted back: "I didn't do it by myself, did I?"

At his question of which of the menservants was the happy father she slapped his face and would have fled had he not caught and held her. They ended by making love and Pearce saying that all would work out and he would take care of everything.

Chapter 4

Kate's reverie was interrupted by a man about Pearce's age bursting into the morning room.

"Pearce, you dog. How romantic, eloping with your bride. I'd never have expected it of you."

He and Pearce embraced.

"We got your telegram yesterday. My mother has been planning events and calls for you non-stop ever since. But why so early? We thought you'd leave your card at a more civilised hour. Your aunt won't be presentable for at least another hour … if then. Which hotel are you staying at?"

He stopped for breath and Pearce finally managed to speak.

"There is a slight problem, Calum. Purely a temporary financial embarrassment." Pearce coughed. "I wondered if we could stay here."

"Oh, I see. Yes, I suppose that would be possible." He glanced at Kate. "Your lady's maid would need to share a room with one of our servants. Oh dear. Your lady hasn't been waiting outside in a cab all this time?"

Pearce coughed again. "Calum, this *is* my wife. Kate, this is my cousin Calum with whom I shared many boyish adventures."

Calum flushed and made a sort of half bow to Kate. "Charmed, I'm sure." Without waiting for any response from Kate, he rushed on: "Pearce, this is not quite what Mama envisaged."

His face cleared. "I see now. This is one of your jokes, that's it. Come now, this would not do for Mama. She would not see the humour of it. Come, let's collect your bride before Mama appears."

"Calum, this *is* my wife." The flat tone admitted no argument.

"Oh ..." for once, Calum was speechless.

Kate said: "I'm very pleased to meet you, Calum."

Calum visibly winced at her accent.

"Oh, dear. Oh dear. No, Mama will not be pleased."

"And what's wrong with my speech? If I may ask?" Kate said.

"Be quiet, Kate," Pearce said. "Calum meant no offence."

"I will not be quiet. It's not bog Irish. My father was a lay preacher."

"Oh dear. No, Mama will not be pleased. Not at all. She isn't even Anglican, Pearce?"

"I'm right here. Ask me. No, I'm not Anglican or Catholic. I'm Baptist."

"Good Lord, Pearce. Perhaps I'd better go and prepare Mama. I don't know what she'll say."

Calum bustled out of the room closing the door behind him.

"This is not going as I had hoped." Pearce frowned. "This is not the Calum I grew up with. He has changed much in six years."

"Or you have, Pearce, working for a living in Canada."

"Nonsense, Kate, I am the man I always was. When my aunt comes down leave everything to me. I'll speak for us."

Kate's reply was lost as the door opened and an elderly lady erupted into the room.

"What's all this nonsense Calum is jabbering about? You've run off with some kitchen maid? I won't have it. I tell you, I won't have it."

"I'm not a kitchen maid."

"I didn't ask you to speak, girl."

"I'll speak when I want to."

The aunt looked open mouthed at Kate. Pearce snorted, threw his hands in the air, and turned his back.

"My father was a lay Baptist preacher."

The aunt gazed wide-eyed at Kate, her lips clamped shut in a thin line.

"I was good enough for Pearce to bed and get with child and marry two days since."

"Well." The aunt glared at Pearce. "What minister did you convince to marry you to this baggage?"

"No priest or minister, lady. We spoke our vows at the Registry Office in Belfast."

"Pearce, I am grievously disappointed in you. That you should descend to this. Take that heretic hussy out of my house at once. At once, do you hear?" The aunt turned and stormed out of the room, slamming the door behind her.

"Phew." Calum sighed. "I knew Mama would not like it. I said so didn't I?"

"Come, Kate. I'll not stay where I'm not welcome." Pearce picked up his bags then hesitated. "I don't suppose, Calum, you could see your way to float me a small loan? Purely temporary, I assure you. Just till I'm settled here and made my arrangements from Ireland."

Calum opened his purse and peered into it. "Four guineas, Pearce. Would that help?"

'*Four guineas.*' Kate thought, '*More money than I've ever seen in one sum before; more than half cook's yearly pay at Laggan House. We're rich.*'

"Thanks, Calum. I'll get this back to you soon."

Without summoning the maid or the butler, Calum saw them to the door himself.

Standing on the step, again clutching her bundles, Kate heard the final clunk of the door closing behind them.

"Come, Kate. We'll get a tram and find a rooming house for a day or so."

Chapter 5

This time it was a relatively short ride to what Pearce told her was the centre of town. There he placed his two bags close to a shop window.

"Kate, set your bundle beside my luggage and sit there with them while I find a policeman."

"A policeman? What do we need a policeman for?"

"He'll know where there might be a convenient rooming house."

Pearce strode off leaving Kate to sit looking glumly around her. To her horror, she hadn't been waiting long before a policeman appeared.

"What are you doing here, lass? No loitering. Pick up your bundles and move on."

"I'm waiting for my husband."

"Oh, Irish are you? Why don't you people stay where you belong and not come here to beg? Now, move on."

Kate was about to argue, but Pearce came round the corner striding confidently towards them.

"Is there some problem, officer?"

His cultured accent and appearance obviously impressed the constable who touched the fingers of his right hand to his helmet.

"No, sir, no trouble at all. I'm just telling this person to move along."

"That person is my wife. She is waiting for me."

"Oh." The constable looked from Pearce to Kate and back again. From his expression, his opinion of Pearce fell considerably.

"Now, my man," Pearce ignored the officer's frown, "can you

direct us to a decent rooming house?"

"None that will welcome Irish such as her. But you might find a place the other side of the Tron in the east end of my beat. A woman there has taken over some single-ends in her tenement by paying the rents of those that couldn't pay then evicting them."

He gave Pearce directions and stood watching as they picked up their belongs and started off.

At the address, Pearce asked an urchin playing in the street for Mrs Ross. She answered their knock on the door and seeing Pearce first, she smiled ingratiatingly, wiped her hands on her filthy, sack-cloth apron, and said in a broad Glasgow accent: "Whit kin Ah dae fur ye, sur?"

Kate pushed forward. "We need a place to stay."

Mrs Ross glared, then the opportunity for profit reasserted itself.

"Ah dae hae a grand wee single-end, fine an cosy, fully furnished an only hauf-a-croon a week. Ye'll no find awthing better than that. There's many a homeless body in the streets that would kill for such a place."

Pearce wrinkled his nose at the woman's sour body odour and rank breath, but Kate said: "We should at least take a look."

In their walk, she had seen many tramps wandering aimlessly.

They surveyed the single-end: A cell-like room with a tiny curtained scullery to one side with a dripping goose neck tap on a black iron sink; above the sink a barred, curtain-less, dirty window; on the other side of the room a wall recess held a double bed covered with a filthy looking cover of little crocheted squares, doubtless someone's pride at one time, but now little more than a moth eaten rag; a damp, dank smell pervaded the air and wallpaper peeled in patches.

Kate glanced at Pearce. His face was a picture of arrogant disgust. Before he could speak, she tugged his sleeve and whispered: "Let's take it, dear. It's some place to sleep for now. I'm completely done in."

Their prospective landlady scowled.

"There's many in Glasgow won't let ony Irish within spittin

distance o their homes. Turn away from this and ye'll see naethin but 'No Irish Need Apply' signs."

Pearce grudgingly agreed, paid the landlady her half-crown in advance, and sat in the only chair, staring around.

Kate was only too well aware that Pearce had never lived in such squalor, with a communal lavatory on the stair-head, and surrounded by poverty stricken neighbours.

Kate soon got to know her immediate neighbours, but disclosed nothing of her circumstances beyond the fact that she and Pearce had emigrated from Ireland to Glasgow in search of work.

Naturally the neighbours were consumed by curiosity about the oddly assorted pair: Kate practical and obviously not gentry; Pearce, who even in his oldest clothes stood out like a sore thumb, a gentleman born, with the assurance and arrogance of a man of substance.

The single-end yielded to Kate's scouring with lye and carbolic. The table, scraped clean and scrubbed, showed a white pine surface; curtains purchased at the Barrows graced the now-clean window; the ragged bedcover thrown out and replaced by sheets and blankets again bargained for by Kate at the Barrows.

Once a week Kate trundled her washing in a borrowed pram to the local steamie.

Chapter 6

Pearce searched for work. Up at dawn, dressed in moleskin trousers, old tweed jacket, long white scarf, and with a flat bunnet jammed on top of his mop of curly, dark hair, he trudged off to scour the East End and the City Centre for work – any sort of work.

Soon, from bitter experience, he learned which firms to avoid – firms where 'No Irish Need Apply' was posted and reinforced verbally. At the beginning he did get some jobs in construction, but it was soon all too clear that not only was he unused to such labour, it was quite beyond his capabilities. Also, although he was a 'Paddy', he was no Irish navvy. His supercilious manner alienated employers and fellow employees alike.

One morning, deep in despair, he set out yet again from the shelter of the close leaving behind him even at this early hour the sounds, sights, and smells of the tenement ... A baby's screaming; the clatter of dishes; the yells of a couple already at each other's throats in the confined cell of their home; the rustle of rats from the odorous back court middens; and over all the gushing of water from the stinking, communal water-closets on each stair-head.

The small hoard of sovereigns had dwindled and all they had left was two of the four Calum had given them. He just had to find work. Kate was due almost any day and there were sure to be added expenses over that.

He stood lost in thought, oblivious of his surroundings, when he heard a voice.

"For the last time, man, are you looking for work or not?"

Pearce shook himself. "That I am indeed."

The man looked him up and down.

"By the looks of you, you're no labouring man. Can you read and figure?"

"Certainly, I can."

"Right, one of my tally men got himself a skinful last night and fell and broke his leg. I need a checker. Let's see how you do."

The man turned and strode off into the dark interior of the Candlerigg's Fruit Market with Pearce hastening after him.

Chapter 7

In the three short months in which they'd been staying in the mean street of squalid houses, Kate's neighbours had already proved their worth. All of them, like herself of Irish extraction, were good to her. Already, she knew all too well it did not do to stray far beyond the confines of her own immediate neighbourhood, for there was much anti-Irish feeling abroad; Irish were not welcome for housing, employment, or even for a place in a lowly soup kitchen. Kate was fully aware in her own street, and indeed, throughout Scotland, there were strictly defined barriers, not only of class, culture, and religion, but also perhaps even more strongly on racial lines.

It had not taken the inquisitive, yet well-meaning, neighbours too long to work out that Kate, although not an attendee at Mass, was still a good living Irish woman. That being so, even despite the mystery of her man who attended the Episcopalian, or Anglican High Church, she was soon surrounded with friendship, kindliness, and endless cups of tea and sympathy. True, there was little enough to spare in the way of food in the other single-end homes, but even so, her new-found friends loved to be able to give Kate what little extra food they could afford.

Each time Mother Murphy did a morning's baking for her own large brood, of steps and stairs bairns, there was always an extra steaming-hot pancake, or soda-bread scone wrapped up in a dish-cloth and sent over to Kate.

Big Betty Donovan took one sympathetic glance at the peaky-looking, undernourished young mother-to-be and said in her forthright manner, and her broad Glasgow accent: "Weel noo, ma lassie, apart frae that bloody big bulge ye've got ther, yer needing for tae be fatted up a bit – wi' sweet bites, dainty tit-bits and such like. And Ah'm tellin' ye this, hen, Ah'm the very one that's goin' tae tak ye in haun' and see tae it."

True to her word, Big Betty would bring in a dish of hot ham and lentil soup or a cup of Scotch broth, or even as on one memorable occasion, a rich creamy egg custard to tempt Kate's appetite.

As she thought of the many kindnesses she had received Kate hummed softly to herself as she worked about her tiny and already spotless home. Cold as the morning was, she nevertheless refrained from yet lighting the fire after she had set it with twists of newspaper and odd bits of coal. What little coal there was left in the hod, she would keep for tonight when Pearce would return, no doubt yet again, cold, hungry, still jobless and low in mind, body, and spirit.

She had just finished sweeping round the hearth and was on the point of lumbering to her feet when she felt the first stab of pain. Strangely enough, the pain was not in her swollen belly as she might reasonably have expected it to be. No, the debilitating pain was low down on her spine. She cried out involuntarily at the same time placing a hand on the painful spot. Then, after having eased herself gently into their one and only horsehair armchair, she placed a cushion at her aching back for extra comfort. No sooner had she done this and finding no instant relief, she decided in her wisdom what was really needed was the stone jar filled with hot water. It was when she rose, or rather tried to rise from the chair, that the excruciating pain shot right through her entire body. With a gasp, she again sank back against the cushion, at the same time wiping the beads of perspiration from her brow with a now-trembling hand.

She thought: '*It can't possibly be the baby. Not yet, another two weeks at least, that's what they'd said at the Panel Clinic on my last visit wasn't it? Anyway, surely if the baby had really started then obviously the pains would be in my stomach. Uninformed I might be, but even I know that, it stood to reason, didn't it?*'

Having convinced herself of her own logic she nodded and again determined to stand up, this time to put the kettle on the hob for a much-needed cup of tea as well as to fill the earthenware stone pig water bottle. If anything, the pain was even worse than before and Kate almost fainted as the waves of pain, fear, and nausea washed over her. It was then it finally dawned on her she would have to seek help of some kind – and be pretty damned quick about it too.

Somehow, she managed to crawl from the chair, pick up the long-handled poker, and then by holding on to the side of the table she eventually reached the side of the bed. Once safely there she stretched across and with as much force as she could manage in her present state she beat a tattoo on the thin dividing wall between her own single-end home and that of Hannah Mary Malone. Still poised uncomfortably against the bed, she listened intently, but as yet could hear no answering tattoo. Drawing the last of her strength to her aid, she banged again on the thin partition wall, but this time even louder and more desperately than before. Then instead of stopping to listen, she banged and banged and went on beating a desperate summons for help. Her last vestige of strength gone, she collapsed on top of the bed, a weeping, pitiful bundle of abandoned humanity. She longed to run away and hide, but not only was flight impossible in her present state, the harsh fact remained, and this kept hammering at her exhausted, befuddled brain, she had nowhere else in the wide world to go. There she was and there she would stay until either a passing neighbour – or perhaps even Pearce – heard her cries of distress, or, and here she shuddered at the awful thought, until she died. Just as this thought crossed her mind, she was aware of the sound of the door opening. This at once gave her hope, for in this neighbourhood nobody ever locked their doors and so neighbours, family, and friends were free to come and go exactly as and when they pleased. So the releasing of the door sneck could mean one thing: help in the shape of a kent face and sympathetic neighbour was now at hand.

Chapter 8

By the time Pearce returned home late that evening from his newly-acquired job, his suffering and exhausted young wife had already been in the agonies of labour for close on twelve hours. As yet, nothing much of any importance had happened. She was being attended by a well-meaning woman, Martha Shaw, who was by way of being the local amateur midwife. This worthy was doing her feeble, but totally ineffective, best to help poor Kate in her long hours of travail. She did this by mopping at the young woman's forehead with a vinegar rag from time to time, while quoting what she in her wisdom thought appropriate: namely long passages from the Guid Book. In addition to being versed in such Bible-thumping, she was also well-versed in such trite sayings as: 'Oh. Sleep, oh gentle sleep. Nature's soft nurse,' and 'Take Time while Time is, for Time will away.' As if this were not enough and about as much good to poor Kate as a silken tea-gown, the stupid woman, throughout her ministrations, Bible readings and brow-moppings used as a sort of Greek Chorus, the promise that all would be well, for it was well known, and in fact, promised by the Guid Lord himself that:

'Joy cometh in the morning. Halleluiah. Joy cometh in the morning.'

In the end, it wasn't Joy that came. It was further excruciating pain, followed at long last by the entry into the world of not one, but two screaming babies.

The arrival of twins was cause for even greater verse speaking by the now flushed-with-triumph Martha Shaw. As she washed each tiny bundle of humanity, she went into ecstasies of praise and thanksgiving to the Guid Lord, high above in his Heaven.

Throughout this seemingly never-ending night, Kate was not the only one to be suffering. Pearce had also endured the tortures of the damned as he listened to his wife's screams, knowing not only he was powerless to help her in any way, but it was all his fault in the first place that she should now be suffering. Through that weary night, he not only battled with his conscience, but also sank ever deeper into a dark pit of self-loathing and guilt.

Yet, when at last the ordeal was over and he looked down at the two babies laid side by side in the large wooden drawer, he felt a wonderful, almost holy upsurge of his spirits.

Perhaps it had all been worth while after all and not just a dreadful mistake? As he gazed in wonder at the two tiny forms, which the midwife had assured him were perfect in every detail with the requisite number of pink fingers and toes, he, there and then, decided in his own mind which child was to be his own particular favourite.

'*Such a bonnie wee lass she is,*' he thought, '*already with a cap of fine golden hair like spun sunbeams, a rosebud mouth, and a good lusty pair of lungs.*'

Despite the midwife's assurance, his own impression was the little boy was not nearly as robust as his sister. With his drawn face and mewling cry, he resembled nothing so much as a wizened old man, who was not only not long for this world, but who was already weary of the struggle for life.

Next day, Pearce, already the proud father, was on hand at the Registry Office the moment it opened for business and with great aplomb, swaggered in and registered the births of his son and daughter. Strangely enough, both he and Kate had liked the name, 'Joy', and had even thought to name their daughter thus. However, after various stanzas of 'Joy cometh in the morning' Kate had voiced the opinion that never again did she wish to hear the word 'Joy'. So it was that Pearce had decided to call the wee girl Angela, since even from his first sight of her, he had called her, my own little angel. Kate opted to name the boy Daniel, after her own elder brother who had emigrated to America.

When later that same week, the twins had been christened in the Anglican Church, it seemed that the Kinnon family life was set fair to continue and prosper for the years ahead. However, that very same evening, tragedy struck.

Pearce's beloved Angela, having given not a moment's trouble or anxiety to anyone in her short life, died from a convulsion.

Chapter 9

In the aftermath of the death of little Angela, poor Kate felt as though the Good Lord who Giveth but also Taketh Away, had indeed taken away not only her precious little baby, but also much more besides. Although Pearce's physical presence was still with her, somehow in his own grief, her husband also had gone from her. Strong and arrogant as he might appear to outsiders with his great height, piercing dark eyes which seemed to bore into one, and his luxuriant, wavy beard, Kate felt his proud bearing was all too often a shield against a prying and unsympathetic world.

This suspicion had been confirmed of late, as night after night when Pearce thought her to be asleep, he would give way to bitter sobs which wracked his whole body, over the death of his own little angel. Kate had never before heard a man weep and such had been the bond between them she longed with every fibre of her being to be able to comfort him. However, on those occasions when she did draw near him and try to embrace him, his only response was to push her away from him, and on rising to face yet another day, to don once again the mask of superiority.

Pearce remained distraught. And as the short winter days lengthened into spring, it seemed nothing or nobody could assuage his grief. Even worse, each time he looked on the puny features of baby Daniel, he felt a wild urge to choke the very life out of him, just as a cruel, unloving God had virtually done with his very own beloved Angela. Feeling as bitter and as unloving as he did, it was hardly surprising that as young Daniel grew into a sickly toddler. It gradually came to the point where it was almost as if an unseen barrier existed between father and son.

What made matters even worse was that Kate now seemed to devote her entire energies and devotion to the youngster, leaving Pearce far behind in her priorities. It was as well that at this point, he had a job on which to concentrate and expend all his energies.

Ever since that first day at the Fruit Market, Pearce had been gainfully employed, bringing home his hard-won wages every Friday night. The overall boss of the market had quickly realised Pearce had a very quick brain and responsibility sat easily on his shoulders. With the right guidance, he might in time even become a section gaffer, as the men called the bosses. So Pearce now had his own high stool and desk in the accounts office and was efficient and conscientious at his work.

On the home front, having by now accepted, albeit unwillingly, his role as an outsider whose sole function was to pay the bills with the money earned from the sweat of his brow, life began to settle into a more ordered existence. With the extra money now coming in from his latest promotion, both he and Kate began to plan for a move to a room-and-kitchen at double their present rent. They'd already had an eye on such a flat for some time. It was not exactly situated in a tiled close – a wally close as the locals called them – nor did it have any better an outlook, but nevertheless, they were both desperate to get it. It was bigger, certainly, but the main advantage was that it was closer to the Fruit Market which would mean less travelling to and from work for Pearce. Better still, he would be able to come home each day at noon for a dish of mince and tatties, or a plate of Scotch broth, or Irish stovies. There were disadvantages, not least that they would have to leave behind the good and supportive neighbours and friends they had already made. But even so, for the sake of a giant leap up the social scale in moving out of the lowly single-end, they were prepared to take the bad with the good.

Having taken the big decision and on the point of going round to the factor with their key-money, the blow fell: Kate was again pregnant. True, with another baby, a larger home would have been ideal. But there was just no way in which their already stretched financial means could be further elongated to finance the move itself, more furniture, a higher rent, and the additional expense of one more mouth to feed.

So the dream of a room-and-kitchen remained, for the moment at least, just that, an unattainable pipe-dream. Equally impossible was poor Kate's homesick dream of ever again being back in her own beloved country. The Ireland of bright peat fires, steaming hot potato-cakes, dew-drenched green fields, the shamrock, the soft rain and the even softer brogue of her adored, but now far-off Emerald Isle. All this and much more, had now gone from her, leaving but a beautiful memory to be cherished in the long dark nights of her troubled soul. No longer would she know the joy of waking to a fresh Irish Spring morning, with the hills dew-tipped and God in his Heaven.

Chapter 10

Six long years after their arrival in Glasgow, Kate was again great with child. Not that there was ever much in the way of loving kindness or comforting caresses from Pearce, but each time that he satisfied his own physical needs, it seemed that inevitably, Kate became pregnant. Perhaps even worse to bear was the knowledge that the only time her husband claimed his marital rights was when he was reeking of whisky

Despite the fact of having given birth to Jenny, the year after twins Angela and Daniel, and Andrew, two years ago – each child as perfect physically and mentally, as any mother could wish for – Kate still worried. Each time she looked at poor baby Hannah with her lolling head, vacant expression, and weird animal noises, Kate fretted that she might again give birth to another severely handicapped child. Strangely enough, her hours of labour which had brought wee Hannah into the world had been the worst of all her births, almost as if the baby had not wanted ever to enter a cruel world.

'Perhaps Hannah was a throw-back in some way? Or is this how God shows His displeasure for my immoral conduct?'

It was just as she was deep in such gloomy thoughts that Pearce came back into their home from his early morning visit to the cludgie – the stair-head communal lavatory.

On his way over to the sink, before starting to wash his hands, he cast her a baleful glance.

"Still seeing the bright side of everything, I see?" he said.

The thought went through Kate's head that had his words perhaps been accompanied by a cheeky grin, then it would have taken the sting out of them. But she knew from bitter experience that was not her husband's way. If Pearce had something to say, then he always came right out and said it, regardless of anyone else's hurt feelings.

By the same token, it would never have occurred to Pearce to put a comforting arm around her shoulders. At the thought of such neglect in her emotional life, tears started to cascade down her cheeks. And once started, she could not stem the flow. Seeing this, Pearce frowned and said: "For heaven's sake, Kate. What's wrong with you now?"

Wiping away her tears with the back of her hand, she gazed back at her husband.

Half an hour later, by which time Pearce had breakfasted well with his usual bowl of porridge, and soda bread and dripping, he was on the point of leaving for work when suddenly he clapped a hand to his brow.

"What a memory. Nearly forgot. It's today you're going out with Betty Donovon and her brood, isn't it?"

Kate looked up from clearing the dishes away from the table. She frowned and chewed at her lower lip.

"Well, the big event *is* today. Sure that's right enough. But I haven't exactly said I'll go."

Her husband shook his head. "Nonsense, Kate. You can't let the children down. Anyway, it will do you all good to get out of this hellhole for a while. Get some fresh air into your lungs."

About to voice her objections, Pearce spoke up first.

"Look, I'd really like you to go. And wee Andrew will love seeing the boats."

Kate had her own thoughts on this matter. '*After all, Andrew was still only two, wasn't he? But, Daniel was five and much more interested in ships, ferries, launches and the like.*' However, rather than start up a family row in accusing her husband of favouring one son more than another, she decided to ignore his words.

Taking her silence for wifely agreement, he put a hand in his trouser pocket and withdrew two precious silver sixpences. Then holding these out to her, he said: "Here you are, Kate. Andrew loves puff candy. Buy a wee bag for him ... and ... er ... for the other children, of course. It will add to the joy of the outing for them."

With these words and a wave of his hand, he was gone.

Later that same day, Tuesday July 3rd, 1883, Kate, her friend and neighbour, Big Betty Donovon, and between them, their squad of children, made their way through the bustling city streets towards Linthouse, near the Govan district of Glasgow.

They knew they faced something of a trek to get anywhere near the launch, so they had packed as many of the children as they could into their two rickety, squeaky prams. The older children trailed along as best they could in their wake.

It was a reasonable morning, neither too hot nor as yet bucketing down with rain, so with the occasional encouragement in the way of chunks of puff-candy, the group made fairly good time on their self-imposed route march. And as they walked, the two women blethered twenty to the dozen. In answer to a question from Kate, Big Betty nodded and when she spoke, there was a ring of pride in her voice.

"Yes. 'Tis my cousin, Declan. A fine carpenter he is. He helped build this fine steamer."

"Isn't he that fine handsome young lad who mended your table for you? I remember seeing him."

Betty grinned.

"Aye, the very one. Came over from Armagh only last year. Lucky enough to get work at Stephen's Shipbuilding Yard. A good lad ... sends most of his wages back home to his widowed mother in dear old Ireland. Just hope we're as lucky with our children when they get to be workers, eh, Kate?"

Kate grinned and nodded her agreement. As she started to speak, her words were lost in a burst of sound and shouts of delight from the children. They had by now approached the gates of the Yard, already black with a seething mass of exuberant, excited humanity.

Flags and bunting waved in the light breeze. The local pipe band, resplendent in full Highland regalia, was even then marching through the gates of the Yard on their way to the launching platform.

Daniel let out a whoop of delight and, with face abeam, turned to his mother.

"This is great, Mammy. It was worth the walk. Thanks for bringin' us."

Kate ruffled his dark hair.

Betty, in high glee, was shouting to make herself heard above the excited, chattering din and the skirl of the pipes all around them.

"Yes, Danny boy, the boat is called the *Daphne* and if ye watch carefully, any minute now, we'll see her slide down into the waters of the Clyde. And do ye know something else?"

Daniel shook his head, agog to get all the information he possibly could about this wonderful event.

"What's that, Aunty Betty?"

Betty paused for dramatic effect, by now thoroughly enjoying the novel experience of having a captive audience.

"See that *Daphne*, son? Well, although ye cannae see them, there's to be more than a hundred men still working aboard her as she gets launched. And my cousin is one o' them. There now, Danny, whit dae ye think o' that?"

Daniel gave a long, low whistle of appreciation, which coming from such a small, earnest boy, caused smiles of amusement from those other spectators around him. One elderly man turned to face Betty and in the broadest of Glasgow accents, said:

"Aye, Missus, and ma three big sons is aboard an aw. Whit a great day it is fur us. Talk aboot the pride o' the Clyde."

Betty nodded, but before she could comment, a youngish woman with a child in her arms and from the look of her, another child in her belly, spoke up: "A great day indeed. Ma man's on the *Daphne* as weel. He really wanted to stay here and watch the launchin' wi us frae the shore. It's by richts his day aff, ye see. But Ah jist tellt him, don't ye be daft, says Ah. You get on board wi' yer pals. It'll be a great experience for ye, Bert. And forbye, we can aye use the extra bawbees."

Everyone in earshot nodded in agreement, for surely there was not a family on Clydeside but needed every farthing they could get in order to keep body and soul together.

Suddenly, there appeared to be some activity from the platform party. A wild cheer went up from the waiting crowds. The elderly man, who had previously spoken with such pride of his three strapping sons, turned to Kate. He jerked his thumb down in the direction of young Andrew who was still holding on to the handle of the pram, for fear of getting lost in the thick of the crowd.

"Listen, Missus. The wee fella will no' see ower much o' the launchin' frae doon therr. Gie's a haud o' him and Ah'll hoist him up on tae ma shoulders."

Kate smiled. "Oh, that's real good o' ye, sir."

The elderly man shrugged away her words of thanks.

"Nothin tae it, Missus. Fine weel Ah ken aw aboot bairns. In fact, Ah must tell ye ... one o' ma lads oot therr on that boat, his wee wifie's expectin' a wean soon ... so ony day noo Ah'm gonnae be a grandfaither. So, Ah micht as weel get in a wee bit o' practice. But quick noo wi' the wee lad. Or we'll miss the launchin' aw thegither."

He raised Andrew high above his head and then positioned the lad comfortably on his shoulders.

"Haud on tight tae ma heid, son. Ye'll get a great view. Aye, this'll be a day for you tae remember when ye're an auld man yersel'."

No sooner were the words out of the proud father's mouth than an almighty cheer went up from the crowd. The pipers again started up their melodies, and amidst scenes of intense excitement and enjoyment flags were waved on all sides and even soft tweed bunnets were taken off and waved vigorously.

Those whose hands were free of children clapped loudly and turned to speak to, slap on the back, or otherwise congratulate perfect strangers. On all sides, snatches of pride-filled conversation could be heard.

"Ma faither's on that big boat, so he is."

"See ma man. Idle for a helluva lang time. Jist got work last week on the *Daphne*. Lucky for him, eh no?"

Kate smiled when she saw Hannah was still savouring a sticky piece of puff-candy, the orange rivulets of which were dribbling down the poor child's chin. Taking a rag from under the sleeve of her dress, Kate spat on the ready-made hanky a couple of times and leant forward to mop at Hannah's face. So intent was Kate on trying to keep Hannah still long enough to get her cleaned up, she didn't see the next part of the launching.

A sudden collective intake of breath from the thousands of watchers on the shore immediately followed by the dying and ragged strains of the pipes as the music drifted away, unfinished, made Kate raise her head in time to see the vessel turn right over and capsize into the murky waters of the River Clyde.

A horrible stillness, a silence which could be felt, followed this unbelievable event. With hand-held flags still in mid-wave, everyone gazed in fascinated horror towards the river, as the *Daphne* was drawn downwards, ever downwards, into the stinking waters of the great river, it was clear that without warning and before their very eyes, the river had claimed its latest victims.

Gradually, as the full horror of the situation dawned on their stunned minds, a new sound was heard: a low, animal keening from the women, young and old, already mourned the loss of a dear one. Strong men wept. With tears pouring down his lined face, the elderly man, the soon to be grandfaither, in an instant grown older than time itself, gently removed Andrew from the perch of his shoulders. With a sorrowful look at Kate, he forced out the words: "Ah'll hae tae get awa hame tae ma wife. She's an invalid, ye ken. Ah jist dinnae ken how Ah'm gonnae break this news tae her. Her three bonnie laddies. All gone. Oh, Christ Almichty. This will kill her. Kill her, so it will. Oh, God help us all this day. Ah still cannae thole the idea."

Now muttering incoherently to himself, he shuffled away, making his way through the crowds of weeping, wailing relatives.

Kate, her arms by now around Betty's shoulders, stroked her friend's hair. And all the while, Betty moaned: "Oh, my poor Declan. And his widow-woman mother. God. Why should this have happened? Why in the name o' Christ, does God allow such sufferin'?"

It was while she was looking over Betty's shoulder Kate saw the young mother to whom they had earlier spoken ... the young, heavily-pregnant girl who had actually persuaded her husband against his will to go aboard the *Daphne* on that fateful day.

The baby still clutched in her arms, the young mother-to-be was gazing about her in shock. It was clear that any minute, once the full impact of the tragedy hit her, she would keel over. Kate eased herself away from a now noisily-weeping Betty. That done, she went towards the young mother and with some difficulty, prised the baby from her clutching fingers. Then, holding the serenely sleeping child in one arm, she enfolded the stunned and shocked young woman with the other.

How long they stood locked in this timeless, wordless embrace, Kate had no way of knowing. How Betty, the distraught young mother, and Kate herself, or even any of their own children got home that day, Kate was never entirely sure. The rest of the day, the struggling, frantic crowds of weeping men, women, and children all became a blur. But forever, she would remember with clarity the shriek that had gone up from the unknown and unnamed young widow: "Oh. Ma man. Ma bonnie man. Dear Sweet Jesus. Gie me back ma poor Bert."

True, Kate herself had not lost a relative nor even a close friend in the *Daphne* Disaster, but the traumatic experience did have one immediate impact on her own life.

That very night, she went into premature labour. As the midwife cleaned up the baby and handed her into Kate's waiting arms, she smiled and said: "Looks like ye've got a real wee beauty here, Kate. She's perfect in every way. So, therr's nae need for ye tae go countin' her fingers and toes. Like a wee heavenly angel, so she is."

Kate gave a weak smile, a sigh of relief and with a wavering right hand, she caressed the baby's downy cheek.

"Thank God for that, Mistress Shaw. Aye. At least there's one happy household in Glasgow this night. Not like all those other poor souls, crazed with grief. I just cannot get out of my thoughts the sight o' yon poor young widow."

"There, there noo, Kate. Try no' tae upset yersel'."

"But if ye'd seen her, Mistress Shaw. Little more than a wee lassie herself. And there she is now … lost her man, left with a babe-in-arms and another wean well on the way. Poor demented soul that she is. I just wonder how in God's name she's goin' to manage. And apart from her sorrow … not even a breadwinner. God help her."

As a very sleepy and exhausted Kate, holding tight to her precious baby, snuggled down in her bed, she yet again thanked God for his blessings bestowed on her own family.

She and Pearce gazed down in love and wonder at the sleeping miracle of their lovely wee Isabella. For Kate and her suddenly enlarged family, the third of July, 1883, had ended on a positive note. But in the annals of Scottish history, it was a black day for all too many working-class folk in Glasgow.

Chapter 11

Pearce's drinking in his off-work hours grew steadily worse, but he was never an uproarious, happy drunk like some of the others in their street. He became morose, silently brooding on the mistakes of his past, his reduced circumstances, and above all the death of Angela, ever ready to lash out at any who crossed him. The children quickly learned to stay out of his way when he came home drunk on a Friday evening, even his favourite Andrew sheltered with Big Betty until Kate knocked quietly at her single-end door with the news that Dadda was safely asleep in bed.

His drinking seriously cut into money available even for the necessities of life and Kate was reduced to searching his pockets, after he fell into a drunken stupor, for whatever coin she could find and hiding it away.

Thus the summer and autumn of 1883 passed. In the winter, diphtheria was rampant in the city and Kate worried herself sick every time one of the children developed a cough. The traditional sugar-coated butter balls to soothe the dry throat of the patient meant no butter or sugar for anyone except Pearce. By February, Kate was beginning to relax. The epidemic was reported as declining, then Andrew started coughing.

Big Betty shook her head sadly at his fever and the development of the diphtheria rash, and in days Andrew was dead.

"How could you be so stupid and so careless?" Pearce ranted at Kate after Andrew's funeral. "Sugar-coated butter balls. Whoever heard of treating diphtheria like that? Ignorant bog Irish peasants like your Big Betty? You should have had the doctor."

"With what, Pearce?" Kate shouted back. "With your drinking there's barely enough to keep food on the table. What was I supposed to pay the doctor with? A doctor won't come to a house like this where he knows there's no pay."

Pearce towered over Kate, then abruptly turned away and strode to the door.

"That's right. Go and drink yourself senseless. Just as you did the night your favourite son died. Lying in a drunken stupor while Andrew breathed his last."

He turned, his face ashen, and looked at Kate, but she felt he looked right through her.

"Christ." He turned away and the door slammed behind him with enough force to shake the whole building.

Pearce didn't return that night and Kate wondered if he was lying drunk in some gutter.

Next evening, at the time he usually returned from his work at the Fruit Market, Pearce walked in. He was red-eyed and tired looking, but there was no hint of alcohol on his breath. The children promptly fled the house, taking Hannah with them.

"Is there food in this house?"

Kate hastened to scrape together a meal from the scraps the children had abandoned in their flight.

Pearce ate in silence.

"You can feed our children better than this –"

Kate was about to launch a retaliatory attack, but Pearce pulled a pay-packet envelope out of his pocket and handed it to her.

"The men at work offered me drink this night – a sort of wake for Andrew, I think, but I'll drink no more. I found this on my desk at closing. No-one would admit to it being his money – this is what we are sunk to – use it for whatever you see needful.

After that, Pearce never came home with liquor on his breath, but his brooding presence cast a pall over the house when he was home. Daniel was beaten on any and every pretext, and avoided his father whenever he could.

Gradually, Pearce began to pay attention to Isabella, the youngest child, and the atmosphere lightened somewhat.

On the first Saturday of November, Pearce pushed his chair back from the table after the evening meal.

"This is our last Saturday here. We're moving to a bigger house."

The announcement was greeted with a startled silence.

"It's not too far from here – Garth Street – but it's a room-and-kitchen. I've made all the arrangements. The coalman will move our bits and pieces on his cart."

"But when will we move?" Kate frowned.

"Next week on Quarter Day, of course. The proper time to end one lease and sign another with the factor."

"You haven't talked to me about this, Pearce."

Pearce's self-satisfied cheerfulness was beginning to evaporate at this less than enthusiastic reception of his news.

"And why should I? I pay the rent. I bring in the pay-packet that keeps this family fed and clothed."

"I keep the house clean and snug for everyone. I should have been consulted."

"Nonsense, woman. This is my business. I have calculated we can afford the extra rent, and I have saved the money needed for the key money and the flitting."

"Maybe if you hadn't drunk so much before, we could have afforded a better house earlier – and Andrew need not have died –"

Pearce's face suffused with blood. He leapt to his feet. Before Kate could move, his open hand slapped her face turning it to one side.

The following backhand blow struck her nose and his ring opened a gash on her cheek.

Daniel jumped forward and got between Kate and Pearce.

"Leave Mammy alone, you bastard," he shouted and kicked as hard as he could at Pearce's shin. The other children screamed.

Pearce looked in astonishment at Daniel for a moment before grabbing him by the scruff of the neck and forcing him face down across the table.

"We'll have none of that language in this house," he snarled, loosening his belt.

Chapter 12

When the November Quarter Day of 1886 came around, right reason or none, and strictly in accordance with Dadda's wishes, the Kinnon family prepared to move a few streets away to their new home. As yet, apart from Dadda himself, not one of the family had even so much as caught a glimpse of the new and bigger house.

Jenny and Andrew were both weeping as if their hearts would break at having to leave not only all their little pals, but also the only home they had ever known in their short lives. Little Isabella, not quite understanding, wept in sympathy. Hannah, to whom one day was much like another, seemed unmoved. Daniel, determined not to give his father the satisfaction of seeing him cry, managed in the midst of all the excitement to keep a stiff upper lip. That is until at the very last when the children were paraded out of the close for the last time and there in the street, at the kerbside, they saw it. The few worldly possessions which the Kinnons owned had already been piled haphazardly on to one of Murphy's coal lorries and even then, father was giving final detailed delivery instructions to the carter.

That done, Murphy doffed his bunnet to Pearce, stirred his great Clydesdale workhorse into action and they were off. The last Daniel saw of the coal-lorry as it rounded the corner into the next street was the sawn-off nursing chair wobbling precariously against the head of one of Mammy's best wally dugs, whose soulful face peered out from a lidless wooden box. As the coal-cart disappeared from view, Mammy, with tears in her own eyes, bent forward, tucked the crocheted knee-rug more firmly round Hannah, already seated in her go-chair, and swallowing back her distress, forced a bleak smile onto her scarred face as she said: "Now then my wee darlings the main thing is not to worry ourselves about all this move. After all, you'll not be all that far away from your pals. And you, Daniel and Jenny, you'll still be at the same school. 'Tisn't as if we were going to another country, though God willing, 'tis fine I would like to be returning to my own Emerald Isle. Ah, well. But mind now what it is I'm telling you … whatever the new place is like, and according to Dadda, it's a palace, but be that as it may, we'll soon be able to see for ourselves, anyway. But just remember one thing is certain and I want you all to hold on to this thought: this is an adventure we're having."

When still there was no answering smile on the children's faces, Kate was on the point of trying further to boost their spirits when a shout from Pearce caused them all to jump. Dadda had already gone striding ahead, leaving Kate to cope as best she could with the weeping, distraught children, a stubborn silent Daniel, and the ever-active yet un-coordinated Hannah. By the time he had realised his wife and family were not close on his heels, Pearce was almost at the corner of the street. He had turned round to admonish them to move along a bit faster when he saw, to his annoyance, that not only were they not close behind him, they had not even set one single step on the road towards their new adventure and what Pearce himself personally regarded as their heft up the social ladder.

At once his face darkened at the imagined slight and he waved his stout walking-stick at the laggards in a beckoning motion. Of course, it would have been easier and much more effective to have shouted his instructions, in the manner adopted by most local people. However, as always, Pearce Claude Kinnon thought himself well above the manners and morals of the other tenement dwellers. It would never have done for anyone to observe, far less hear Mr Kinnon acting in a coarse manner, devoid of all social graces. No, he had his standards to keep up and it would take more than a few recalcitrant children to make him change his inborn and, as he saw it, socially correct habits of a lifetime.

Catching his meaning of the impatient beckoning with his walking-stick, Kate at once gathered her brood around her, but not before she had given them one last word of hope and encouragement for what they obviously saw as a very uncertain future. Bending her face close to them, she looked into two pairs of tearful eyes and the openly rebellious face of Daniel and said: "Right, then, you lot. We had better get our skates on before your poor Dadda bursts a blood vessel or else his walking stick bursts into flames with impatience." Here the children giggled. "Now, you lot, quick march."

They set off to walk the few streets to their new and as yet, unseen room-and-kitchen home. At that very moment, Dadda was hastening round the corner of the street, so the now-biddable children, always susceptible to Mammy's gentle brand of coaxing, made every effort to catch up on Dadda, as all the while their little legs went like castanets and the clatter of their boots echoed off the cobbled street.

Once arrived outside the new tenement building, before which Dadda, a frown of impatience on his face, was already standing, both Kate herself and the children looked with interest at the once-blond, but now blackened with soot and age, fabric of the tall building. To all intents and purposes, it looked much the same not only as the building they had just vacated, but also as a thousand other gaunt tenement structures which abounded in the City of Glasgow.

As the family procession entered the close, already they felt quite at home, for not only did the dank walls look the same as their old close, the smell was exactly the same, being a mixture of cats' pee, dogs' shit, stale vomit, and the stench of human excrement issuing from the constantly running lavatory on the half-landing.

With the habit born of years, and almost as an automatic action, Kate and the children stopped outside the first door on the left as they entered the close. Pearce, who had been giving final instructions to the carter for the uplifting, disposal and proper placing of his few sticks of furniture, now hurried into the close after his family. He gave a puzzled frown when he saw them all huddled round the doorway just inside the close.

Fixing his wife with a beady eye, he asked: "Why on earth are you all standing there, like orphans of the storm. This isn't our old close, you know. This isn't the house I've chosen for you, you know."

It was Kate's turn to wear a puzzled look and after pulling her Sunday-best shawl closer to her neck, she replied with a touch of asperity in her voice: "Well, you might know exactly where we're headed. But since you've told us nothing, other than it's a room-and-kitchen, how on earth can you expect us to know which door it is that we're looking for?"

Having delivered herself of her protest, Kate then shepherded her brood across to the door opposite. Seeing this, Pearce burst out angrily: "Oh, for heaven's sake, woman. Did I say that our new home was on the ground floor? Honestly, how stupid can you get? Come on, now, follow me. And quick about it, for the carter is right behind you with the kitchen table balanced on his shoulder. Follow me."

As her husband made as if to start climbing the stairs, Kate stopped him with a hand on his sleeve.

"Hold on a minute, Pearce. Are you saying that our new home is upstairs? Mind you, I grant you it will be lovely to be one up and that bit removed from the noise and stench of the Saturday night drunks, who as we all know to our cost, use the common close as their nearest and most available lavatory. Oh, yes, one flight up will be just grand. Just one slight matter, we'll need to take Hannah out of her go-chair. Maybe you could carry the wee darling upstairs and Daniel can hump up the pram one step at a time. All right, Pearce?"

With a face like sour milk, Pearce looked at wee darling Hannah as if he could have wished her at the ends of the earth. Even so, he bent down to untie the leather straps which held her and, that done, he raised his head and looked Kate square in the eyes.

"Just one thing, Kate, before we start climbing the stairs. Yes, the new house is above, but not on the first flight, as you so fondly seem to imagine."

Kate cocked her head on one side and, with a speculative look on her face, waited for her husband to go on. Her instinct told her what she was about to hear was not in any measure going to be to her liking. Nevertheless, she still said nothing, but the tight, angry white line of her pursed lips already spoke volumes. She did not have long to wait to hear the words she dreaded.

Pearce, with a kicking, restless Hannah now in his arms, peered over the child's head and in a voice devoid of all emotion, said: "The new room-and-kitchen is on the top floor."

At this piece of news, there was a sharp intake of breath from the already burdened carter. The man said not a word, but with a great show of injured and betrayed feelings, he lowered the table to the damp floor of the close. Then, fixing Pearce with a fish-eyed stare, he dusted his hands down the length of his leather jerkin and said with great deliberation, in his coarse but telling Glasgow accent: "Here jist a bloody minute, Mister Kinnon, sur. When ye asked me tae humph all yer bits and pieces tae yer new hoose, ye never said a fuckin' word aboot any four flights of stairs. And because ye yersel' never mentioned it, I never thought tae ask. Ye see, man, most folk roon' aboot here when they're daein' a flittin', at least hae the common decency fur tae at least tell the cairter that's he's gonnae be daein' a spot of mountain-climbing. But, see ye, ye sneaky bastard that ye are, ye never let slip a single word aboot me havin' tae climb up and doon Ben Nevis with yer bloody furniture. And speakin' o' which, even with all yer airs and graces, I've saw better stuff gettin' chucked oot at Paddy's Market."

By now, Pearce was fit to be tied. Heaving Hannah over so her weight now rested on his left shoulder, thus giving him a better view of the rebellious carter, Pearce said in his usual genteel voice, but one which now dripped with ice and venom: "See here, my man, I'm paying you and paying you well for your services. And as I recall the deal was that you would remove and then reinstate my goods and chattel to my new home. Is that not factually correct, my good man?"

The carter took off his flat cloth bunnet, and with black-rimmed finger-nails enjoyed a good scratch at his balding head. That done, and with a great show of mute insolence, he studied his fingernails, as if seeking, if not actually counting, the day's crop of head-lice. Only then did he leer up at Pearce and say: "Maybe if ye took the gob-stopper oot yer mooth, I'd ken better what it is ye're trying fur tae·say. But one thing Ah did get ... that 'my good man' business. Weel, Ah'll tell ye this, Mister Kinnon, there's one thing sure, Ah'm no yer good man. I'm a fine upstanding Irish Catholic and let me tell ye this, boyo –"

Pearce hoisted Hannah back off his shoulder from where the poor child was already dribbling a stream of saliva down his back, and instead reseated her in the go-chair.

"Right then, Murphy, that's quite enough of that. We're not needing to let the question of religion enter the lists, for what we're talking about is –"

The carter took a red spotted rag from his trouser pocket, and after giving his bulbous nose, which matched the colour of his makeshift handkerchief exactly, a loud blast, he then proceeded to study the contents of the handkerchief in much the same manner as he had done his stock-taking of head lice.

That it was a studied insult was not lost on Pearce. Now free of his burden of Hannah, he advanced towards the man and, tapping the latter on the shoulder with the head of his cane, he said in a voice which, although overly polite, was nevertheless tinged with menace: "That's quite enough of that, Murphy –"

With a ham-like fist, the carter brushed away the walking stick, at the same time saying: "Mister Murphy, if ye don't mind, my good man."

That did it. Pearce saw red. Throwing his stick to the floor of the close, where the steel ferule clattered noisily, he then grabbed the carter by the scruff of the neck.

"Listen you, I've met your sort before. No wonder you give the Irish a bad name. You'll neither work nor want. Now let's get this straight, I've paid you good money, ten shillings of my hard-earned cash, and you'll take my furniture up stairs to the topmost flight and do it now, do you hear, Murphy?"

The man shook himself free, and with a murderous look in his eyes, said in a voice which carried not only an air of authority, but also the ring of finality: "Listen, yourself, Kinnon. Ah've met yer sort before. And if ye want that bloody rubbish carried up four flights of stairs, then there's little problem and but one answer to it. Do the fuckin' job yersel', bastard that ye are."

The man turned away from Pearce with such force that he crashed into the table, which in turn ricocheted off the wall with a splintering sound as if one of the already not too stable legs had given way under the strain. As all the while the man's progress was watched in open-mouthed horror by Kate and the children, they heard Pearce muttering dire threats about sending for the police who would soon sort out a wild Irish Paddy like that. But nothing would stop the man in his determination to leave the scene with all possible speed. However, when he reached the end of the close, the carter did take time to turn and with a strange, almost pitying look on his face, say: "Listen, Kinnon, if ye find yoursel' in a mess noo, then ye've only yersel' tae blame. A wee bit o' common courtesy, not to mention an extra couple o' bob in ma haun', an Ah'd hae been glad fur to help ye upstairs with yer stuff. But, see ye, ye're that bloody high-and-mighty – twisted, in fact. Weel, ye've made yer bed, so now ye can just lie in it ... that is when ye finally get it hauled up aw thay stairs."

At his own witticism, the carter let out a great belly laugh which shook all eighteen stone of him.

For his part Pearce was turning away to assemble his brood and his worldly goods, and work out his strategy, when he again heard the coarse voice from the still-chuckling carter.

"One thing Ah will dae and that's tae lift yer stuff off my coal-cart. Ah'll leave it on the pavement here, to await yer lordship's convenience. And just one last thing; Ah must say it's yer poor wee wife, a real decent wee woman, that I'm sorry for. God help her. Lumbered with a bloody milksop like ye. And as to how ye ever got up enough gumption for to father aw those poor wee weans, weel, it fair beats me, so it does."

At this point Kate had to lay a restraining hand on Pearce's arm as he made to race after the man. Even so, the carter had not yet finished with him. He pointed a beefy hand at a by-now trembling Kate and in a voice of doom, said: "Aye, that poor wee God-fearin' woman. Heaven alone kens what she ever done to deserve a man … humph … man, did Ah say …more like a bairn … like ye. And anyway, maybe ye'd better think on a bit, *Mister* Kinnon, *sir* … just how the hell is that wee woman supposed to manage to struggle up and doon aw thae stairs day and daily with that poor handicapped bairn and her go-chair. Seems to me, ye'd hae been far better aff staying where ye were in yer single-end. At least there, ye were on the ground floor. And noo Ah'll bid good-day to ye, *sir*, and let ye get on with yer flittin' before the rain and dark sets in. Good-day, *Mister* Kinnon, *sir,* and good luck to yer wee wife … she's gonnae be needin' aw the luck she can get."

With that, the man was gone, leaving not only a sour taste of defeat in Pearce's mouth, but also a very clear echo of his words in Kate's already overtaxed brain.

"How will she manage up and down all those stairs with a handicapped bairn and her go-chair?"

'*How indeed?*' wondered Kate, to whom the thought had already occurred that life four flights up with Hannah, her go-chair, buckets of washing for the steamie, and bags of shopping to be carried in every day to feed her growing family, was going to be no picnic. Even worse, suppose the unthinkable happened and she ever became pregnant again with another child, how on earth could she possibly cope?

Then, with a deep sigh, Kate turned towards the stairs. She knew in her heart of hearts that somehow – as yet she had no idea as to how she would achieve the miracle – but somehow, with God's help she would cope. After all, she had no alternative. As the carter had said, they had made their bed, or rather, they would make it, once Pearce and little Daniel managed to struggle upstairs with their burden. Kate gave her own burden – weeping, tired, and irritable Hannah – a playful tweek of her tartan ribbon, which she always wore as some sort of talisman, gathering the child into her arms for the next stage of their journey.

Chapter 13

With her family eagerly gathered about her skirts, and a now somewhat mollified Pearce at her elbow, they made the grand tour of their new abode. As Kate already knew, there were definite and very real disadvantages to living in such an eyrie high above the City streets. Even so, she was generous-spirited enough to acknowledge to Pearce that, 'yes' she could already see the good points about their new situation. First, of course, as she had already surmised, was the more pleasant aroma at being thus far removed from the stinks and appalling messes to be found in almost any Glasgow close. Not only that, but with its being a room-and-kitchen this meant that the best front room overlooked the street, and given the height of their window, they had an excellent view of the surrounding district, even with what Kate was sure was a patch of green in the far distance.

But surely the greatest benefit of all lay in the fact of their now having their very own tiny water-closet which was wedged into a corner of the minute hallway. This edifice was as the seventh wonder of the world to Kate and her family, for it meant that never again would they have to creep out in the dead of night – nor at any other time, come to that – to a freezing cold, stinking lavatory on the stair-head. In her joy that never again would she need to keep a chamber-pot under the bed, far less carry the disgusting object down to the stair-head cludgie, Kate chuckled to herself: '*Cludgie, indeed. No wonder the Glasgow folk call the communal outside lavatory such an expressive, ugly name. It somehow describes it more accurately than a whole dictionary of words.*'

Her thoughts were interrupted when Pearce, with a hand at her elbow, said: "Well, we've seen the best front room and having now duly marvelled at the glory of our very own water closet, shall we now take a look at the kitchen?"

Kate, by now, already sold heart and mind on the new home, allowed herself to be led into the back kitchen. As Pearce threw back the dark, wood-grained door with a certain panache, she stopped in the doorway with a cry of delight.

"Oh, no, Pearce. I don't believe it. It's … why it's all truly wonderful. Wonderful. And quite beyond my wildest dreams."

As she gazed through a blur of tears at the gleaming, well-polished kitchen-range, a bigger, better and altogether much more up-to-date model than the one she had left behind in the single-end, she found that coherent speech was almost beyond her. But even so, the thought went racing through her over-excited brain: '*Oh, Pearce, Pearce, you stupid man. If only you had gone about it all differently … treated us as a united, caring family with rights, ideas and even wishes of our own, how very different things would have been. If only … if only you had thought of me as a person in my own right, just for once. If you had let us – or at the very least, let me – come to see the place first, rather than taking the law into your own hands, then we would never have had that awful row. You would never have had cause to hit me. I would have realised at once, the very moment I'd seen this, this mansion, I'd have known you had our best interests at heart. Oh, Pearce, I can hardly bear to think of it … that terrible row … and in front of our young, impressionable children.*'

Kate wiped away with her sleeve the tears which were then coursing down her cheeks, as she squared her shoulders and took comfort from the thought: '*Yes, young, impressionable minds. But never worry, I'm sure that no lasting harm was done. Couldn't possibly be, for children soon forget and move on to the next bit of excitement in their lives. Still, it is indeed terrible to think that that ugly scene could have been avoided altogether. For one thing's sure*

... although the children may forget, I never shall, not if I live to be a hundred.'

While these thoughts had been coursing through her mind, unbeknown to herself, Kate had been absently touching at the area of her face which still wore the bruises and healing scar of their fight. Seeing this, Pearce, for once in a rare outward demonstration of affection, threw his arm around her shoulder, and pulled his wife close.

"Katie, we've had our troubles, our differences ..." he whispered. "Do you think, my dear ... could we possibly look on this as a new start? After all, I don't suppose anybody's marriage is perfect, is it? It's something which has to be worked at day and daily. So ... what do you say, Katie, lass, can we start again?"

At these words, not least the look in his eyes and his use of the pet name Katie which she had not heard him call her in many a long day, Kate blushed and like a newly-wedded girl. With stars in her eyes, she allowed herself to sink into the deep well of love and affection which she could read in Pearce's eyes.

She nodded her assent and, as she reached up to plant a light kiss on his bearded cheek, she was surprised to find the eyes of young Daniel watching her every move. A momentary shiver of fear went through her body, but she at once dismissed it with the positive thought:

'No, it can't be I must just have imagined that look of hate in Danny's eyes. No. The children have already forgotten that terrible row. Of course they have. And that's a God's Blessing, if ever there was one.'

By half past nine that very same evening, all the bits and pieces of furniture had been not only transported upstairs, but also arranged to Kate's satisfaction, although even she, optimist that she was, had to admit that scattered over a room-and-kitchen, not to mention a razor-thin strip of hallway, her belongings now looked even more sparse than had been the case in the humble single-end. Transport was thanks to a friendly neighbour, Buddy Robertson, into whose door Pearce had at one point inadvertently crashed with the brass bedstead. Buddy, who had obviously drink taken, came out on to the landing in the first instance prepared to do battle with whoever it was who was banging at his bloody door. However, on seeing Kate, he at once demanded to know what the hell she thought she was doing in dragging an end of a heavy bedstead, when there were plenty strong, willing and able men around, ready to do her bidding. With the exaggerated mannerisms and supreme gallantry of the gloriously drunk, nothing would do Buddy but that he would at once relieve her of her burden. And in effect, fleein' drunk with booze or not, her knight in a greasy boiler suit and ragged neckerchief soon proved his worth. When all the furniture, or what passed for such, was all finally installed, her saviour left with a courtly, if somewhat unsteady, bow and again navigated his way back down to his own flat.

Daniel was not impressed with their spacious new eyrie. He had not forgotten – nor indeed, he vowed, would he ever forget – that black Saturday. In that moment as he saw his Mammy again apparently being won over by the 'Beast of Candleriggs' he made a solemn oath to himself ...

His own dear, lovely Mammy might have lowered her guard. But, he, Daniel Robert Kinnon, never. Never would he do likewise. From that day on, each Saturday in life as the anniversary day came around, he would deliberately relive the ghastly scene in his mind.

That would be his role in life. And, one day, it was sure, one day Pearce Claude Kinnon would rue the day he ever lifted his hand to his long-suffering wife, Kate.

That day would surely come, as certainly as night followed day, as surely as the dark days of winter burst into spring. Yes, indeed, that day of reckoning would come.

Chapter 14

Hardly had they completed the final adjustment of their furniture, than there was a strident ringing of the doorbell. Kate and Pearce looked at each other in amazement, but it was Kate who found her voice first: "Now, who on earth can that be? Surely not our first visitor before we've even got the kettle on the hob."

Pearce shrugged his elegant shoulders.

"One person I know it won't be, and that's Spud Murphy round to apologise for his boorish behaviour. Not an ounce of good manners in him, that fellow."

Kate smoothed down the front of her dress.

"Well, only one way to find out. And that's to open the door."

Since neither one of the children nor even Pearce himself made the slightest move to do so, it was left to Kate to pick her way past the now-empty tea-chests which still cluttered the kitchen and the tiny hallway.

On opening the door, she was taken aback to be confronted by a wizened old woman, dressed from head to toe in sombre black. Even more amazing, the crone carried somewhat precariously, on account of its burden, a heavy wooden tray. Set out on this, on top of a snow-white cloth with crocheted edges, was a selection of enamel mugs, a china teapot, a tin of Nestlé's milk and an assortment of scones and pancakes. As the tray wobbled and came perilously close to falling at Kate's feet, she instinctively put out both hands to grab hold of it. With the tray now steadied and held safely between them, Kate was at a loss to know how to greet this stranger standing uninvited on her new doorstep.

The problem was solved for Kate when the other woman opened her mouth and, in a soft Irish brogue with only a hint of Glaswegian in it, said: "Hello, Missus. Sorry, but I don't know your name yet. Anyway, I'm your next-door neighbour. I live in the wee single-end, just through the wall from your front room. I'm Mrs Abigail McGarrity, but most folk here call me Granny Gorbals.

Kate, whose own arms were beginning to wilt under the weight of the heavily laden tray, quickly introduced herself.

"Well, my dear Mistress Kinnon," the old lady said, "I just wanted to welcome you to your new home here in Garth Street. And this wee cup of tea and plate of sweet bites is my way of saying, welcome. I hope that we'll be good neighbours to each other in the years to come."

At this kind and totally unexpected gesture, Kate could feel a lump in her throat, and she had to gulp a couple of times before she could trust herself to speak.

"That's very kind of you, Mistress ... Mistress McGarrity and –"

Her visitor shook her head and the movement of her body caused further danger to the tray.

"Ach, my dear, we might as well start as we mean to go on ... just call me Granny. Everybody else does."

Kate smiled her acknowledgement of this, and gathered the tray and the now-cooling tea into the safety of her own hands.

"But what are we doing standing out here, talking on the doorstep? Come in ... Granny, come in."

Granny needed no second invitation, and once rid of her burden of the tea-tray, stepped with alacrity into the narrow hallway.

Once Granny had been formally introduced to the children and to Pearce, Kate was amused to observe their different reactions. Hannah started to cry, the other children herded together as if against a common enemy, and Pearce, at his most haughty, looked down his patrician nose at the witch-like creature standing crouched before him.

Not only seeing this, but also sensing their unspoken antipathy and indeed fear of the crone, Kate put herself out to be at her most charming to their visitor:

"Just you sit yourself down, Granny. And you'll stay and join us in this feast of goodies which you so generously, and so very thoughtfully, have provided."

Over tea, the atmosphere lightened somewhat, especially when the children and Pearce realised not only had Granny provided the tasty bites, she had also baked them herself, and especially for the Kinnons, no less, in honour of them and their removal to their new house.

Conversation was flowing easily and well, up to the point where Kate suggested that Granny might care to be given the grand-tour of the Kinnon's new abode.

The old woman smiled over her one remaining tooth, which so exactly matched in colour the rest of her ensemble.

"Thank you kindly, Mistress Kinnon ... Kate, but really, there's no need for that. You see, I already know this house like the back of my hand."

Never one to miss a trick, Pearce was right there with the inevitable question.

"Oh, indeed: And might I ask why that should be the case?"

Granny cackled, so overcome with her own private joke she began to splutter and cough. It took a mug of cold water and a couple of hefty slaps on her back before she recovered sufficiently.

"Well, Mr Kinnon, sir, it's a wee bit delicate ... But the fact remains that the last tenants, real kindly souls they were from Ballygally, they allowed me the free run of their water-closet, be it day or night."

This astounding statement was greeted in stunned and total silence, Then, seeing the horrified look on her husband's face, Kate decided on a delaying action.

"And how ... just how do you mean, Granny?"

The old woman sighed, pushed back the stretched over-long sleeves of her ancient cardigan, then as if explaining matters to a not very-bright child, said: "Well, it came about like this. The Monaghans, the last tenants, and real decent Irish people, like ourselves, when they got on a bit on in the world, street-traders they were and making money hand over fist and –"

At this point Pearce, with a frown on his face and a note of irritation in his voice which declared to the initiated that this was *not* how he had envisaged the first day in his grand new home, said: "Yes, yes, Mistress ... Mistress McGarrity I rather think that we have now got the message about what splendid people the previous tenants were. But I still don't follow, I'm afraid. What on earth has all this to do with us and with our water-closet?"

Granny shook her head and tutted, and when she spoke, there was a matching note of asperity in her own voice.

"Sure, and is that not just what I'm trying for to tell you, Mr Kinnon, sir. When the Monaghans made their pile of money, they got a plumber – 'twas their cousin from Galway, if I remember right – anyway they had him fit up their very own water closet out in your hall there. 'Twas the talk of the neighbourhood. The only one like it – a real nine days wonder, especially when all the rest of the commonality have to use the communal cludgie out on the stair-head."

Granny paused for breath and Pearce took the opportunity to slide in a word.

"But even so, Mistress McGarrity, I still don't see that you –"

Granny smiled at Pearce, as at an errant schoolboy.

"Bless you, sir. It's no great mystery. With nobody ever locking a door hereabouts and with me getting on in age a wee bit ... the Monaghans – lovely people, the pride of the Irish – they *insisted* that I treat their water-closet as my very *own*. No need to stand on ceremony, no knocking at doors. 'Come right in, anytime, day or night, Granny. 'Tis what they used to say. No, and begorrah, we're not having a fine old Irish lady like your dear self standing out in a freezing cold close, waiting her turn for the cludgie. Our home is your home ... 'twas what they used to say."

Her monologue over, Granny then sat, hands folded in her lap and looked expectantly first at Pearce and then at his wife. If the expression on Pearce's face was anything to go by, it would be a cold day in Hell before he, like the 'so-good Monaghans', extended a similar invitation to the almost toothless crone whose sour breath could have felled a weaker man than Pearce.

Kate bent forward, and smiled.

"Well, Granny, I can't see any great difficulty. Seems to me as if you could find your way into this house in the dark. So, just you keep to your usual routine, my dear. No need to change it on account of us."

By way of reply, the old woman, with tears in her eyes, reached up and kissed Kate on the cheek. Kate caught Granny's withered hand between her own, and in that moment, it was as if a bond of friendship had been forged between them. Again Kate smiled.

"Thanks again, Granny, for that lovely surprise tea and baking. Don't you trouble yourself about the tray. One of the children will bring it through to you later."

Accepting that she might just possibly be on the point of overstaying her welcome, Granny rose to her feet, all the while her arthritic knees sounding their clicking castanets.

"Thank you kindly, Kate and you too, sir, for your offer of help. And it's been just grand meeting your lovely wee family. Yes. I've really enjoyed my visit."

The old woman was dragging her twisted, bent body through the kitchen doorway when the sound of Pearce's voice stopped her.

His voice rang out like a pistol shot.

"Mistress McGarrity. I am so glad that you enjoyed your visit – for it will be your last."

Kate drew in her breath, her face ashen, almost as if she had received a physical blow.

"Pearce."

With a wave of his hand, he dismissed that one shocked word from his wife.

"No, I will not be stopped. I will have my say, Kate. We have moved here to better ourselves. And if that includes having our own exclusive water-closet, then that's our good luck. We are not running a public lavatory here ... and most certainly not for such as you, Madam."

The previously garrulous old woman was, for once, struck dumb, but the offended look on her care-worn face spoke volumes, and none of it complimentary to her new neighbour. Kate was ashamed, appalled, and bitterly hurt on the kindly old woman's behalf. Too stunned by emotion to speak, she could yet again utter only that single word.

"Pearce."

Her husband now turned his fury on her, after having first, with an odd flapping motion of his hand, banished the listening children to the hallway beyond. He glared at his wife, who by now was standing with a comforting arm around Granny's bowed shoulders.

"Kate, you can stand there calling, Pearce, Pearce, from now until Kingdom come, if it so pleases you. But I will not be swayed from my decision. We have come here to give ourselves a lift *up* the social scale, not be dragged into a slum by some filthy peasant straight from the bogs of Ireland."

At these words, Granny stretched out a bony claw and clutched on to Kate for additional support. As the younger woman looked into the rheumy old eyes, she could see at a glance how deeply hurt had been the kindly old neighbour.

Kate knew within herself she could now have found the strength, the impetus, and the courage with which to face up to her husband. But knowing that any further angry exchange of words would only mean additional hurt for Granny, she resisted the impulse.

Drawing the bent figure closer to her bosom, she stroked down Granny's wispy hair which had escaped the steel-pinned cage of her bun.

"Right, then, Granny, my love, let's get you home safely to your own fireside," Kate said, speaking into Granny's hair. "I'll sit with you a wee while. You'd like that, now, wouldn't you dear?"

Granny's only reply was a snuffle as she was led away.

Game to the last, Pearce shouted: "Kate. Get you back into this kitchen. This minute, do you hear me? God Almighty woman, you're far too vulnerable for your own safety. Get back here now. Do you hear me?"

This latest outburst was too much for the old woman, who was now visibly trembling. Not so, Kate, who, once her Irish temper was roused, was a match for any man. Turning her body round to face him, she spoke clearly, but without obvious rancour and in a cold, yet controlled fury.

"Hear you? Oh, yes, I hear you all right, Pearce Kinnon. But heed you? Never in a million years. And while we're at it, you can forget all about cosy reconciliations. As far as I'm concerned, you've made your new beginning. So get on with it."

And with this parting shot, Kate led the still-trembling old woman out of the door and back into the safety of her own humble, yet welcoming, single-end.

A new stage in the life of Kate Kinnon had just begun. And at least one thing was sure: she had found a new friend.

Chapter 15

It was fast approaching another Hallowe'en and Kate could hardly believe the year had gone so quickly. But even if a glance at the calendar had not reassured her of the date, then the fact of children all clamouring for odds and ends of cloth, wool, any scrap of rag with which to dress-up would have done so. Kate had a rueful smile on her face as the thought came to her: '*Poor souls. They don't seem to realise that whatever rags we have we're wearing them.*'

Even so, she determined that somehow or other, she and Granny Gorbals would get Hallowe'en outfits of one sort or another codged up, so that the children could then wander the gas-lit streets for the traditional guising rites. As with everything to do with the Kinnon children, Granny threw herself into the project with enthusiasm. She raided her clothes chest and even tore up an ancient lace-trimmed petticoat, just so that Isabella could go as a fairy, the one costume on which she had set her heart. One way and another, by the time October 31st rolled along, each child was suitably outfitted. Daniel as a pirate with a black rag patch over one eye, dressed in flowing robes and a tall hat; Jenny as a witch; and Isabella, the aforementioned fairy. Even Hannah was not left out of the excitement, but since she, of necessity, had to travel in her go-chair, it was decided that she should be a baby.

Daniel, being the senior, was put in charge of the expedition, with strict instructions to keep to their own street and call only at the doors of those neighbours known to them. The excitement was particularly intense when, once dressed, he made them all go through their party pieces yet again, so that they would be word perfect. He had even worked out a little pat-a-cake routine which Isabella was to perform with Hannah.

As Kate waved them off, she tousled Isabella's fat sausage curls.

"Right, off you go. And mind now, be polite. Remember to say 'Please for my Hallowle'en' when you go into folks' houses. Then, don't stand there giggling. Get on and do your party pieces, just the way you've rehearsed."

A quiver of excitement went through the group as they looked at each other and tried desperately to remember the words of poems and songs and the various dance steps. The motley crew had already started on their way to the next close when Kate's voice halted them.

"Danny, listen, son. When you get back with your Hallowe'en spoils, instead of coming home, go straight into Granny's. All right? And you never know, there might be a wee surprise there for you."

Having seen the children safely off the premises, Kate raced back up the stairs, two at a time. As she entered Granny's single-end, she could see the old woman was already hard at work. There in the centre of the tiny room stood an enamel basin, which Granny was in the process of filling with saucepans of cold water from the goose-neck tap at the sink. On the table, waited in readiness, four rosy red apples, a large soda scone already liberally smeared with treacle, and a hollowed-out turnip into which the features of a face had been etched. The old woman raised her head as Kate entered the room.

"We're nearly there, Kate. I've got the candle ready for the lantern, and we'll light that as soon as we hear them coming up the stair. You can put the apples in the basin, then get a fork and a chair for them to kneel on for the dookin' of the apples."

Kate nodded and bustled about the room, doing Granny's bidding.

With gnarled hand on the small of her back, Granny eased her arthritic frame as upright as it would go. She surveyed her handiwork and nodded with satisfaction.

"Right. That's us. I'll just get into my costume now, while you go into your own house to get yours fixed up."

Kate's eyes widened in alarm.

"Oh. but, Granny, I haven't got a fancy dress. I never thought for myself."

Granny, far from being put out in any way by this piece of news, instead grinned in delight.

"Aye, I thought as much." Here she bent down and retrieved a newspaper-wrapped bundle which she then held out to her young neighbour. In some wonder, Kate unwrapped the parcel. Inside was an old bit of blanket, cut into a triangular shawl pattern, and over the rough material were several scorch marks as if a flat iron had rested too long.

Kate, totally bemused by now, frowned.

"But ... I don't understand, Granny ... what's it supposed to be? What am I to do with it?"

Hardly able to contain her mirth, Granny stood back, arms akimbo, and cackled: "Nothing to it, lass. Just away next door for ten minutes, brush out your hair, as if getting ready for your bed. Throw the bit blanket round your shoulders and carry a wee candle in a candle-stick. And that's you dressed for Hallowe'en."

Having delivered. herself of this speech, Granny started giggling like a naughty schoolgirl to such extent that she had to hold on to the table for support.

"But Granny ... I still don't get it."

Granny Gorbals wiped the tears of laughter from her eyes.

"Kate. You're not very quick on the uptake, are you? Do you still not see what it represents?"

Again Kate shook her head.

"Kate. It's a night with Burns. You know ... they say he was a great one for the lassies. So ... night with Burns. Get it?'

Kate put a hand to her mouth, as if scandalised.

"Granny, I'll wear it ... but just to please you, mind. And for goodness sake, don't let on to either Pearce or the bairns as to what it's supposed to be. Just let them think what they like."

On a wave of laughter, Kate left Granny to get her own fancy dress ready, whatever that might be.

On her return, Kate was surprised to see that the old woman looked much as usual, except that she was now wearing a tall black hat.

Granny grinned.

"Ach, well. Folks hereabouts say that I look like one anyway. So, no better time to be a witch than at Hallowe'en."

When the children came back with their spoils of a few farthings, toffee apples, and puff candy, they were already in a high old state of excitement. But when they entered Granny's darkened room in which the only light came from the eyes and mouth of a turnip lantern, they really went wild with excitement. When they saw Granny with her tall witch's hat and even Mammy dressed up as a rag wife, their excitement knew no bounds.

Granny leant forward and, drawing her adopted family close, she intoned in what she fondly imagined to be a witchy voice: "Now we're going to dook for apples. Right, Daniel, you can be first. Show the wee ones. Kneel on that chair, hold on to the back of it, hold the fork in your mouth and when I say the magic word, abracadabra, you drop the fork and try to spear an apple."

By the time that each child eventually had his or her own apple, everyone was drenched and the linoleum floor was awash with a puddle of water.

Granny gave Kate a rag with which to mop up the floor, while she herself watched in delight as the children devoured their hard-won apples.

There was yet one more surprise which Granny had in store, but for added excitement, she wanted the children themselves to be the first to discover it. As yet, not one of them had paid it a blind bit of notice.

She chuckled to herself at the thought: '*I wonder if they think I normally have such items hung up to air on my clothes pulley?*'

Since still nobody had remarked on either the pulley or the strange object dangling from it, Granny raised her eyes and gazed heavenwards. As is the way with people everywhere, if one person looks up with a puzzled frown as if trying to identify something, then others are sure to follow suit. Soon the children and Kate were gazing upwards in stupefaction. It was left to Hannah, always on the lookout for something to eat, to clap her hands in delight and say: "Jeely piece, Granny. Jeely piece."

Granny hugged Hannah, all the while telling her what a clever wee girl she was. The old woman laughed.

"It's not exactly jam, nor jelly either, darling. But it's treacle on both sides of the big soda scone. And all you have to do is jump up and try to catch a bite out of it."

There were whoops of delight and at once and without further invitation, all the children, with the exception of Hannah, strapped into her go-chair for her own safety, started jumping up and down.

Seeing this, Kate became mildly alarmed.

"Oh. Granny … do you think this is such a good idea? What about your poor neighbour below?"

Granny chuckled,

"Ach, let the bairns enjoy themselves. Let them jump up and down all they like. It's only that old misery downstairs – Emily McAnulty – yon dried up prune of an old maid. Honestly. she bangs the ceiling with a broom handle every single time my pulley squeaks whenever I raise or lower it for my wee bits of washing. So tonight, we might as well give the old witch something to moan about. Being Hallowe'en she'll maybe think it's ghosts trying to get at her. One thing's sure: she'll know it isn't a man. For no man would be seen dead with her."

And there the matter had rested, with three exuberant children jumping up and down, screaming loudly each time they got a belt across the face from the swaying, treacly scone. If anything, the intermittent banging sounds issuing from the irate downstairs neighbour only added to the general enjoyment.

When at last Kate managed to prise her children away, one and all agreed, treacle-covered faces and all, it was a night to remember.

Chapter 16

The excitement and promise of the forth-coming International Exhibition of 1888 had been building up for many months past. Ten-year-old Daniel Robert Kinnon was ecstatic. His own Primary School had organised to take its senior pupils, of which Daniel, happily, was one, along to Kelvingrove Park on opening day. There, complete with Union Jacks, they would join the many hundreds of Glaswegians lining the route outside the Hillhead entrance with its triumphal arch.

Quoting his teacher, Daniel would tell anyone who would listen to him that Glasgow, with a population of 761,000, was now the Second City of the Empire and was poised to stage its first major International Exhibition. The largest in Britain since the London show of 1862. True, there had been other smaller Exhibitions in the interim: in Edinburgh in 1886, and the Royal Jubilee Exhibition in Manchester 1887. However, the watchword now was: "Manchester and Edinburgh may try it, but Glasgow can do it."

The long-awaited eighth of May dawned at last and Daniel was the first member of the Kinnon family to rouse from his bed, without the usual prompting from Mammy. Still in his bare feet, he padded across to the front-room window and looked down into the street. He smiled when he saw that instead of the feared rain or Scotch mist, the day looked set fair for a day of bright sunshine. Not only that, but from the scraps of newspaper blowing along the pavements and gutters of Garth Street, it would seem that there would certainly be breeze enough to do justice to his precious flag.

Some half-hour or so later, as Daniel spooned his porridge, Mammy grinned across at him.

"'Tis a grand day you're getting for your outing, Danny. So, you be sure to sup up all that porridge – give you strength to cheer the Queen and wave your flag for her."

Daniel, never sure when Mammy was being serious or just trying to wind him up, put down his spoon with a sigh. Then with all the superiority of his school-learned knowledge and the confidence of his ten years, said: "Mammy, it isn't the Queen herself who's coming. It's the Prince and Princess of Wales. And he's to open the Eastern Palace with a gold key."

At this nugget of information, Kate shook her head in wonder.

"A gold key, indeed. My, my, and I wonder where they get the money for such extravagant frivolities? 'Twould be more like the City Fathers to provide decent houses for its workers. But there, 'tis the way of the world. And nothing the commonality – and Irish scum at that – can do about it."

Since young Daniel had no answer to this complex problem of the hated wild Irish in overcrowded Glasgow he instead concentrated on finishing his bowl of porridge. That done, he asked: "Please may I leave the table, Mammy?"

Permission graciously given by a slight nod from Mammy's head, Daniel then went over to the cupboard by the sink. He bent down and, after extracting the old tomato box of shoe cleaning materials, he got down to business. A supply of old newspapers was also kept in the box, for quite apart from its use as protector of Mammy's clean linoleum, odd bits of newspapers were used to stuff the toes of thin and shoddy footwear soaked in any one of Glasgow's famous downpours.

By the time that not only his boots were mirror-image clean, but also his unruly mop of hair had been slicked down, and even the back of his neck washed in honour of the great Royal occasion, Daniel Robert Kinnon was a joy to behold.

Mammy, one hand on hip, an appraising look in her green eyes, looked him over from top to toe.

"Yes, Danny Boy, you'll do. In fact, if the Prince of Wales himself looks any more handsome … well, I'm the one that will be fair cheated."

Unused to such praise and lacking the necessary élan with which to deal with such compliments, Danny took refuge in toeing the rag rug with his booted foot. Kate, who had put out a loving hand with which to pat his smooth cheek, thought the better of it. Instead, she diverted her hand to smoothing back a stray lock of her own hair.

'*Yes, Danny Boy, you're growing up. So I'd better not go chucking you under the chin or patting you like a baby. That would never do, to upset your manly pride.*'

Knowing all the while that she would have loved to gather her son up in her arms, Kate ignored the compulsion and instead concentrated on making him a special piece for his sweet bite which he always enjoyed at his school playtime. In honour of the Royal occasion today, her own darling Danny Boy would have, instead of the usual dripping, a taste of Granny's lemon curd.

As she handed over the newspaper-wrapped pack of thick bread slices, Kate smiled fondly at her son.

"Now, Danny, have a wonderful time at the Great Exhibition. And your teacher's got the money all gathered together to get your class in, isn't that right?"

The boy nodded, hardly able to contain his impatience to get going. However, polite as ever, he answered: "That's right, Mammy. Mind, we've been paying it up a farthing a week since March. Creepy Connor said it was cheaper going with the school – tuppence each instead of sixpence."

Kate smiled despite herself, but even so, she felt a mild rebuke to be in order.

"Danny. That's enough of that Creepy Connor talk. No way that to speak about your headmaster."

Daniel pressed his lips together then, lowering his head, looked up at his beloved Mammy.

"Sorry, Mammy. But you must admit he is a bit creepy the way he sneaks about with his big Lochgelly belt in his hand. Just fair looking for folk to punish."

Kate laughed.

"Away with you, cheeky wee rascal that you are. And you'd better hurry or you'll get a doubler from his belt for being late."

At this threat to end all, Daniel was halfway out the door before his mother stopped him with a restraining hand on his arm.

"No need to take me at my word quite so fast, Danny. Anyway, you've forgotten something."

He frowned and looked around the kitchen, and finished by patting his Sunday best jacket pocket to check that his pack of bread and lemon curd was safely stowed therein. Kate watched this performance then, without a word, she walked over to the mantelpiece and lifted down the highly-polished best tea caddy. With eagerly seeking fingers, she scrabbled around the inside of the caddy. Then, as her fingers closed over something, she withdrew her hand and again approached her son.

Whatever it was, she kept it in her tightly bunched fist. Then with a mock-serious expression on her face, she smiled at her adored son.

"Danny. Close your eyes. Then just you hold out your hands. I'll give you a creepy Kinnon doubler. See how you like that."

When Daniel again opened his eyes and looked in wonder at his upturned palm, a slow smile crept over his face.

"Oh, Mammy, Mammy. Two whole silver threepennies. For me?"

Kate threw back her head and laughed, delighted that the planned surprise for which she had also been saving at the rate of a farthing a week had proved so acceptable to Danny. Again, she laughed.

"Of course it's for you, Danny. To spend at the Exhibition. And listen, it couldn't possibly be two half silver threepennies, now could it, you daft gowk. Away with you – you can't keep Royalty waiting. And mind and use that rag I gave you for a hanky. Would never do to let the Prince of Wales think that we're all Glesga Keelies in this benighted City – even though we are Irish."

75

As she waved her son off from the front-room window, Kate found herself wondering: '*What tales would he have to tell on his return.*'

Since she herself had never been to an Exhibition of any kind, be it international or otherwise, she had no way of knowing, or any possible conception as to what delights may or may not be awaiting him. But knowing Daniel, she knew he would be full of it on his return home. Her one remaining hope was that Pearce would, for once in a lifetime, take time out to listen to his son. As she turned away from the window, having caught Daniel's last cheery wave as he turned the corner, she thought: '*Ah well, time will tell. Meantime I'd better see to Hannah and the girls. Can't stand here day-dreaming for ever more: much as I'd like to.*'

Chapter 17

When later that same day Daniel arrived home from his visit to the Exhibition in Kelvingrove Park, from the bemused expression on his face, it was clear he was still slightly shell-shocked from the impact of the wonders he had seen. The family was seated round the kitchen table and with the exception of Hannah who as usual, understood little or nothing but her own immediate needs, it was to an enthralled audience that Daniel spoke. Amazingly, even Pearce seemed not only attentive, but also even somewhat impressed. He allowed the boy to finish speaking, all the while stroking and smoothing down his handsome black beard.

"Yes. Daniel, I am indeed pleased that you've been able to give us all such a comprehensive report of your visit. Yes, that twopence was most certainly money well-spent."

Daniel's eyes widened as he started to correct Dadda as to the total amount of money spent. He got no further than: "Oh. but Dadda, I had –" when catching a warning look from Mammy, he at once changed tactics, and to cover his confusion, started coughing and spluttering, as if something had stuck in his throat.

Kate immediately got to her feet, returning a second later with a mug of cold water. With a twinkle in her eye and a conspiratorial air for his eyes alone, she held out the mug, with the tongue-in-cheek words: "Something go down the wrong way, Danny?"

When he again sufficiently recovered, Daniel resumed answering the eager questions still being fielded by Jenny and even wee Isabella whose eyes were out like organ stops in amazement. Much to Daniel's enjoyment of the unique situation, even Dadda seemed to be hanging on his every word.

"But Daniel, is that really true?" Isabella said. "What you told us about the statue heads – made out of soap?"

Daniel nodded so emphatically that a lock of hair fell over his brows.

"Honest, Isabella, it's true. I swear it. How could I even make up such a thing? There was a head and shoulder ..."

Here Pearce, ever one to educate his children interposed: "It's called a bust, Daniel. Such a carving, no matter of whatever material – it's called a bust."

Daniel digested this fact and went on: "Well, there was a bust of the Queen, Queen Victoria herself, with a crown on her head. And one each of the Prince and Princess of Wales. And Robert Burns, and Walter Scott and David Livingstone. And lots more. Wonderful to see. And all made out of soap. Now what was it called ... oh yes ... white Windsor Soap."

From then on, even after tea was well finished, Daniel was allowed, for once in his life, to hold the centre stage and regale his audience with wonders untold. There was the gigantic corncob archway with the words picked out on it; there was a full-size reproduction of a miner's workplace with the new marvel of the age – electric lights; there were dozens of ship models, including that of *Livadia*, the fantastic steam yacht recently built for the Czar of all the Russias; there was a special Exhibition of the Queen's Jubilee presents from all over the world.

"Imagine it," said Danny, with shining eyes, "eight hundred presents. Silver boxes, jewels, books, silks and satins, medals, and even slippers."

At this revelation, the girls clapped their hands in delight, as they ooh-ed. and ah-ed, all the while trying to form a mental picture of eight hundred gifts. But such a feat was beyond them, so it was left to Daniel to go on.

"There's even a whole Indian Street where you can buy ..." he cast a sideways glance at Mammy, "… if you've any money, that is, you can buy fancy sweeties in lovely tins and even in carved boxes."

Pearce laughed.

"But not, I hope, carved in Windsor soap, eh, Daniel, my boy?"

By this time, the girls were almost hysterical with laughter, as was Daniel at his father's rare joke.

"And Dadda, there's even a switchback railway. Yes, and they've got attendants stationed down below, ready to pick up any articles that get lost in all the excitement. Isn't that just grand, Dadda?"

Pearce nodded.

"Mm, Yes, grand perhaps, but not entirely educational. I rather think we could do without the switchback railway. Never mind, Daniel, you have certainly used your ears, your eyes and your tuppence all to good effect. I do congratulate you, son."

At this rare and totally unexpected praise being heaped on his unsuspecting head, Daniel was momentarily at a loss for words. Then he decided to press home his advantage for the sake of the common good.

Greatly daring, he ventured: "Dadda, do you think maybe you could take us all one of the days to see the Exhibition? There's plenty more I'd like to see or even get a closer look at. And the girls would love it, Dadda."

Pearce sat further back in his chair, folded his arms across his chest and with pursed lips appeared to think deeply before giving his 'yea' or 'nay'.

All the while he was mentally deliberating, the rest of the family, including a flush-faced Kate, held its collective breath. The only sounds were the ticking of the clock, the distant clang of a screeching tramcar, and the sucking sounds from Hannah as she chewed at the fingers of a long-suffering and somewhat mutilated Raggy-Aggy.

At length, Dadda cleared his throat. Never had he had a more appreciative or expectantly hushed audience. Leaning far back in his chair, he inserted his thumbs under the topmost part of his waistcoat, and from this stance of authority, he surveyed his audience.

"Well now, let's see: a family outing to see for ourselves the wonders of the Empire and of the world on display at Kelvingrove Park.

Again that silence.

"Just one proviso: we leave Hannah with Granny Gorbals. 'Twould be too much for the poor child, what with the crowds, the noise, and the bustle. We do that ... and yes, I think such a visit would indeed be feasible."

The girls looked at each other in disbelief, clapped a hand to mouth and ended by flinging their arms wide and hugging each other.

Daniel got to his feet, walked around the table, and shook Dadda by the hand.

Chapter 18

The summer was going on and as yet, Dadda had not fulfilled his promise to take the family to Kelvingrove Park, there to see the wonders of the Exhibition. True, he had been on the point of going towards the end of May, but then the weather had broken and there were fierce storms, and he decided to leave it until a later date. What further strengthened his resolve was that there had been reports of a number of leaks in the Exhibition's main roof and he decided in his unassailable wisdom that this would be harmful to Wee Isabella's somewhat delicate constitution. To drive home the point, he had even brought back from the Fruit Market a cutting from one of the newspapers. Under a report of the problems of the leaking roof, there was a cartoon picture of some Glasgow street urchins standing in front of the White Windsor display of soap carvings of such notables as Queen Victoria herself, the Prince Consort, Burns, Scott, and Livingstone. The aptly-worded caption read: 'THE GREAT UNWASHED get a free tub at the Exhibition during a thunderstorm.'

Pearce nodded his head sagely.

"I have already said we will go, and go we shall. But we'll wait until there are no more leaks in the roof or until the weather improves. Whichever is first."

And there the matter had rested, with no amount of cajoling, coaxing or ever tears of any avail in making Dadda change his mind.

By the time that the month of August was drawing to a close, the sun was again shining from a cloudless blue sky. Not only that, but on the 22nd of August, the streets of Glasgow were ablaze with colour of a different variety. From the topmost of every building, from each Civic office hung flags and bunting. In short, Glasgow itself was decorated to the hilt. Further, it was being said that not only had there been a flurry of repainting and an additional ornate porch added to the Main Building of the Exhibition, but also the statue of Robert Burns had been removed from the Grand Hall, there to make way for an impressive, blue bedecked throne.

"Yes, it's true, Isabella," Daniel said. "The Queen herself is coming to Glasgow – and this very day."

Isabella clapped her hands in delight, and this action was soon copied by Hannah, for whom movement and laughter of any kind was always a delight.

Daniel ruffled Hannah's coarse black hair affectionately as he passed her go-chair. Then, looking up at Mammy, with head cocked on side, he said in his quiet, thoughtful way: "Mammy. There's far more flags and excitement in the streets now for the Queen's visit than there was for the opening day itself when the Prince and Princess of Wales came. Why do you think that should be?"

Kate raised her head from the pile of freshly ironed clothes which she was about to hang up to air on the overhead wooden pulley. Glad of a break from her over-warm task, she sank with a sigh into the nearest chair.

"You're perfectly right, Daniel. People hereabouts are much more impressed. at the prospect of this visit. Of course, many a one thought she should have made an effort and opened it herself. But there's another reason …"

Danny's face posed the question and Kate went on: "Well, the truth of the matter is this: Her Majesty has only once been in Glasgow, close on forty years ago, if I understand it right. Seems she hated the grim, grey skies, was appalled at the state of our slums, and said that she disliked the City of Glasgow so much that she never wished to return."

Daniel smiled.

"Seems like she's changed her mind then; at least about never coming back."

Kate nodded.

"A woman's privilege, Daniel. And if any woman knows about privilege then it's our beloved Queen Victoria. Mind you, I agree with her about the state of Glasgow. Just wish that I could have taken one look, turned my back on the grey, horrible place, and then dismissed it from mind. But then, of course, I'm not a queen: not even the Queen of our close."

Danny laughed, knowing instinctively that his own kind, loving, gentle mother was much too backward at coming forward ever to aspire to be that formidable matron who kept tramps, drunks, and wayward children at bay: namely, the Queen of the Close.

She was, however, strong enough an authority in her own household to chivvy her troops, lest they were too late for the grand parade along Sauchiehall Street.

Rubbing her hands together in anticipation, Kate smiled at her son and said: "Come on, Danny Boy. Let's get a move on. Or it'll be another forty years before we see her Britannic Majesty and Queen Empress. You lift Hannah's go-chair down the stairs for me, and I'll bring Jenny and Isabella – not forgetting our pack of cut-bread and dripping. We can all wave our flags and then eat our pieces in the park. Right, here we go."

It was a tired but happy crew of children who returned later that evening after a feast of flag-waving and cheering. And it later appeared that no less a personage than the Queen herself had also had a good day.

For instead of just stopping-by on her way to her beloved Balmoral, as had been her stated intention, she visited again privately two days later, when she showed 'appropriate interest in the Women's and Indian Section.'

Better still, as far as the Kinnon family were concerned, with the stamp of Royal approval now firmly adhering to the entire concept of The Glasgow International Exhibition, Pearce decided the time had now come for his own family, with the exception of Hannah, to make a cultural visit.

Chapter 19

The day chosen by Pearce for the family cultural outing was a fine sunny Saturday at the end of August. By dint of working additional overtime, not only had he amassed an extra spot of money for the great event, he had also gained the rare privilege of a free Saturday afternoon. As the children and Kate herself bustled about getting ready, Pearce sat at the kitchen table, his money spread out before him, as he counted it into separately allocated bundles.

"Right. Now as to the cost of admission: it will be a shilling for you, Kate, a shilling for me, and sixpence each for Isabella, Jenny, and Daniel. I make that three and sixpence altogether."

It was a statement rather than a question, but even so, Kate shook her head.

"Not so, Pearce."

Her husband pursed his lips in annoyance.

"Forgive me, Kate," and this in a tone of voice which begged for no forgiveness, neither brooked any meddling by a stupid, uneducated woman.

He cleared his throat and repeated: "Forgive me, Kate, but if there's one thing I do know about, it's counting. After all, I am working with figures, and large columns of them at that, every day of my life at the Fruit Market."

Kate nodded, but beyond that made no comment.

"So, my dear good woman, if I say that the total admission fee comes to three and sixpence, then that is exactly right."

Again Kate shook her head, if anything even more vigorously than before.

"No, Pearce, I'm sorry, but isn't the entrance fee higher on a Saturday?"

At once enlightenment dawned on his face and happy, as always, to be able to correct her, he said: "You are correct in one point, Kate. Yes, it is more expensive one day a week, but fortunately for us, not on a Saturday. For some reason best known only to our City Fathers, on the Thursday of each week, the entry fee jumps to an astronomical half-crown."

Kate looked suitably impressed with this nugget of information. Even so, she again, and much to the interest of Daniel, said: "Your total is still wrong, Pearce. You are forgetting another sixpence for Hannah."

At once her husband's face darkened, and he pounded a clenched fist on the table with such force that his carefully constructed piles of money disintegrated and scattered in disarray across the width of the oil-cloth covered table. He half-rose to his feet.

"Kate, let me get this straight. Right from the word go, I said that this family cultural and – I hope – highly educational, visit would exclude Hannah. Quite apart from the needless extra expense, it would be of no possible interest to one of her mentality."

Kate sucked in her breath over her teeth then, without a minute's hesitation, she launched into the attack.

"Pearce. You talk about a family outing. I would remind you that Hannah is a member of this family and a much-loved one at that. And let me tell you this; if Hannah is excluded from the outing, then we all stay at home. Of course, you yourself are at perfect freedom to attend alone in all your glory."

Even as she spoke, Kate was conscious of three pairs of young and somewhat anxious eyes fixed upon her face.

The thought went through her mind: '*I'll hate to disappoint the others. But if that's what I have to do, then so be it. For we are not setting foot beyond this door without Hannah. And I'll hate worst of all to let Danny down, especially after he spent some of his precious money at the Exhibition on buying me a wee souvenir box of sweets. Still, the decision is Pearce's, not mine.'*

Later that same day and after a right Royal battle of wills, the family set out en mass on the great adventure.

Once arrived at the Exhibition, they wandered around the sights, stalls, and exotic smells of the wide Main Avenue, while from the Grand Hall beyond could be heard the strains of the daily organ recital. Daniel was particularly enamoured of the many splendid ship models from such famous shipbuilders as Fairfield Co. Ltd, who built not only cargo ships, but also ironclads, luxury liners, and even millionaires' pleasure boats.

When it became obvious not only that the rest of the Kinnon clan had had more than their fill of ship models but that Daniel wanted to linger longer at this display, it was Pearce himself who came up with what appeared to be an amicable and universally approved suggestion. Turning to his son, he leant forward and, at his most majestic, said: "Listen, Daniel, this is what we'll do: you stay on here with Hannah; after all, it doesn't much matter to her what she sees. I'll take Mammy and the other two girls over to the Van Houten's Dutch House. I believe that they serve excellent cocoa there at tuppence a cup. And wee Isabella will enjoy having it served by the girls in their national dress."

It was arranged that they would all meet up later in the Indian Street where it was felt there would be plenty with which to amuse even Hannah, since many of the stallholders there sold all varieties of rich Indian sweetmeats. Pearce was just turning away when suddenly he put a hand in his pocket and, returning to his son's side, held out a handful of coppers and two silver threepenny bits.

"Here you are, Daniel. Treat Hannah and yourself to some sweets. But not too many, we don't want any upset stomachs. Right. We'll be off for that cocoa. We'll meet up with you later. Good-bye for now."

A bemused expression on his face, Daniel looked down in wonder at the sum of money, far more than he had ever before received from his father. He smiled. Oh. Yes. He would do Dadda's bidding in getting a wee treat for Hannah and himself. But in addition to the already mentioned sweets, he had an additional treat in mind. It was one that he knew Hannah would love – even though, for once, it had nothing whatever to do with eating.

It was an hour or so later when the family finally met up again.

"Well, Daniel, I see from the way your jaws are going that you found the sweet stall all right."

Here, Pearce cast a fleeting glimpse at Hannah whose jaws also were working overtime.

Pearce, in a rare good humour at the excellent way his two girls and his wife, without the encumbrance of Hannah, had conducted themselves at the Van Houten Dutch House, now detailed their next move.

"We'll have another half-hour or so in looking at the working models: see how they make comfits; prepare sacks of Scott's Midlothian Oats; and if we're lucky, we might even catch a *glimpse* of the Power Drop Biscuit Machine. After that ... well, I'm going to treat us all to a High Tea. After all, this is a real occasion in our lives. "

When, sometime later, it was time to choose which tea room they would favour, again Pearce took charge. He refused absolutely, and somewhat surprisingly, since he himself was now teetotal, to set foot into Jenkins Temperance Refreshment Rooms.

But the reason became clear, to Kate at least, when on closer examination, she saw that the restaurant was further billed as Working Men's Dining Rooms. The thought went through her mind: '*Oh, dear me, no. That would not be sufficiently grand for our high-born Pearce. And tucked in here between the Dynamo Shed and the Machinery Court. 'Twould never do.'*

Some half-hour and footsore miles later, the family, somewhat to their own surprise, found themselves ensconced in the genteel Royal Bungalow, which itself occupied a prime position not only overlooking the river, but also the bandstand and the beautifully illuminated Fairy Fountain. In such an elegant setting, while Pearce seemed perfectly at home, Isabella and Jenny did their best to cope with the stress of it all and when they spoke at all, it was in the hushed tones normally reserved for the rare occasions when Pearce took them to Mass at the High Anglican Church. Kate extended her little finger, or pinky as Glaswegians called it, in what she thought to be the formally correct mode of raising a cup to one's lip in polite society.

As Pearce looked round his family seated upright at the snowy-white, linen-covered table with its heavy, silver cutlery, from the self-satisfied smirk on his face it was clear to even the most casual observer that he was congratulating himself on his well-behaved brood.

Jenny had been spooning up another helping of food for Hannah. At that moment the unfortunate child moved, gagging on the food already in her mouth. With a loud retching sound, which could be heard, much to the disgust of the elegant ladies and their handsome escorts, all over the opulent restaurant, Hannah vomited the mess far and wide. If ever there was a display of projectile vomiting then this was it. Some of the spewed-forth vomit now dripped from Isabella's lovely golden ringlets, there were splashes of the foul-smelling mess on Pearce's best and only silk waistcoat. Even worse, a well-upholstered and richly-dressed matron at the next table had been the recipient of a goodly share of the vomit which had now come to rest on the ledge of her well-endowed bosom. On all sides, there was much confusion and pushing away of well-filled plates, as with expressions of disgust and much wrinkling of patrician noses, the patrons decided that the meal had come to an untimely finish.

Even greater confusion reigned at the Kinnon table, as Kate both tried to mop up Hannah with a convenient table napkin and at the same time round up her brood.

As they left in some disorder, Kate was sure she heard a comment in the tortured vowels of the refined Kelvinside accent from one over-dressed, over-fed, and over-bejewelled matron to the effect that: "Can't imagine how that lot of scruff got in here. Don't they know there's a working men's dining establishment for the likes of them?"

Daniel, as he trailed out after the rest of his family, was conscious of two facts: the first, he and his family were the centre of all eyes, every stuck-up toff, every la-de-dah snob in the place had studied the Kinnons and found them wanting. Not only were they scum, they were Irish scum at that; the second, once safely home in Garth Street, he was set fair to get the thrashing of his young life from Dadda.

For not only had he been the guilty party, who had stuffed Hannah to capacity with a variety of rich Indian Sweets, there was still that other matter. He knew in his heart it would be bound to come out, one way or another. So he might just as well confess to it ... aye, he had taken Hannah on the switchback railway. And not just once. She'd had two rides on the thrill-a-minute coaster. And if that plus the glut of sweets had made her sick, then yes, of course, he was sorry.

But Hannah had squealed with delight throughout her exciting, never-to-be-repeated journeys. All right, she had been sick afterwards, but if they were apportioning blame, whose choice had it been to make them all suffer the torment of the damned high tea, no less in that temple to high fashion and false manners, that swanky restaurant in which they had no place, nor indeed any idea of how to conduct themselves?

True, she could equally well have spewed forth her meal in the Working Men's Dining Room. But somehow Daniel had the feeling, rightly or wrongly, that it would not have caused such a furore there, nor been regarded as a studied affront to the other diners – all of them as lowly born as the Kinnons themselves.

Chapter 20

The day had started like any other in their small, cosy and now fairly-well furnished and equally well-run home. After the upset of the move from their old home and the debacle of the flitting itself, all the children and Kate herself had settled well into their new abode. In the two-and-a-half years that had since passed, the children had made new chums in the neighbouring streets. Kate also had cultivated new, and in at least a couple of cases, better friendships; Pearce plodded along as usual in his job at the Fruit Market. Kate often pondered the truth that beyond the fact her husband worked at the Market, and brought home his wages faithfully every week, she knew very little about either the Fruit Market itself or about Pearce's place there in the hierarchy

On the few occasions that she had tried to pump him for information, he had replied: "Look, Kate, you know that the Market is just around the corner, for you must pass it every day. You know that I work there and that I bring home a living-wage, sometimes with enough left over for those little ornaments you so delight in. Honestly, I don't know of any other woman in the Candleriggs who is the proud possessor of three pairs of wally dugs."

Kate had laughed at that, for it was true enough. While Pearce might deny her much in the way of loving affection, he did, however, humour her in her passion for cheap china knick-knacks, or what she herself chose to call her wee bit dabbities. But when she dared to ask him about his job, his face darkened.

"Kate, you do your job in the home, and I'm bound to admit, you do it well. The place is always gleaming, polished to an inch of its life with your vinegar-soaked cloth, or whatever it is you use. Well-cooked meals are always on the table at exactly the right time. And the children are growing up to be a credit to you. But having said all that, you do your job and I'll do mine. That's all you need to know, especially as long as I bring home sufficient money with which to feed, house and clothe us."

Despite having been overwhelmed at such unexpected praise being bestowed upon her blushing brow, Kate had been forced to leave the matter there.

Such had been the thoughts going through Kate's head that spring morning when she first awoke, that for once she was loathe to leap out of bed in her usual fashion. However, with a deep-felt sigh, she rubbed her eyes awake with knuckled hands, knowing as she did, if she wanted the range cleaned out, relit with twists of old newspapers and spent coals, then she had better get on and do it. For as Pearce had so rightly said, and that on more than one occasion:

"You do your job, Kate. And I'll do mine. A woman's work is in the home."

And there the strict delineation of work had stayed. In good days and bad, in fine weather and foul, in sickness and in health. Pearce would no more have thought of lifting a nugget of coal with which to replenish a dying fire than he would have dreamt of going to work without his gaffer's bowler hat. For Pearce, entirely due to his own hard work, had come on in the world. With a number of young clerks working under him, he was the boss of that particular section and as such, entitled to wear that much aspired-to badge of office – the gaffer's bowler hat. At the way her thoughts were wandering this morning Kate shook her head of rich, nut-brown hair, so vigorously that the two fat plaits danced around her.

Then, speaking quietly to herself, she said: "Come on, Kate, my girl. Never get the porridge on the fire at this rate. Nor the bairns ready for school."

She sidled her bottom over to the edge of the bed. taking care not to waken a still sleeping Pearce, nor even the three girls lying on the hurlie-bed and over whose still forms she would have to step in order to reach her clothes. Keeping a wary eye on the four recumbent bodies, she dressed quickly and expertly in the curtained dark before reaching up to the gas-mantle. That done, she brushed out the thick pigtail plaits, which, thus released, fell in a cascade of waves to her slim waist. Then, with a couple of deft and long-practised movements, she swept the mass of hair up into a coil which she in turn skewered with steel pins on top of her head. She then went into the front room to waken her son and on the way back through the narrow, dark hallway, paid a quick visit to the water-closet. Back in the kitchen, she washed her hands under the tap at the sink, and started her daily routine. The pot of porridge oats had been steeping overnight, so once she had finally coaxed the fire in the range into active life and added another scoop of coal as added encouragement, she positioned the pot and then set about laying the table. As she bustled about filling the kettle for Pearce's early-morning cup of tea, she hummed softly to herself, already happier that the well-oiled routine was moving smoothly.

Later, having devoured his tea, porridge, toast and dripping in complete silence, Pearce eased his chair back a bit from the table, patted his stomach as if congratulating it upon the fine job it had just done and, with unaccustomed bonhomie, smiled at Kate.

"My, and that was grand, Katie lass, just grand. Just the thing to set up a working-man for the day's toil ahead of him."

Kate somewhat flustered by the unaccustomed praise, Pearce's good humour, and his surprising use of her pet name, smoothed down her apron and smiled uncertainly, as she waited for him to go on.

His keen, piercing eyes which never missed a thing, be it a speck of dust or an unwashed mug, looked her over from top-knot to toe. Then, as if liking, perhaps even more, approving, what he saw, he leant forward and, taking her work-worn hand in his, said: "Katie, listen, my darling girl. I've been thinking." Here he cast a surreptitious glance over his left shoulder at the three forms still in the hurlie bed. Satisfied they were in fact still asleep, he moved his hand further up her arm and in a grand conspiratorial whisper said: "Yes, thinking, a good deal of late. Now that I'm earning a good steady wage week after week, and thanks largely to your good management, we have no outstanding bills. Well, the point I'm trying to make is this: how would you like a –"

Kate, her green eyes wide with astonishment and perhaps even a measure of fear as to what on earth might be coming, decided, if nothing else, to put an end to the agony of suspense, to make a joke of it, clutching one hand to her bosom and raising the other to her furrowed brow in the classic pose of the abandoned drunkard's wife about to be thrown out into the snow, she screeched:

"No, Pearce, no. Not another house move. I don't think I could stand that. Not so soon. Not just after three short and – may I say happy – years here in Garth Street."

Pearce laughed appreciatively and not least at the effect his own words had had on his wife. He allowed himself the rare luxury of a tight, self-satisfied little smile. It was still playing about his lips as he said in what was, for him at least, a coquettish tone of voice: "Katie, my own dear girl, you should have been an actress. But listen. Do be serious for a minute. Bear with me. It is not a house move which I have in mind, but –"

Still enjoying to the full their rare moment of intimacy and shared innocent fun, Kate could not resist prolonging the delightful event. Again clutching one hand to her breast, she laid the other hand on Pearce's arm and with her eyes raised to heaven in mock distress, she moaned: "Oh. Sir, kind sir. Tell me what my fate at your hands must be. Tell me. For I am but a poor unschooled country maid and not wise in the ways of a cruel, wicked world."

Pearce started to laugh and went on laughing until he had to hold on to the back of a kitchen chair for support. Then at last, he wiped his eyes with the back of his shirt-sleeve.

"Katie, Katie. Honestly, we're both behaving like a pair of naughty, over-exuberant school children. And look, there's poor Hannah stirring with all the commotion. Well, I can see I had better tell you quickly and have done with it."

Kate dropped her hand from his arm, lowered her head, and then, looking up between girlishly, shy, half-closed eye-lashes, said: "Tell me, kind sir, for I am totally at your mercy. What now is to be my fate?"

He reached out and clasped her round the waist in such a bear-hug as she had never before known. Then, speaking close to her top-knot, he said: "What I have in mind is this, my dear; a family holiday, no less."

Chapter 21

Kate was stunned, but she managed to recover herself sufficiently to say in a tone of wonder: "A wee holiday, did you say, Pearce? By all that's miraculous, that would be truly wonderful. In all the long, weary years we've been here in this grim, grey, accursed city, the furthest I've ever been from Candleriggs is a wee outing to Glasgow Green and Kelvingrove."

Kate frowned, then slapping the palm of her hand against her forehead, she exclaimed: "No, I'm sinning my soul by telling a lie. I remember now you once took us to that lovely Rouken Glen for an afternoon. But a wee holiday. Now that indeed would really be something. But, Pearce, do you really mean it? I beg of you, please don't make sport of me, for that I just could not bear."

He laughed good-humouredly, and not least at her recently adopted Glasgow accent, which contrasted oddly with her soft and attractive Irish brogue. He leant over and, as if to lend weight to his words, patted her bare arm gently.

"A little holiday, I said, my dear, and that is exactly what I meant. If it pleases you to do so, then look on it as a reward for the job, the grand job, I may say, that you're doing in rearing our family in this alien environment. With the exception of poor daft Hannah, who'll never be anything other than she is, they are all turning out much better than I could ever have expected or even hoped for."

He beamed his approval at her and although Kate could well have taken umbrage at his comments with regard to Hannah – for she alone knew how very hard she worked with the poor soul – she decided instead to bask in the glory of the moment. That being so she pushed back an overhanging lock of hair, smoothed down her sack-cloth apron, and smiled back at her husband.

"Yes, Katie, my girl, you're bringing them up just fine, to be decent citizens. Not like some of the riff-raff we see around here. They're polite and well-spoken, albeit with lapses into that terrible, guttural Glasgow patter. I swear to God, they're bi-lingual. And well-read too."

His eyes blazing with excitement, he leant forward and grasped her hands between his own.

"Katie, as you know, I really do detest either you or any of the children adopting this vile Glasgow accent. Even so, the locals have a very apt turn of phrase for what it is I'm planning."

He paused to let his words sink in. At this, Kate leapt from her chair, as if shot from a cannon. Her green eyes aglow, she stared at him in disbelief.

"Pearce. You don't mean ... you can't mean ... it would be just too wonderful for words."

Pearce too rose to his feet and, with a beaming grin, he held wide his arms to her, as at that exact moment, and like a couple of excited school children, they shouted in unison: "A wee trip doon the watter."

He hugged her to him then, as they drew apart, with a delighted grin still on his face, he laughed.

"And apart from the pleasure it will afford the whole family, there's something else. We can look on it as a special birthday treat for wee Isabella. How would that be? Good idea, don't you think? After all, we'll never forget the day of her birth, will we? With that awful launching tragedy on the Clyde. Still, we're lucky, we're together. And the mighty River Clyde will be our friend, our means to take us doon the watter to the lovely Island of Bute."

Kate was overcome with joy, as her eyes took in and tried to comprehend the rare sight of her husband's face, happy and carefree at last.

She began to hope in her heart perhaps at long last he was getting over the death of his beloved and sorely-missed, dearly departed Andrew and Angela.

As she waved her husband off to work, and then cleared away his breakfast things, before getting the children up, the phrase kept going round and round in her head.

"Just a wee trip doon the watter."

Unable to restrain her exuberance, she hiked up her skirts and did a spirited Irish dance right there and then by the side of the kitchen sink.

The thought came to her:

'Honestly. I can hardly wait to tell the. children. But, perhaps I'd better wait until things are definitely arranged. It would never do to disappoint the wee darlings.'

She started re-laying the table in readiness for the children, then, with hand poised over the table with some spoons, she paused. Her face lit up with her sudden, bright idea.

'That's it. That's exactly what I'll do. I'll go round and have a word with Big Betty Donavan. Seems to me she went doon the watter last year. I'll find out all about it from her. Then once everything's settled, all cut and dried, like, that's when I'll tell the children the good news. But not before.'

That point happily settled in her own mind, she bustled about the kitchen getting both herself and the children ready to face another day. She smiled and hummed to herself, secure in the knowledge that right at that moment life was good and even seemed, amazingly, to be getting better all the time.

Chapter 22

Glasgow Fair Saturday dawned at long, long last. Although by tradition this great day always fell on a day in mid-July for all the sunshine, so little light that penetrated Kate's back kitchen, it might just as well have been a day in the gloom of November. Small wonder then that Isabella had asked for about the fiftieth time in as many moments: "Mammy, is it really true? Are we really going away to the seaside for a holiday?"

Kate nodded happily, already busy in trying to slick down Hannah's coarse dark hair in order to make the poor child as presentable as possible for the great adventure. Despite the gloom of the weather, inside the overcrowded kitchen even at that early hour, there was already an air of carnival. In one corner, Daniel was crouched low over a sheet of newspaper as he blackened and brushed his best Sunday boots. Young Jenny was already wearing, at a rakish angle, her straw sun bonnet, which although new to her, had already weathered a lifetime of summers, before finally coming to rest in Paddy's Market, from which a bargain-hunting Kate had rescued it in exchange for handing over to the stall-holder one silver threepenny bit. Kate smiled as she recalled how Jenny had carefully climbed on a chair to place her precious hat on a high shelf well out of the grasping reach of her younger sister.

Isabella, who had packed and repacked her leather school bag at least a dozen times, with increasingly disastrous results, was at that very moment doing her best to stuff back inside the bag an overhanging length of cotton petticoat and one draw-string navy knicker leg. When the latter item, which seemed to have a life of its own, again cascaded over the edge, she gave a tut of annoyance and threw the bag angrily into the corner where it just missed the open tin of greasy black shoe polish. More to divert her Mother's attention from the near disaster in the corner than for any other reason, Isabella turned and again asked: "Mammy, is it really today we're going on that big boat? Honest and true?"

Kate gave a final pat to Hannah's hair, secured with a Kirby grip the child's favourite tartan ribbon which she had already tied into a chocolate-box bow, and then turned to face her youngest daughter.

Then, holding her arms wide, she gathered Isabella to her bosom and gave her a reassuring kiss.

"Yes, my darling. It is indeed true. We are going this very day. And no mistake. Even if I have to drive the boat myself."

Just at that moment, Pearce came in from the hallway, and, catching the last of Kate's words, he gave a hearty laugh.

"You drive the boat, did you say, Kate? Humph. And a grand job you would make of it too. Like as not, we'd all end up in the nearest tenement close, and not a very salubrious one at that, I'll be bound, probably round the corner from Govan Wharf.

The children all laughed uproariously at this. Then as their laughter died away, Pearce, as if again back to his usual strict manner, frowned.

"Well now, children, it's high time we were all ready. If we fritter away the morning like this, I'm sorry to tell you that there's only one thing we'll catch. And it won't be the *Marquis of Bute* at that."

Daniel looked up from where he was engaged in clearing away the boot cleaning materials.

"But Dadda, if we don't catch the big boat, what will we catch?"

Pearce gave them all a wicked grin, with the nearest thing to a twinkle in his eye.

"The only thing we're likely to catch, son, is a head cold."

With the exception of Daniel, who blushed scarlet and felt that he had been made a fool of, the rest of the family roared with laughter.

Half an hour later, amid a welter of bags, cane-baskets, hampers, children, buckets and spades, and the ever present go-chair for Hannah, the Kinnon clan finally emerged from their close and headed in procession along Argyle Street towards their first port of call at the Broomielaw.

As they marched along, the first thing that Kate noticed was that the normally busy streets were, much to her surprise, strangely deserted. In fact, instead of the usual noises of the City, the pounding of horses' hooves, the screech of tramcars, the cries of the street traders and all the other ever-present sounds now so familiar to her, today there was nothing. Whatever distant sounds there were, the barking of a dog, the screaming of a child, all seemed strangely muted.

Never the less despite the somewhat eerie atmosphere, their family procession kept steadfastly on its way with, as usual, Pearce striding on at its head, walking-stick in one hand, holiday hamper in the other, the children, also encumbered with various items of luggage, following in Indian file, with Kate bringing up the rear with Hannah in her ancient go-chair packed with parcels, sun-hats, stretched woollen cardigans, and even an umbrella and a brightly-painted parasol with which to cover all eventualities. It was when they were walking under the Highlanders' Umbrella further along Argyle Street that Kate realised what a difference the absence of its usual traffic, people, noise, and bustle made. In this covered space under the railway bridge, the screech of Hannah's rickety go-chair echoed all around them, as did the clank of the older children's tin buckets and spades as they from time to time clattered against the enamel mugs which each child wore on a neck-string, almost as a badge of office.

Kate had a quiet smile to herself when she thought of the name, Highlanders' Umbrella. Many people thought it had gained its name on account of the many immigrants from the Highlands of Scotland being mean with what little money they had and sheltering from the rain under the covered area, rather than go to the expense of buying an umbrella.

But thanks to the knowledgeable Granny Gorbals, Kate knew

different. The reason for the name had nothing whatever to do with the supposed thriftiness of the Highlanders. No, it was quite a different reason. Over time it had become a meeting place for the hundreds of young men and women, homesick for their beloved glens, braes, and Highland crofts left far behind them, who had, of necessity, come to the City of Glasgow to seek work. On their one free day, the Sabbath, they would congregate under the Highlanders' Umbrella, there to meet with other homesick exiles and speak their own beloved, lilting Gaelic language.

Kate had never seen the Sabbath meetings, but again according to Granny Gorbals any Sunday afternoon or evening, in front of every closed shop, there would be little groups of people from Mull, Mallaig, Inverary, or any other part of the Scottish Highlands one cared to mention.

Kate was shaken out of her reverie when there was an explosive sneeze from Hannah. At once, Kate ground the go-chair to a halt, withdrew a rag from under the sleeve of her best navy serge dress, and prepared for battle.

If there was one thing which Hannah, normally fairly biddable, really hated, it was having her nose wiped. She would squirm her body away, toss her head from side to side, and then retch loudly when her Mammy's rag finally made contact with the dribbling green slime. Pearce had also stopped and with his walking-stick was indicating that they should hurry along. Then, in case his wife had still not got the message, he cupped a hand to his moustached and bearded mouth and yelled.

"Kate. For heaven's sake, do get a move on. The *Marquis of Bute* won't wait for ever, you know, and certainly not on our convenience. Hurry up."

Kate took a wild swipe at Hannah's face, and much to the latter's displeasure, scored a bull's eye. That done, she went hurrying on to meet up with her husband before he could get a chance to berate her further for her tardiness.

"I was just thinking back there," she said, "how lucky the

Highlanders are with their own meeting-place. Must be grand that, when you're feeling homesick. 'Tis a pity we don't have an Irishman's Umbrella. Now wouldn't that be something?"

Pearce, intent on making sure that he got his brood to the Broomielaw dockside with all possible speed, without even slackening his pace, turned his head and looked at his wife as if she had taken leave of her senses.

"What? What's that? Oh yes, I see what you're on about now. But you're forgetting surely. The Irish in Glasgow do have a meeting place. Of course they do."

It was Kate's turn to look puzzled. Then her face cleared and she smiled.

"You're right, Pearce. How could I have forgotten Paddy's Market especially since every stitch the children and ourselves wear comes from its stalls. Paddy's Market, yes, you're right."

Pearce's only reply was a dismissive shake of his head, as if in this way, he could wave aside her words. He frowned at her.

"No. That's not the meeting place I meant. I was referring, of course, to the Ship Bank Tavern, a pub which has long been the unofficial headquarters of the Irish in Glasgow."

Kate frowned.

"Oh, can't say I ever heard of it."

Pearce allowed himself the luxury of a superior smile. Looking down at her from his great height, he replied:

"Well, naturally, my dear. After all, a public house is no place for a respectable matron like yourself. But of course, I personally have always been aware of its existence. They do say that if you come from Donegal, Cork, Ballygally, or any place in Ireland for that matter, all you have to do is go along to the Ship Bank Tavern in the Briggait, and within minutes, you'll be given the address of, and I daresay a helping hand from, another immigrant from your own area. No problem at all."

Kate stopped so abruptly that with the judder of the go-chair, Hannah's uncoordinated fingers loosed their hold on her rag doll, which jerked out of her hands and fell down on to the pavement, just missing a puddle by inches. As she stooped to retrieve poor Raggie-Aggie, Kate fought hard to keep the anger she felt out of her face and her voice. Her common sense told her to let the matter rest there, but even so, she could not resist one short barb.

"Pearce, do you mean to say you knew about that pub when we arrived, poor, lost souls, that awful day at the Broomielaw? You knew there was help readily available? You mean we need never have gone through that demeaning scene with the high and mighty lady whatsit? Oh, Pearce, Pearce."

His lips twisted in a sneer of scorn.

"Look, the past is over and done with. But if you must know, yes, I was fully aware of the existence and of the actual location of that Irish pub in the Briggait."

Kate opened her mouth but so great was her white-faced shock that no sound issued from her lips.

"Yes, Kate, of course I knew. A rough fellow on the boat across from Ireland gave me full directions as to how to find the place, and also a contact name to ask for. But let's face it, my dear, I also knew, without ever seeing the Tavern, that it would not have been my sort of place. And you could hardly have expected me to mix with a rabble: common Irish peasants straight from the bogs, all penniless and looking for a hand-out, now could you?"

Kate's answer was lost, for at that moment, they rounded the corner and found themselves at the Broomielaw Wharf. What first struck them was the appalling noise.

Pearce, blissfully unaware of the seething emotions still boiling in Kate at his recent revelations, turned to his wife.

"Aha, so now we know why Argyle Street was so quiet. It seems that everyone else in the whole of Glasgow got here before us."

Kate gazed about her, a look of disbelief on her face, her eyes still on the seething mass of noisy, excited, and voluble would-be passengers.

"But Pearce, surely one boat is never going to take all these people? We'll be killed in the rush. That we will."

Pearce did not deign to answer what his superior look obviously classed as an ignorant, ridiculous question. Instead, with a jerk of his thumb, he indicated the many boats tied up to the quayside, boats with names like *Benmore, Columba, Sultana, Viceroy, Undine, Guinevere,* and half a dozen more and each one with its own wooden destination board with such names as Rothesay, Kirn, Innellan, Dunoon, Lamlash, Brodick, Whiting Bay, and many others.

Kate made a long whistling sound of relief and turned back to her husband with a smile on her face.

"Well, thank goodness for that. I was worried for a minute there. But listen, I've never heard of half these places."

It was her husband's turn to grin, pleased as ever to air his superior knowledge.

"Well, just concentrate on Rothesay. You've heard of that and that's where we're bound. Some of the others, likes of Brodick, Lamlash, and Whiting Bay, they're on the Island of Arran. At one point, I did think we might have gone there. I believe you get a better class of person there. But then the fare decided it for me. As far as I recall, it costs roughly two shillings per head more to travel to the Island of Arran than it does to that of Bute. Anyway, Royal Rothesay is known as the Madeira of Scotland, so at least the sun should be shining there."

Kate nodded, all the while with her eyes on the ant-hill of men, women and children, all at a rare pitch of excitement and all desperate to get on to their respective boats and on their way far from the city streets for fourteen glorious days.

She reflected that ever since young Andrew's tragic death from diphtheria, Pearce, at first lost in the depths of depression, had finally emerged from the black cloud to choose yet another favourite from his, by now, somewhat depleted family. Kate smiled grimly to herself as the thought rose unbidden to her mind.

'*His latest favourite. Humph. An easy choice that, I must say. He detests Hannah, can't even bear to look at the road Daniel is on, and wee Jenny, young as she is, is far too much like himself in temperament – aye, and I must say it though God forgive me – she's too much like his old father in appearance for his lairdship's liking. She reminds him too much of people, places and past events in Ireland which he'd much rather forget.'*

She nodded sagely.

'Aye. Not much of a choice. That left only the fair Isabella, didn't it? No wonder that she's now his bright shining star.'

Kate was interrupted in her musings. Some sort of bitter altercation was going on between a man standing nearby and some tongue-waggling children. His face puce, the man was bawling at the world in general, and at any child in particular who would stop their wild games and studied insolence long enough to listen. Up till then, apart from the gangway-bashers who were annoying nobody but those unfortunate, more timid children still meekly awaiting their shot, the gangs of screaming children chasing each other had been proving a real menace to everyone. Given the press of humanity, it meant that every time a child raced past, then at least one bystander received a hefty blow from an enamel mug, which swung from the neck of every child.

The irate passenger, whose cheap cardboard suitcase had already been sent flying, and at one point had been in danger of himself falling into the water as he had rescued it from where it teetered on the edge of the quay, had had more than enough. That last blow on the jaw from a flying enamel mug had been the last straw.

"See you kids. You wee brats. Just one more belt from those bloody mugs. Just one more, that's all. And you lot of nitwits are all for the high jump. Dae you hear me? Get the message, eh? Or do I have to shove the message right into your lugholes? Aye, and with a belt on the ear to go with it."

At this outburst, most of the children took the warning and sped as far away and as quickly as they could from their tormented victim. It was left to one particularly brave, tousle-haired youngster to make a rude gesture at the kilted holidaymaker, at the same time chanting:

Kiltie, Kiltie, cauld bum, big banana feet
Cuddles a' the lassies and farts in his seat
Kiltie, Kiltie cauld bum, big –

On hearing this, the enraged man roared like a bull and would have pursued the fleeing youngster had it not been for the concerted cheer which just then went up from the crowd, thus announcing without the benefit of any official notification that the gangway had now been placed in position, in readiness for the passengers to get on board the *Glen Rosa*. At once, a tremor of excitement went round the ranks as those passengers who intended to board this boat, started to gather up bits of luggage, shuffle forward and finally, search frantically for those missing members of their family who, up until then, had been amusing themselves in doing exactly as they wanted, be it playing on the gangways, chasing each other, or annoying other passengers. The air was rent with a cacophony of such panic cries as,

"Jamesina, come here."

"Henrietta, come over here tae your Granny at once. At once, I say. Dae ye hear me, you wee midden."

And the threat to end all:

"Willie McKitterick, if you don't come over here this minute … Aye you. You wee toe rag, this very minute, the only bloody boat for you will be the Training Ship. And you can soon see how weel ye like that, my fine laddie."

Pearce, oblivious to the chaos around him, was lost in his memories. He and Calum had sailed thus as children down the Clyde, so long ago, buffered from the crowd by two stout footmen, supervised by Calum's sour faced tutor determined to turn the excursion into an educational event. He smiled, remembering their escape from the tutor into the seething mass of passengers and playing hide and seek, unwilling on his part, with the tutor for the better part of the morning till hunger drove them to meet him in the restaurant. There had been other holidays with Calum in Ireland when Calum was as adventurous and mischievous as he had been. Happy days, indeed.

Kate's voice broke into his pleasant reverie.

"Well, Pearce, not be long now, eh? Strange being back again at the Broomielaw, isn't it? Remember last time?"

He turned on her a look of loathing.

"No need to remind me, Kate. If anyone knows where this charade of family life began in this God forsaken City of Glasgow, then that person is me. I do assure you."

Kate stopped rounding up children, pram, Hannah, and luggage. The colour faded instantly from her already pale face, as she rounded on him, and oblivious to the inquiring stares of bystanders, and the perked-up, intently listening ears of her own children, she said in the loudest of stage whispers: "Charade of family life, did you say, Pearce? Well, by God. And if anyone has made it a charade, then it's you. You yourself, the Laird of Candleriggs. Lording it over all and sundry: Lording it here, there, and yonder. But your own family. Humph. Never, never there for your family. May the Good Lord above forgive me, but for all you either know or care, we might as well not even exist. Do you hear me, Pearce?" At this point, her voice rose almost to a screech. "These precious wee bairns and I might as well not exist. You treat us like scum. Like the very dirt under your feet."

All around them, interested bystanders were beginning to nudge each other in the ribs and then either point or nod surreptitiously towards the Kinnon clan and then titter behind cupped hands. Seeing this further development of such unwanted attention being bestowed on them, Kate blushed scarlet with shame and humiliation, especially when she found the other passengers were beginning to shuffle forward, ever nearer to herself and Pearce, the better to hear the rowing couple's angry words. Pearce, suddenly aware of this public interest in his most private life, drew himself to his full six foot two inches height, stared down coldly at his wife and said in his most haughty manner and cultured voice: "Kate, I rather think we will pursue this ... discussion on arrival at our destination. Meanwhile, let us now board the waiting vessel. See. The gangway is now in position."

Amid a welter of leave-takings of those less fortunate mortals being left behind in Glasgow, cries of delight, shouts of anxiety, the passengers all finally boarded the gaily bedecked vessel. Then, as it pulled away from the dockside at the Broomielaw, the ship's horn sounded a farewell blast, which caused those of a more nervous disposition to cry out in alarm. This was followed by shouts of relief when they realised there was nothing to worry about, it merely signalled the fact that at long last, they were finally underway.

Despite the earlier gloom of the day, and as if also to cheer the *Marquis of Bute*, the sun was now breaking through, with the promise of a fine summer's day to follow. Between that and the prospect of two weeks' holiday spent doon the watter and far removed from the grime of the Glasgow city streets, there was an air of festivity aboard. And well to the fore was the usual Glasgow camaraderie and brilliantly warm sense of humour. On all sides, total strangers were laughing and joking and calling each other Jimmy, Jock, or Shuggie, no matter what their proper name might be, and no-one seemed to mind in the slightest.

In the Kinnon clan, relations were obviously still greatly strained between Pearce and Kate. However, the latter, for the sake of the children at the start of this unique event in their lives – a holiday, no less – was making a colossal effort to appear as carefree and as happy as any of the other travellers. In such a mood, once having settled Hannah, for whom the ship's siren had sounded a harsh note of total panic, she then pointed out to the other children the many ships spread out along the Clyde. Daniel, Isabella, and Jenny were over at the ship's rail, jumping up and down in their excitement. It did Kate's heart a power of good to see how obviously delighted and carefree they all were. Seeing the joy on each little face, she had to fight back tears of happiness.

The first part of the journey passed all too quickly, so that almost before they knew it, the *Marquis of Bute* was slowing down for its first scheduled stop at Govan Wharf. As she looked round the already overcrowded boat, its decks seething with a boisterous humanity, Kate wondered where on board the next lot of passengers could possibly get so much as even a spare inch of space. Soon, however, the newcomers and their bairns, baskets, and hampers were safely aboard, and in high good humour, everyone squashed up to make room. and the boat again got under way, once more to three hearty cheers for the Captain and his gallant, if by now somewhat deafened, crew. Every inch of boat-rail was manned by the eager passengers and everyone was waving frantically, regardless as to whether or not they knew the watchers on the shore. They were steaming along at a steady pace, when suddenly the woman standing next to her clutched at Kate's arm and at the same time let out an ear-splitting yell.

"Oh, my God. Would ye look at that."

Kate's eyes followed the pointing finger, but apart from a number of people waving from the shore, she saw nothing untoward. However, as the other woman's fingers tightened their grip, closer examination revealed that one of the waving figures on the shore seemed to be head and shoulders above everyone else.

"And no wonder," agreed her new-found friend, "for that's my bloody holiday hamper she's standing on."

There was a moment's stunned silence, followed by sympathetic mutterings from those within earshot, and one philosopher made so bold as to say: "Ach weel, hen. That's life. You'll just have to do without your precious hamper. Never mind, hen, you never died o' summer yet."

But the young woman was made of sterner stuff and at once it was clear that she, for one, was not prepared to accept the inevitability of the situation. With a determined look in her eye, she asked of the world in general:

"Right then. Now where do I find the driver of this boat? Tell me that."

An older man, more respectably dressed than the other holidaymakers, and with his gaffer's or boss's hat prominently in place, at once took charge.

"If it's the Captain you mean, Missus, then that's him, with all that gold braid. Look. Up there on the bridge."

At once the woman plonked her baby into Kate's arms, hiked up her skirts and, keeping a firm grip on her flying shawl, raced with all possible speed for the bridge and its ACCESS FORBIDDEN TO PASSENGERS notice. She bounded up the companionway, two steps at a time, unhooked and threw aside the chain meant to keep the common herd at bay, and then marched up to the *driver*, a handsome, bearded figure resplendent in gold braid and gold-rimmed peak cap. There was much flailing around of arms, gesticulating, shouting and even at one point, the distraught woman's forefinger scolding and then finally prodding the shoulder of the august person. At length, the *driver* nodded his assent, courteously escorted his tormentor and critic of his hard won navigational skills from the sacred precinct of his bridge and next thing they knew, and to the utter amazement of all, the boat started going backwards.

When she rejoined Kate, the younger woman made a show of dusting off her hands and putting her shawl to rights. Then as if addressing a public meeting, and with a defiant gleam in her eye, said: "Aye. I soon told him. There was no way I was going doon the watter to Rothesay withoot my holiday hamper. Apart from anything else, he surely couldnae expect my poor wee bairn to suffer the one nappy for two whole weeks."

There was a whoop of delight, not only at these words themselves and the fact that this domestic problem had been discussed with the gallant Captain no less, but also at the mental picture of both sight and stench which they conjured up in the minds of her audience.

Once the ship had reversed all the way back again to Govan Wharf, the woman, with her daintily booted foot, stirred her still somewhat inebriated husband into action. With suitable expletives for the daft scunner, that he most assuredly was for having left the damned hamper on the quayside in the first place, she sent him on his route down the gangway. By the time, obviously still in a drunken haze, he staggered back on board with his burden, to the shouts of encouragement and ribaldry of his fellow passengers, an impromptu choir, faces abeam with delight at this diversion, were already singing with verve, gusto, but little accuracy for the known words:

Oh, we're no awa tae bide awa
We're no awa tae leave ye
For we did come back to see ye.

The voyage doon the watter to Rothesay was at last well and truly started. This time, there would be no going back.

Chapter 23

The German Band was still playing as the *Marquis of Bute* sailed majestically on, in calm seas past Toward Lighthouse. With the sun shining down from a cloudless sky, most people were sitting out on the top deck, where every inch of space on the slatted wooden seats was occupied, as indeed was every upturned suitcase and each wicker hamper.

On all sides, passengers lazed away the trip, all the while tapping their feet in time to the music. Even so, the faces of most of the passengers were turned not towards the musicians, but instead were tilted up to the sun. By now, most of the men had loosened their ties and unfastened collar studs. Some had even freed their ties altogether and these garlands were now waving in the gentle summer breeze. Sunday-best jackets had been discarded and the metal clips of a variety of braces and armbands glistened in the sun and sent off shafts of light which dazzled the eye. Like badges of office, the knotted, squared-off handkerchiefs posed atop each boiled beetroot of a perspiring face. Scraps of conversation batted back and forth, a dog barked, children laughed or screamed, and over and above it all, the band played a medley of light airs.

Then, at a nod from the violinist, they launched into a different time, the words of which invited all and sundry to 'Come and see the baby, any time they cared to call.' At once, people sat up straighter and tapped their feet with greater urgency as they hurried in full-flight of imagination to see the baby who 'Looks sae neat and swanky, like a dumplin in a hanky.' Even Kate, although not actually joining in the singing, nevertheless relaxed sufficiently to drum her fingers on top of the ship's handrail in time to the rhythm.

Had the song been Irish, the words of which had been known to her, then Kate would have been singing as heartily as the rest of the holidaymakers. However, for the moment, she was more than content to enjoy the sun, the balmy sea breezes, and the music. Had Kate been able to make time stand still, then that very moment was the one she would have chosen to preserve for eternity. Immersed in the heady, electric air of carnival and gaiety, with her family around her, the sun shining high above, and the vessel sailing along in tranquil seas. At that exact point in time, life was good, oh, so very good for Kate Kinnon.

But time, indeed life itself, stands still for no-one and almost as if they realised it, suddenly the children at her side began fidgeting, already bored with gazing out dutifully at the waves, the screeching seagulls, and the mainland hills beyond. Pearce was sitting at some little distance from his wife and family. Although in the middle of a crowd of excited chattering holidaymakers, he alone was no part of it. Engrossed in reading his favourite and well-thumbed anthology of poetry, there he sat, a rock of stolid respectability and calm, in the midst of the seething, shouting, laughing, and lustily-singing mass of humanity on all sides of him.

Kate sighed at the sight of him in such a situation. At this distance and observing him as she would objectively assess a total stranger, she had to admit: '*Yes, you're a handsome devil. With that sprinkling of grey at the temples you're looking more distinguished than ever. From the look of you, you could be an eminent professor or some such grand person. With your dark good looks and superior air, that way you have of tilting your head and looking down your nose at the common herd, you stand out like a sore, if definitely highborn, thumb.*'

Kate sighed again.

'*The day I see you sitting out on the deck of a Clyde steamer in your braces, with a knotted handkerchief on your head, that'll be the day you've decided to join the rest of the human race.*'

Even the mental picture of her husband thus attired brought a smile to her face and it was with the laugh of a carefree holidaymaker that she bent down to attend to the children.

"Danny Boy, why don't you and Jenny go for a wee walk around the top deck? She would like that and as long as you keep an eye on her, she'll surely behave herself. All right, son?"

Danny, although not exactly over the moon with anticipation at such a prospect, did however agree.

Then, astute as ever, with a twinkle in his eye:

"I know what you really mean, Mammy, You want me to keep her as far away from Dadda as possible. Right?"

Kate, despite herself, burst out laughing. Then, assuming a mock air of censure with pursed lips and an admonitory finger, she leant forward.

"Tut, tut, Daniel, my boy. That's quite enough cheek from you. Any more of that and you'll be at the receiving end of what your pals back in Glasgow call a skelpit bum."

Jenny and Daniel collapsed in gales of laughter. It was not merely their Mammy's ineffectual attempt at a broad Glasgow accent which had amused them, they were almost hysterical with delight at her use of the word bum, a word normally banned in the polite Kinnon household.

Still laughing, Kate leant forward and ruffled her son's curly dark hair, which despite his many plastering-down efforts, always managed to spring back to vibrant life. She smiled fondly at his freckled, cheeky little face.

"Right. my lad, be off with you before I put my threat into action. And mind now, keep a good eye on Jenny. For she's up to more tricks than a basketful of puppies."

Kate turned to Isabella who for the past ten minutes or so had been dancing an impromptu and completely unselfconscious Highland Fling in time to the German Band's lively music. The nearby holidaymakers, with wild cheers and ribald comments, had applauded her exhibition. Now, flushed with triumph and slightly out of breath, Isabella was holding on to Hannah's go-chair for support.

Isabella's lovely hair was as blonde as Daniel's was raven black. With her recent exertions, the broad tartan ribbon, especially bought for the holiday, had come loose. In the normal way, Hannah was the only one of the girls to sport a ribbon in her hair, but on one of her recent visits to Paddy's Market, Kate had been lucky enough to buy cheaply an end roll of brightly-coloured tartan ribbon. It was a riot of various shades of red and yellow, which the stallholder, eager to make a sale, assured Kate was the official dress MacMillan tartan.

Kate now bent forward and retied the length of ribbon, then finished by taking one of Isabella's fat, sausage ringlets in her hand and twisting the heavy yet silky blonde hair over and around her fingers.

Isabella looked up and smiled her own special sweet little smile at her Mammy. With the sun on her face, and its rays sending off shafts of pure spun gold from her mass of ringlets, Isabella looked like an angel – almost too pure, too perfect and altogether too ethereal for this cruel world.

Kate's cup of happiness was complete as she looked at this lovely child of her heart, so different in every way from poor Hannah, with her coarse dark hair, her sloe-eyes, and her poor deranged mind.

With her other hand, Kate stretched forward and stroked Hannah's cheek.

'*'Tis no wonder that Isabella is Pearce's favourite child. With those delicate looks, that colouring and her inborn air of elegance, she'll be a beauty by the time she's in her teens. Even more, she'll be a real lady.*'

Kate had a secret smile to herself as she thought: '*Much as it grieves me to admit it, but my wee Isabella takes after Pearce's side of the family. Nothing of the starving, poverty-stricken Irish peasant about her. No wonder that Pearce has such great plans for her in the years ahead. Wouldn't surprise me in the least if he were to return in triumph to Ireland with a grown-up Isabella on his arm. and insist that his family pay her due homage, perhaps even hold a coming-out ball at Laggan House for the young beauty. Ah, well, Kate my girl, time will tell.'*

Chapter 24

The first morning of the holiday, they awoke to brilliant sunshine spilling through the partly-closed curtains. Kate stirred lazily in bed, and for a hazy, still half-asleep moment, she wondered where on earth she could possibly be. Then, as she stretched her arms luxuriously and her splayed hand finally came to rest on Pearce's arm, it all came back to her in one glorious, mind-boggling rush of wonderful realisation. Of course. She was on holiday and not only on the first holiday of her life, but also for the first time in years, she was *truly, in every sense,* in her husband's bed. She smiled a secret smile and felt the blood rush to her face as she thought: '*Wasn't last night glorious? Oh, if only life could always be like this. But who knows? Perhaps this is the start of something new and better than I've ever known? Well, time alone will tell, Kate my girl. Meantime, enjoy this heavenly experience and make the very most of your two weeks.*'

Pearce was still sleeping soundly so, removing her hand from where it still lay on his arm, she then edged over to her own side of the bed and crept out as quietly as possible. That done without causing more than a slight moan from her husband, Kate then put on her outdoor coat over her best nightgown.

'*Who knows,*' she thought, '*perhaps one fine day Pearce might even buy me a lovely dressing gown such as the fine ladies in the Big House used to wear. Imagine it. Me, a lady's maid, with a quilted, satin dressing-gown. Now, wouldn't that be something to tell the neighbours?*'

She was still smiling at this happy thought and on her way to check on the children in the next room, when she stopped with her hand on the door handle. An even stranger thought had just come to her: '*After the carefree passion of last night, my girl, it won't be a swanky dressing gown you'll be after wanting. No, more like it would be a bell tent, voluminous nightgown. Something to cover the bulge of your belly rather than a glamorous dressing gown.*'

Like a mischievous schoolgirl, she giggled into her cupped hand as she allowed her thoughts to wander idly.

'*To think such a thing should happen now – especially after Betty's warnings about the strength of the Rothesay air. Shouldn't be surprised if I take more than a stick of seaside rock back to the Candleriggs as a wee souvenir.*'

She was still smiling as she went in to rouse the children in good time for the cooked breakfast which Mrs Graham had promised them. Normally loathe to get up on mornings back home, on this occasion the children needed no second bidding and were soon diving about the room in various stages of undress. With the promise that Mammy herself would see to the brushing of Hannah's hair, which was always something of a trial, Jenny was delegated to the task of getting Hannah dressed in her best summer frock.

Later that same day, replete with food, the family gathered in the lush acre of garden, ablaze with hydrangeas, fuchsias, and a myriad of other flowers whose name they had not yet been told. The garden of Ardbeg House overlooked the seafront and on such a day, with the sun overhead, yachts sailing along effortlessly over the waves, and the urgent cry of seagulls above them, the children and Kate thought they were in Paradise.

Having drunk their fill of the exquisite scenery, there was some dissension as to exactly what plans should be made for the glorious summer day now lying so invitingly before them. Jenny wanted to take her bucket and spade and head without a moment's delay for the beach at the Children's Corner, there to delve into the making of sand castles with all possible speed; Isabella desperately wanted to go and see the

Exhibition of Highland Dancing, the advertisement for which she had spelled out carefully and laboriously while on the boat coming over to the Island; Daniel, with every fibre of his being, wanted to accept Mrs Graham's kind offer of the use of the little rowing boat which she kept permanently moored at her own private stretch of beach just across the road; Pearce wanted to walk for miles and on the way, explore the flora and fauna of this magical island with its magnificent palm trees and its sun-kissed shores lapped by the warming balm of the Gulf Stream; Kate, still feeling mellow and drunk with happiness, would have been happy to fall in with anyone's plans so long as it did not necessitate her leaving this Madeira of Scotland.

When things were beginning to get a bit out of hand, and the discussion was fast developing into a good-going family row, Pearce, in his usual way, took total command of the situation. He clapped his hands once only, and immediately, without a word spoken, his troops fell into line.

"Now then, here is what I would suggest … Jenny wants to make sand castles? All right, so she and Hannah can both go to the beach with Mammy. And yes, since it's a holiday, I'll even give them all money with which to buy ice cream."

There were whoops of delight at this suggestion, for perpetually befogged or not, Hannah knew the words *ice cream*. So, as soon as she heard the magic words she started a none-too-rhythmic banging of her bunched fist against the metal sides of her go-chair.

"Nice cream. Nice cream. Hannah good girl, Dadda. Hannah like nice cream. Good girl, Dadda."

The appealed-to Dadda cast her one of his usual looks of utter loathing and distaste that he had fathered such a creature.

"Yes, yes, Hannah, my girl. I think we've all got that message loud and clear, thank you."

Just then, Kate happened to look over at Isabella who, despite a brave attempt to keep her composure, nevertheless could not still the trembling of her lower lip. Not wishing the slightest thing to mar this wonderful holiday, Kate hastened to point to Isabella.

"And what about poor Isabella? Is she to be left out of all these lovely treats? What about her, Dadda?"

At once Pearce's face softened, and although he did not say so in so many words, it soon clear he had left the best treat of all to the last, as if wanting to savour it and hug it to his heart. He smiled at Isabella and it was a smile such as he never at any time bestowed on the rest of his brood. With the eyes of an adoring father, he at once stretched out a hand and stroked his favourite daughter's ribbon-held ringlets.

"Forgotten my wee Isabella? Of course I haven't forgotten her. What a question. No, here's the master plan for her … She has set her little heart on seeing the Highland Dancing Display, so that is exactly what she will do and have ice cream too. In fact, I myself will take her. I gather it is being held at the little village of Port Bannatyne. A pleasant walk on such a day, according to our esteemed landlady. So if we walk there and back, see the display, and at that same time, see something of this beautiful island, that will suit us both just fine and dandy. That not so, eh, Isabella?"

Dadda chucked her under the chin. Isabella had no need to reply to the hypothetical question, for her beaming face said it all. And best of all, her delighted grin acknowledged how pleased she was that she, out of all the family, would have Dadda to herself.

As yet, nobody had thought either to mention Daniel or enquire as to what his wishes might be. Painfully aware of this fact, the unhappy boy, all the while toeing patterns in the stone path with his new holiday sandals, was trying his best to look as nonchalant as possible. He raised his head with a jerk the very moment he heard his father address him by name.

"Right then, Daniel. I expect you would like to get off on your own and do what most lads enjoy on seaside holiday – a spot of fishing. How about that?"

At once Daniel blinked in utter disbelief at his own good fortune and, as the full meaning dawned on him, his face broke into a delighted grin. Go fishing, on his own, and in Mrs Graham's wee cracker of a boat. Perhaps his Dadda did trust him, did harbour some fatherly love for him after all.

He opened his mouth and had started to stutter his heart-felt thanks when the voice of his father overrode that of his own.

"As I say, Daniel, a spot of fishing. And who knows, you might even catch a tiddler or two for our tea. Ha ha. How about that, eh? Mind you ..." Pearce wagged a playful yet at the same time admonitory finger, "... just one thing to remember ... whatever fishing you do, is to be done from the pier. And not – I repeat NOT – to be done from that boat of Mrs Graham's. Do I make myself clear, Daniel? You are to leave that rowing boat strictly alone. Now, do you understand?"

Daniel, his face by now a picture of misery, could only choke back his bitter disappointment, at the same time nodding in stunned agreement with his autocratic father.

Seeing this reaction, so different from those of the other children on being told of their respective treats, Pearce frowned.

"I must say, Daniel, a vestige of enthusiasm would go a very long way, my boy. However, be that as it may, I shall of course, give you sufficient money to buy a fishing net, and if you make your purchase prudently, then who knows, there may even be enough money left over with which to buy an ice cream wafer, for I think you are now rather too old for the childish pokey-hat."

Poor Daniel, with an obvious effort of will, tried his level best to appear suitably grateful for such parental munificence. But even this watery smile misfired, and his father fixed a beady eye on the hapless youth.

"On the other hand, instead of guzzling ice cream, you may prefer to use any extra cash towards the improvement of your mind. Use the money to pay for your entrance to Rothesay Castle. Learn something useful for a change. I believe the castle dates back to something like the thirteenth century."

Kate had a pretty shrewd idea as to what her first-born was mentally saying. That being so, she flashed a quick, sympathetic smile

122

as the boy caught her glance. She knew in her heart of hearts that poor Daniel would have given anything for even a crumb of fatherly love or even attention. But she knew also that the deprived lad was too unsure of himself and too certain of his father's quick temper ever to voice aloud such private thoughts. The pity was she knew he never would.

Chapter 25

The rest of the week passed just as happily as that first glorious day. As in sunshine, which seemed as if it would go on for ever, the Kinnons played and relaxed together as a united family on the shores of Sweet Rothesay Bay. Early on the Saturday morning, Kate stood at the bay window of their bedroom and looked out over the already sun-dappled Firth, stretching her arms luxuriously above her head as she thought: '*How beautiful. Thank you, God, for yet another lovely day.*'

Later that same morning, as they sat round Mrs Graham's dining table, Kate exulted in the fact that for the first time ever they seemed to be a real family at long last – even the tension between Pearce and Daniel seemed to have softened. They had all just enjoyed a cooked breakfast and were still on the toast and marmalade stage as Kate poured out extra cups of tea from the elegant silver teapot. Pearce looked on approvingly at her dainty, refined manner of playing the society hostess in such a rich setting, and smiled fondly at his wife.

"Yes, Kate Mavourneen, we'll make a lady out of you yet."

Kate stopped with the teapot poised over Daniel's still-empty cup and glimpsed up at her husband with twinkling, impish eyes.

"Well, now, Lord Pearce. If it's all the same to you, kind sir, we won't be starting all that up again. What you see before you is all the lady I'm ever likely to be. So, I beg of you, sir, let's just leave that flea stick to the wall."

Pearce threw his head back and gave a great belly laugh which gladdened Kate's heart to hear. But it was his next words which brought a beam of delight to her face, and an even greater lift to her heart.

"Kate, I've been thinking. I've just had a wonderful idea. Kate my girl, how would you like it if we were to get a little flat, or cottage even, down here in Rothesay, or at least somewhere on this lovely island? Then for future holidays, it would be so easy. We could come and go as we pleased."

Kate's grinned and could hardly speak, so surprised and delighted was she.

"Pearce, do you really mean it? Could we possibly do such a thing? You're not just teasing me, are you? Not just giving me a touch of the old Irish blarney now, are you? But how could we afford it? Where's the money to come from?

Pearce nodded sagely.

"I've been keeping it as a surprise and this seems as good a moment as any to mention it. You see, I'm doing well at my job now. In fact, recently there have been strong hints of a possible promotion. Between that, and a bit of extra overtime on other nights besides Fridays, I'm sure we could take on that lovely little cottage which Isabella and I saw yesterday. Isabella's quite fallen in love with it, you know. Isn't that right, Isabella, my dear?"

Isabella beamed from ear to ear. Seeing this, Pearce leant across the table and patted the child fondly on the hand.

Kate did not doubt his words for one moment, but even so, there were a. dozen questions which at once sprang to mind.

"But Pearce, where is this dream cottage? And how could we get it?"

Pearce held up a hand.

"No problem there, my dear. It had a TO LET notice on it. And to tell you the truth, had today not been a Saturday, I would have been on the estate factor's doorstep at dawn, down on my bended knees, begging to be allowed to become their new tenant."

The idea of Dadda ever having to beg for anything, far less abase himself in such a way, was too much for the family. The mental picture of their strict Dadda on his knees in supplication made them look first at each other in amazement, then burst out laughing.

At this point kindly Mrs Graham came back into the room to see if they wanted more toast or a fresh brewing of tea. Having ascertained that more would be welcome, she said: "My and it's just grand to see you all enjoying yourselves so much. The Rothesay air's certainly doing you all a power of good already. Surely these nut-brown bairns can't be the same, wee peelly-wally city sparrows that arrived here only last Saturday? If you don't mind me saying so, it sounded is if you were all having a right good laugh a wee while since. So tell me this and tell me no more, is it a private joke, or can anyone join in?"

Pearce beamed, then at his most gracious and without a moment's hesitation, said to the rotund and jovial landlady: "No secret at all, Mrs Graham. I was just telling the family about the fact that I'd seen a lovely cottage to rent. Then I said I would even go down on my bended knees in order to get the keys of that particular little kingdom."

Again everyone laughed noisily and as Mrs Graham wiped the tears of laughter from her eyes, she said: "Your family's right, Mr Kinnon, sir. You are much too distinguished a gentleman ever to have to beg for anything. Now, if you don't mind my asking, sir, which particular cottage would that be?"

"Let's see now. I'm afraid I don't know the name of the road, but I could take you to it. Turn left from your own garden gate and walk on out past the Thomson Fountain and it's a wee cottage in the second line of buildings overlooking the sea front."

At once Mrs Graham clapped her hands.

"I ken exactly where you are, sir. It's one of the original old fisherman's cottages. I ken fine the one you mean."

"Right then, first thing on Monday morning I'll be on the doorstep of that factor."

"Yes, my wee pets," Kate said. "It's all going to be wonderful. We'll be able to spend whole summers down here, like lots of other families already do, with Dadda coming down on the last boat on Friday nights for the weekend. It's wonderful. A dream come true. And our life together is all going to be so different."

Chapter 26

Still bouncing about on a wave of euphoria, the family set about making plans for that day. Jenny had already entered her name for a special sandcastle building competition. As a result of her improved relationship with Pearce, Kate had persuaded him they should both accompany Jenny and give her some moral support on this highly important day in her young life.

"It would be a real treat for her, Pearce, especially since you went out with Isabella yesterday. Anyway, the other children will be just fine. They can play around on that bit of private beach over the road. Mrs Graham's very kindly given them her permission. Honestly, she's so kind, anybody would think that they were her own grandbairns. She's told them to look on that stretch of beach as their own wee hideaway. Would you believe it, she even promised to give them a wee picnic to take with them. Now isn't that kind? So, they'll be fine over there. Within shouting distance of the house, I can't see that any harm can come to them."

Pearce, having heard his wife out in silence, was still undecided and chewed at his lower lip in hesitation and perplexity.

"Mmm. Can't say I'm overjoyed at the prospect. Still, let's see."

He turned to Daniel.

"Here's what we'll do, Daniel. I'll place you in charge of the other two children, right? Hannah will be perfectly safe sitting in her go-chair at the sea shore, tossing stones into the water. She'd like that. Isabella can amuse herself and play with Hannah. You can use the time to improve your mind a bit – perhaps make a study of the tiny creatures in all those fascinating rock pools."

Daniel looked somewhat nonplussed at this, but nevertheless nodded his head in ready agreement as his father went on: "Anyway, we should be back around noon. So surely no harm should come to any of you in that short time."

Pearce then turned to his wife with a worried frown on his face.

"You know, Kate, I'm still not too happy about this. Look, tell you what. You take Jenny to the competition and I'll stay here with Isabella and the others. Yes, more I think about it I'm sure that would be the best plan."

Kate, who had at once noticed the immediate trembling of Jenny's lower lip, hurried to say: "Oh, Pearce, please do come with us, it would be so nice, just the three of us off on our own for once in a lifetime. Please. Please say you'll come. Anyway, apart from anything else, it makes it rather look as if you don't trust Daniel."

Kate's observation struck home. With an impatient wave of his hand, Pearce indicated that the matter was resolved. But even so, just before setting out with Jenny and his wife for the Children's Corner, he turned to his son.

"One last thing, Daniel, my boy. You see that rowing boat of Mrs Graham's? I believe I've already warned you on that subject. Well, you leave that strictly alone, boy. Do you hear? Is that fully understood? Fully understood, I repeat. That boat or indeed any unattended boat is strictly out of bounds as far as you and your sisters are concerned. Is that crystal clear?"

Daniel, greatly daring, cleared his throat.

"Dadda, a moment ago you thought of staying behind here with Hannah, Isabella, and myself. Would you not change your mind and perhaps even take us all out in the boat yourself? That would be a real treat for us. Would you do that for us Dadda?"

Pearce's reply snapped back immediately.

"No, Daniel, even if I were to remain with you, I would most certainly not be messing about in any boat with you crew. In fact, were I to stay, I'd be sitting against the sea wall with my book of poetry.

Merely keeping an eye on you. So, you can disabuse yourself of any idea of my setting out to sea with you lot."

At these words so harshly and thoughtlessly spoken, even Kate felt affronted. And so closely attuned was she to her dear Danny Boy that she could almost guess at the thoughts going through his head right at that moment.

The look on the boy's face spoke volumes:

Father, could you not just once in your life give into my wishes. I've heard you boasting to neighbours, yes, and even to Mrs Graham about what a fine oarsman you were in your youth. Well, why not take me out in the wee boat and show me how it should be done. Surely that wouldn't kill you, now would it?

Right. If that's the way you want it. Then strangers is what we'll be. Never again in my life will I ask you for anything. No, in future, no matter what happens, I wouldn't even give you the time of day, far less my friendship, love, or even a scrap of respect. As of now, father, you're a big round nothing in my life – at least until the day comes that I get my revenge. Meantime, father, thanks for nothing as usual.

Chapter 27

For Jenny and her parents, their morning at the Children's Corner had been a great success. Despite the many other excellent entries, Jenny's creation, a handkerchief-beflagged sand castle with its own shell-edged moat, had won first prize in the girls' section. The three of them strolled along in the sunshine, her mother and father arm-in-arm, taking in the sights, sounds, and smells of the crowded promenade, where excited children dashed about, dogs barked, seagulls squawked overhead, and the smell of seaweed wafted over the rocks.

Jenny clutched to her bosom her hard-won prize for the competition. Every so often, she would look at her prize, convinced she was the envy of every other girl in the whole Island of Bute on that lovely summer's day. Her first prize had taken the form of a beautifully-dressed china doll, with whose sweet face Jenny had already fallen in love. Catching her daughter's look of pride, Kate nudged her husband.

"My word, Pearce. But isn't that a lovely doll? And wasn't our Jenny a clever wee lass to win it all by herself?"

In a rare good humour, and always one for success of whatever nature, Pearce beamed down at his ten year-old daughter.

"Clever, did you say, Mother? Yes, indeed. I'm sure she's the smartest girl in the whole of Rothesay."

They all laughed and in high glee, and Jenny went skipping along the promenade ahead of them.

Arriving at the Bathing Station, she stopped to peer through the railings at the busy scene below on the shore. She was pushing her head further forward when there was a warning shout from her mother.

"Jenny lass. Take care. Mind you don't fall through."

Still keeping a firm hold on her already-precious dolly, Jenny drew back from her precarious situation.

"I know what, Mother. If it's adventure young Jenny wants, let's all go for a wander in the forest – in Skeoch Woods. You'd like that now Jenny, wouldn't you? And who knows? We might even meet some little elves and fairy folk. You never know."

Kate laughed, but looked uncertain.

"Shouldn't we be getting back to the others? It's already past noon and Mrs Graham will be sure to have our meal on the table on the very dot of one o'clock. You know fine what she's like. Anyway, the other three will be looking out for us. We did promise to be back by twelve o'clock, didn't we?"

Pearce frowned then, waiving aside all of Kate's objections, he took Jenny by the hand.

"Nonsense, Kate. We're on holiday, woman. No need for us to be running to a time-table. Plenty of time for a spot of adventure in the enchanted forest. Anyway, the fairy-folk are good friends of mine from my boyhood days in Ireland. They'll simply wave a magic wand and get us back in lots of time. So, no rush at all. Let's go."

When finally the three happy holidaymakers emerged tired but triumphant from the dense woods, they were still laughing and joking together as at no other time in their past family life.

Removing his pocket watch, Pearce studied it then, in voice of mock alarm, said: "Ten minutes till mealtime. Looks like my fairy friends let me down after all. Come on then, you two, best hurry along – or Mrs Graham will indeed read us all the Riot Act."

Again they laughed even more heartily than ever when Dadda broke into an anxious exaggerated and hurried turkey-trot. All this while, Kate mentally hugged her happiness to her heart.

'Oh, why can't life always be like this? This is wonderful. Never before have I seen Pearce so relaxed. What a great holiday. And a cottage to see about on Monday. Oh, dear God, thank you. What

have I ever done to deserve such happiness?'

As they were nearing their boarding-house, Jenny noticed a crowd of people congregated over near Mrs Graham's own stretch of shore. She tugged excitedly at Dadda's hand.

"Oh, look, Dadda. Is it another sand castle competition, do ye think? Can we go and look at it?"

Pearce smiled fondly at his daughter.

"Well, my dear, I should say it's highly unlikely to be another competition. Not over there, anyway. And, no, I don't think we've got time to take a look at this stage. After all, dear Mrs Graham will be dishing out the mince and tatties any minute now, as your Mammy pointed out earlier. It really isn't fair to keep the poor woman waiting. You know how delicious the food is, always piping hot, and she does take such a pride in it."

But Jenny looked so crestfallen that her Dadda laughed and, quite unlike his usual brusque city manner, he once again acted the carefree holiday-maker and relented without further ado.

"Well then, Jenny, if it means all that much to you, perhaps another couple of minutes won't make all that much difference to the scheme of things. Over we go. Who knows, perhaps someone has caught a giant fish, or even a whale like Jonah. Now wouldn't that be something to tell your friends back in the Candleriggs?"

The trio crossed the road and joined the outer edge of the visibly excited, shuffling, yet strangely quiet crowd of people. When, after a couple of seconds, they could still see nothing of any interest, Pearce turned to another bystander.

"What's going on, sir? Why the crowd? Damned if I can see anything."

The other man turned to his questioner.

"I suppose the excitement, if that's what you could call it," he said quietly, "is all over, bar the shouting, as they say in these parts. The other one is being tended up yonder in the big hoose the noo. But, the other poor wee bairn ... weel ... I'm afraid it's ..."

The man shook his head sadly, as if words were beyond him.

Pearce's face went ashen, despite his fine Rothesay tan. He grabbed the man roughly by his sleeve.

"What other one? What other poor wee bairn? What in God's name are you talking about, man?"

The man shook off Pearce's hand, and shrugged his shoulders.

At that point, another bystander, obviously still buoyed up by the excitement of the occasion and eager to get his sixpence worth in, leant forward.

"Aye, man. Ah seen the whole bloody business. It was two weans – some o thae holiday kids, city slickers most like never even seen a boat aw their life afore. Weel, man, Ah'm telling you, it was …"

Pearce grabbed this long-winded witness by his jacket lapels, and shouted hysterically at the man.

"For God's sake. What exactly did you see? Quick. Tell me, for the love of God."

The man angrily shook himself free of Pearce's grip.

"All right, man. Keep yer hauns to tae yersel'. Ah'll tell ye aw ye want tae know."

Pearce stepped back.

"It wis twa weans in a boat. A lad and a lassie. The lassie stood up and widnae sit doon tho the laddie shouted at her. Wan o' the steamers wis jist comin intae the pier and ye ken the kind o' wash they make. The laddie either didnae ken tae turn his row boat bow on tae the waves or maybe he wis too busy trying tae get the lassie tae sit, but anyway the bout couped o'er and they baith fell in. Some others, once the waves died, rowed like hell fur the upturned boat, but they only found one bairn hangin' on tae it."

"Which bairn?" Pearce shouted.

"Ah dinnae ken, but they're still lookin fur the other yin …"

Kate didn't wait for anything further. With a scream, she ran over the road towards the house, with Pearce and Jenny in hot pursuit.

The sight they saw on entering Mrs Graham's kitchen froze them to the spot.

Hannah sat on one side of the fireplace placidly munching on a biscuit.

On the other side, wrapped in a blanket, Daniel, with a hangdog expression, held a mug of steaming liquid in a trembling hand.

As if frozen to the spot, Kate and Pearce stood still as statues as they took in this tableau. Kate was the first to recover her composure. She dashed over to her son and threw her arms protectively around the trembling child.

"Oh my wee darling, Danny. Poor wee soul. Thank God, at least you're safe. Thank God."

The only sound in the kitchen was the ticking of the grandfather clock as Kate rocked her son to and fro in an ecstasy of relief.

Pearce, with a yell like a wounded animal, shattered the silence. Roaring like an angry bull, Pearce took a step over to his wife and, in one furious movement, wrenched her away from her so recently rescued son.

Like one demented, he roared at her: "Thank God, did ye say, woman? Thank God? For what? That He left that alive...." he gestured at Hannah, "that useless lump of fat ... that imbecile ... that bloody fuckin' cretin ... and took away my lovely Isabella. Is that what you're thanking God for? Christ Almighty."

There was a shocked intake of breath from Mrs Graham.

"Mister Kinnon, sir. I will not have language like that. Not in this Christian household. Of course, sir, fine weel Ah ken ye've had a terrible, truly horrific shock, otherwise at the very first hint of such foul language, ye would have been oot o' that door wi' yer bags and baggage. Aye. and quicker than ye could say Jock Tamson's bairns."

Pearce rounded on the hapless woman.

"I'll thank you to keep your stupid mouth shut madam. The loss is mine, not yours. That being so, I'll say exactly what I like, when I like and to whom I wish. Is that perfectly clear, madam?"

After having first cast a warm and sympathetic glance at a still-weeping Kate, Mrs Graham turned to face Pearce.

"Mister Kinnon, if you please, one thing does seem to have

escaped your notice: the loss is not yours alone. What about your poor, dear, wee wife? And not forgetting your other weans. Surely they too are grieving sore enough without hearing you blaspheming and cursing and swearing like some drunken lout. If you can't show any common decency in ma ain hoose, at least spare a kind thought and maybe even a wee cuddle for yer poor bereaved family in their sad loss. Surely that's not too much to ask o' ye, noo is it?"

"Madam," Pearce said in his most regal voice. "What concerns my wife and my weans as you call them is my concern, not yours. Anyway, one thing is certain. We will be out of here before nightfall, that I do assure you. So you've no further call for worry. Do I make myself clear?"

"Very well, Mister Kinnon, that's as you wish. But never let it be said I put you out into the street. Anyway, in the sad circumstances, I will not, of course, be rendering any account. I feel it's the least I can do."

Pearce's face suffused with colour.

"Thank you, but *no*, Madam, I would have you aware that the Kinnons have always paid their debts – of whatever nature."

With these words, he cast a bitter look at Kate, who at once caught his unspoken meaning and went into a further paroxysm of uncontrolled weeping. If anything, this served only to further infuriate Pearce, especially when his son, Daniel, rose somewhat unsteadily from his seat and went over to offer his dear mother what little comfort he could.

No sooner were Daniel's arms around Kate's neck than Pearce let out a howl of rage. In one bound, he was at their side. Without another word, he grabbed his son by the scruff of the neck and threw him with maniacal force across the room, where he collided with a sickening crunch against the opposite wall.

This was altogether too much for Mrs Graham, who at once strode to the centre of the room and stood there, arms akimbo.

"That, Mister Kinnon, sir, is quite enough," she said in a quiet, controlled voice. "I demand that you leave this room ... my kitchen, may I remind you ... and leave at once. Do you understand me, sir? At once, I say. I take it that you have finished with this disgusting display of violence?"

Pearce sneered.

"Finished? Finished, did you say? No, indeed, I have not yet done with it. In fact ... if truth be told ... I'm just getting started."

He grabbed hold of Jenny's lovely new doll and, swinging it by its fancy lace dress, he threw it wildly against the opposite wall, as if aiming directly for Daniel's tear-stained face. It just missed Daniel's head. The doll's pretty little head ricocheted off the wall and smashed to smithereens on the stone floor.

Amidst a flurry of lace petticoats, fur-trimmed bonnet, and ribbons, there the doll lay, battered beyond recall.

Part Two – Life Goes On

Chapter 1

A year after the fateful holiday, by nine o'clock on a Friday evening, the Kinnon Ceilidh, as Kate called it, was in full flight. Started to raise the children's spirits from Pearce's frequent black moods, these evenings were the ideal time since Pearce was never home before eleven o'clock on a Friday. Kate had her own suspicions as to why, but thrust them aside to join the children in merry making.

Much of the puff candy had been eaten and Kate, laughing and protesting all the while, had been prevailed upon to execute a spirited Highland Fling. Hannah was laughing noisily and rocking to and fro in her own peculiar way, and the other two, Jenny and Daniel, were clapping hands and alternately imitating both the actions and the ear-splitting squeal of playing the bagpipes. Into this hive of riotous activity, the door of the kitchen suddenly burst open – and there Pearce stood, his face suffused with rage.

For an instant, it seemed he was almost too angry even to be capable of speech. But despite this, the wild staring eyes themselves spoke volumes. When eventually he did manage to splutter incoherently, it was the ravings of a man pushed to the very edge of sanity by his bereavement. When at last in control of himself, he stared with loathing at the erstwhile merrymakers and yelled at them in a voice which could no doubt be heard by the half of Candleriggs.

"And just what the bloody hell is going on here?"

The very sight of him, far less his harsh words, was enough in itself to halt Kate in mid-Schottische. She stood there in an agony of misery, embarrassment and indecision, one hand on one hip, the other raised high above her head.

She felt she was standing there with her mouth agape, not only at the interruption but also at the surprise, indeed the shock, of seeing Pearce home so early on a Friday night. Almost without volition, she said the first thing that came into her head.

"Pearce. You're home early. But ... it's Friday. So ... what's happened the night?"

Looking at her as if she'd taken leave of her senses, the enraged figure, still framed in the kitchen doorway, waved aside her words, and said: "What's happened indeed. I'll tell you exactly what's-happened – I've come home early from work after working my fingers to the bone to provide for you all and keep you in a measure of comfort – I've come home early from work and caught you all out. That's what's happened, my fine lady Kathleen. And just how long has all this been going on – all this unseemly merriment in our house of mourning? How long? Just tell me that."

Unable to take in this new and unnerving situation and still totally ignoring his question, Kate said in a voice tinged with wonder: "But, Pearce. You're never home early on a Friday night. That's been your habit for more years than I care to remember."

His face darkened and the beetle brows drew even closer together as he thundered at her: "Woman. Are you daft? What is it with you? It's Fair Friday. We can finish work a bit earlier, if we wish. But in past years, I've never chosen to claim that special privilege; preferring rather to work on the additional hours for the sake of the extra money, for our common good, I might add."

Kate put out a hand, about to speak, but Pearce had not yet finished.

"You may remember – even last Fair Friday night, I worked late as usual – to get extra money for our ice creams, donkey rides and other treats during that accursed, ill-fated holiday. You can't have forgotten that. Although when I see all this jollity ... on what is almost the very anniversary of poor wee Isabella's death ... well, it just beats me. It really does."

At this point Kate laid a placatory hand on her husband's sleeve.
"Pearce, my dear, listen. It isn't at all what you think and –"
With an angry gesture, he shook himself free of her hand.

"Kate, what I think is this: I came home early for once in a lifetime of Fridays, because I just could not concentrate on columns and figures, nor indeed on any other aspect of business. My mind kept going back in time to last Fair Friday night, and how very happy we all were, at the prospect of our first ever holiday doon the watter and ..."

At this mention of Rothesay and the scene of his own shame and self-reproach, there was a strangled cry from Daniel who was sitting on the stool before the fire. It was this sound more than anything which as yet had been said, or even worse, left unsaid which finally finished what was left of Kate's composure.

Like the old woman she now felt herself to be, she lowered her arms with a great effort, almost as if they were dead weights. Then with a cry like that of a wounded animal, she sank, utterly exhausted, into the nearest kitchen chair. Like one in the throes of a nightmare, she looked around with a dazed expression. Then as the full realisation, not only of the loss of her wee Isabella, but of the way in which she had misjudged her husband finally dawned on her, she started to weep and went on sobbing as if her heart would break. All the while wild thoughts went racing through her brain.

'*My God. How I've misjudged him. All these long years, all these Friday nights of our Kinnon Ceilidhs this last year. He really has been working overtime. To provide for us. Not dallying with some fancy woman, as I had thought. Oh. my God.*'

As it finally dawned on her just how very wrong she had been in her rash assumptions, she knew in that moment that nobody is totally bad – not even Pearce Claude Kinnon. By now, almost in a state of shock, she held out a trembling hand to him and pleaded.

"Oh, Pearce. Will you ever be able to forgive me?"

Pearce, who assumed it was the riotous party scene which had met his arrival home Kate was pleading forgiveness for, stared at her, then thundered: "Forgive you? Humph. When what you've been doing is little short of dancing on poor wee Isabella's grave?"

For a moment, words failed him. Then, raking his fingers through his hair, he said: "Forgive you, did you say, woman? No. Never in a million years."

With tears of rage, frustration, and grief spurting from his eyes, he turned on his heel, went out of the door, and left the flat.

On his return next day, after a night of wandering blindly, aimlessly through the Fair Friday streets of revelry and drunken debauchery, he was a changed man. He steadfastly and cruelly ignored Kate and the three remaining children, just as, as he told them, they had ignored not only the death, but also the extended mourning period he himself deemed necessary for his own, but dearly-departed Wee Isabella.

As the autumn slowly gave way to winter Pearce's behaviour at home alternated between long periods of silence when he would sit for hours blank eyed in his chair beside the kitchen fire, and outbursts of rage when Kate would hurriedly take the children to Granny Gorbals until the manic spell had passed and the shouting and swearing gave way once more to a deep lethargy.

Chapter 2

In the second week of 1891 Kate chanced to be passing the entrance to the Fruit Market when she heard some sort of disturbance just inside. Men were shouting and swearing, not that swearing was an unusual occurrence at the Fruit Market, but the voices sounded angry. One of the voices was Pearce's, she was sure.

Venturing closer to the uproar, she saw Pearce brandishing a tally board.

"Your tally is wrong," Pearce shouted. "You're not going to get paid for stuff you didn't deliver."

"Even with your bowler and your fancy talk you can't add up right. I'll not be cheated again. Last week you cost me money. Today I had a witness do my tally."

For a moment, it looked as if they would come to blows, but a second bowler hat approached and demanded to see Pearce's tally board and that of the witness.

The witness started to say something but was waved to silence by the authoritative newcomer who studied both boards.

"Aye, they don't agree."

The carter pointed at Pearce. "He missed the count. He was standing there in a dwam. You could have walked Barnum and Bailey's circus past and he wouldn't have noticed."

Murmurs of agreement sounded from the men standing round.

The newcomer initialled the witness's board and turned to Pearce.

"My office, Mr Kinnon, if you please."

"You're going to take his words over mine, Cameron?" Pearce blustered.

"Mr Cameron, if you please. Yes, you're out here tally clerking because you were making too many mistakes in the ledgers at your desk and blaming everyone else. Now it seems you can't even be trusted to do this job. You can pick up your pay poke at the office on Friday as usual. We'll pay you up to today."

Kate hurried away from the market before Pearce saw her.

Pearce arrived home late that evening, surly, morose, but – Kate was relieved to see – quite sober.

"They're letting men go at the Market. There's not enough work."

Kate waited in silence.

"I'll need to start looking for other work," Pearce finally said and sat staring at the fire with his back to Kate.

Next morning, Kate was up betimes and got Hannah washed and dressed earlier than usual. Danny, Jenny, and Pearce were all still sleeping, so she wheeled Hannah out of the door as silently as the squeaky old go-chair would allow. She had no compunction about going to Granny's door this early, for like many old people of her generation and class, the habit of early rising was a deeply ingrained one and the hard-working Granny would have counted it a mark of shame to be still abed beyond the hour of six o'clock, whatever the morning.

As she and Granny sat over their ritual cup of tea, Kate poured out the tale of Pearce's loss of his job.

"There, there, Kate, don't worry, dear, everything's going to turn out all right. You'll see."

It was Granny's kind words and sympathetic manner which finally broke the dam of Kate's misery. After the storm of weeping had subsided, Granny said with all the wisdom of her seventy-five years.

"Kate, when you've lived as long as I have, you learn what are things worth worrying about. There's no point crying over what's past and can't be mended. What you have to think about is what to do next."

Granny's cure for all ills was a wee sweet bite and she urged her young neighbour to accept a pancake liberally spread with some of her latest boiling of blackcurrant jam. By the time Hannah too had been provided with a nice jammy doorstop, Kate was once again in control of her emotions. She cast a speculative look at Granny.

"Granny, how is it you can take things so calmly?"

Granny opened her mouth to reply, but just then she caught sight of Hannah. By now the girl was covered in blackcurrant jam from ear to ear, while what looked like a purple stream was meandering down the front of what had been a fresh white blouse. The fingers which Hannah was waving around in her usual un-coordinated fashion were also thick and sticky with blobs of blackcurrants. Granny, with a smile, rose to her feet to get a damp cloth from the sink with which to mop up Hannah. Only when that was done and the soiled cloth again rinsed out and draped over the goose-necked tap, did she return to her battered horsehair armchair. She looked intently at Kate, as if weighing up in her own mind exactly what she wanted to say.

"How do I keep so calm, you ask? Well, no secret. Nowadays I know better than to question the Will of God, I just accept it, that's all. Mind you, when my dear Patrick died, I took it really hard. Why him? Why him? I kept asking."

Kate cleared her throat, as if uncertain as to whether or not to speak.

"Granny, please don't talk about it if it upsets you. But … what … what exactly was it that happened to your husband? You vaguely mentioned once to me he had been killed in an accident. But you didn't go into any details. Was it at his work? Was that it?"

Granny shook her head sadly and the movement caused one of the steel pins to become dislodged from her bun. It fell to the floor, but contrary to her usual houseproud antics, Granny left it where it lay at her feet. It was clear to Kate that her innocent question had triggered off a painful memory for the old woman.

"No, Kate, he wasn't killed at work. It might have been easier to accept had that been the case. I still … even after all these years … still find it difficult to talk about. But here, wait a minute. You can read, can't you? Just give me a second."

Granny got to her feet and moved over to a ledge above her wall-bed. With some difficulty, on account of its great weight, she finally managed to lift down her Family Bible, which she then bore back in triumph on her outstretched hands. With great reverence, she placed the Bible on top of the oil-clothed table and then after some fumbling of the brass clasp with her arthritic fingers, she lifted back the heavy gold-tooled leather cover. Inside, next to a single pressed flower, there was a newspaper cutting, now yellow with age. This she lifted carefully and handed over to Kate.

"Just read that, my dear. I think that this is the right time, for it often helps when in trouble to know that others have travelled an even harder road in this journey of life. My prayer is that you yourself will find comfort once you realise what I have endured."

By now thoroughly intrigued at this unexpected development, Kate just could not imagine what she might be about to read. Resting the fragile piece of paper in the palm of her left hand, she bent her head to read as best she could the faded print.

As if Granny could not even bear to look at the scrap of paper, far less even think of the message it carried, she went over to Hannah and together they played a noisy game of pat-a-cake.

Thus left in peace, Kate read the bare facts of an appalling tragedy on Monday February 19th, 1849, when seventy people were trampled to death in Glasgow's Theatre Royal at Dunlop Street. It seemed there had been a little smoke and some sparks from the front of the gallery. But this had at once been extinguished by the simple expedient of one theatre-goer stuffing his cap into the outlet pipe. The band, which had stopped playing on the dreaded shout of "FIRE," again started playing, there were relieved shouts of, "All's right."

One galleryite had even called for three hearty cheers. The tragedy, the awful irony, of the situation was that before they reached the third cheer, a fireman appeared. There were renewed shouts of, "FIRE", immediately followed by blind panic and a mass exodus towards the one and only stairway ...

"And your poor husband was one of the seventy killed, is that right, Granny?"

The old woman turned away from a now over-excited Hannah and again approached the table. She nodded.

"Aye, indeed, Kate lass. My poor Patrick. His night at the theatre. He had saved up for weeks. It was to be a grand treat. 'Twas the great new Irish comedian you know, Hudson, direct from London's Covent Garden, no less."

"Oh, Granny, what a terrible waste of life. I wonder you can bear to think of it at all, even after all these years."

Granny dabbed at her rheumy eyes with a rag which she had hurriedly taken from the pocket of her sack-cloth apron.

"The truth is, Kate, I can't. But, like I say, I thought it might help take your mind off your own worries. You see, in that awful tragedy, most of them were just young men, either just starting out on life, or with wee bairns and wives at home. And then there were three wee lassies and even a bairn of three tender years amongst the victims."

"Oh Granny; but you know, you're right. Even just hearing about it all puts my stupid worries into perspective."

With all the wisdom of her years, Granny nodded. She patted Kate's hand.

"That's the best news I've heard in many a long day. Meantime, what about a wee taste of the cup that cheers? I've just had an idea as to how we can help your finances, now that they're taken a tumble.

As the two women later sipped the hot, sweet tea, they put their heads together to discuss Granny's brainwave.

The idea was so simple that Kate could hardly wait to put it into practice. With such a business head on her bowed shoulders there was no doubt about it; Mrs Abigail McGarrity, otherwise known around the Candleriggs as Granny Gorbals, was a true survivor.

Chapter 3

Kate made her way through the cold streets of mid-January 1891. After Pearce's increasing lack of concentration and irascibility at work had finally been too much for his employers and he had been dismissed, Granny Gorbals had suggested that for a determined woman there was always work to be found in the more affluent neighbourhoods where proud housewives would pay to have someone else take their turn to wash the tenement stairs. So Kate trudged on to an area of wally closes and affluence. If anything, the horse-drawn traffic seemed even heavier than usual and Kate had to step nimbly to avoid being drenched with the upthrown filth, slush and horse-dung emanating from the filthy gutters.

Even at that early hour, the pavements were black with pedestrians; in the main, women with babies happed up tightly in shawls and held close to protect them from the cruel, biting wind. But Kate noticed ahead of her a frail looking woman hobbling along with the aid of a stick and clutching a shopping basket in her other hand. By this time, most of the younger men, those who were lucky enough to have found employment, had already departed for their own labour, be it in foundry, shipyard or chemical factory. Here and there, a sprinkling of older men, with hand-me-down suits and worn, cracked boots loitered around the many street traders' barrows, in the often all too vain hope of securing a morning's work in lifting packing cases or some such menial and poorly paid task. Work that Pearce was not physically suited for, even if he would condescend lower himself that far.

Kate's eyes took in the busy scene all around her. Then catching sight of a group of unemployed younger men hanging around the corner of Glassford Street, she hurriedly averted her eyes. With the cancer of unemployment spreading its tentacles throughout the Second City of the Empire, such aimless groups of dispirited men hanging about the street was nothing new. On nearly every street corner, on every bit off waste-land, groups of such men were huddled together for mutual support in their misery.

With head bent low on her chest, Kate neither heard nor saw the horse-drawn tramcar until it was almost too late. Had it not been for quick thinking on the part of one of those very same unemployed men, then the old lady with the stick would most assuredly have been killed. As it was, the man's puny, undernourished arms dragged her back from the horse's hooves just in the very nick of time. He wheeled her round and threw her over to the safety of the pavement, where she landed with a crash as her spine collided with the stone wall of a warehouse. Then, with the sudden force of the action, the man himself overbalanced and for a horrifying and mind-stopping second, he teetered on the edge of the pavement, from where, had he toppled over into the roadway, he himself would have been trapped under the tramcar. As it was, by the grace of God and by a superhuman effort on his own part, the rescuer managed to right himself sufficiently to keel over to the pavement rather than to the roadside. So, the brave man landed in a heap at the old lady's feet. Like a tableau of the '*Drunkard and his Wife*' such as Kate had often seen at one of the enjoyable Penny Geggy dramas in the park, or even at a Temperance meeting, the two participants remained frozen to the spot in statue-like pose.

The man was the first to recover his wits, as somewhat gingerly he rose to his feet and dusted down the threadbare suit. He rescued his flat tweed bunnet from the filthy gutter where it now lay.

Kate rushed up to the pair and helped the old lady to her feet, steadying her as she trembled. The man was wiping bits of mud and horse-dung from his bunnet with his jacketed elbow. Then, grinning sheepishly at them, he said in the broadest of Glasgow accents:

"Uch. never mind. It's supposed to bring good luck."

Kate smiled back at him.

"Good-luck, did you say, sir?" the old lady said in a quavering voice, "If anybody's lucky today its me. Had it not been for you, your quick thinking, your bravery ... I shudder to think what might have – indeed, what would have happened."

Her rescuer gave his bunnet a last spit and polish with a rag which he removed from his trouser pocket. That done, he jammed it on his head, gave it a ritual tap and pulled the skip low over his eyes. He peered up at her from under the rim.

"Best thing, Missus, try not to think aboot it. It was a bloody close shave, I'll grant you that. But it seems you're not wanted jist yet awhile up there with all the heavenly angels. When your time's up, you'll be the first to ken. Will ye be aw right to gae hame?"

Kate nodded

"I'll see her home if you could pick up her bits o' messages?"

Feeling that she really must do something to repay the man for his brave and unselfish act, Kate started fishing around inside the depths of her own wicker basket. However, one horrified glance from the eyes squinting up at her from under the bunnet's rim, was more than enough to strangle at birth any idea which she might have harboured as to making any monetary recompense to the old lady's saviour. Seeing that she had changed her mind, the man gave her a cheeky grin.

"Well, hen, here's her basket. Much as I'd love to stay here bletherin' with the pair o' ye aw day, I'd best be gettin' back to my pals. They'll be takin' the mickey oot off me, thinkin' I've clicked with a new girl-friend. So, tata the noo. And for the love o' God, mind how you go, Missus."

He had already turned away from them and was heading back towards his mates on the corner, when the old lady's voice halted him and caused him to turn his head to catch her words.

"I said, thanks again. Is there's anything I could do?"

The man raised his bunnet and, groping under the rim with his fingers, gave his head a good scratch, as if this somewhat aided his mental thought-process. Then, as if someone had turned on a switch, his lantern-jawed face lit up.

"Aye, hen. There is something you could do. Maybe you'd be kind enough to light a wee candle and say a Novena for my wife and bairns? Would you do that?"

"I'll see you home, Mistress …?" Kate said.

"Mrs Scott," the old lady said. "I'd really appreciate that. It's not far but I do feel a bit shaky."

Mrs Scott lived on the ground floor of one of the wally closes that Kate so envied. She invited Kate in and insisted on making them a nice cup of tea. Kate looked round in admiration.

Seated in the front room, Mrs Scott glanced sideways at Kate.

"Mrs Kinnon, that young man asked me to light a candle and say a Novena for his wife and children. I must confess I wouldn't know how to do that. I'm not Catholic. Could you …?"

Kate laughed. "I'm sorry. I'm not Catholic either, I'm Baptist. – at least my father was a lay preacher."

Mrs Scott clapped her hands. "What a coincidence. I'm Baptist too. I daresay the Lord will take the intention for the deed."

As they talked, Mrs Scott learned that Kate had been on her way to seek employment washing stairs.

"Would you consider a different kind of work, Mrs Kinnon? I'm bad with arthritis and find it difficult to get about. I was out today for a bit of shopping because the woman who usually 'does' for me has left Glasgow – her husband has managed to get a place with some relative on a farm near Ayr."

"What would you need me for?"

"Well, she used to come in on Monday, Wednesday and Friday to clean and shop for me – and to give me a bit of company. Sometimes she'd make a stew or a casserole for me that would see me through the weekend …"

"Yes, I could certainly do that."

Kate left Mrs Scott feeling very satisfied with her morning. She now had a job that paid more than she could have expected for washing stairs all week without the tiring, back-breaking work that would have entailed.

She soon settled into a routine. On the mornings she went to Mrs Scott she could still have breakfast for Pearce, and for Danny and Jenny before they left for school, leave something for a mid-day meal and be home in the afternoon to prepare an evening meal. Tuesdays and Thursdays she could leave home later in the day to wash the limited number of closes and stairs she had decided to take on after all.

Pearce gave up any pretence at seeking work. His moods alternated between the depths of gloom when he ignored everything and everyone, and violent rages.

Kate and Mrs Scott began to form a relationship that was much closer to friendship than to that expected between employer and employee.

Chapter 4

Some months after taking up employment with Mrs Scott, Kate was increasingly worried about Pearce, who showed no sign of interest in anything or anyone.

She waited till Pearce had gone out of the kitchen to use the toilet before she took three sixpenny pieces from the old tea caddy at the back of the top shelf above the sink.

With the money clutched in her hand, she felt happier walking down the street than she had done for months. Although in her heart she knew it to be an extravagance, she knew exactly where a shilling of her money was going to be spent. With the other sixpence, she determined to buy the ingredients necessary for Pearce's favourite tea – a plateful of Irish stovies. Surely he won't chuck that back at her?

She headed at high speed for the consulting room of Doctor Desmond Aloysius Clancey. By the time she entered the converted shop, it was already packed to capacity. The women, most of whom had crying bairns happed up inside their shawls, were pale-faced with the burden of poverty and excessive child-bearing. The men, in the main, were thin, lantern-jawed spectres. Like a uniform, the men wore suits of the cheapest materials, long off-white, fringed scarves and flat bunnets. The air was thick with tobacco-smoke and those who were not smoking the cheapest of cigarettes were instead puffing away at clay-pipes.

This crowd of would-be patients with their variety of ailments were ranged round the tiny room, seated on a hard wooden bench and an ill-assorted collection of rickety chairs

In stark contrast to the normal Glasgow camaraderie and social chit-chat, there in that Holy of Holies, Doctor Clancey's consulting-room, not one person spoke. The only sounds were the screaming of the babies, the frantic tamping and puffing of a smoker as he struggled to rekindle his pipe, the coughs, the sneezes without benefit of handkerchiefs, and the occasional shuffling of bottoms and creaking of chairs each time the distant ping of the doctor's bell announced it was now the turn of the next claimant on his time, knowledge and medical expertise.

At last the bell pinged for Kate, who went with all possible speed into the inner sanctum.

After having first deposited her two sixpences into the saucer kept for the purpose on Doctor Clancey's roll-top desk, Kate sat down.

The doctor, in his rich Irish brogue which a lifetime of medical practice in the Second City of the Empire had done nothing to tame, smiled kindly.

"'Tis yourself, Mistress Kinnon."

Kate nodded.

"And what seems to be the trouble, my dear?"

"'Tis my husband, Pearce, Doctor, sir. I'm worried about him. Never a patient man, even when he was well, he has recently become violent And truth is, I just don't know how to cope with him."

"Mrs Kinnon, I cannot diagnose someone I haven't seen, let alone examined. Can you tell me what his symptoms are, or better yet send him in to see me himself?"

"Since our youngest daughter drowned almost two years ago, he has been moody, surly even, and not able to concentrate on anything. It's been bad enough that he's lost his job in the Fruit Market – he couldn't set his mind to the figures in the office."

"What age is your husband, Mrs Kinnon?"

"Fifty-four. Why?"

"Some men do go into deep despair and black moods over the loss of work at an age when other work is unlikely; some take to the drink …"

"No, it's not the drink. Not this time."

"It sounds like a melancholia brought on by the tragic death of your daughter and made worse by the loss of his job. Time and patience may be the only cure."

Kate sighed.

"In marrying me, he married out of his class. Had to give up family, friends, country estates, a privileged way of life. No matter what I do, say, or even suggest, it is like a red rag to a bull."

Dr Clancey leaned forward.

"It may be small comfort, my dear, but his present attitude possibly has nothing whatever to do with you and your early days of married life. Quite the reverse in fact, the melancholiac frequently turns against those nearest and dearest. So, that would rather prove not only have you been greatly loved in the past, but that his present behaviour has everything to do with his melancholia and nothing personally to do with you, my dear."

Kate gasped.

"I didn't know that, Doctor, sir. Oh, what a relief."

Doctor Clancey nodded.

"If it's any help, just you hold on to that fact."

"Your words are indeed a great help, Doctor. You see, all along, I've been blaming myself for poor Pearce's condition."

The doctor smiled and eased his chair back slightly, indicating in this subtle way that the interview was now, or at least should be, drawing to a close. Then, almost on second thoughts before rising to his feet, he frowned.

"But surely you are not alone. Aren't your children now of an age to help you in dealing with your husband?"

Kate shook her head.

"Three of my children are dead. Poor Hannah is severely handicapped, both mentally and physically. My daughter, Jenny, reminds Pearce of what he has lost, and he blames Danny for Isabella's drowning."

Dr Clancey threw his arms wide in a gesture of despair as he let them fall and slap against his trousered thighs.

"My dear woman. Life has treated you ill, hasn't it? But life goes on. And we must each get on with it as best we can."

Kate made no reply beyond a despairing nod of her head, as her tears trickled down her cheek. Dr Clancy patted her gently on the shoulder.

"There, there, my dear, don't take on so. What you really must do is get yourself a hobby of some kind; knitting, sewing, crochet, or reading. Get something – anything – that's for you and you alone. Then whenever your husband is asleep or even in one of his quieter spells, you'll have something else to occupy your mind."

As she turned to leave, already mentally bracing herself for the irate stares and angry mutterings of the other patients, who would no doubt consider that she had outstayed her welcome, she was stopped by the doctor's hand on her shoulder.

"Hold on. I'll give you a bottle of my special red tonic. On the house, my dear."

Kate gasped.

"Oh, Doctor, that's real kind of you, sir. And will this mixture make my man well again?"

Doctor Clancey looked serious.

"No, my dear. I couldn't prescribe for a patient I've never seen. Anyway, I know of no medicine to cure melancholia. The bottle is an iron tonic for you. Between that and your hobby, the world should look brighter."

Before Kate could launch into an ecstasy of thanks, he walked her to the door.

"Best be off with you now, before I have a revolution on my hands with that bunch of folk next door. Good-bye, Mistress Kinnon. Remember: the tonic, a hobby and for once in your life, put yourself first."

Chapter 5

By the spring of 1892 Daniel had was fourteen and unlike other local boys was still at school. Pearce insisted if Daniel wasn't working, he should take every advantage of education. Instead of the handsome lad for whom his mother had so fervently hoped, he had turned out so far to be a miserable looking, lang drink o' watter, as her Glasgow neighbours would say. Not only that, but his thin, pasty face was pitted and marked with pimples, while an angry looking boil on his neck seemed on the point of eruption. Kate sighed as she looked at her first-born and his latest harvest of pimples. For a moment, she could almost have sympathised with Pearce in his constant and everlasting grief over the loss of their other lovely children. Almost, but not quite, for the fact remained that Pearce was always so much against poor Daniel that with her maternal instincts roused, it was only natural that her sympathies lay with the introverted youth.

Whatever the boy did, did not do, said, or even suggested was wrong in the eyes of his hypercritical father. Even worse, his constantly irate father made no bones about telling the lad he was useless on every possible occasion. Earlier that very morning over the breakfast table, the pair of them, father and son, had almost come to blows. Had it not been for Kate's urgent and insistent intervention, she still shuddered to think how the matter might have been resolved. As it was, Pearce had gone off to sulk in splendid isolation in the good front room, while it was left to Kate to restore what little she could of Daniel's fragile self-confidence.

She glanced again at the morose youth sitting slouched over the table, then with greater animation in her voice than she felt, she asked: "Right, Daniel. How about you and me having a nice wee cuppa? And a wee blether now that the coast's clear. If we're lucky, I think there's a crumb or two left of that clootie dumpling I made yesterday. Do you fancy a wee slice fried in dripping, son?"

"Fried dumpling did you say, Mammy? That would be great. For fine well you know it's my absolute favourite. But listen, I thought you said I was to keep off fries, and chips and all that kind of stuff, leastways till all my spots and boils had cleared up a wee bit. Is that not right?"

By way of reply, Kate stepped over to the table, and gently ruffled her son's hair.

"Och, listen, son. One wee slice of my good clootie dumplin'll not do you one wee bit of harm this morning. Who knows? It might even cheer you up a wee bit. Even if it does give you another plook on your face. Right, son?"

Daniel smiled his assent and, while he waited for his mother to get busy with the frying-pan, he chuckled. Hearing this, Kate turned round from the kitchen range, a look of surprise on her face, delighted that her son had so quickly recovered his good spirits. Of course, she had to admit whenever he was away from Pearce and, better still when on such rare occasions as this, had his Mother all to himself, then he was happy.

As she set the generous slice of dumpling into the frying-pan, Kate, anxious to bolster even further his raised spirits, asked over her shoulder: "Aye, and jist what is it that's amusing you so much, my fine laddie?"

Again Daniel laughed, this time even more heartily.

"You've just done it again, Mammy."

With a puzzled frown, Kate asked: "Done what, for heaven's sake?"

Daniel got up from the table and after first looking round the door to make sure that his father was nowhere near, he settled himself into the one and only armchair. There, lolling at his ease, his eyes twinkled at his Mother.

"It's your voice, Mammy. Nowadays, for some reason best known to yourself, you seem to speak in a mixture of Irish accent and straight Glesga patter. I mean, here you are talking about plooks like any Glaswegian."

Kate threw back her head and laughed.

"And since when did you become an expert on accents? Cheeky wee midden that you are."

Daniel joined in her laughter. Then as it died away, he looked at his mother for a long moment, as if wondering how much he could venture to say without in anyway hurting her feelings.

Finally he spoke: "Well, I've noticed when you're speaking to Hannah, Jenny, or me you speak as near like a native Glaswegian as makes no difference – except of course for that wee bit Irish brogue. We all speak the same as our pals from the school, so we understand you, Mammy. But when you're talking to him, if you get my meaning, then you aye use your posh pan-loaf voice. Am I not right?"

Kate placed the fried dumpling on to the two plates and grinned at her son.

"Well, I'll say this, Danny Boy, and in any accent ye care to mention, for somebody who normally doesn't say much, you miss nothing, do you? Seems to me, nothing going on in this house escapes you, now does it?"

Daniel merely grinned.

"Better eat that while it's hot, son. Later on, when you've demolished it, we'll have a talk about this morning's contretemps with Dadda. Aye, and if it pleases you son, I'll be happy for to talk as posh as you like just to get to the bottom of this morning's carry on; whatever that was all about."

The slices of fried dumpling safely disposed of, mother and son then got down to a blether about the morning's events. It was all exactly as Kate had feared. Yet again Pearce had been attempting to impose his own strict ideas on an unwilling young man who was gradually evolving his own theories about life in general and his own outlook in particular.

Kate placed a gentle hand on her son's arm.

"Now then, Danny Boy, exactly what did Dadda say to upset you this way? Honest, son, I could see you were nearly in tears – greetin' – before he'd finished with you. Tell your Mammy, son, what was it?"

Daniel took a deep breath, then after only a second's hesitation, he plunged straight into his tale of woe.

"Well, Mammy, you see it was like this: Dadda says that now he's out of work …"

Daniel paused, his eyes filled with tears, and he angrily knuckled his eyes.

"Dadda blames me for his ill-health. The shock of Isabella's tragic death brought it on, he says. He was fair harping on about it, it was all my fault. … It was and it wasn't, Mammy … I was going to go out on the row boat by myself. Isabella screamed at me that she'd tell Dadda if I didn't take her with me. She said she'd say I'd gone out even if I didn't and I knew I'd get a thrashing … so I let her get into the boat. She wouldn't sit still … I shouted at her to sit down … she just laughed and said she was going to dance … I shouted at her and she said she was going to tell Dadda anyway since I shouted at her … the boat was rocking so I let go the oars to try and make her sit down … then a big wave hit us. I don't know where it came from. The boat turned over and I grabbed hold of a rope that was hanging from it. I couldn't swim … and there was no sign of Isabella …

Kate, tears streaming down her face, gazed across the table at Daniel.

"Oh, Daniel, why have you never told anyone this before?"

"Do you think it would make any difference to him? He's had his mind made up all my life I could do nothing right."

"It was God's will that poor Wee Isabella died," Kate said. "Did you tell Dadda this, this morning? Is that what the fight was about?"

Daniel's voice broke with emotion and it took some gentle persuasion from Kate before the upset youth could continue speaking.

"No, even if I'd wanted to, Dadda wouldn't listen to me. He said, now that he can no longer work, I'll have to become the breadwinner and look after the family. Honestly, Mammy, I have looked for a job, but there's nothin' to be had and it's Dadda himself that makes me keep on at school. The thing is, he wants for me to try to get a job of some kind in the shipyards of all places. Mammy, sorry. I'm not lazy nor nothin' like that, but to work in the shipyards. It's the very last thing I'd want to do. Honestly. I'd just fair hate it. All the noise with the hammerin', rivetin', and bangin', the freezin' cold and all that. I just couldn't stick It Mammy. Anythin' else, but not the shipyards"

Kate leant across the table.

"Listen, Danny. I'm real sorry your father has been having another go at you about Wee Isabella's death. That wasn't fair of him, son, and if it were not for fear of starting another argument, I would be the first to tell him so."

Danny's pale face grew even more ashen and he put out a hand as if to wave away the very suggestion that his mother should take up the cudgels on his behalf. Seeing this, Kate at once reassured him.

"It's all right, son. I'm not that daft. Anyway, if I know my own Danny Boy, I think you've already made up your mind as to what you want to do with your life. Am I not right on that score?"

Danny's face coloured painfully and with his mass of spots thus highlighted, somehow he seemed even more than usually vulnerable.

"I think," Kate said, "knowing you as well as I do, I could make a good guess at your secret ambition in life. You'd like to run away and join the soldiers. You fancy yourself in a uniform and wearing it as far away from the Candleriggs as possible. Is that right son?"

"Mammy, you've got the wrong uniform. I do want to run away, that's true enough. But I want to go to sea. I'm set for a sailor boy, that's me."

Kate's eyes widened in amazement.

"A sailor indeed. My, my, and that's very strange, for nobody in my own family back in Ireland ever went anywhere near the sea, far less wanted to sail on it."

Kate sat lost in thought for a few minutes, gazing at a past which only she could see.

"And now my son, my first-born and now my only son, wants to be off to sea. Forgive me for saying it son, but especially after what happened … the accident and that, you must be really keen, that's all I can say."

After further discussion, Daniel agreed not to rush headlong into the sea-going idea, but to save it for later. He yielded to her wish that he would hang on for another six months or so in the hope of getting a shore job to his taste. But if nothing turned up during that spell, then, yes, he could go to sea and with her full understanding and blessing.

Chapter 6

Kate had always got on well with the local shopkeepers and not just on account of her always paying her bills strictly on time. She was always able and happy to pass the time of day, inquire after the shopkeeper's family, and generally be sociable. With her pleasant personality, courteous manner, and soft Irish brogue, over the years, she had gained not only friendship but also various perks from the shopkeepers. It was not unknown for an extra tomato, a chipped egg, or even a wee bag of broken biscuits for Hannah to be slipped into Kate's basket by a friendly shopkeeper.

Shopping, after her session with Daniel, the local newsagent had asked: "That young lad of yours still not got a job, Mrs Kinnon?"

Kate shook her head sadly.

"No, nothing doing so far. But at least it's not for the want of trying, Mr McGregor."

The newsagent nodded.

"Oh, fine well I know that, Mistress Kinnon. He's a grand lad. Not an idle bone in his body. Not like some of the layabouts round here. Some of that lot will neither work nor want. Mind you, it must be said, times is hard."

Kate agreed and Mr McGregor went on: "The thing is this, and I wouldn't say this to anybody else, but I know you're a lady of discretion. I'm beginning to feel my age a wee bit. I could do with an assistant. and with my own boy away, emigrated to America, I've no family to help. I've been thinking I could maybe train up a likely lad like Daniel ... if he took to the business, that's to say. What would you think of the idea?"

"Oh, Mr McGregor, do you mean it, sir?"

The kindly face beamed and his chins wobbled as he laughed.

"Too bloody right I mean it, if you'll pardon my French. I'm getting too old for all this early-rising carry on. Between that and having to look after my invalid wife. Anyway, don't take this the wrong way, Mistress Kinnon, but I've an idea that as well as helping me, the extra money wouldn't go far wrong in your own household these days, am I not right?"

Kate, choked with emotion at the man's offer, had to swallow several times before she could trust herself to speak.

"Extra money useful, did you say? Man, you never spoke a truer word. Especially as ..."

The newsagent finished the sentence for her.

"Especially with your husband being the way he is now? Not able to work and that. Does the Panel Doctor hold out any hopes for him?"

"He won't hear of going to the doctor. Says a doctor can't do anything for what ails him. The death of his lovely Wee Isabella has gutted him and left him unable to concentrate on anything else. That's how he lost his job at the Fruit Market; he made mistakes in his figures." Kate sighed. "For all that he's a big man, he's no labourer. He wasn't brought up to it. When we came here first, he tried heavy jobs, but he wasn't fast enough or strong enough ... Now, he scarcely leaves the house. He doesn't even read any more. Just sits in front of the fire for hours staring into space, ignoring everyone. Mind you, that's better than his raging tempers over nothing."

"Well, then, my dear, just you send young Daniel along. We'll make a newsagent of him yet. Just you see if we don't."

Again, Kate thanked him profusely and was on the point of leaving when Mr McGregor exclaimed: "Oh, I nearly forgot. I've another wee snippet of news for you, my dear.

"As you know, I put those wee adverts in the window as an obligement for folk ... well. they do bring me in an odd shilling as well. Anyway, when a Mrs Delaney came in with her wee message about wanting to rent a room in a good God Fearing household, well, I thought of you right away. I said to the good lady I wouldn't bother displaying her advert but instead I would give her your address and tell you to expect her round to have a word with you. So, she'll be round to see you on Saturday night. The arrangement might turn out to be mutually agreeable and beneficial. Anyway, Mrs Kinnon, you can see what you think once you've met the widow-woman and made your own judgement."

"Oh, Mr McGregor," Kate said, "you're far too good to me. Such kindness I'll never forget. Never, even if I live to be a hundred – which God forbid."

With loud cries of thanks being heaped on his head, the balding, rotund newsagent blushed like a discomfited teenager. To hide his embarrassment, he waved her words away, at the same time thrusting into her hands a couple of bars of Highland cream toffee.

"Here, away with ye woman, yer haverin that ye are. Take these toffee bars out to Hannah, for fine well I know that she always likes her wee sweet bite."

Kate left the shop and flew home on wings of hope pushing an enthusiastically-sucking Hannah in her now too-small go-chair. The poor child now seemed to be all knees and elbows in the rickety old pram and her head lolled like a puppet's with the movement of the wheels. As she so often did, Kate talked to Hannah as they went along the busy streets. She would point out to her the strong Clydesdale horses pulling the heavy-laden carts, the tram cars with their important sounding bells, the many street traders who not only trundled their barrows, but who often had a distinctive cry for their wares, like the fish-wife, who announced her coming with loud blasts on her bugle. Hannah particularly enjoyed the fish-wife's bugle and it kept her entertained just searching the busy streets in the hope of catching a sight of the sack-cloth aproned woman, wearing a man's flat bunnet. Best of all, and what really tickled Hannah's fancy, was when she spotted a horse doing its business in the middle of a stream of traffic.

They had now entered a quieter side street and to keep Hannah amused, Kate started telling her all about the latest news. The fact that poor Hannah perhaps recognised, far less understood, only about one word in thirty was not important, the point was that Mammy was talking and paying attention to her and that, Hannah loved.

"What do you make of that, Hannah, my love? Our Daniel's to get a job and real training for to become a man of business. And your old Mammy ... well, she's maybe going to be getting a lodger. My, things are really looking up, eh?"

Already Kate's mind was racing ahead of her as she made plans for the prospective and as yet still-to-be-met lodger.

Beaming with happiness, she gazed fondly at the sticky mess which was now Hannah's face.

"I've got it all arranged in my head already, Hannah. Here's what we'll do. Since your Dadda now spends all his time in the back kitchen anyway, we'll all move in there. That will leave the good front room for Mrs Delaney. Is that not a great idea, Hannah?

"Well, now, we had best get our skates on. I've still got a lot of work to do. Especially if I'm to get the best front room ready for my lodger. I'll have to get it looking really nice so that the widow-woman likes it and wants to become my lodger. So, maybe I'd better not count my chickens just yet awhile. Oh, dear Lord above, please let the widow-woman like the room and agree to take it. I don't care how hard I have to work. I'll work my fingers to the bone, that I will, but please let it happen."

Chapter 7

As had been previously arranged, Mrs Josephine Delaney turned up at Kate's door on the following Saturday afternoon, by which time Kate had cleaned the best front room from top to bottom. Not only had she rearranged the furniture to the best advantage, but also she had polished the old wardrobe to within an inch of its life, and, from a length of material bought at a jumble sale, she had even made opulent new curtains with which to frame the inset wall-bed. Then as a last, pretty little touch, the previous evening she had crocheted a couple of small doyleys which she then arranged tastefully on the knee-hole dressing table.

Kate bustled around putting the final touches to the best front room. Finally, she rubbed down the dark, wood-grained varnish of the door and as a grande finale, gave a ceremonial flick of her duster at the picture of Highland stags at bay in pride of place over the fireplace. That done, she stood back and, hands on hips, surveyed and admired her handiwork. She nodded her self-satisfaction.

'*Yes, Kate, my girl. It will do very well. I'm sure there's not a finer, nor a cleaner room to rent anywhere in the whole of Candleriggs. Come to think of it, even if Mrs Delaney doesn't like it or want it after all, then there are plenty more herring in the sea.*'

On that happy and positive note, she then went into the kitchen to attend to Pearce and make him a cup of tea, while she awaited Mrs Delaney's arrival. They had just finished their tea and scones when the door knocker sounded. As if shot from a cannon, Kate leapt to her feet and almost ran to the hall in her eagerness to open the door, so anxious was she to start on this new phase of her life. She opened the door and there on the landing stood a tall, striking-looking woman whose very bearing pronounced she was a lady of quality. It took all of Kate's will power not to give a quick bob of a curtsey, as she had been trained to do whenever, and if ever, she chanced to meet any of the fine ladies at Laggan House.

As if innately sensing the younger woman was somewhat discomfited, Mrs Delaney took the initiative. Holding out her gloved hand, and in a very cultured Irish accent, the visitor said: "You must be Mrs Kinnon. I believe you are expecting me? Mr McGregor gave me your name and address and suggested that I call round to see you today. I'm Josephine Delaney – Mrs Delaney, that is."

By now, having recovered her composure to some extent, Kate invited her visitor into her home and set about making her feel welcome. As she showed her guest into the freshly prepared front room, she first gave a nervous cough.

"Here it is, Mrs Delaney, the room I can offer you. I've arranged the furniture to make it a bed-sitting room, and with that little table over by the bay window, I'd be able to serve you all your meals, which I'd cook for you in the back kitchen."

Kate stole a quick look at Mrs Delaney's face to gauge the woman's reaction. But all she could see was a poker face giving not the slightest clue to what the woman was actually thinking.

In her acute nervousness, Kate babbled on.

"Of course, if you preferred only attendance, by which I mean you would buy and bring in your own food, do your own marketing, in other words, then, of course, I'd be happy to cook it for you and serve it in here at whatever times would be most convenient for you. And of course, I'd be happy to attend to your laundry needs if you wanted me to and …"

At this point Mrs Delaney peeled off her fine kid gloves then, holding them in her left hand, she held up an elegant, be-ringed, and well-manicured hand as if to stem the flow of Kate's tirade. In her superior way and looking down her nose at her would-be landlady, she drawled: "Steady on there, Mistress Kinnon. At this moment, I am still only at the stage of looking and assessing the accommodation on offer, before I make my final decision. Nothing whatever beyond that. And most certainly, no fait accompli, I do assure you, Madam. I do still have another couple of possibles to see and consider as yet. That other newsagent, the big shop round in Argyle Street, he had a discreetly-written notice in his window which rather attracted me. Something about a large, bright airy room with elegant furnishings and attendance. And, would you believe, overlooking Glasgow Green and a ... let me see, how did they phrase it?"

The pompous woman put a forefinger to her head in an elegant pose as she supposedly pondered the wording of the advertisement.

Somehow, Kate, with a quiet smile to herself, had the feeling that the well-corseted and upholstered woman before her knew exactly what the notice had said. Her suspicions were confirmed when, with a trilling laugh as of a young self-conscious girl, Mrs Delaney simpered.

"Oh, yes, I remember now. How very stupid of me to forget. The advertisement said: 'such a rich setting would be the ideal location for a Lady of Quality'."

Again she laughed her girlish trill, which contrasted oddly with her sergeant major physique. Recovering her poise, she shrugged elegantly, at the same time holding out her splayed fingers as if to encompass the mean room in which she currently found herself. As one handing out charity to the workhouse poor, she smiled kindly and gave Kate a crumb of comfort.

"Of course, my dear, that room may already have been taken. I do realise that. But even so, as far as your own room on offer goes, well, as I say, as yet, no fait accompli. Obviously, I do appreciate that in no way whatsoever can you compete with the elegance of Monteith Row and its Glasgow Green setting."

Kate frowned, for the very mention of Glasgow Green, far less Monteith Row was enough to upset her. Deciding on the instant that attack was the best form of defence, she rallied her thoughts and the turmoil of her emotions.

"Monteith Row indeed, Mistress Delaney. Humph. I would not have thought the grand gentry set of people there would have need of a paying lodger."

It was Mrs Delaney's turn to look surprised, but even so she was not about to be spoken to in this manner by a person of the lower classes. She looked down her fine patrician nose.

"Oh, so you know the area, do you? Perhaps you've done some cleaning, stair washing, or the like there, is that it?

Kate folded her arms across her chest, holding to herself the wild surge of glee which raced through her body.

'*Why not?*' she thought. '*Why shouldn't I mention it, do a spot of name dropping? After all, the high and mighty Mistress Delaney is obviously a snob of the first order. Right, Kate, my girl, here goes.*'

She smoothed back her hair, then smiled innocently at the smug woman before her.

"Cleaning? Me? In Monteith Row? Oh, hardly that, Mistress Delaney. You see, I have visited, as a house guest there, in fact, at the home of my husband's aunt. Perhaps you know her?"

Mrs Delaney's face was a study of conflicting emotions as, holding a hand to her bulging neck, she inclined her head on one side.

Kate swallowed hard a couple of times, more to bite back her mirth than anything else, then speaking in an exaggerated tone of great confidentiality, she said: "We don't normally let on about our relations in high places hereabouts, but I know I can trust you not to betray a confidence."

The tall feather in Mrs Delaney's over fussy hat bobbed its easy acceptance, as it all but poked out Kate's left eye. Holding her head somewhat to the side to avoid further confrontation with the William Tell monstrosity, Kate nodded sagely.

"Like I say, you may already know my husband's aunt, what with you, from the look and sound of you, moving in high circles. She's the Lady Christabel Telfer-MacPherson. But of course, Monteith Row is just her Town house. She keeps an estate in Argyll you know."

Plain, untitled Mrs Josephine Delaney, widow-woman with high social pretensions, was visibly flabbergasted. Almost as if she expected the Lady Christabel to come strolling elegantly through the door at any moment, she smoothed down her already immaculate dress. When she again spoke there was a trace of wonder in her voice.

"Lady Christabel Telfer-MacPherson. Why, she's one of the leading society hostesses in Glasgow. During the season, of course." She frowned. "No, I can't say that I know her personally. But, of course, it goes without saying that I do know of her – through mutual friends, you understand?"

Kate did understand. And perhaps even more than Mrs Delaney knew, in that moment, Kate was aware she had found herself a paying lodger.

Chapter 8

In the days that followed Mrs Delaney's moving in it was soon clear not only had Kate gained a lodger, she had more or less lost a husband. By the end of her first week in residence, Pearce not only knew all there was to know about Mrs Delaney, he also knew that he had found his long-sought-after soul mate. For Josephine Delaney was one of his sort of people.

Pearce and Josephine soon found that, although apparent strangers, nevertheless it seemed that their paths had often almost crossed in the far off and privileged days of their youth, in the grand country houses of dear old Ireland. Because of the relatively closed circle, they had former acquaintances in common and, had Pearce not been banished to the colonies when he was, they would undoubtedly have met each other at some point.

Josephine's life story and fall in social standing was amazingly similar to Pearce's own sad tale. She had fallen hopelessly in love with her father's handsome young stable-lad, who had looked after Josephine's horse, and had been cut off from her family with only the clothes she stood up in and with whatever jewellery she was already wearing at the time of her banishment.

Her husband, before they left Ireland for good, had surreptitiously entered her parent's home one night and 'retrieved' her jewellery, her personal box, and as many clothes as he could throw out the window and they could carry. That had finally severed her connection with her family.

As Kate entered the room bearing a loaded tray with the vital requisites of scones, pancakes, fingers of shortbread and other such delicacies for a satisfying afternoon tea, she was in time to hear a burst of laughter from the precious pair. In fact, so engrossed in each other and in their shared reminiscences were they, that neither of them so much as looked up or in any way acknowledged Kate's presence. Seeing this and feeling very strongly that she was the odd man out, Kate smiled grimly to herself.

'*Humph. That's rich, I must say,*' she thought. '*It looks as though their Highnesses have put me firmly into my rightful place, straight back to where I started, a humble, servile and damned overworked lady's maid. That's all I'll ever be, a bloody skivvy.*'

Her thoughts were interrupted when she heard Mrs Delaney give another girlish giggle.

"And that, in a nutshell, my dear Pearce, is how I came to be in this hell-hole they call Glasgow."

Kate could not have cared less how Josephine Delaney came to be in the Second City of the Empire. As long as she paid her lodging and attendance fees regularly each Friday, that was all that really concerned Kate. However, in an effort to make her presence felt and insinuate her way into the conversation, she cleared her throat and asked of her lodger: "If I might make so bold as to ask, Mistress Delaney, what did bring you from Ireland to this dirty, drunken city of Glasgow?"

Mrs Delaney looked put out at this direct questioning of her high-and-mighty self by one of her social inferiors. Then perhaps remembering her own place in the scheme of things in the Kinnon household, she decided to make a joke of the matter. She cocked her head on one side, made a great show of considering deeply the posed question.

"What brought me from Ireland to Scotland, you ask? Well, now, let's see. I do know that it wasn't my Fairy Godmother. That much is sure. So, that being the case, I guess it might just have been the overnight boat from Larne to the Broomielaw, don't you agree? And, of course, one's handsome young lover of a stable lad, Dominic."

At this riposte, Pearce threw back his head and roared with laughter, obviously on the same wave-length of sophisticated humour as his new found friend. In that moment, Kate knew with absolute certainty that from hence, it was going to be a case of two is company; three is an upper class couple and their well below the salt maidservant. And no prize for guessing who would fill the latter humble, yet necessary and overworked role. Kate sighed. She had indeed made a rod for her own already overburdened back.

She smiled grimly as through her mind raced an old Scots saw which she had recently heard one of her Glaswegian neighbours quote in an hour of sore travail.

"Och, weel. The guid Lord above shapes the back for the burden."

Kate pursed her lips.

'If that's true, then the good Lord has recently been hard at work in reshaping my back for this latest burden. For one thing is sure, it is myself that will have to carry the pampered Mistress Delaney and her voracious appetite. Myself and none other.

Chapter 9

Daniel jumped at the chance of the job with the newsagent and happily took over Mr McGregor's early morning stint; opening up, unpacking the morning's papers, and serving those men lucky enough to be employed with their early edition, and cigarettes or tobacco to see them through the day. That rush over he swept up; tidied up generally; cut and weighed out the larger tobacco packages into the one ounce, half ounce, and quarter ounce packets their customers could afford; and had the kettle on for tea for Mr McGregor's arrival. Although that really completed the morning's work he was paid for, Daniel, having left school on taking the job, stayed around, serving customers, reading the papers and the magazines – the penny dreadfuls – and running errands.

In the evening Daniel again unpacked the late edition and the racing paper, bundled up unsold papers, and generally made himself useful.

At the end of his first week he precipitated a major row when he refused to hand his shilling wage over to Pearce, instead insisting on giving it to Kate.

"That's no fit job for a man, anyway," Pearce finally shouted.

"But's one job more than you've got," Daniel shouted back, and fled the house.

Kate pacified Pearce, but kept the shilling.

As the year wore on, between Kate's work with Mrs Scott, her cleaning jobs, Daniel's minute wage from the newsagent, and Mrs

Delaney's lodging and attendance fees, Kate managed to keep the house with just under half of what Pearce had been earning at the Fruit Market. Granny Gorbals took care of Hannah when Kate was out working and although reluctant to do so at first was prevailed on to take sixpence a week for her trouble.

Pearce, with Mrs Delaney to converse with, spent a great deal of time in the front room with her, and was more animated, at least when he was with her. With his family in the kitchen he still tended to sit in morose silence at the fire, but the violent outbursts of temper became less frequent. He and Daniel avoided each other when they could and when contact was unavoidable, as at a family meal, each behaved as if the other was not present.

Daniel had a growth spurt over the year and although not yet as tall as his father, he began to fill out and show signs of becoming a well built young man.

Just before Christmas, Mrs Scott had Kate do a special clean for her and buy in all sorts of Christmas treats. Kate wondered if Mrs Scott was going to have visitors and if that would involve much of a clean-up later. When she arrived at her usual time on Friday, December 23rd she was surprised to find the table set for two and a mouth watering smell of cooking and baking permeating the air.

"Who are you expecting, Mrs Scott?"

Mrs Scott smiled at her.

"You, Mrs Kinnon. Since you won't be back now till after Christmas I thought we would have a little celebration today, just the two of us. Sit down."

"Oh, I couldn't do that. You sit and let me serve you."

"This is my house and today you are my guest. Sit down."

For the first time in her life, Kate sat at table and was served her meal. Compared to what she usually ate this meal was gargantuan. She finally pushed back her chair.

"I couldn't eat another bite."

"I have a little medicinal spirit, Mrs Kinnon. Will you take a drop with me?"

Kate nodded and they toasted each other and drank.

"I'll clear up now," Kate said. "You have a seat."

"You'll do no such thing. We'll clear up together. You can wash or dry. You pick."

Finished, Kate insisted on making a pot of tea for them and they sat chatting.

"I'd better get started or I won't finish today," Kate said.

"No, I had you do a special clean on Monday and Wednesday so that we could have this little party today. Before you go, I have some cake and shortbread wrapped for you to take with you."

Kate was overwhelmed by Mrs Scott's kindness. She had felt that the pair of them had got on very well together, more of a feeling of one friend helping out another than the mistress servant relationship she knew only too well, but she had not expected this.

At her usual time to go Kate put on her coat and hat then collected the parcel Mrs Scott had ready for her. As she turned to leave, Mrs Scott handed her a crown, twice her usual weekly pay of two shillings and sixpence.

"I can't take this, it's too much," Kate protested, trying to thrust the money back into Mrs Scott's hand.

"Nonsense, girl. It's only money and what else do I have to spend it on? I've never stopped blessing the day when I was nearly run over by that tram car. Take it and welcome. Merry Christmas."

Chapter 10

Dazed, Kate left Mrs Scott's home, but instead of heading straight for home she turned and walked in the direction of the book barrows. These handcarts, a Glasgow institution in their own right, were to be found throughout the city, sited on many a busy street corner, when they were not actually being trundled through the dense traffic.

Today one book barrow, just off Hope Street, caught her attention and she stopped to browse through the selection of second hand books on display. She had taken Dr Clancy's advice to heart and taken up a hobby, reading, and found she could lose herself and forget the trials of her busy life immersed in the pages of a book. First she had read the books that Daniel brought home from the library, but had come across the book barrows and found the books there were affordable and, better still, some of the owners would let her exchange books she had read for a different book. Some charged a small fee for this, some didn't, and Kate enjoyed the haggling involved.

Today as she rummaged through the books on the barrow she was aware of the owner watching her for some time before he stepped forward.

"Are you looking for something in particular?" he asked in a soft Irish brogue very like Kate's own.

"No, just something to read."

He laughed. "I think you may find something here. As you see, I don't sell fruit or vegetables."

Kate smiled, more at his accent than at the feeble joke. "Aye, that I can. I'll just look for myself, thank you."

"They're arranged more or less by subject." He came and stood beside her. "To the left of this cardboard up to the end of the barrow you'll find text books and non-fiction. Between the two cardboards is all fiction, and in the last three rows you'll find poetry."

"I don't think any of the other barrows do that," Kate said. "It's very helpful."

He laughed again. "And good for trade. Students from the Uni know just where to look for used texts without wasting time going over my whole barrow." He turned to face Kate. "You have a lovely accent, mistress. Have you been in Glasgow long?"

Somehow it seemed quite natural to talk to this complete stranger and Kate replied: "Since 1877."

"And have you never been back to the Old Country since?"

"No, never."

"I go back every now and then to buy books and visit my old mother."

He shook himself as if suddenly aware they were drifting away from business.

"Just take your time then, Mistress …"

"Kinnon, Kathleen Kinnon," Kate said, without pausing to think.

"Terence O'Neil, at your service, Kathleen Mavourneen."

Kate left Terence's barrow with two books and a feeling that she would be back soon.

Over time, Kate became something of a regular customer. Terence, in addition to a fine stock of second-, third-, and sixtieth-hand books, also had a grand line in Irish banter – definitely one who'd kissed the Blarney Stone. Each time he saw her approach, his laughing Irish eyes would sparkle and he'd call out: "Why, if 'tis not Kate Mavourneen herself. And 'tis Terence O'Neil here, entirely at your service, Ma'am."

No matter the day, the time, or the weather, the genial greeting never changed. And somehow, the panache, the cheeky grin with which he so obligingly offered his services, always left Kate with the feeling there might well be other commodities on offer apart from the more mundane books. No matter what her family problems, Kate always felt the better for a chat, no matter how brief, with Terence.

After the first few visits, Kate took to bringing with her a few fresh baked scones and they would stand by Terence's barrow discussing the books Kate had read. Terence introduced her to the pleasures of poetry – something Pearce had never attempted although in their early days she had often asked him what he found so enthralling in his books of verse.

Chapter 11

The morning of Monday, March 20th, 1893, started off like any other day for Kate, and she set off reasonably contentedly for Mrs Scott's. There she and Mrs Scott chatted as Kate went about her work, then, as usual now, they sat and gossiped over a cup of tea before Kate left.

'*I'm really lucky,*' Kate thought. '*Things are working out pretty well. Mrs Delaney seems to keep Pearce happy and quiet, and even though she can be a nuisance, her money is regular. Jenny is doing well at school and Pearce has agreed she can stay on and maybe even become a teacher. Danny seems happy enough with Mr McGregor, even if he'd like a job with a bit more money. And I've got a good job and a good friend with Mrs Scott.*'

Kate surfaced from her daydream and looking round her, realised she wasn't on her way home. She was headed towards the book barrows.

'*Well, why not? It's a fine day. I don't need to rush back to make a lunch for Mrs Delaney; she said she would be out till time for her afternoon tea and there's plenty of bread and cheese in the house. Pearce can fend for himself for once.*'

Terence saw her approach and met her with his usual effusive greeting. They stood side-by-side at his barrow animatedly discussing a book Terence had recommended to her.

"Excuse me," a familiar voice said from the other side of the barrow, "I asked how much this book would be."

Kate looked up and there across the barrow was Mrs Delaney staring at her.

Terence took the book and named his price.

Mrs Delaney paid without quibble.

"My landlady, Mrs Kinnon, can take it home for me to save me carrying it about town. Don't let Pearce see it. It's a surprise for him. Put it in my room."

She turned and walked off without a backward glance.

"Now there's a polite one," Terence said. "Not as much as a, 'Nice day,' or 'How'd you do,' to you, and you her landlady." He glanced at the book. "And I don't think much of her choice of poetry either. Here, Kathleen, I hope her husband enjoys it."

Kate didn't correct his misconception. The day was spoiled. She said her goodbyes and left for home.

She entered the house to the sound of raised voices. Hurriedly, she hung up her coat and hat and walked into the kitchen.

Pearce and Daniel stood facing each other on either side of the table.

"I will not make your damned tea," Daniel shouted. "What did your last slave die of?"

"Don't you use that language to me. You are my son –"

"Then treat me like one. Mr McGregor's more like a father to me than you've ever been."

Kate stepped forward.

"Sit down both of you. You're quarrelling like children over who's to make the tea? I'll make it."

"Who cut off his legs?" Daniel said. "You're out working all day, every day, while he sits here on his backside ordering everyone about – "

"That's enough out of you," Pearce shouted. "You're not too old yet for a thrashing–"

They were both on their feet again and Pearce stepped to one side. Kate moved to step between them and Pearce with an oath pushed her. She stumbled, her foot caught on the rug, and she fell heavily. Ignoring her, Pearce advanced on Daniel, slackening his heavy leather belt as he did so.

"Not again, Dadda, never again," Daniel said, and taking advantage of the fact that both his father's hands were engaged, landed one heavy blow on Pearce's midriff, followed by a right uppercut to his jaw.

Pearce fell and, before he could rise, Daniel looked down at him.

"If you're wondering where I learnt to do that, I had a fight near everyday at school just because I was the son of the Laird o' Candleriggs."

Daniel turned and walked out of the house.

Kate struggled to her feet. She put out a hand to Pearce to help him up, but he ignored her and stood by himself.

"If that boy ever sets foot in this house again, I'll thrash him within an inch of his life."

"Don't talk daft, Pearce. Don't you see he's way past that. He's not a wee boy to stand still for a leathering. He's nearly your height. He'd fight back."

For answer Pearce kicked Kate's basket across the room. It tipped over and Mrs Delaney's book fell out. Pearce pounced on it.

"More rubbish from your damned book barrows?"

He glanced inside.

"Aye, rubbish it is. Can't you even recognise bad poetry when you see it? Here, take your damned book."

He threw it across the room at her and turned around to see who she was staring at.

Mrs Delaney stood framed in the kitchen doorway.

"Mistress Kinnon, your ruffian son almost knocked me down on the stairs. I'll not put up with it. I'll have my afternoon tea now, if you please. Pearce, would you care to join me?"

With Pearce and Mrs Delaney ensconced in the front room with their afternoon tea, Kate took the opportunity to go to Mr McGregor's shop. As she suspected, Daniel was there.

"Are you all right, Mammy? I'm sorry, but he was after me all afternoon, the tea was the last straw."

Mr McGregor appeared at the counter.

"Mrs Kinnon, come away into the back shop and have a seat. Danny, put the kettle on and make us a cup of tea –"

He looked puzzled when both Kate and Daniel burst out laughing, and Kate hurried to tell him of the afternoon's event.

"Danny can stay with us for a spell, Mrs Kinnon, if that will help."

"We wouldn't want to put you out," Kate said.

"Nothing grand, we have a wee truckle bed that he can sleep on in the hallway of the house or we can bring it down here for him to sleep on in the back shop."

"Thank you, Mr McGregor. I'll bring your stuff down to the shop for you, Danny. I don't think you should be up there for a while.

Chapter 12

Over the next few weeks calm reigned in the Kinnon house. Daniel's name was mentioned only once, when Jenny asked where he was, fortunately out of Pearce's hearing. Mrs Delaney made no mention of the book of poetry she had bought, or of seeing Kate at the book barrow.

Kate dropped in to the newsagent's shop from time to time to chat to Daniel and on one occasion Mr McGregor made a point of sending Daniel out on an errand.

"I don't want to interfere, Mrs Kinnon, but Daniel knows I know some of the sailors that ship out of here and that I could probably get him a place as a ship's boy ..."

"Has he asked you to get him a ship?"

"Well ... not in so many words ... yet ... but I don't think it will be long before he leaves us. He wants some adventure – more than running a wee newsagent's – and he wants to earn some more money."

"Then he'd be better placed by someone you know than chancing his luck by himself, wouldn't he?"

"I hope so. Then, if he asks, I should talk to my friends?"

Kate sat silent, thinking for a spell.

"If he's as close to just going as you think, Mr McGregor, maybe you should broach the subject yourself. I'll be sad to see him go, but I think there's no stopping him now."

Two weeks later Kate was not surprised when Daniel told her he would be shipping out as a ship's boy the next day.

"But if your ship's registered here, you'll be back from time to time, right?"

"No, Mammy, the company sails out of Liverpool. The ship only called in here with cargo of tobacco. It's not her regular run. Their ship's boy broke his leg. That's why they've got a spot for me."

Pearce shrugged when told the news, then after a long silence told Kate and Jenny to sit down.

"With Daniel gone, one source of income for the family is gone – "

"Pearce, he didn't bring in very much," Kate objected, fearing what was coming.

"Never the less," Pearce continued, ignoring Kate, "it means less income. Jenny will leave school and seek employment at the mill. They're always looking for girls there."

"But, Dadda, you said I could stay at school and maybe become a teacher," Jenny said.

"I've changed my mind, and there's an end to it. It's foolish to give a girl an education. Years without income to the family and then they're off to get married."

Despite Jenny's tears and Kate pleadings, Pearce's mind was made up and he would not be moved.

So Jenny, at fourteen, much against her will, left school and went to work at the local mill. Kate came to an arrangement with Mr McGregor to take over some of Daniel's jobs in the newsagents, dropping her stair cleaning activities, but keeping her job with Mrs Scott. It wasn't quite as convenient to Mr McGregor since Kate's times had to be fitted round feeding Mrs Delaney and Pearce, and her mornings with Mrs Scott.

Relative peace, if not harmony, returned to the Kinnon household. Jenny bitterly resented having to leave school, but when Pearce suggested to her it was Daniel's fault for having run away, she vigorously defended Daniel, saying he wouldn't have needed to leave home if he'd been better treated there.

Chapter 13

Almost two years after Daniel left home, sixteen-year-old Jenny still detested her job at the mill and at home was barely polite to her father, avoiding him whenever she could. A works outing was announced and Jenny was reluctant to go, saying she saw enough of the girls at the mill on a daily basis and had no desire to spend her free time with them. However, Kate persuaded her to go, pointing out there would be all sorts of other employees there from different parts of the mill and other shifts.

About a month or so later, when the Works Day Outing was but a memory, young Jenny seemed happier than she'd ever been in her life before. She went around the house singing, even offered to do the odd household chore like cleaning the brasses on a Friday night without even once being asked to do so, and strangest thing of all, she went off to the mill each morning not just with stars in her eyes, but even earlier than she needed do. In fact, there was such a dramatic change in her that one morning over breakfast Kate felt compelled to remark on it.

"Jenny, lass, I've been meaning to say, it's so good to see you happy these days. Does that mean you've finally accepted your lot in life? Or is there some other reason? Are you in love or something? Is that it?"

Jenny coloured then, bending her head over her plate, she became intent on breaking pieces of bread into tiny pellets which she pushed to the rim. Obviously, Jenny was loathe to pursue the subject, but Kate persisted.

"You don't need to tell me, Jenny. I can see it from your face, lass.

You've got a lad, haven't you?"

When there was still no reply and the only sound in the room was the ticking of the clock and Pearce's intermittent snores from the haven of the wall bed, Kate took a deep breath and, determined to get to the bottom of the mystery, decided on one more try.

"Well now, Jenny, it's really nothing to be embarrassed about. After all, let's face it; you're growing into a real bonnie young lass. It would more surprise me if the fellows hereabouts were not flocking round you. So, tell me, dear, did you meet somebody special at the Day Outing, is that it, eh?"

Jenny, having now transferred her attention from the bread pellets to her bowl of porridge, pushed the already congealing mess around with the edge of her spoon and, keeping her eyes down, still made no reply. Kate sat down to join her with a welcome cup of tea and after idly stirring in a spoonful of Nestlé's milk which did double duty both as sweetener and milk, she cleared her throat.

"Come on, Jenny, lass. You can tell your Mammy. To tell you the truth, there's nothing I'd like better than to see you fixed up with some decent young chap, married and settled into a cosy wee single-end of your own. That's my great ambition for you, darling. If nothing else, it would get you safely out of this existence we have here; what with the problems we have with Hannah, not to mention your Dadda, and his black moods and terrible rages."

This last comment was made in a whisper, accompanied by an anxious glance over at the huddled figure beneath the patchwork quilt.

"Mind you, dear, I'm not meaning any disrespect in talking about your Dadda like that ... we all know it's just his illness ... and poor Hannah can't help being the way she is. But the point is, that's my cross to bear. That's not to say that you have to suffer it along with me, dear. You're young, you're a lovely looking fresh faced young lady. So I suppose what I'm really trying to say is ..."

Jenny opened her mouth and pushed back a stray lock of hair.

"It's all right, Mammy, I think I get the message. I know what you're trying to say. And believe me, I'm grateful to you for confiding in me like this. I know you'd like fine to see me married and settled in a wee place before I'm too old and maybe left on the shelf. Is that it, you don't want to be lumbered with an old maid, eh?"

Kate reached across and laid a hand gently on her daughter's arm.

"You an old maid? I don't really think there's much danger of that. And mind you, you're young enough yet in all conscience. But the thing is; if you're starting to be interested in boys, going about with them and all that, well, I thought we'd better just have a wee chat about it. You see, dear, there's two kinds of men, those that are willing to enter the married state and those … er … those that are dead keen to enter the marriage bed but without going through the formalities … if you get my meaning.

Jenny blushed to the roots of her hair and made as if to get up from the table, but her mother's hand detained her.

"No, listen to me, darling, for I know what I'm talking about. And let's face it, how often do we get a chance of a real heart to heart talk? But for once, with Hannah and your Dadda both sleeping and …

"Yes, indeed, Jenny. Marriage to a good man. It would be the making of you, girl. But I've been going all round the house this past ten minutes in trying to spell it out for you. you must remember to keep yourself and your body pure. Till your wedding night, give nothing away, nothing, until you've got that gold wedding ring on your finger. Do you understand, darling?"

Jenny finally raised her head, with a face the colour of boiled beetroot.

"Ach, for goodness sake, Mammy. I've only just met the lad. The way you're going on anybody would think that I was engaged or something."

Delighted to have her suspicions confirmed that there was indeed someone on the romantic horizon, Kate, determined to ignore the rebuff, pressed on with her speiring for news.

Smiling happily, she leant back in her chair.

"Oho, so I was right. There is a young man. Yes, I knew it. But what did you say his name was?"

Jenny smiled.

"Mammy, you're the absolute limit, do you know that? Talk about fishing for titbits of news. You're even better at it than old Nosey Parker Gordon in the next close. Anyway, as you very well know, I did NOT mention what his name was."

Kate took a leisurely sip of her tea.

"No, but you are going to tell me, aren't you, dear? And before you go out that door to the mill. Right?"

"Mammy, you wouldn't keep me late for my work? That new gaffer is the limit. Two minutes late and he docks your pay."

Kate sat silently until at last Jenny blurted out: "Well, if'n you must know, his name is Ross. There now, will that satisfy you?"

Jenny at once got to her feet and taking her heavy cardigan and her outdoor coat from the peg, behind the door, she made as if to leave. She was already halfway out of the door when her mother, with a worried frown on her face, stretched a detaining hand out to Jenny.

"Here, Jenny, just wait one minute, my girl. There's only one man I know round about here who's called Ross. It's not all that common a name, you must admit. Round here, it's nearly all Patrick, Terry, Jimmy, or Jock. Like I say, the only Ross I have even heard of in this district is that layabout Ross Cuthbert. Lives in that stinking slum just round the corner. Not that I'd hold that against him, you understand, but local gossip has it that he's not just lazy, bone idle in fact, but he's a drunkard, a womaniser .... and God alone knows where he gets the money for that style of living, and even worse, he's ..."

Jenny, her face puce now, which in itself was reply and confirmation enough for her mother, pushed away Kate's hand.

Then, with the light of battle in her eyes, she yelled: "Yes, Mammy, it is Ross Cuthbert I've been seeing. But he's nothing like what you say. He's a lovely fellow, not a drunkard, not a womaniser and as to the thing you were about to mention ... something even worse, I just cannot imagine what you mean.

Kate, furious, with an admonitory finger, spelled out for Jenny exactly what she meant.

"Womaniser I said, and womaniser I damn well meant, my girl. Even worse, he's not even a decent church or chapel going man. And he's years older than you."

Jenny opened her mouth to speak but her mother had not yet finished.

"I doubt that it would be marriage of any kind which that scum would want. No, he'd be after just taking what he could get, what was on offer, like. Then, true to form of his kind, he'd run off like a yellow coward, leaving you with a full belly and a lifetime of disgrace before you. Take it from me, marriage is not for the likes of him. That's the very last thing he'd want. Oh, yes, happy enough to accept and enjoy to the full the pleasures of marriage, all the home comforts of wedded bliss. But without the formality of a wedding."

There was a wild look in Jenny's eyes.

"Well, Mammy, I don't know where you get your information from, but I'm happy to tell you that you're dead right on at least two counts: he doesn't attend any church or chapel, because he doesn't believe in any god, and yes, the women flock round him. If that makes him a womaniser, then you're right there as well."

Kate took a step back from the fury which she could not only hear but also see in her daughter's face. Then she held her splayed hands out towards Jenny as if in this way she could somehow stem the flow of bitter, angry words. But it was not to be, for without even pausing for breath, Jenny continued.

"What you may not yet realise, not only is he a very handsome lad, a real dark-haired charmer, but … yes … I will say it, I love him."

Kate drew back in shock then rallied.

"Oh no, Jenny, you don't mean it. You can't mean it. You could never be happy with a wastrel like that. Apart from anything else, there is just no way that I could stand aside and see you, a good, well brought up Christian girl, throw yourself away on a heathen the likes of him. Don't do it, I beg you, please don't do it."

Jenny looked her mother up and down.

"You're a fine one to talk, Mammy. He's years older than me, you say? Dadda's twenty-two years older than you – and he was when you were wed. You don't go to mass at Dadda's High Anglican church or attend any other church I know of. Anyway, who said anything about marriage? Nobody but yourself even mentioned the word marriage. Your gossips should keep up to date with the news. Ross is married already. He had to get married – a shotgun wedding, isn't that what they call it? Big Aggie's father would have killed my poor dear Ross if he hadn't married Aggie to give her bairn a name. But he doesn't love Aggie, he loves me."

"And Aggie's bairn was an example of immaculate conception?"

Kate wept as she watched her daughter secure the Tam O'Shanter on her head, give a last tweek to her long knitted scarf, and make for the hallway. In the background, Kate was dimly aware that over in the wall-bed, Pearce was stirring and cursing as he slowly opened his eyes to the rude awakening. Hannah too was making the odd grunting noises which usually presaged a temper tantrum.

Ignoring both her mother's bitter weeping and the extraneous noises from the two beds, Jenny turned on her heel to give her parting shot.

"Right, then, that's me. I'm off for another fun day of bloody hard work at the mill. But there's just one thing I've decided; there must be more to life than this constant misery. Danny made it away and good luck to him. So if ever Ross Cuthbert asks me to run away with him, I'll not need to be asked twice. I'll be off like a bloody shot and as fast as I can and as far away as I can get, to put as many miles as possible between me and this ... this fucking ménage, with daft Hannah and her fits, screams, and tantrums. And I'll tell you this, Mammy, I would elope with the very Devil himself if I thought he could get me far away from that old bugger ... that bad-tempered old bugger of a father."

As the door crashed behind her fleeing daughter with a force that seemed to shake the very foundations, Kate looked round, as one in the grip of a nightmare from which there could be no possible awakening.

Chapter 14

In the weeks which followed the row between Jenny and her mother on the subject of Ross Cuthbert, to Kate's vast relief, his name had not been mentioned again. True, Anne-Marie Caughlan, one of the Kate's acquaintances, had whispered to Kate that she had seen Jenny and the young man walking along the street together on several occasions. However, closer examination of the scrap of gossip revealed only that the two had occasionally walked together to and from work.

When Kate discovered this, her feeling was one of relief as she thought: *'Well, as long as that's all they're doing, I've no call for worry. After all, nothing much can happen in those circumstances, especially right in the middle of busy city streets and in full view of such nosey parkers as Anne-Marie Caughlan and her meddling cronies.'*

What further reassured Kate was that apart from never once mentioning Ross's name, at least in her mother's hearing, Jenny had taken to going out with a girl friend from the mill every Saturday night. For the past month, every Saturday night, Lizzie Fergus turned up faithfully at Kate's door to meet Jenny. Then together, the pair of them would set off happily for the weekly soiree run by one of the churches. True, Lizzie herself was a bit more loud-mouthed and common than Kate would have chosen as a bosom friend for her daughter to go around with.

Even so, just once or twice of late, Kate had begun to wonder, when late each Saturday night the girl came back from the soiree with stars in her eyes, a lilt in her voice, and a spring in her step.

'*Meeting him on the quiet?*' Kate thought. '*Perhaps that loud-mouthed Lizzie is really just a front, a cover-up? Oh, no. I can't believe that of Jenny. She may have her faults – who doesn't – but I can't accept that she would ever be so devious. Not Jenny.*'

Thus reassured, for the moment at least, Kate accepted the situation at face value, and plodded along reasonably happily each day, all the while working on her long-held tenet, the blissful assumption that no news is good news.

Matters continued fairly smoothly until one morning when, unusually for her, Jenny had difficulty in rising for work in her usual bright and breezy manner. After much cajoling, prompting, and finally an ultimatum from her mother, she eventually did surface. With her pale face and red-rimmed eyes, she was indeed a sorry sight across the breakfast table. As if that alone were not enough, so unlike her usual cheery manner, not only did she seem disinclined for idle chatter, but also she was as irritable as a cage of bears with outsized headaches.

Finally, when Kate could stand her rudeness not a minute longer, she fixed her daughter with a steady gaze and said: "All right, let's have it. What in God's name is wrong with your torn face this morning? That's what I'd like to know."

Asked a direct question in this way, it was impossible for the sullen young woman to ignore it. However, she did the next best thing, by averting her gaze from her mother, and then staring down into her bowl of porridge.

"What's wrong did you say, Mammy? Nothing, at least nothing more than usual. You know I hate that damned mill, always have, and always will. But for your sake, I do try to make the best of it. After all, I know it wasn't your fault that you had to break the promise to me about staying on at school and going for Teacher Training."

The girl cast a bitter look over at the sleeping hulk of her father in the wall-bed.

"But apart from anything else, you know that I hate to have a rush in the morning. I like to take my time and get into the day gradually before I've to face another day in that stinking mill."

Kate, who had been spreading a dollop of dripping on to a piece of toast, laid down the knife with an air of finality.

"Well, Jenny, let's put it this way: if you're late this morning, then it's nobody's fault but your own. I certainly called you in plenty of time. If you were stuck to your mattress like glue to a hairy blanket, then that's your fault, not mine. So think on that, my fine lady, if you're apportioning blame."

The only answer to this was a tut of annoyance from Jenny as, at the same time, she clattered her spoon on to the porridge bowl, thus causing some of the milk to spurt up and over the wax cloth. Seeing this, Kate pushed back her chair with an angry movement and went over to the sink to get a damp cloth with which she wiped the mess on the table. That done, and with the wet cloth, to which adhered blobs of porridge, still clutched in her hand she pointed a warning finger at the unhappy young woman before her. Then, with each word she spoke, she emphasised her message by shaking an admonitory forefinger, so that Jenny would be left in no doubt as to her meaning.

"Yes, my fine lady. You can chuck the cutlery about as much as you please. And you can sit there tutting with that mumper face on you that would turn milk sour. But while you're at it, there's one more thing. You can sup up the rest of your porridge. For I'm telling you this. You are not leaving this house on a cold morning like this with an empty belly."

Fully aware of the warning look still in her mother's eyes, she again, and with a great show of reluctance, lifted the spoon and half-heartedly chased the now-congealed porridge around the bowl. That done, she lifted a tiny spoonful to her mouth, but as the cold porridge touched her lips, she retched and had to replace the spoon hurriedly, albeit more carefully than before. There was a silence between them during which Jenny sat with her head in her hands and Kate mulled over what she had just witnessed. The noise of a spent coal clunking into the ash-can had the effect of rousing them both. It was Jenny who was the first to speak.

"Mammy, honestly. I'm just not hungry this morning."

But Kate, by now the incensed housewife, the very one who had been up at five-thirty that morning to clean the fire, set it and make the porridge in good time for Jenny's early start at the mill, finally saw red. She banged the flat of her hand on the table with such force that even more milk and porridge splashed over on to the table. However, this time there was no rush to mop up the mess, even though the wet cloth was still in her hand. Intent on teaching Jenny a lesson, she lifted the spoon and, shoving it close to Jenny's face, in a voice quiet with menace she said: "Jenny Kinnon. You are not – I repeat NOT going out of this house this day until and unless you have eaten at least a few spoonfuls of that porridge. It might not seem much to you, but apart from anything else, having your welfare at heart, the fact remains that not only have I spent good hard-earned money to buy the oats in the first place, but I'm the one that's been slaving away since break of day … in fact even earlier, for it was still dark when I got up at half-past five. And for what? So that your ladyship can sit there, turning up her nose at the wholesome food. And not even put tooth to the damned stuff. Oh no you don't, my fine lady. Now, not another word, moan, or retch. Get it down you into that belly of yours."

In amazement, Jenny looked at her mother, for Kate in a temper was indeed a rare occurrence in the Kinnon household. Jenny frowned, suddenly aware that what they were talking about here was more than just a few spoonfuls of the hated porridge. However, to try to defuse the situation, she lifted the spoon to her lips. She managed, with a supreme effort of will, to get the first three spoonfuls down. It was when she attempted to swallow down the last of the slithery mess that she again started retching and just could not stop. Lifting a handkerchief to her lips, with porridge already spilling from her mouth, she rose quickly from the table and raced from the kitchen. Kate watched the departing girl and then heard her bolt the door of the water-closet. The sound of retching could be heard in the kitchen even over the noise of the running tap which Kate had hurriedly turned on in an attempt to keep the noise of her daughter being violently sick away from Pearce, who was already stirring restlessly. It was at this point that Pearce woke up and from the cosy warmth of the wall-bed at once demanded to know what all the racket was about.

"Is my mug of tea ready yet, woman? And I'll have some hot toast and dripping, if you please, and quick about it too."

Kate immediately skewered a slice of bread on to the toasting fork, and without so much as an answering word to her husband, was bending down to the bars of the grate when she heard a sound at her back. Swivelling round, she was in time to see a white-faced Jenny re-enter the kitchen. That the girl was distressed was plain to any but the most casual observer. However, before Kate could comment or even question her further, Jenny quickly snatched up her coat, scarf, and Tam O'Shanter beret with its knitted, bobbled top-knot. With her eyes fastened to the floor, Jenny mumbled the words, 'Right. That's me. I'm off to work', and without so much as a farewell 'cheerio' or even a wave of the hand, she sped out of the door.

Kate, with a sigh and a sorrowful shake of her head, turned back to the task in hand. She had just finished scraping some dripping on to the freshly-toasted slice of bread when she happened to raise her eyes in response to an impatient call from the still-waiting and hungry Pearce. She frowned at what she saw. Draped over the chair in front of her was the long, grey cardigan which Jenny always referred to as her mill cardie. As a rule, and no matter what the season of the year, she took it with her every day, since in the chill of early morning, it was always cold and damp in the mill. Seeing this essential item of clothing thus left carelessly behind, Kate shook her head and gave a tut of annoyance. She laid down the plate of toast on the table then, after having first wiped her hands down the front of the sack-cloth apron, she lifted the cardigan, intending to run down the stairs with it, in the hope of catching up with Jenny. But as she lifted it, Pearce called from the bed, demanding to have his toast while it was still hot. In a spurt of irritation, Kate threw the cardigan back down on to the chair and turned to attend to her husband. It was when she was returning to the table that she happened to glance down and saw a scrap of paper lying on the floor. She frowned, then, realising it must have fallen from the pocket of Jenny's mill cardie, she bent to retrieve it. On the point of tossing the torn-off piece of paper into the fire, since it offended her housewifely eye, she noticed what appeared to be a message of some sort printed on it. This at once stayed her hand, but fearing to attempt to read it in front of Pearce, she grabbed up her glasses, and without further ado, retreated at high speed for the seclusion of the water-closet.

Once safely installed there, with the door snib firmly in place, she smoothed out the paper and struggled to read it in the dim borrowed light from the transept window overlooking the hallway. The letters appeared, as if of their own volition, to jump off the page and hit Kate between the eyes. She gasped in horror, unable, or perhaps unwilling, to believe the evidence of her eyes. She scanned the words yet again, as if in this way trying to re-form the letters into a different and more acceptable meaning. But no matter what her hopes and wishes, and try as she would, the message remained the same.

I'LL WAIT AT THE TOLLGATE TILL NINE ON WEDNESDAY NIGHT. WE'LL RUN AWAY TOGETHER. IF YOU DON'T COME, JENNY, THIS IS GOODBYE. YOUR LOVING, ROSS.

As the full implication of the words sank into her brain, Kate gasped and she thought, '*No. It can't be true. Not my Jenny and that no-good womaniser, Ross Cuthbert.*'

Then, realising that she could not stay in the water-closet for ever, she got slowly to her feet from where she had been perched on the edge of the toilet-pan. With her now-trembling fingers, it was all she could do to unsnib the metal fastener on the door. Then she trailed one foot wearily after the other, back into the kitchen.

Every minute, every hour of that endless day she went about doing her chores at Mr McGregor's in a wooden, mechanical fashion, not her usual cheery self with her customers. The words, as if branded on to her brain, kept hammering away, Wednesday night. We'll run away: Wednesday night. Run away. Your loving, Ross. We'll run away. How she got through that day without betraying by either word or look the inner turmoil she felt, she would never afterwards know. But survive it she did, as indeed she had already survived so much in her life. Later, on her way back with a laden shopping basket, she suddenly stopped as she turned the corner into Garth Street. By the time she had reached her own close entrance, she had it clear in her own mind as to exactly what she would do.

The thoughts raced. '*Right. My so-called intelligent Jenny, you that was the pride and joy of the family with your brains and your aspirations to be a school-teacher. Now all set to run away with a married man. And him with a child, and all. Well, I'll soon see about that.*'

In a more determined, if not exactly happier, frame of mind, Kate climbed the stairs to her top flight flat. As she pushed open the outer door with her right shoulder, she had a final thought: '*No, Jenny. We're having no truck with that daft carry-on. Not only would the disgrace of that go with me to my grave, even worse – the scandal of it all would drive away my good paying lodger. And that would never do.*'

When Jenny returned from work that same evening, she found a lovely hot meal awaiting her, her mother happily bustling around the kitchen, and her mill cardie still hanging over the chair exactly where she had left it. Casting a surreptitious glance at her daughter's anxious face as she hunted through first one pocket, then the other, Kate had the satisfaction of knowing her suspicions had been proved right, especially at the look of intense relief on Jenny's face when she withdrew the scrap of paper safely from its supposed hiding place. Kate quickly averted her eyes as Jenny advanced to the fireplace and tossed the paper into the fire, where the flames soon devoured it. However, the words of the message were engraved not only on Jenny's heart, but also on that of her anxious, disappointed, but nonetheless determined mother.

Chapter 15

When the next evening, Jenny arrived home, tired-out as usual from her day's work at the mill, the tea table was already set. And much to Jenny's surprise, her Mammy had obviously made a special effort in that the meal consisted of all Jenny's favourite foodstuffs. There was a steaming plate of delicious, savoury-smelling Irish stovies, rich with the flavour of onions, carrots and mutton stew, which had obviously been simmering on the hob for the entire day. Despite it being her favourite, it was clear to Kate's experienced, motherly eye that her daughter was having some difficulty in finishing her portion. Seeing this, Kate made neither sign nor comment, but kept her innermost thoughts to herself. The stew was followed by a helping of clootie dumpling apiece, which Pearce tucked into with great energy and aplomb. As she watched in fascinated horror her father's determined attack on the mound of moist, fruit-laden pudding, Jenny, by now looking somewhat pale around the gills, was forced to replace her spoon on the table with pudding still untouched.

"Mammy, it looks lovely. But after all that stew, I honestly don't think I could manage another mouthful. Sorry, but my belly's full."

With great self-restraint, Kate refrained from commenting on this last observation, but even so, the fleeting thought went through her head: *'So, your belly's full, is it, my girl? Aye, indeed. And maybe even fuller than you realise.'*

With the sweetest smile she could summon, given the circumstances and her own secret knowledge, Kate looked at her daughter and nodded.

"No need to worry your head, Jenny. Dadda will soon demolish your helping as well as his own."

Pearce, with bulging cheeks and busily chewing teeth, merely nodded his delighted acceptance of the generous offer.

Kate turned to face her daughter. Then, keeping strictly to her previously well thought out and prepared plan of action with which to combat this latent family crisis, she smiled sweetly and in the voice of a caring, considerate mother, she said: "Well, then, Jenny. If you've had enough to eat, away with you into the hall and get ready. Take your time, dear, for I'll do the tea things tonight. You'll want to look smart for this special occasion."

Jenny jerked her head up and, with a look of alarm on her face, stuttered in some confusion: "Special ... special occasion? But what do you mean, Mammy?"

Kate shook her head, as if gently reproving her daughter.

"Jenny, lass. What a memory. Do you not remember? You mentioned it to me only the other day."

But still Jenny looked not just puzzled, but also downright scared at what she was about to hear. Kate laid a hand on her daughter's arm and was not in the least surprised to find that it was trembling.

"You said you were going out tonight to .... to help with a new activity group, or some such .... for unemployed youngsters."

Jenny had the grace to look somewhat shamefaced, but before she could speak, Kate hurried on.

"That's why I prepared your favourite tea tonight. Least I could do, if you are doing a fine charitable act like that for the deprived. Now then, off with you and get ready. Give me a shout once you've changed and you and I will have a wee cup of tea together before you go. All right, dear?"

By the time Jenny came back into the kitchen some half hour or so later, Dadda, replete with the excellent meal just consumed, was already noisily dozing off.

From where she stood at the sink, Kate swivelled her head round to speak to Jenny. But the words froze on her lips. In some weird way, it suddenly appeared as if Jenny had gained an inordinate amount of weight within the last thirty minutes or so. In a flash of inspiration, the truth dawned on Kate.

'*Of course. So that's it. Why, the devious little bitch. Well now. If that's your game, we'll soon settle your hash.*'

She walked over to the range and piled on to an already bright fire, extra coal which she then prodded with a long-handled poker into life. That done, she then insisted that Jenny take the seat nearest to the fiercely burning fire while Kate poured them both a cup of tea. A swift glance was enough to show Kate that already her daughter was sweating profusely. But even so, she still could not believe that her daughter would really be so devious. Excusing herself briefly, Kate went out into the hallway where she at once opened the cupboard which did double duty as a wardrobe. The row of empty coat-hangers was the final proof that she needed.

Kate's lips pressed together into a thin, straight line, as a firm resolve took hold.

'*Right, my girl. If that's your sneaky little game, two can play. Two can play at lying, cheating, and devious conniving. And I know exactly what my first move is going to be.*'

Kate crept along to the end of the hall where, with great secrecy and speed, she worked to put the first spoke in the wheel of her daughter's escape plan.

Once back in the safety of the over-warm kitchen, she again sat down, having first of all given a ritual tap to the pocket in front of her floral apron.

No sooner had she sat down, than her daughter rose to her feet.

"Well, Mammy. I'd best be off now."

Kate made no verbal reply, but simply nodded and watched Jenny leave the room. In two seconds flat, the girl was back in the kitchen beside her, a look of amazement on her still fire-flushed face.

"Mammy. I don't understand. I can't get the front door to open. And the key that always hangs on the wall, it seems to have disappeared."

Kate said not a word, but held out her hand, in the palm of which rested the key which she had earlier taken from its usual perch.

"This what you're looking for, Jenny?"

With mouth agape, Jenny stared down at the key.

"But you never lock the door. Far less lock it and remove the key. What's the big idea?"

For reply, Kate laid the key on the table between them, but with the tip of her forefinger resting lightly on the fulcrum. Slowly, she rose to her feet. Then with great deliberation and with every syllable crystal clear, she said: "The idea is really quite simple, Jenny. Yes, I have indeed locked the door. I have the one and only key and I have decided that you are not leaving this house tonight. Do you understand?"

Jenny frowned.

"Oh, I understand the words you're saying, but what escapes me is their meaning. What about the club for the unemployed?"

Kate smiled grimly and nodded her head.

"Yes. What about your grand Christian mission? If you think I'll believe that, my girl, then you must think I came up the Clyde on a barrow. And if as you say, the meaning of my words escapes you, then that's the only thing that will be escaping this night. Perhaps you can understand that?"

"But I promised ... I said I'd meet Lizzie and we'd both go together and ..."

Kate looked in disgust at her daughter, still lying in her teeth. She leant forward, holding a bunched fist under the girl's nose.

"Listen, Jenny. As far as your dear pal Lizzie is concerned, I happen to know that you promised her nothing. Nothing, do you hear? You see, my darling daughter, it so happens I know what you're up to."

Jenny's eyes were wide with astonishment.

"But how ... What ...?"

This was to be Kate's big moment and she resolved to relish her victory.

"The only one you've promised anything to – and quite a lot at that, as I understand it – is that bloody wife-deserter, Ross fuckin' Cuthbert."

Jenny paled and for a moment, she looked to be on the point of collapse.

"Mammy. What's got into you? I've never heard you swear before."

Kate gave an angry toss of her head.

"'Tis enough to make a saint swear. But the fact remains, there is no way you are ever going to leave this house to run away with a married man. And most certainly not with that damned Ross Cuthbert. Is that clear?"

"But Mammy, I love him."

"Love him? Well, if he's that keen to have you, the bastard will first have to break down my front door and deal with me first."

Jenny sank back into the chair and laid her head on her hands. Then, she slowly raised her gaze.

"Listen, Mammy. You might just as well face it. I do love Ross, but he's not the only reason I'm leaving home."

Here she let her eyes rove round the cluttered kitchen: a forest of clothes hanging from the wooden pulley above them, Hannah snoring in her hurlie bed, and Pearce slumped, asleep, in his easy chair. She sighed, and with a sweeping gesture of her hand, indicated the room and all it stood for. Seeing this, Kate at once leapt to the defensive.

"Oh, and just what is that grand gesture supposed to indicate, my fine lady? Would you tell me that?"

"If you must know, Mammy, I told you before. I cannot stick another moment in the same house, far less the same room as that miserable old curmudgeon of a father."

Since there was little that Kate could have said to defend Pearce and his black, explosive moods, she made no answer. It was the next cruel barb that found its mark and really hit hard.

Jenny pointed a trembling forefinger towards the sleeping Hannah.

"And that useless lump of blubber … that daft idiot. Honestly, Mammy. I'm ashamed to be seen out in the street with her, pushing that rickety old pram and …"

Jenny never got to finish her sentence. Kate's hand shot out and she slapped her errant daughter with such force that the sound echoed in the quiet kitchen.

Jenny gasped in pain and horror as she held a soothing palm to the side of her face. She opened her mouth, but no words came.

"Jenny, there's plenty more of that, if required. And like I say, if that accursed Ross Cuthbert wants you, then he'll have to come in person and beat that lion's head on the door. After what you've just said about poor Hannah ... well, I might just hand you over to him. And good riddance to bad rubbish, say I."

"Mammy."

Kate shook off her daughter's hand.

"Mammy, nothing. But if you're going to sit there weeping all night, while awaiting your love, at least have the decency to weep quietly. We're not wanting your Dadda and Hannah to waken. To say nothing of disturbing the peace of that nosey Mrs Delaney in the front room."

Ross Cuthbert never did beat a tattoo on the brass lion's head, or make any attempt whatever to claim his bride. He had flown, free as air, leaving his abandoned Jenny to face alone the consequences of their brief, if ecstatic and entirely illegal, union.

Chapter 16

In the days that followed that never-to-be-forgotten Wednesday night, Jenny went skulking around the house in the greatest huff, not even sparing a loving gesture, a kind word , or so much as a disinterested glance for poor Hannah. The only sounds coming from Jenny were in the early morning when she could be heard retching in the water closet.

One morning it got to be so bad that Mrs Delaney was prompted, with an assumed air of innocence, to ask of Kate when the latter brought in her early cup of tea and biscuits: "Is Jenny not too well this morning, then, Mrs Kinnon?"

Keeping a poker face, Kate laid the tray down on the bedside table.

"Oh, nothing for you to worry about, Mrs Delaney. Just a wee bilious attack, I think. She was very prone to them as a bairn, you know, and I have heard it said that you never really grow out of them."

Even as she spoke the words, Kate already knew herself to be lying in her teeth.

'Bilious attack, did I say? Humph. That will be right. But at least there is one thing true ... there is nothing for you to worry about, Mrs Delaney. But plenty to keep my mind troubled for many a long day, if I'm not far mistaken.'

Even so, and despite the telling sounds each new morning, with Jenny in her present dark and uncommunicative mood, no words were spoken between mother and daughter, and certainly no reference was made to the subject uppermost in the minds of both women. Finally, it got to the point that Kate felt she would have to ask Jenny the question which had been on the tip of her tongue for weeks now.

On the following Saturday night, Jenny had gone out with Lizzie, supposedly to the weekly soiree at the local church hall. And no sooner were they out the door than Kate made a decision, and one which she knew she should have taken weeks ago. As she sat at the kitchen table with a pile of darning in front of her, she resolved, that very night she would sit up, awaiting her daughter's return and then finally have it out with the girl once and for all. Having come to this decision, she already felt happier in her own mind as, with a smile on her face, she drew the basket of darning towards her and set to with a will on the ever-present task. As she plied her needle, her thoughts kept on racing even faster than her nimble fingers. If the situation was exactly as she feared, then she knew that come what may, she would still be able to face this latest challenge, as she had already faced so much in life. She would weather the storm. And in view of her own history, she would also be able not only to sympathise with her daughter, but also stand by, encourage, and help her in her hour of need. She nodded her head with satisfaction.

'And another good thing, at least we'll be having no dealings with that bastard Ross Cuthbert. He's done a runner to Edinburgh, they say.'

As she got up to make herself a mug of cocoa, she stretched her arms above her head to ease her aching muscles. As she again lowered them to her side, she glanced over at both the hurlie bed and the wall-bed to check that their respective occupants were sound asleep. Kate stretched forth a hand, meaning to stroke Hannah's brow, but then thought the better of it, lest she should awaken the girl, who would then start demanding a mug of 'ko-ko, ko-ko' for herself. Instead, Kate tip-toed over to the range. As she heated up the pan of milk, the thought came to her: *'Well, Jenny lass, I just hope that when your time does come, the child will be perfect in every detail and not in any way like poor Wee Hannah, God help her.'*

As she sat at the oilcloth covered table and stirred her mug of steaming cocoa, she gave free rein to wild thoughts of young Jenny left not only with a bastard child, but one who was even more physically and mentally handicapped than her own Hannah. Sinking ever deeper into a pit of depression, she shook her head, as if in this way she could abandon such gloomy thoughts.

She bunched her fist and, raising her arm, pounded the air, with all the while, a look of vehemence on her face.

'*Men. Humph, every one of them are absolute bastards. Never met a good one yet. Out only for that one thing. Then it's off with the old and on with the new. Bastards. Never mind, Jenny lass, you and I will struggle through somehow. And surely we couldn't end up with two damaged bairns in the one family? No, the wee one will be fine. And come to think of it, it will be real cosy having another wee bairn about the house. Yes, we'll manage just fine.*'

This thought was still uppermost in her mind when, having finished her bedtime drink, she was just sitting in reflective mood before the dying embers of the fire. She shivered as the room started to grow cold and would have liked to add a few new coals to the fire, but considered this an unwarranted luxury, especially since she knew that Jenny would be in soon and then she could get to bed and snuggle into Hannah's warm body. She rose to her feet and turned down the gas mantle to its lowest peep. Taking her plaid wool shawl from its hook behind the door, she cowled it around her head and waited in what comfort she could for her daughter's return.

Always a positive thinker, Kate mentally planned what knitting and crochet she would need to do in readiness for the baby's coming. She still had the Christening Robe and beautifully hand-made shawl which a kind neighbour had gifted to her in an effort to assuage her grief and pain over the difficult birth she'd had with Hannah and its dire consequences. So those two items would be at least a start. In addition, she could have a good scout round the Clothes Market, which Glasgow Corporation had opened round in Greendyke Street, and from which piles of fine old hand-me-downs were periodically sent to Ireland. From the waiting bales of cloaks, jackets, gowns, petticoats, shirts and shifts, she would be able to extract something which with a little alteration could be adapted to fit the needs of a new baby. Yes, the more Kate thought about it, the more enthusiastic she became, and the more eager for Jenny to return from the soiree.

Already in her own mind, she had decided exactly what she would do ... the very moment that Jenny arrived back, she would fling her arms around the anxious young girl.

"It's all right. Don't you worry yourself any more. You see, I know. And we'll manage fine together and without the help of any of those bastard men."

In her mind's eye she could see the look of amazement on Jenny's face, not only that at long last her guilty secret was out, but also at the understanding and totally unexpected way in which her mother had so obviously accepted the unlooked-for news. Her cosy mental picture expanded to the sight of a softly-weeping Jenny, huddled against her mother's breast. She even had a little joke, or play upon words with which she would lighten the tense, fraught situation.

She would hold her daughter close and murmur into her hair: "That's right, darling. Just you have a bit weep to yourself, you'll feel the better for it. Then we'll get on with the business in hand, or maybe to be strictly accurate, I should say, the business in your belly."

She was sure that Jenny would have a real good laugh at that.

In her mind's eye, she could see her daughter, with much of the tension already removed from her face, throwing back her head and giving her old, infectious, and almost school girlish giggle.

With the big decision taken and thus feeling happier in her mind than she had done for many a long day, Kate soon drifted off to sleep; a lovely cocoa-induced sleep. When she awoke with a start, it was to the realisation the fire had long since gone out, she was feeling cramped and cold and she was alone in a silence that could be felt. Her first thought was to check the time. She got slowly to her feet, and in the dim gaslight peered at the grandmother clock above the mantelpiece. With a gasp at what she saw, she drew back. Then in disbelief, she again crouched closer for another look at the dial with its pattern of painted sun, moon, and stars. The hands still pointed to three o'clock. Seeing this, she frowned, then with a tut of annoyance decided in her own mind that Jenny had already arrived home but, finding her mother asleep before the fire, rather than disturb her, had instead crept off quietly to her own sofa-bed out in the narrow hallway. Kate frowned even more deeply and she slapped a bunched fist into the palm of her left hand as the realisation hit her.

'Damn. So much for my grand plan of a reconciliation scene. I really did want to be awake to give the poor lass the big welcome home and assure her that I would definitely be sticking by her. And now, dammit all, I've missed the perfect opportunity. I'll just have to wait till another time now. Nothing else for it.'

Deciding since that was obviously the case, she might just as well get ready to pop into bed beside Hannah, she first tip-toed out to the water closet to pay a last visit before settling down for the night. Reaching the door of the cludgie, she looked over to her left, to see Jenny cosily tucked under the patchwork quilt on the horse-hair sofa, a recent purchase from one of the many street-traders. But to her amazement, the bolster and patchwork quilt itself were still neatly folded at the end of the sofa, still awaiting Jenny's return.

Kate, with all thoughts gone of settling herself for the night, stumbled back into the kitchen in a state of shock. In the dim gaslight and now with her entire body trembling like a leaf in a gale, she again peered at the clock. Yes. She had been right, it had not been a figment of her imagination, not an isolated part of a dream, although nightmare it most certainly was. The hands on the clock now showed a few minutes after three o'clock and still there was no sign of Jenny.

Kate sat down heavily into the one and only armchair which was normally reserved for Pearce, but right at that moment, she could not have cared less had it been reserved for His Holiness the Pope himself.

'Where on earth can Jenny be till this time? She has never been this late in her life before. Not even when she was secretly seeing that accursed Ross Cuthbert. Suppose she's been in an accident? Knocked down and killed by a runaway horse? Oh, God, where is the girl?'

Then an even darker thought flashed through her head as she pondered the fate worse than death.

'*Worse still, what in God's name can she be doing till this ungodly hour of the morning?*'

Kate did not have long to wait for an answer to her prayers. Just a few minutes later, she heard the sound of the front door opening and closing. This was followed by slow, rather hesitant footsteps in the hall. Then the door burst open and her daughter was there with her in the dimly-lit kitchen. The moment she saw her, Kate immediately leapt to her feet and went towards the girl. Kate froze to the spot. For the Jenny who had reeled into the room was a totally alien person, never before seen by her loving mother.

The girl was riotously drunk, and sodden with the sweet-cloying stench of gin. Looking at the scene through an alcohol haze, Jenny swayed on her feet and would have fallen but for the quick thinking of her mother. Just in time, Kate stretched forward and grabbed hold of her daughter before she fell headlong across the table. As Kate tried to get her seated in the armchair, it was like trying to cope with a rag-doll. Finally, with great difficulty, she got the girl seated and threw a crocheted shawl around her shoulders. With a wary eye on the sleeping Pearce, she knelt before Jenny and tried to make some sense of her drunken ramblings.

"Lizzie. It was Lizzie. Yes, Mammy, she told ..."

When after several minutes of this, of which Kate could understand nothing, she finally rose to her feet and bustled about making the semi-conscious drunk a mug of hot sweet tea. Then, holding it up to her daughter's lips, at the same time almost throwing up with the stink of gin, she said: "Jenny, listen to me. Drink this down you. Then, hopefully once you've sobered up, if it's the last thing I do, I'm going to get some sense out of you. Yes, and this very night."

Kathleen further insisted that Jenny also get some food down. So, eventually after almost force-feeding her with one piece of soda-bread after another, and two cups of tea, Jenny slowly began to sober up a bit. Suddenly aware of her surroundings, she blinked a couple of times and gazed around as if coming out of a very deep sleep. When she saw this latest development, Kate immediately asked: "Now then, my fine lady, and what exactly is all this about? What in God's name has happened to you this night, Jenny?"

Eventually, after a long look at her mother and an even longer silence, hesitantly at first, Jenny started speaking.

"Oh, Mammy. It was terrible, so it was. Just terrible. You see, Lizzie made me drink that stuff. I gagged and retched something awful at the very taste of it. But Lizzie made me drink it all up, said it would help my problem. And would make an end to it."

Kate took hold of her daughter's hand and held it so tightly with her nails digging into the flesh that the girl winced and would have withdrawn her hand, had such a thing been possible. But Kate held on like grim death, all the while urging her daughter on with her sad tale.

Apparently, the well-meaning, if misguided, Lizzie, who seemed to be knowledgeable about such matters, had proffered yet another piece of advice in addition to the efficacy of drinking a large quantity of gin. Hearing this, Kate frowned and said: "Oh indeed, and what exactly did the famous Lizzie tell you to do? Or, if I'm not much mistaken, Jenny, what did the stupid little bitch tell you to take?"

That last barb really struck home. Even so, it took a bit more prompting on Mammy's side before the whole degrading story was finally out in the open.

As if deep in thought or prayer, Jenny held her head in her hands and it was left to Kate to prise them away so that she could better understand what it was the girl was muttering.

"It was Lizzie, Mammy. She told me to take some pills that she had managed to get for me. She said that between the pills and the booze … well, that should do the trick. It was Lizzie. Honestly, Mammy, Lizzie told me to take them."

Kate's eyes were wide with disbelief and, had it not been for the sleeping forms of Pearce and Hannah, she would there and then have given her daughter the loudest telling-off of her young life. So, controlling with the greatest difficulty her urge to shout and yell obscenities at the hapless girl before her, she stage-whispered: "Oh, indeed, madam. So Lizzie told you to toss back a box of pills and a bottle of gin to wash it down. That's right, eh? Well, and I suppose if the bold Lizzie told you to go jump in the River Clyde, then you'd do that too? Is that so? Anyway, don't you tell me that dear Lizzie, just out of the goodness of her heart, spent all her hard-earned money on a tramp like you? If you think I'll believe that, madam, then you must think I'm really simple."

Jenny made no answer beyond a heart-felt sigh. Kate went on: "Oh no, my fine lass, the money must have come from somewhere, for such items do not come cheap. Mind you, lately I've noticed the odd threepenny bit, yes and now I come to think of it, even a whole sixpence missing from my purse. I said nothing at the time, but I'm ashamed to say I suspected poor Hannah. Not that she would either know the value or have any use for money, but I thought perhaps the twinkling silver had attracted her."

The look on Jenny's face was confession enough

"Aha, so that's the lie of the land. And no doubt while you were stealing the bread from our mouths, you were also raiding my savings from my best tea-caddy?"

Kate rose to her feet and went towards the mantelpiece on which rested the gleaming brass caddy. Jenny put out a restraining hand. Her mother looked down in disgust, then slapped away her daughter's hand, but still made no move to lift down the cache of carefully-hoarded farthings, halfpennies, threepenny bits and sixpences. There was no need to investigate further, for already she knew what she would find.

Feeling that she had aged ten years in as many moments, Kate sank into the chair opposite and studied her daughter, as if seeing her for the first time. Then, as if dragging the words up from a long way, she said, still in the hoarsest of whispers, so as not to disturb the sleeping forms in the two beds: "So your dear friend Lizzie, who would appear to be something of an expert in such matters, told you that the pills and the booze would do the trick. Dear God in heaven. Do you know what it is exactly that you're saying? There's a very ugly word for what you've done."

Unable to restrain herself a moment longer, Kate got to her feet and, stretching across the table which lay between them, she grabbed hold of her daughter by the scruff of the neck. Then, with the girl's face close to her own, she whispered: "God Almighty, Jenny. Do you know exactly what you've done? And oh, my God. The shame of it. To think a man has brought you to this. That you would steal from your own mother. Steal the very bread from our mouths. And then enlist the help of ... a trollop like that common Lizzie ... and procure an ... an abor..."

The hated word stuck in her throat, so that Kate who, in impotent fury felt that she must lash out at something, finally vented her spleen on the cause of Jenny's fall from grace.

Her face contorted with anger, Kate said: "Well, I don't think much of you, Jenny. I think even less of your pal, Lizzie. But that bloody bastard Ross Cuthbert. That wee Glasgow nyaff that got you into this mess in the first place ... well, I say bugger him. May he rot in Hell. Bugger him to everlasting damnation."

Jenny stared in disbelief at her mother, for seldom had she heard her mother swear in this fashion. And in a strange way, the very fact of her having of necessity to keep her voice low, somehow it made it seem that much worse. It would have been less disturbing if her mother had been able to give free rein to her fury and had actually shouted the words at her.

But shouted or not, as far as Jenny was concerned, the message was crystal-clear: her mother now knew exactly what had happened. As she looked into the white, care-worn face of her mother, Jenny was totally unprepared for the next words which issued from the nerveless lips.

"Well, Jenny, and you've done it now. Believe me, the awful tragedy of it all is this; if only you had spoken to me, instead of to that bitch Lizzie. But even apart from that, dear, I already suspected. No, I knew in my heart of hearts what had happened. And you can believe it or not, and you've only my word for it but I waited up specially tonight to tell you … tell you …"

Choked with emotion, Kate collapsed back into her chair.

"Mammy, what is it ? What were you going to tell me?"

Kate bit at her lower lip as she pondered the advisability or otherwise of confiding in her daughter what she had had planned for earlier that evening, now in experience and sorrow a whole lifetime away. When eventually she did open her mouth and relate to Jenny what she had had in mind, the news was the final straw for the unhappy girl. With the cry like that of a wounded animal, she raced from the room and out into the darkened hallway.

Kate knew better than to follow her daughter, for what more could be said that had not already been told? With a long sigh, she got to her feet and automatically started getting undressed. And all the while, her mind was racing. Unless she was very much mistaken, and although she had no experience of such matters, there would be no new baby for which to plan ahead. She knew instinctively her own most immediate job would be to clear away and wash blood-soaked sheets on the morrow. And then, having done that, to nurse her shamed daughter back to health, and all in the short space of time available, that of a single Sabbath day.

That way, the stupid and hopelessly naive girl could at least get back to her work at the mill on Monday morning, as usual, and with nobody except the famous Lizzie any one whit the wiser.

Chapter 17

As Kate had predicted, she managed to get Jenny back to the mill, certainly looking like death warmed up, but no-one except Lizzie knew what had happened. Jenny no longer went out with Lizzie, indeed she scarcely went out at all except to the dreaded job at the mill, and would spend long hours at home sitting in the kitchen, silent and sullen, retiring early to the sofa bed in the hall.

After nearly two years of depression, Jenny started to brighten and with a new girl friend again ventured out of a Saturday evening to the soiree hosted by a local church.

"Don't worry, Mammy," she said to Kate, "Lizzie doesn't seem to be around any more. At least she's left the mill and I don't see her or want to see her. I've learnt my lesson."

Kate still worried, but was pleased to see Jenny regain her health and energy as the year wore on.

Christmas of 1897 was relatively happy. Kate had her usual pre-Christmas party with Mrs Scott, and, greatly daring, had bought a half bottle of good Irish whisky and presented it to Terence the week after he had given her a leather bound volume of poems. At the Hogmanay party Jenny had shyly introduced a young man to the family, Brian McCardle, a joiner who had just finished his apprenticeship.

"This time," Kate said, "keep yourself pure, Jenny lass. Get that gold band on your finger before you give him any favours of a physical kind – you certainly know what I mean, Jenny darling. Take my word for it. Keep Brian dangling on a string till your wedding night. You're really lucky, dear, for he doesn't know anything about that other dirty business. Don't forget, no man wants used goods and cast-offs from any other fellow. He'll find out soon enough on your honeymoon, but by then it will be too late, for you'll be safely married. Do you get my meaning?"

Jenny assured Kate that she had no intention of making the same mistake twice and that Brian was a nice lad.

He certainly seemed to be quite different from Ross Cuthbert. Soft spoken and polite, he even impressed Pearce, talking knowledgeably about his work in the shipyard.

One afternoon, rather than going straight home from Mrs Scott's, Kate, thinking of the particularly upsetting row with Pearce that morning, again sought her usual solace of the book-barra and its cheerful, fascinating and – it must be admitted – handsome owner. As she picked her way carefully through the overcrowded streets with the ever-present smells, jostling humanity and screeching tramcars, she found herself thinking: '*Yes, a wee blether with Terence O'Neil. 'Tis just what the good doctor ordered.*'

And now here she was, not only with quickening step but with a heightened bit of colour in her cheeks and fluttering at her heart at the very thought of seeing Terence again so soon. Kate smiled.

'*Ah, yes, my girl. Seems to me that the handsome bookseller is of more importance these days than the books themselves.*'

Not that there was anything clandestine about their meetings – after all, how could there be, with half of the worthy citizens of Glasgow looking on? But the element of essential secrecy from her husband lent a certain excitement to the occasion and for a fleeting moment, she felt she could almost have sympathised with Jenny in her hopeless passion for the unsuitable and already much-married Ross. Not wishing to dwell too long on that particular problem, Kate started humming a haunting little Irish air to herself as she hurried along.

'*Perhaps things are starting to work out better for me. After all, I've never had a special man friend before. One I could talk to about books and the like. Imagine it, me, Kate Rafferty talking all knowledgeable-like about books.'*

A secret little smile softened her work- and worry-worn face and she was still humming the tune as she rounded the corner. She just couldn't believe her eyes. True, the well-laden book-barra was there in its usual stance, but of Terence there was not a sign. Another man, a perfect stranger, was selling the occasional book and in a broad Glasgow accent trying to chivy up those browsers who'd obviously been there long enough without attempting to make a purchase or even to bargain with him. Kate, feeling as if a rug had been pulled from under her, hesitantly approached the barra and its new attendant. She went through the motions of lifting and looking at first one book, then another, then finally, with a sigh of deep frustration, gazed at the barra boy, wondering how best to approach him.

Then a thought flashed through her mind: *'Perhaps Terence is off just for a few days – with this terrible cold germ? Yes, I'm sure that's all it is. After all, if he'd been leaving surely he'd have mentioned it to me last week? Yes, I'll bet he'll be here, large as life, next week again. So, Kate my girl, say nothing to the barra boy, no need to make a damned fool o' yersel'.'*

On the point of turning away and back again homewards, she lifted up an attractively-bound book of poems which was wedged at the back of the cart and near to the man's hand. It was a volume which she and Terence had discussed some weeks previously and he had promised that if he got a fair copy of it at a bargain price he would keep it for her. She riffled through the book and then, with a sigh, replaced it exactly where it had been. As she did so, the barra boy laughed. "A good job yer no' wantin' that yin, Missus. It's reserved. Terry himself, before he went away like, told me to save that yin for some special friend of his, and ..."

Kate's face paled.

"Terence, away? Is he ill? A wee touch o' the rheumatics, eh? Something like that?"

The man laughed and shook his head.

"Rheumatics did ye say, Missus? No a bit o' it. Skipped away like a Spring lamb, off back tae his benighted Ireland – that's what he's done. Back to his Emerald Isle. All the same, these Paddies, if you ask me."

Almost unable to believe her ears, Kate clutched on to the barrow's shaft for much-needed support. Seeing this, the man peered closely into her face.

With typical Glaswegian humour and kindliness, he said: "Heh, lissen, hen. If yer gaun to be faintin', away and do it some where's else. Right? Bad for business. Folk might think it's my prices is gein ye the heebie-jeebies."

Despite herself, Kate laughed out loud and the man patted her shoulder.

"That's mair like the thing, hen. Feelin a wee bit better noo? Or dae ye want te sit doon on that orange box for a wee while?"

Kate shook her head and hurriedly gathered her wits.

"No, no, I'm fine. But thanks all the same. Anyway, I'll get away and not keep you from your good work."

"Listen, hen, if yer a regular, maybe you could help me. Happen you might know who that book is reserved for. Terence wrote something on the fly-leaf. But Ah'm no' that good at the readin'. Terence did mention something – the name o' a song. But damned if I can remember it."

He frowned in concentration

After a moment Kate murmured: "Kathleen Mavourneen? Would that be it by any chance?"

At once his face lightened and he grinned at her over the graveyard of his teeth. After first spitting on his hands, rubbing them together, and finally wiping them on his moleskin trousers, he stretched across the barrow and delved into the pile of books.

With the gold-tooled, leather-bound volume of poetry safely in his hands, he opened it at the requisite page with the inscription before handing it to Kate.

As she gazed at the words, she felt her eyes mist over.

As if unable to believe the witness of her own eyes, she read the inscription several times over. "Listen, Mister ... er ... sorry I don't know your name. Mister?"

He raised his flat tweed bunnet, and with questing fingers, scratched his head before laughing.

"Mister, nothing. Listen, hen, nobody in Glesga ever cries me nothing but Shuggie. I wouldn't know myself as a Mister."

Kate laughed, already feeling very much at home with this kindly man, his beaming grin and his pawky, ready Glasgow wit.

She nodded. "Right then, Mister ... er ... Shuggie. I've read this wee message. It does say to 'My dear Kathleen Mavourneen.' And also ..."

Shuggie slapped his thigh in delight.

"Then it's definitely meant for you, hen. You yourself said the name of the right song. And if ever anybody looked and sounded like a Kathleen Mavourneen, then 'tis yourself, Missus, with that lovely, soft Irish accent."

Kate felt herself blush, something she hadn't done in years. But it wasn't so much the compliment which caused her confusion so much as uncertainty as to how to phrase her next words.

"Well, Shuggie. 'Tis like this. The rest of the message in the book ... it's well ... it's rather private and personal, you see and ..."

At this revelation, Shuggie grinned like a delighted schoolboy who had just been told a dirty joke.

"You mean, like, it's a love letter, or what the Frenchies call a Billy-dux. Is that it, hen?"

By now Kate's face was beetroot-red.

"Well, I don't know that I'd put it quite as strongly as that."

Shuggie waved her words aside.

"Listen, hen, a love letter's the same in any language, even if it is written inside a book. But imagine, Terry O'Neil, a real hard-man, tough as nails. Him writing you a Billy-dux. The auld bugger. Mind you, hen ..."

Here he peered, in a highly confidential manner, into her face.

"That book must have cost Terry an arm and a leg – ten bob at the very least, or I'll be far cheated. So, he must think real highly of you, hen."

Kate's eyes opened wide in amazement and she was about to speak, but Shuggie beat her to it.

"Listen, hen, whatever words the old lothario wrote are for your eyes alone, and just you remember that. The book is obviously a gift for ye. So take it and enjoy it, hen."

If Kate had fallen into the Clyde and come up with a gold watch, she could not have been anymore delighted. And even though, as Shuggie had indicated, Terry had gone back to his native Ireland, the printed words he had left behind gave her hope for the future.

TO MY DEAR KATHLEEN MAVOURNEEN, DUTY CALLS ME TO IRELAND MEANTIME, BUT WE'LL MEET AGAIN. LOVE FROM TERENCE.

There was love and joy in her heart and a spring in her step as she headed home to Garth Street and whatever new family crisis awaited her there.

Chapter 18

Kate was sitting in the kitchen sewing, with Pearce dozing in his chair beside the fire, on a January afternoon. She was thinking over the events of the years since Danny had left home and wishing he had been present at the their last Hogmanay party when everyone had seemed reasonably happy.

She was startled out of her reverie by a series of sharp knocks at the door.

'Now who can that be? It can't be Granny Gorbals, she would just walk right in, and so would most of the neighbours with maybe one knock and a shout "hello".'

Sewing laid aside she hurried to the door.

A young man stood out on the landing smiling at her.

It was Pearce as Kate remembered him from their first meeting at Laggan House.

"It's me, Mammy."

"Danny." She threw herself into his arms, hugging and crying.

"Can I come in?" Danny said after their first greeting had calmed down.

Kate pulled the door almost closed behind her.

"Dadda isn't quite the man he was, Danny. He's sixty, going on sixty-one. He never really recovered from that melancholia and this last year, one morning when he woke his hands trembled something dreadful. They still do and he's not too steady on his feet. He's still sharp as a tack though."

"What does the doctor say it is?"

Kate laughed. "You know your father, he won't hear of seeing a doctor. Would you stay out here for a minute while I tell your Dadda? I wouldn't want to risk shocking him with you just walking in."

"That I will, Mammy. Take your time. I won't run away."

Kate went straight into the kitchen with the intention of speaking to her husband. But Pearce was dozing noisily in his chair. His steel-framed reading glasses had slipped halfway down his pinched beak of a nose. Taking her courage in both hands, Kate leant forward and gently tapped his cardiganed sleeve. It was her third attempt which finally aroused him when, with a start, he looked up into her eyes.

"What's the matter? What's wrong? I was sleeping, woman. Can't a body even get to sleep in peace here?"

Ignoring this petulant complaint, Kate leant further forward and whispered into his ear: "Now just keep calm, Pearce. It's nothing for you to get alarmed about. But ... well ... the thing is ... you've got a visitor."

At this startling news, he immediately struggled to sit more upright in his chair. He frowned in perplexity.

"A visitor? For me? Who would want to visit me? Humph. The only person who ever comes to visit me is that old Granny Gorbals, and even that is because she's looking for a free tea and pancakes. Yes, funny thing that, now I come to think of it. She always, but always, comes on your baking days. Yes, that's the only ..."

Kate laid a gentle hand on his shoulder.

"Now, Pearce, you know that's not true. A real faithful friend and visitor, is Granny Gorbals."

Pearce opened his mouth to protest, but, for once, mindful of Danny Boy still waiting out on the landing, Kate was too quick for her husband.

"No doubt about it, Pearce. You do have a visitor and believe it or not, it's your long lost son. There now. What do you think of that? Danny Boy is out there on the other side of the door, waiting to greet you after all these years."

For a second, Kate thought he was about to explode, so sudden was the rush of colour to his now normally pallid face. Then, just as suddenly, as if all the fight had gone out of him, he exhaled a long, whistling sigh of defeat. Then, looking at his wife, and in a voice drained of all emotion, he said: "Well then, if Daniel has now condescended to visit us, after all these years, you had best show him in."

Kate felt a measure of relief at Pearce's quick and apparently ready acceptance of the fact of Daniel's return.

She smiled with gratitude and happiness.

"That's the ticket, Pearce. Just one thing ... let me comb your hair again, give your face a bit dab with a wet flannel and then I'll look out a clean fresh cardigan for you. Must have you looking smart to greet your only son, eh?"

By way of reply, Pearce's face at once suffused with rage.

"No need to put on the Lord Provost's Show for that scum: Let the bastard see me as I am. Let my errant son see exactly what he has wrought with all his crazy shenanigans. So, just you keep your fussing, housewifely hands off me."

Pearce looked up in bewilderment and wonder at the handsome, strapping young man before him, amazingly, an exact replica of what he himself had been as a young blade. Kate, fervently taking in the scene, rather fancied that for a moment she caught a fleeting glimmer of pride in her husband's eyes. He even went so far as to hold out a trembling right hand, which Daniel immediately grasped and shook firmly in man-to-man fashion.

"Father, it's me. I've come back to see you."

Whether or not it was real emotion, or simply a cruel side-effect of his illness, Pearce's eyes filled with ready tears. It was a moment before he could speak and even then, all he could manage was: "Daniel. Daniel. My son, it's been a long time."

With these words, Kate knew that for the moment at least, her son had been welcomed back, amazingly enough, into the bosom and to the hearth and home of his own family.

Her face radiant with joy, she leant towards the two men and rubbed her hands as if in anticipation of some rare treat.

"I know exactly what you two need right now. And that's a wee cup of tea. But laced with a spot of Granny's best medicinal Irish whisky."

The two men beamed and nodded their approval of this excellent suggestion.

"I'll just put the kettle on the hob. Then I'll pop next door and give Granny the great news, and at the same time borrow a wee dram of her whisky. Good old Granny; always ready to help in an emergency."

Kate charged out the door and ran into Granny's single-end. In the event, by the time she had related the exciting news to her old neighbour, the decrepit old woman was herself in need of a reviving measure of the health giving, golden water of life. That done, and with a quick hug and a kiss for Hannah, Kate then beat a hasty retreat, with the half-empty whisky bottle clutched in her trembling fingers.

As she re-entered the kitchen of her own home, Kate grinned in delight and she felt her heart give a lurch of happiness at the scene which confronted her. Her normally morose husband and her son were already deep in conversation. As she bustled happily about, every inch the contented housewife and proud mother, Kate happily and quite shamelessly eavesdropped on their fascinating talk. True, it was her own Danny Boy who, totally unlike his former, shy self, was doing most of the speechifying, but even Pearce was taking an active interest in what was being said, and spurring his son on to even greater heights of rhetoric with the occasional nod or grunt of assent, amazement, or feigned disbelief. Right at that very moment, Danny Boy was deep in some tale about the volcanic Mount Cameroon which he had seen when his ship docked in the baking heat of Tiko wharf in West Africa.

"And father. You should have seen the witch-doctors. All dressed up like a dish of fish. And the drums from the workers' camp on a Saturday night. Enough to make your spine tingle and your hair stand on end. Yes, it's true, father. That part of Africa – they're deeply into witch-craft – what is it they call it, now? Voodoo, or some such name. No, I tell a lie. It's ju-ju magic. And they even make sacrifices to appease the mountain, keep it from erupting again. Honestly, what a place. I couldn't begin to tell you of its fascination – the scenery, the people, the climate."

All the while her cocked ear was eavesdropping on this entertaining travelogue, Kate was deliberately taking her time in preparing the whisky-laced tea and in liberally spreading jam on some pieces of her soda-bread. She frowned momentarily, when suddenly remembering Danny Boy's fondness for sliced 'clootie' dumpling, she berated herself for having used up the last of it only the previous evening.

'Oh, if only I had known in advance of his visit, what a feast I would have prepared. It would have been a banquet to outdo any New Year celebration. Ah. well, can't be helped now.'

She smiled with delight as, bearing a loaded tray over to her two men-folk, she heard Pearce say in a voice tinged with awe, wonder, and incredulity: "Daniel. What a wonderful story. But surely it cannot be true? Do people really live like that in this day and age?"

Danny Boy grinned from ear to ear then nodded, obviously more than happy with the effect he was creating.

"True? Yes, father, every single word of it."

Pearce adopted a skittish attitude as, reaching over and giving a playful tweak to Daniel's luxuriant, dark beard, he laughed.

"Go on with you, Daniel. It's havers, all nonsense, my lad. Begod, if ever anyone kissed the Blarney Stone, 'tis surely your good self, Daniel Robert Kinnon."

By now fully entering into the spirit of the thing, Daniel again grinned, a poignantly boyish grin, strangely at odds with his manly physique and bearded face.

"No, Father. Blarney Stone be damned – if you'll pardon my French, Dadda. 'Tis the God's honest truth. Oh, many the story could I tell you. Like the time our Chief Steward got blind drunk in Capetown. Then got himself robbed in a back alley, didn't he? And arrived back on board early next morning, wearing only a newspaper."

Pearce laughed wildly at this and slapped his knee in delight. As

Kate handed round the tea and tasty bite, with her free hand she patted the side of her husband's face, so delighted was she to hear him laugh again, after all these sad, lonely years.

Daniel, his mouth full of soda-bread, took a gulp of his tea then, with twinkling eyes, he stared at both his parents with a speculative look in his eyes.

"Yes, Dadda. Many a weird and funny tale could I tell, but most of them, I think I'd better keep for a man-to-man only discussion."

Here he cast a cheeky glance at his mother, who opened her mouth to protest. But Daniel was too quick for her.

"Mammy. There is one story I know that you'd enjoy hearing."

Kate put the empty tray down on the table.

"Oh, and what might that be?"

"Well, I mentioned our Chief Steward. On one of our trips, that same fellow – we were outward bound from Liverpool to Southern Australia – you'll never guess what he did."

Pearce, already agog, was hanging on every word, as he silently shook his head and waited with what patience he could muster for his son to go on. Daniel needed no further prompting.

"Again, the damned fellow got roaring drunk, spent the crew's food allocation money. No, not on drink for himself, although even that would not have surprised us in the least."

Pearce frowned and urged: "Then what? What did he do?"

Daniel shook his head with the remembrance of it.

"Instead of buying us a variety of foodstuffs with which to keep body and soul together until our next port of call, he spent all the money, yes, every last allocated farthing on a consignment of – of all things – cases of dried apricots."

Kate put a hand to her mouth to stifle her ready amusement.

"Oh no, Daniel. You're joking."

Again Daniel shook his head and then took another gulp of his whisky tea.

"I wish I was joking, Mammy. For we had apricot pie, apricot pudding, apricot flan, apricot stew, apricot flambé. As if that hadn't sickened us, we even had apricot cakes and bread. Not to mention Irish stew à la apricot. There now, what do you make of that?"

Pearce and Kate both laughed. Pearce, with a look of pride on his face at what a fine, upright, and entertaining young men his estranged son had become, gently pushed at Daniel's uniformed shoulder.

"Get away with you, Daniel. Blarney Stone talk that is, if ever I heard it."

Daniel laughed and crossed his heart in the way that small children do when they went grown-up people to believe their stories.

"'Tis on my sacred word, Dadda. And believe me, if you've never tested Irish stovies made from apricots, apricots and even more of the damned things – then you can take it from me – you've missed absolutely nothing."

As Kate prepared a fresh brewing of tea, she gazed in fascination at the two men in her life, now together and possibly for the first time ever, not locked in either sullen silence, mutual dislike nor even angry and heated exchange.

' *'Tis a miracle. And long may this happy truce continue, God willing.*'

Chapter 19

With Mrs Delaney occupying the front room, Jenny had to join Hannah in the hurlie bed to let Daniel sleep on the sofa bed in the hall.

"It won't be for too long, Jenny," Daniel said. "I've only got five days before I have to leave to get back to my ship in Liverpool."

In the following days, both Daniel, the sailor home from the high seas, and Pearce, his stay at home father, travelled the world together on a crest of euphoria, as they visited strange, faraway places. Many a good laugh they had together over Daniel's remembered and re-enacted diverse exploits in places as far removed as Cardiff and Capetown. Right up until the very evening of the third day of Daniel's visit, it seemed to Kate that not only had virtually every country under the sun got a mention, but also that Daniel and Pearce were getting on like a house on fire. The only country not so far mentioned was Kate and Pearce's own dear homeland, the Emerald Isle. Although she herself had been well aware of this, she felt it only politic to keep silence on the subject.

On the morning of the third day of Daniel's visit, a Thursday, almost as if the past few days of concord and strife-free pleasant social intercourse had placed too great a strain on him, Pearce awoke in a foul temper. Right from the word 'go' that morning, whatever Kate did, said, did not do, or even suggested, was anathema to him. Strangely enough, it was left to Daniel himself to calm down his father's ruffled feathers. He did this by sitting down opposite him when, with knees touching, they shared a pot of tea together. Then Daniel went on to a further chat about some of the more amusing of his

229

sea-going adventures. At one point, the old man threw back his head, laughed, and slapped his knee in delight.

"Daniel, I just don't believe it. 'Tis a vivid imagination you have, to be sure, boyo."

Daniel grinned in delight at his enjoyment of the many far-fetched sea stories. Placing a hand on his father's shoulders, he gave a reassuring squeeze.

"'Tis the God's honest truth, Dadda. Honestly. We cured the Chief Steward of his alcoholism that way."

Then turning round to include his Mammy in the audience, he smiled and gave her a wink.

"Just you listen to this, Mammy. Then you could perhaps take your good self next door to Granny's for a wee cup of tea?"

Kate caught his meaning at once. With Pearce suitably entertained and already in a much more pleasant, amenable mood, Kate should seize the opportunity to make herself scarce, while the going was good. She smiled and nodded her understanding and acceptance of her son's suggestion, then with arms akimbo and a look of mock ferocity in her eyes, she said: "You don't really mean it, Daniel. You do have at least one story which is fit also for my ears? My, my, aren't I the lucky one?"

Danny Boy grinned back at her and smoothed down his wavy beard before commencing his story. He cleared his throat a couple of times then, confident that he had the full attention of his parents, he started.

"Well now, let's see. It was in South Australia, at a two-horse station called Woomeroo. One of the work-horses had just breathed its last on the wharf. The poor beast just dropped dead from over-work in hauling logs to the ship. Well, we couldn't leave the poor animal just lying there, now could we?"

Pearce and Kate both shook their heads, intrigued as to what could possibly be coming.

"Right. So we were hoisting the dead horse with rope and tackle and it was swaying somewhere between dock-side and shipboard. Just at that moment, Chiefie comes out on deck, doesn't he? Half-cut, as usual. And in the half-light, sees the swaying lifeless horse high above us. Right?"

Pearce nodded his eagerness to hear the punch-line of this weird tale and even Kate herself was hanging on every word. Danny pursed his lips, as though biting back an unbidden smile.

"Well, I can still see it. Chiefie points up to the sky with a trembling finger and says,'My God. There's a horse. Flying through the sky'."

Pearce leant forward and placed his hand on Daniel's knee.

"And you and your shipmates? What did you say, Daniel?"

Here Danny allowed himself the luxury of a broad grin.

"Oh, nothing much. Just asked, 'And what particular horse would that be, Chiefie? For in this dim light, we don't see so much as a mosquito flying through the air, never mind a bloody horse'."

Pearce gave a great belly laugh.

"And do you mean to say, that really cured the poor man of his addiction to the demon drink? Is that what you're after telling me?"

Daniel looked reflectively at his father for a long moment, all the while stroking his beard. Finally, he grinned boyishly.

"Well, now, let's just say he never, to my knowledge at least, touched another single drop of the water of life all the way back across the Indian Ocean to Capetown and points north. And that is the God's honest truth."

While Pearce was still laughing, Danny turned aside and with his thumb jerked an 'on your way' silent message to Kate. She, for her part, needed no second bidding.

Chapter 20

No sooner had she stepped out from the close than the wind screamed at her in all its January fury. She shivered.

'Thank God I'm only going as far as Mr McGregor's wee shop on a morning like this.'

So intent was she on battling against the elements that she almost cannoned into someone coming in the opposite direction and would, in fact, have done so had it not been for quick thinking on the part of the other person.

"Oh, 'tis yourself, Mistress Kinnon. My and you're in a fine old hurry this morning."

Kate blinked the sleet out of her eyes, then wiped the ice-cold moisture from her frozen cheeks. When her vision was again clear, she found herself looking into the kindly eyes of Willie Goddart, the local postie.

"Hello, there, Postie. Some morning, eh?"

Willie grinned and nodded.

"Aye 'tis that. And I'm the one that knows all aboot it. Been oot tramping the streets, up and doon closes, in and oot yon stinking wynds since five o'clock this morning." Here he gave an expressive shiver. "What a bloody life, eh, Mistress Kinnon?"

Kate smiled and laid a hand on his uniformed sleeve.

"Never mind, Willie, it's a grand steady job you've got. And there's not too many of them round about these parts."

Postie nodded reflectively.

"You never spoke a truer word, Missus. Aye, you're dead right."

Kate grinned.

"Tell you something else, Postie. You'll not be needin' to climb the stairs to my top flat for a month or two yet. My Danny Boy's home."

Postie smiled.

"Isn't that the grand news? Aye, you'll be the happy woman."

"Happy, I am. Not only is Danny home, but he and his father are getting on just great; swapping stories, laughing together. And you want to see the beautiful fan he brought me from Spain."

Postie hoisted his bag higher on his shoulder and with his right thumb, jerked back his uniformed cap. Then he grinned.

"A lace fan indeed. My, my, just the very thing you need in the Candleriggs on a January morn."

As they surveyed the grey streets in which daylight was having its usual battle to pierce the blackness of the high tenements, they laughed in unison. Kate pushed his arm away with a playful gesture.

"Away with you, Postie. The thought was there, don't forget. And anyway, he gave me more money than I've ever had in my hand before."

The man grinned.

"Well, Missus, it's grand to hear of somebody in this God-forsaken dump getting' a bit of good luck."

"I'm off to Mr McGregor's wee shop. I want to get some sweeties for Hannah and Granny Gorbals. A great pair that; only happy when their jaws are working overtime. Anyway, I want to tell Mr McGregor the good news about Danny. He used to work there, you know."

With a cheery wave from Kate, and a forefinger to skipped bunnet from Postie, the two parted company as, all the while, the wind and sleet screamed around them and sent litter dancing along the road and the pavement under their feet.

As Kate entered Mr McGregor's wee shop and heard the bell ping behind her, she could hardly contain her impatience until such time as he had served and conversed at length with the customers already crowded into the cosy warmth.

Chapter 21

When Kate returned some half hour or so later to the warmth of her cosy kitchen, the first thing that met her at the door was the sound of male voices raised in anger

'*Oh, no. I knew it was too good to last.*'

The moment she entered the room, the two men, both red-faced with fury, stopped speaking, almost as if someone had turned a switch.

In the ensuing, uncomfortable silence which could be felt, it was finally left to Kate herself to speak. With great finality, she put her purchases down on top off the table, and faced them.

"Right. Now, what's all this hullabaloo about?"

Her men looked at one another, then as quickly glanced away again before finally letting their eyes fall to a minute examination of finger nails in the one case, and booted feet in the other.

"Pearce. Are you going to tell me? Or do I have to drag it out of you?"

Her husband frowned, not least at being thus addressed in front of his son. Then, like a petulant and naughty schoolboy, he inclined his head towards Daniel and mouthed the words.

"It was his fault. 'Twas your precious son who started it."

Then, as if this cryptic statement explained in full their earlier dramatic outburst, he shut his mouth like a clam.

Kate's face now suffused with colour, for it was already apparent to her that this could be a long-drawn-out discussion. She banged a clenched fist on the table with such force that not only did her items of shopping jump, but Pearce himself started, as if shot from a cannon.

"Listen, the both of you. I demand to know what has happened."

Daniel opened his mouth to reply but his father was too quick for him.

"Oh no, you don't, m'lad. I'll have my say first, even if it kills me."

By now, almost puce in the face, Pearce was half-way out of his chair as if preparing to do battle with his son. Seeing this, Kate frowned and, laying a hand on her husband's shoulder, eased him back to a sitting position.

"Kill you? Humph. Keep up that rage and it might very well do just that, Pearce. For goodness sake, calm yourself."

"Calm myself. Calm myself? Good God Almighty, woman. Do you know what your precious, wonderful son did? When he was in Ireland, no less. Aha, and we didn't hear a word about his exploits there in the first few days of his visit. Oh, no. We've been all round the bloody world and planets beyond, listening to a lot of stupid blethers about flying horses and the like and …"

Pearce stopped to regain his breath, if not his composure, and although Kate knew there was much that she could have said in reminding him of what enjoyment and laughter he'd had from those very same tall-tales, she thought it expedient at this point to hold her tongue.

It was instead Daniel himself who jumped into the breach.

"Mammy, I'm not ashamed of what I did. I did it for the good of the family."

No sooner were these words out of Daniel's mouth, than his father grabbed hold of his walking-stick and, waving it in his son's face like a man demented, he screamed: "Liar. Liar. You bloody bastard, Daniel Kinnon. You did it to shame me. Good of the family be damned. You wanted to shame me with your devilish plot."

At this fresh outburst, Daniel looked to be on the point of collapse, as he nevertheless got to his feet and took a step back from the still frantically waving walking-stick. Kate, between the heat of the room and the intensity of hatred generated from the two men in her life, felt physically sick and mentally exhausted. She put her head in her hands and awaited the denouement of this drama, which she knew was bound to come any minute now.

With a renewed strength born of his hatred for his only living son, Pearce rose unsteadily from his chair and, by leaning heavily on his walking stick, tottered across until he was standing eyeball to eyeball with Daniel. Then, throwing his stick to the floor where it clattered and bounced off the gleaming brass fender, he clutched for support at the front of his son's jacket. Then pulling the ends tight, as if he had it in mind to throttle the life out of his first-born, he glared into the face before him.

"As of this minute, you're no son of mine. So take yourself and your ill-gotten gains and get the hell out of it. Do you hear? Get to buggary."

"Pearce. For heaven's sake. Do modulate your language. Granny Gorbals will hear you."

Still clutching on to Daniel, her husband swivelled his hand and cast her a look of utter loathing.

"Listen you; I don't care if the whole world hears me. I want this useless windbag out of here and damned quick about it. He can take the spoils, the loot of his ill-conceived venture, and go."

"God Almighty, Pearce. You keep going on about ill-gotten gains, loot, spoils. What in God's name did Daniel do? Rob a bank or something, is that it?"

For reply, Pearce almost spat out the words at her.

"Worse. Much worse. He shamed me. Why, he actually –"

When it seemed that words had failed his father, Daniel brought his own hands up in front of his chest then, throwing them wide apart, he managed to cast off his father's strangle-hold on him. This was done with such force that Pearce, caught completely off-guard, tottered and fell back, giving his head a glancing blow on the table's edge as he crashed to the floor. Like a stranded whale, there he lay, a look of stunned amazement on his face, especially when neither Kate nor Daniel made the slightest move to assist him to his feet.

In the heavy silence that followed, Kate was aware of the sound of a distant tramcar. The next thing she heard was Danny Boy, yelling.

"Right, father, if that's the way you want it, so be it. You can believe what you like, but the only reason I approached your sisters and brothers at Laggan House was to tell them you were destitute. And that's why your sisters gave me some of their jewels to sell. They had no difficulty in believing that I was who I said I was. It seems I'm now the image of what you were as a young man. When you got dear Mammy into trouble and –"

As if her head weighed a ton, Kate shook her head wearily and held up the palm of her hand.

"Daniel, no more. Please. But, is it really true? Did the Kinnon sisters give you jewels? To help us?"

Danny Boy nodded.

"Aye, that they did, Mammy. And Uncle Desmond gave me a velvet bag full of golden sovereigns and –"

Pearce had by now crawled further along the floor where, by holding on to the leg of the table, he managed to drag himself upright. Drawing together whatever small semblance of dignity he could muster, he drew himself to his full height.

"Right, Daniel, we'll have no truck with mention of Uncle Desmond, the Kinnons of Laggan House nor their jewels and money."

Here he pointed a trembling forefinger to the other side of the room:

"There's the door. And I want you out of it. Take the booty with you and –"

Here Daniel started to protest but, with a fierce shake of his head, his father would have none of it.

"You've utterly shamed me before my own family. Destitute, indeed. Humph. So we want not a farthing. Not a farthing do you hear? Now get the fuck out of it."

As when he had left before, Kate found Daniel in Mr McGregor's back shop.

"I'm really sorry, Mammy. I did do it for the best. If he wasn't so damned pig headed he'd see it. His father's dead and his brothers and sisters can now admit it was Dadda's fault, not yours – not that that would make them any readier to accept us, but they do see it as unfair that he should be penniless. His sisters gave me this jewellery – they said it was Dadda's share of what his mother left – and Uncle Desmond gave a velvet purse of sovereigns – I used some coming up here from Liverpool."

Daniel placed two soft cloth pouches on the table in front of his mother.

"Danny, I can't use any of this. Dadda wouldn't let me. It would kill him to think we were living on his brothers' and sisters' charity.

"Well, I'm not taking it back." Daniel shrugged. "I got it for you and Jenny and Hannah anyway. He can't live for ever."

Mr McGregor agreed to keep the pouches for Kate hidden under the floorboards in a tin cash box.

That night. not long after Daniel had packed his kitbag and taken a tearful farewell of his Mammy in the privacy of Granny's single-end, Pearce brought the day to a dramatic conclusion.

In a screaming fit of impotent fury, he collapsed and Dr Clancy had to be called at last.

"It's his heart," Dr Clancy said, shaking his head. "I should have seen him long before this. A severe attack, and he is showing signs of having suffered a brainstorm of some sort in the past. I'll give you a prescription ... but really ... try to keep him quiet ..."

The thought of how he had been shamed before his family in Ireland by his only son, Daniel, grew like a cancer within his brain. For days and nights on end, he would sit, sunk in apparent apathy, muttering obscenely to himself about that bastard boy.

Daniel Robert Kinnon had at last got his revenge on his father.

Chapter 22

With Daniel gone again life continued as before, but Pearce was now definitely an invalid and if anything more irascible than ever. The bright spots for Kate in the week were her mornings with her friend and employer Mrs Scott.

Jenny by comparison was happy and cheerful, being in the house with Pearce as little as possible and spending all the time she could with her boyfriend Brian.

Early in April she told her mother that Brian had been saving hard and they thought they could be married in June. Kate was ecstatic.

"Jenny, that's great news. A June wedding would be lovely. You and Brian can find yourselves a nice wee single-end nearby. It will be grand to see you settled."

However, in the last week in April, Jenny came home from a meeting with Brian in tears. She refused to talk to Kate about it and retreated to her sofa bed in the hall. Next day she was at the mill as usual and instead of meeting Brian as she usually did, she came straight home.

"Have you and Brian had a wee fall out?" Kate said.

Jenny burst into tears and fled from the tea table to her sofa bed in the hall.

"What's got into that damn girl now?" Pearce said.

Kate followed Jenny out to the hall.

"What's wrong, darling? Lovers do have these quarrels. It can be a frustrating time. I'm sure everything will be all right."

Jenny clung sobbing to her mother. "Brian won't see me again ...

we were on the Glasgow Green ... it was a lovely evening ... just getting dark ... and I let him ... it was the most wonderful night of my life."

Kate shuddered.

"You gave yourself to him?"

"Oh, Mammy, he said I'd been with another man ... how could he know? He said he wasn't taking second hand goods and the wedding was off."

By the third week in May, Kate's worst fears were realised. Jenny was pregnant again. This time there would no abortion. Jenny would carry the baby to term – a January baby – and Kate was determined she would stand by Jenny and her baby come what may.

The one problem could well be Mrs Delaney, but Kate would face that difficulty in due course when Jenny began to show.

As the months passed and Jenny's bulging belly was witness to the whole world of the result of the most wonderful night of her life, there were several immediate repercussions. The first thing that happened was that the financial mainstay of the Kinnon household, the high and mighty Mistress Josephine Delaney, opted to take herself, her voracious appetite, and most importantly, her money out of their house of shame. Kate's cheeks still burned with embarrassment every time she thought back to the day that Mrs Delaney had given her ultimatum.

"I tell you now, Mrs Kinnon, either that unwed mother leaves or I do: It's as simple as that."

Kate made as if to put the coal-filled hod down on the hearth, while she mentally debated the best way to tackle this latest threat to her family's security. But even before she could get a single word out, she found her red-faced lodger was too quick for her. Mrs Delaney pointed a podgy finger at the gleaming copper hod.

"And while we're at it – there's no point in your leaving extra coal for my fire, thanks all the same, Mrs Kinnon. For I shall not be here to use it. I've given you my ultimatum; either Jenny – that dishonoured girl – goes from this house or I do. It's perfectly simple, you know, a clear-cut choice."

Kate rose from the hearth and turned to face her lodger.

"Mistress Delaney. You surely don't expect me to throw my own daughter out into the street?"

The woman's only reply to this was a vigorous nodding of her head. Kate watched in fascination as Mrs Delaney's double-chins wobbled like jellies, while her flint-hard eyes bored into her. There was a silence between them which was accentuated by the delicate ticking of Mrs Delaney's antique clock on the mantelpiece. When the silence became unbearable, Mrs Delaney put a hand to her over-fussy hair-do and, as she patted it into place, the firelight caught the diamonds in her rings and gave off great beacons of light which all but dazzled Kate. Even so, rather than feeling intimidated by the other woman's wealth Kate, in some strange way, found strength, and anger even, to face up to this spoiled, selfish, over-rich woman.

"You may have diamond rings, my fine lady, but you're still my lodger. And what I say goes in this house."

Kate squared back her shoulders with a new resolve.

"Right then, Mrs Delaney, if you insist that I choose between you and my daughter, let's face it, there really is no choice. You are the one who will have to go, and as you yourself have said, the sooner the better."

The decision taken, Kate walked to the door and was turning the brass knob when Mrs Delaney's voice stopped her.

"Mrs Kinnon, I think you'll find your dear husband does not agree with your decision. In fact, he told me only yesterday that as far as he is concerned, it will be the workhouse for Jenny."

Kate's face suffused with rage and she had to control a wild urge to walk over and slap the self-satisfied smirk from the stupid woman's face. Instead, she held on to the door knob as if her hand were welded to it, as she fought to regain her composure.

"Oh indeed, Mrs Delaney. Well, of course I do know you and Pearce have shared many a confidence during your long years under my roof. And those cosy little afternoon tête-à-têtes with me running myself stupid catering to your sweet-tooth. And we can all see the result of that over-indulgence too. Seems to me that poor misguided Jenny isn't the only one to have a fat belly."

There was a sharp intake of breath and a fluttering hand raised to the region of her heart, as the obese woman stared in horror at her suddenly voluble land-lady.

"Mistress Kinnon, nobody ever spoke in such a manner to me in all my life. I would ask you to remember your place, my good woman."

Kate, ever aware of, and hyper-sensitive to, any reminder of her humble beginnings, suddenly saw red.

"Oh, I'll remember my place, all right. My place is here. It's your position that concerns us right now. What I say goes. I demand that you leave. Pearce is in no position to order anyone about, far less demand that his poor, misguided, wronged daughter be sent to rot in the City Workhouse. But you, madam, you can go to hell, and be quick about it."

That very same evening, a somewhat subdued Mrs Delaney left in a decided huff. She took with her a crocodile-skin overnight case which would be sufficient for a short stay at a city-centre hotel and indicated to Kate that a carrier would collect the rest of her belongings in due course.

Apart from the loss of income accruing from Mrs Delaney's departure Kate felt herself to be well-rid of the spoiled, useless bitch. Perhaps Jenny had, all unwittingly, done her Mammy a favour after all.

Life settled down to some sort of pattern for the Kinnons, Hannah and her inseparable rag-doll as usual spending the days next door with Granny Gorbals. Kathleen, devoting Mondays, Wednesdays and Fridays exclusively to the arthritic Mrs Scott, the kindly old woman in Garnethill who already had proved herself to be more good friend than demanding employer and with her re-acquired bucket and deck-scrubber, setting out on one or other of her cleaning jobs on Tuesdays and Thursdays. The majority of the stairs she swept, washed and disinfected were reached via beautifully tiled entrance closes, and like so many other poverty stricken immigrants to the Second City of the Empire, it was the height of Kathleen's ambition that she herself would one day live in a wally close. On Saturdays she took over the running of Mr McGregor's newsagent cum sweetie shop.

A sigh escaped Kate's lips on the morning of December 23rd, 1898 as she set off yet again. While she kept the dream of living in a posh building with its tiled wally close and stained glass windows, she knew in her heart of hearts that, for the moment at least, she was certainly not even an inch nearer to achieving her ambition.

'*Ah well,*' she thought, '*at least I'm now working in such grand settings. And while I sweep and scrub the stairs, and dust down the ornate doors and banisters, I can still dream. Lucky to have all these wee jobs – things could be a lot worse.*'

Kathleen wrapped her coat closer against the biting East wind and, with head bent against its bitter onslaught, she battled out to face yet another day.

Meantime, back in the family's top-flight room-and-kitchen, another equally well-ordered routine had become established over the past few weeks and months. Pearce was now ministered to by Jenny. Each morning, the minute that poor Hannah had been wheeled away from the scene of operations, a set pattern of events got underway. It was now his disgraced daughter Jenny who, day after weary day, cared for the irascible and ungrateful old man, sunk back into his depression, lethargy, and frequent temper tantrums following the departure of Mrs Delaney.

If ever the old saying about familiarity breeding contempt was true, it was certainly borne out in the execution of the essential daily rites in the Kinnon household. Each day it was not only the girl's belly which grew in size. Almost in equal proportion grew each day the mutual dislike, if not the downright hatred, between Jenny and her father. That particular morning, in the last month of her already difficult pregnancy, no sooner had Jenny waved off her Mammy from the front-room window, than matters which had been simmering for so long suddenly boiled over.

Apart from being ungainly as she bore all before her with the enormous bulk of the unborn child in her belly, Jenny always felt particularly nervous and awkward when dealing with her father. Quite apart from anything else, like a hawk with hooded eyes he watched her every movement as she lurched and clattered her way around the crowded kitchen.

This was the situation every day, but that particular morning it was clear, from the very first moment when she slopped his tea over into the saucer, that they had got off to a bad start. It mattered not a jot that Pearce himself, with his shaking hands, more often than not, spilled his tea. What offended him was that his slovenly slut of a daughter had had the temerity to present the cup and saucer in such a state. His face contorted with rage as he shouted at the hapless girl.

"Good God Almighty. Can you do nothing right, girl?"

What further infuriated him was that rather than answer in kind, Jenny instead chose the path of silent insolence. As so often in the past, notably in his dealings with Spud Murphy the carter on that memorable day of the flitting, silent insolence was the one thing which Pearce either could not or would not suffer. So on seeing the look of utter disdain on Jenny's face, he clattered the half-empty cup back down on the saucer with such force that the teaspoon fell to the linoleumed floor. In his rage, he looked first of all at the teaspoon where it lay, at the cup sitting in its puddle of now cold tea, and finally at Jenny.

"Jenny;" he roared, "I demand that you start all over again. Take away this damned cup. Bring me a napkin and a fresh cup of tea, and for the love of God, serve it decently."

Still without a word, Jenny, with elaborate care removed the offending cup, and set about doing his bidding. As she this time prepared a tray, her seething thoughts were bubbling inside her brain. She knew, of course, her father was already in a foul mood.

Had she taken Mammy's advice to heart, then by now she would have been safely settled in her own wee single-end home, with a loving husband by her side and far removed from this hated room and its equally detested occupant. She just could not believe how naïve she had been – especially after the dire consequences of her first sexual experiences with that married wastrel of a so-called man, Ross Cuthbert. How could she have been so daft? Well, thanks to her own stupidity, Brian had found out her guilty secret long before the planned wedding date. When, from their night of illicit passion in Glasgow Green, he had discovered he was quite clearly not the first on the scene, he had beat a hasty retreat in search of a fresh young virgin for his bride. Last thing Jenny heard of him was that he had emigrated to Canada – a land where it was rumoured the authorities were giving away free, with both hands, huge tracts of Prairie land to pioneer settlers.

Jenny sighed with despair, frustration and an intense longing for what might have been had she heeded her mother's warnings. Hearing this discontented sound, Pearce at once reacted in like-fashion.

"Jenny, what in God's name is wrong now? Is it not enough that you have brought shame on this household? And lost us our lodger – the one bright spark in my life – and my only true friend, Mrs Delaney. Now there was a real lady for you; well-born, mannerly and with a proper respect for the rightness of things. Yes, a lady, Josephine Delaney."

At once Jenny turned to face him as she shouted back, giving him as good as she herself had received.

"What's wrong, did you say, Dadda? I'll tell you what's wrong I'm sick, fed-up with waiting hand and foot on you."

Pearce's already pasty complexion went ashen

"Listen you … you pregnant hussy. Believe me, I would die rather than ask your help."

Just at that point, a wave of nausea and faintness hit her and she had no alternative but to stand there, clutching on to the edge of the still-uncleared kitchen table. Suddenly, as if matters were not already bad enough, she felt a spurt of wet warmth trickling down from between her legs. She knew enough of the facts of life to realise what was happening. Clutching a trembling hand to her forehead, and in the greatest blind panic she had ever known in her life, she screamed at the top of her voice: "Oh my God. It's started. The baby. It's started. God help me."

In one last desperate bid to reach the door and whatever help might be found beyond the suffocatingly-warm kitchen and its other occupant, she lunged her ungainly body away from the mainstay of the table.

It was then that she fell in a dead faint just in front of the closed door. As she fell with a crash that shook the foundations, her last coherent thought was: "The baby – it's started. And who in God's name is going to help me now?"

Chapter 23

It was some five or six hours later and well into the afternoon before Kate finally got back to Garth Street. In the normal way, she would have been home much earlier. However, something so unusual had happened that she felt justified, at least for once in her life, in making the most of it.

Mrs Scott had, as in the years before, insisted that she and Kate have their annual pre-Christmas party. As usual Kate had thoroughly enjoyed herself and to her surprise and delight Mrs Scott had given her five guineas. When Kate had tried to refuse, Mrs Scott had been adamant. Kate could take the five guineas or she could stop coming to work and chat.

To even the most casual bystander, it must have been apparent that right at that moment, all was well with the world of Kate Kinnon. She almost danced along the street in her delight at her unexpected good fortune, her face shone with happiness and from time to time, she hummed a catchy Irish tune.

'Just fancy Mrs Scott giving me all that money. It could not have come at a better time. Lucky me.'

She was actually heading home, desperate to tell Jenny and Granny of her good fortune, when all of a sudden she stopped short in such a manner that the shawled woman behind her all but cannoned into her. The other woman was obviously not having such a good day, for at the near collision, she let out a stream of expletives which left Kate blushing and profuse with apologies.

Anyway, having gone to such trouble to change course in mid-

247

stream, Kate decided to proceed with her bright idea. Glad to see the back of the other woman, she grinned.

'Yes. I will do it; why shouldn't I steal a couple of hours? After all, it isn't as if anyone will be needing me right now. Hannah is safely under Granny's wing. Jenny still has a few weeks to go to reach her time. Anyway, she's looking after Pearce. Right. Here goes.'

She retraced her steps and instead headed towards the Briggait and from there to Shipbank Lane. Her final goal was Paddy's Market and the many second-hand stalls which were sited in the archways under the railway line.

When she arrived, it was to find the usual scene of noise, laughter and. bustling activity. There was much evidence of the usual Glasgow bonhomie and ribaldry, as stallholders, browsers and buyers alike traded not only second-hand goods but friendly insults.

Altogether, the atmosphere of the place exactly suited her mood, and not least on account of the air of added excitement and suspense as everyone kept a weather eye open for the polis, as members of Her Majesty's Constabulary were known locally.

Kate would have loved to dawdle over the hats, coats, bed linen, tablecloths, and even books. But on this occasion, she had come with a specific purpose in mind and she determined not to be detracted from it. She already knew that if there was a bargain to be had anywhere in Glasgow, then this was the place for it. So in this Aladdin's cave under the railway bridges of the Second City, she started her hunt. She scoured from one end of Paddy's Market to the other, but nowhere could she find what she wanted. At last she sighed, and with a deep frown on her face, all her earlier jubilation gone, she was on the point of giving up the search when she spied a face she recognised. It was old Shuggie, the kindly soul she had met before at the Book Barra in Stockwell Street. But as far as Kate could see, this time it was not a barrowload of books he was trundling. Kate shook her head in disbelief.

'I just don't believe it. This must be a dream. Surely I couldn't

possibly be lucky twice in one day?'

She awakened from her reverie when she heard her name being called, and glancing up, with a questioning look in her eyes, she found that she was being hailed by the very man himself, old Shuggie.

"My, my. And if it's not Kathleen Mavourneen herself, my lovely Irish colleen."

Kate laughed, willing herself to keep her eyes on old Shuggie and well away from the contents of his barrow, even though she felt their magnetism drawing her. It would never do, she realised full well, to evince too much interest. The only result of that would be to put the price up.

But she had reckoned without old Shuggie's friendly and direct manner.

"Nice to see ye, hen. But if you're looking for books from me the day – as I mind, it was poetry you were after? Aye, never could stand the bloody rubbish myself. If it's books you're after ... weel, hen, not to put too fine a point on it, you're shit out of luck."

Kate gave a broad grin.

"Well, that's the wonder of poetry disposed of Shuggie, and no mistake."

They laughed together in easy companionship, with all the while Kate wondering the best way, without appearing too obvious, to broach the subject uppermost in her mind. Fortunately, Shuggie put her out of her misery.

With a disparaging wave of his hand towards his overloaded barrow, he shook his head.

"Not a book in sight. Bugger my luck. No, hen, I'm stuck with this barra-load of rubbish.

When he again indicated with a grubby forefinger the contents piled high on his barrow, Kate this time took a closer look. Her eyes grew wide with amazement. Seeing this, the old man grinned.

"No wonder you're near losing your eye-sight, hen. A right barrow-load of rubbish for a respectable book-dealer like me to be wheeling aboot the streets of Glasgow. I feel a right big Jessie. Just hope none o' my drinking pals see me."

In her excitement, Kate had to gulp a couple of times before she could speak. Even then, when the words came, they had an odd husky quality. She pointed to the object of Shuggie's scorn.

"And what might you be planning to do with that … er … that barrow-load of rubbish, as you choose to call it?"

Quick as a flash came Shuggie's reply.

"See Ettna Cassidy's stall over there? Weel, I'm hoping that good old Ettna will give me ten bob for the lot and let me get the hell out of here."

Kate gulped. She could hardly keep the excitement out of her voice.

"Ten bob, eh? Listen, Shuggie, how would you like to double your money at one fell swoop, as it were? I'll give you a golden sovereign for the cot and the pram."

Shuggie's eyes widened with surprise and delight, but before he could say anything, Kate went on.

"Just one thing, though. I'd need to ask you to wheel the load round to Garth Street for me. Then hump it up four flights to the top flat. Do you think you could do that?"

Shuggie half-raised his bunnet and, with black-rimmed fingers, groped underneath the skip of his cloth cap as though seeking something of value which he had lost. At length he grinned over the stubs of teeth which so exactly matched his finger-nails.

"Listen, hen, for a golden sovereign – well, let me tell you this – I'd even sell my Granny, never mind take a wee jaunt round to Garth Street. Aye, I'd be happy tae wheel this bloody lot of rubbish tae Kingdom Come for ten bob, nivver mind a golden sovereign. Must be my lucky day."

"Lucky day. You and me both, Shuggie. Tell you what, I'll give you the sovereign now, we'll walk round to my house together. Then, after you've unloaded the stuff – well, there might even be a wee cup of tea and a hot potato cake for you. How would that suit you, Shuggie?"

The old man nodded his assent.

Then, with a great display, he spat first on the palm of one hand, then on the other, rubbed them together and finally grabbed hold of the shafts of the barrow. He grinned.

"Right, then. Nae more talk. Lead on, MacDuff. And I'll tell you this – I could murder for a drink even if it is only the cup that's supposed to cheer."

So it was that in high good humour the oddly-matched pair set out, with Kate's purse now a bit lighter. Even so, she felt that it had been money well spent. Now she was assured that when Jenny's bairn would be born, probably in another two or three weeks, then it would be the first child in the Kinnon family to have its own satin-lined Moses basket. There would be no kitchen dresser drawer for her grandchild. Even better perhaps was the carriage-built high pram which she knew that she herself or Jenny would be proud to wheel through the streets of Candleriggs. Yes, while it was certainly true that Jenny's baby, at least in the eyes of the law and of enquiring neighbours, would be born a bastard, nevertheless from that moment, Kate decided that nothing but the best would be good enough for the new baby whenever he or she decided to arrive.

Chapter 24

Half an hour or so later, Kate, Shuggie, and the overloaded barrow arrived outside her own close in Garth Street. That in itself would have been excitement enough for the interested and highly inquisitive neighbours who, if nothing else, always loved a removal, or a flittin' as they called it. However, given the knots of overalled, beshawled women already gathered at the close-mouth, it was at once clear that something of even greater moment had already taken place. As Kate approached the first group of whispering women, they immediately stopped all efforts at conversation, and instead, after a commiserating glance at Kate, moved aside to let her pass. By now highly intrigued as to what could possibly have happened in her absence to occasion such underlying excitement, Kate cocked an enquiring head. But on seeing this, most of her neighbours at once lowered their eyes, as if bent on making a minute study of the pavement puddles at their feet. It was left to Big Beanie McGuire to act as spokeswoman.

This formidable lady lived on the ground floor, and on account of her white-scrolled and disinfectant-scrubbed door-step and her child-chasing efforts, she was known as the Queen of the Close. She it was who assuming command of the situation, stepped forward and taking Kate by the arm, said in her broad Glasgow accent: "It shouldn't be too long now, Mistress Kinnon. It's five hours ago and more since the midwife went up there. And even before that we heard the screams of the poor lassie. But God willing, it won't be long now."

Kate clutched the other woman's hand, and her eyes wide with fear and amazement, she asked in a hoarse voice: "Poor lassie? Midwife?

Surely ye don't mean … no, it can't be Jenny. She's got close on another month still to go. Tell me, ye don't mean it."

Beenie, every inch the Queen of the Close, patted Kate's hands as if conferring a blessing or an award on her loyal, if humble, servant. Then, standing with arms akimbo and smacking her lips, as one about to retell a prime piece of gossip, she leant closer to Kate, and stage-whispered for the benefit also of the bystanders: "Near another month, you say? Aye, well, that's as maybe, Mistress Kinnon. But we all know fine well that Nature's its own master; doesn't have any truck with calendars and the like. And of course, that accident this morning could well have hurried things on a wee bit. I'm sure that's what has happened."

There was a murmur of assent from the onlookers who, it was clear from their facial expressions, were enjoying every moment and every nuance of the drama being played out.

All thoughts of a patiently-waiting Shuggie and his barrow-load of goods still at the close-mouth vanished from Kate's mind.

"Accident, what accident? For God's sake, Mistress McGuire – Beenie, tell me."

Obviously highly pleased with the effect that her news had had on the now distraught woman visibly wilting before her, Beenie, perhaps because she genuinely did not know as much as she had implied, or perhaps even to prolong the dramatic effect, shrugged.

"The accident? Well, now, Mistress Kinnon – Kate, my dear, you'll have to ask Granny Gorbals about that. Seems she was there, or thereabouts, anyway, at the time it happened."

Kate did not wait to hear another single word but, summoning up all her reserves of strength, she took to the stairs which she raced up two at a time.

By the time she had reached the third flight of steep stairs, Kate was forced to stop for breath. As she stood there, clutching on to the banister, gasping as if her last breath had come, with the sharp and agonising pain of a stitch in her side, it suddenly dawned on her exactly what form the reported accident must have taken. In her bones, without any busybodies telling her any more half details, she knew instinctively that her wee Hannah was dead. As her frantic brain raced ahead, she could see in her mind's eye the scene – Granny had perhaps dozed off as she was prone to do, and Hannah, with her fascination for fire, had somehow toppled from her go-chair and been burned to death.

At this point, Kate shook her head, as if not only to wipe the mental image from her mind, but also to clarify a few points.

'No, that can't be it. Surely there would be a smell of burning on the stairway. And wouldn't poor old Granny have burned to death too? Got it. Poor wee Hannah – she's choked to death – on one of Granny's fresh-from-the-griddle scones. It's been too hot for Hannah and she's choked, God help her.'

Kate, although still painfully aware of the stitch in her side, had one last boost of energy – sufficient to get her up the last flight of stairs.

At last, finding herself outside Granny's door, she at once flung the thin plywood door wide and breenged in without even the customary cry of, "Yoo-hoo. It's only me, Granny."

The moment she entered the single-end, the sight that met her eyes pulled her up short, so that she had to hold on to the door-jamb for much-needed support. As she stood there, breathing heavily and taking in the unusual and totally unexpected scene, she felt as though she herself were far removed from it. And it was as if the scene were being enacted on a brightly-lit stage, the actors going about their business while she, the audience, was somewhere beyond the footlights and beyond their ken.

It was Hannah who was spot-lighted first. She looked as though she had been freshly washed and groomed for, with face aglow in the firelight, and every coarse black hair firmly in place, she was at that moment greedily and noisily sucking at a large candy-apple, the juice of which was dribbling down her chin. Suddenly, perhaps sensing the presence of her Mammy, she raised her eyes.

"Mammy, Mammy, Hannah a good girl. Jenny a bad girl. Jenny screaming. Jenny shouting bad words. But Hannah good for Granny."

Almost as an automatic reaction, Kate, with one hand still on her throbbing side, went over to Hannah and patted the girl's head. But all the while her physical presence was with the self-righteous Hannah, her eyes never left those of her other daughter, at that moment cosily tucked up in Granny's wall-bed. Seeing this, Jenny gave her Mammy a sweet, shy smile, after first gazing down with wonder at the shawl-wrapped bundle in her arms.

"Mammy, what are you waiting for? Are you not going to come over here and say hello to your first grand-bairn?"

Kate needed no second bidding. The next instant found her perched somewhat gingerly on the edge of the bed, as she too gazed in awe at the baby now nestling in its mother's arms.

Kate laid a hand on her daughter's pale cheek, and she stroked it lovingly.

"Oh, Jenny, lass. It's true. It's all over. But although I'm glad for you, dear, I'm that sorry I wasn't here to help you in your hour of need."

Jenny shook her head and her eyes filled with tears.

"Oh, Mammy, Mammy. Please don't fret yourself. The main thing is it's all over. And Granny there, she was a tower of strength. In fact with her quick thinking, you could say that she saved my life."

Kate rose to her feet and, stretching a welcoming hand to Granny, drew her into their private group at the bedside. Then, after having planted a kiss on her daughter's head, Kate peered down at the bundle in Jenny's arms.

"You … and the bairn, you're both all right? You still haven't told me … what is it, boy or girl?"

Granny Gorbals, a broad grin splitting her face from ear to ear, and mightily pleased as if she at her great age had given birth, at once rushed in to answer the new grand-mother's question.

"The wee bairn is grand. As perfect a specimen of humanity as I've ever seen. And don't forget, I've been on nodding terms with quite a few new-born babes. It's got the right number of everything: ten tiny fingers, ten twinkling wee toes, a mop of black curly hair, a wee rosebud mouth. There's only one thing missing …"

Kate at once frowned in apprehension.

"Something missing? Granny, for God's sake, what do you mean?"

Granny gave a wicked smile and a naughty wink, as if she knew she was about to scandalise the strait-laced Kate.

"The only thing missing? One of them funny dangly things that wee boys come ready-equipped with into this world. And damned soon learn to use, if I'm not much mistaken."

Despite herself and probably more from a sense of relief than from anything else, Kate burst out laughing.

"Oh, Granny, what a terrible way to talk."

Then, as the full meaning of what Granny had just said dawned on her, Kate stood with mouth agape, face aglow, her voice tinged with wonder.

"Oh, Granny, Jenny. Do you mean it? I've got … I've really got a grand-daughter?"

The old woman nodded, her own face glowing with pride, delight and an almost proprietorial air.

"Are you daft or something, Kate? Of course you've got a grand-daughter. Is that not what I've been trying to tell you for the past ten minutes? And while we're at it, I'll tell you something else. Blood relation or not – and I don't care what anybody else says or thinks – as of this minute, I'm looking on that wee bairn as my very own great-grandchild. So there, Kate Kinnon; you can put that in your pipe and smoke it."

Again Kate laughed and without another word spoken, the two women fell, half-laughing, half-weeping into each other's arms. Friends and neighbours for so many years, through dark days and fine, their tears now mingled in happiness at the birth, the safe delivery and above all, the perfection of this bastard child.

When at last they drew apart, both women dabbed at their eyes, Granny with the edge of her best pinafore which she had obviously donned in honour of the occasion, and Kate with a rag which she withdrew from the sleeve of her working serge-dress.

Suddenly, with hand now lowered to replace the rag, she stopped with a puzzled frown on her face.

"But wait a minute. Big Beenie down in the close she mentioned something about an accident. What was that all about?"

Granny made a grand dismissive gesture with her work-worn hand,

"Accident? Ach, I would not give it such a name. More like a wee mishap, and certainly nothing for you to get your knickers in a twist about, Kate; it was just ... well ... Pearce got his hand in the way of some hot water that cowped. Nothing for you to worry about. But you know what men are like; talk about a fuss. Anybody would have thought that he was giving birth, instead of your brave wee Jenny there."

Kate was still not entirely convinced.

"But, are you sure he's all right, Granny?'

The old woman nodded.

"Fine. Grand and as happy as a pig in shit. Mind you, I made him a wee herbal infusion. Then I got Aggie, the midwife, to take a wee look at him for good measure. But for all that, he was making such a hullaballoo – he was disturbing Jenny rather than the other way round – that Aggie and I brought her in here to get on with the important job of birthing in peace and quiet and without the so called help of any bloody man."

As if right on cue, and as if to disturb their own peace, Hannah having overheard the word Aggie at once thought it referred to her doll, Raggie-Aggie, still lying on the floor from where it had previously been abandoned, in favour of the then greater attraction of the toffee-apple. However, with the latter now but a sticky, glorious memory, Hannah at once started banging the sides of her go-chair and yelling: "Raggie-Aggie, Raggie-Aggie, Hannah wants Raggie-Aggie:"

Granny and Kate exchanged sympathetic smiles, but it was the older woman, ever-mindful of the needs of her adopted charge, who was first on her feet.

"Right, my lovely. In this house, whatever Wee Hannah wants, Hannah gets."

She bent her arthritic frame to retrieve the doll, handed it over to the young woman, and chucked her under the chin, which she then wiped with a damp cloth before creaking her way back to her seat.

As she settled the cushion at her back, Granny grinned over.

"Right, that's another crisis solved; Pearce will still be sleeping like the big baby he is, after that herbal mickey-finn I slipped him. No, my dear," and here she leant over and patted Kate's arm, "no, you've nothing to worry about. Oh but wait a minute, I tell a lie. There is indeed one wee worry

Kate, knowing now beyond a doubt not only that all members of her family were safe, but also that from what she had reported, Granny had coped magnificently, at once thought that Granny was on the point of making one of her rather near-the-knuckle jokes.

However, feeling that in the circumstances the least she could do was to humour Granny, Kate at once assumed an air of the most frantic worry, at the same time grabbing hold of the old woman's hand.

"Oh, Granny. What now? What final worry could there possibly be?"

Granny first cast a glance over to the wall-bed, to the drowsy Jenny and the sleeping, and as yet un-named, new born baby.

"Well, it's two things I'm worried about, if you must know. One is, what are we going to call the wee darling? I know what I call her, my own wee Rosebud. But what is to be her baptised name? And the other problem: it seems a real shame to me, to have to bed the wee precious in a kitchen drawer. If only we had a nice wee cradle. Ach, well, maybe some day ..."

Kate, as if she had taken leave of her senses, leapt from her chair.

"Oh, my God: Shuggie."

Without a word of explanation to Granny, she raced to the door, with Granny's gob-stopper eyes following her until she disappeared from sight and fled from the room. She raced down the stairs at a high rate of knots, with every step of the way, the words hammering at her brain.

"He'll have disappeared. I just know it. He'll have vanished into thin air with my gold sovereign, the carriage built pram and that lovely crib. How stupid of me. If only I'd waited until he had delivered the goods, and then paid him. Oh, well, it's done now."

Chapter 25

When Kate reached the close and peered out into the street, her worst fears were at once confirmed. Of Shuggie, his barrow, and her own bought and paid for goods, there was not a sign. Between her disappointment at that her own stupidity, her misplaced trust in Shuggie, and the intense emotion of all that had happened, it was suddenly all too much for her. Great, shaking sobs convulsed her body. At last, when the storm of weeping had somewhat abated, she straightened her body and took stock of her situation.

'Well, Kate my lass. You've been a bloody fool. No denying that. But at least, even if you have lost the crib and the swanky pram you still have that lovely wee grand-child upstairs. Aye, and now no place to bed the wee darling. Honestly. And anyway, you've still got your best friend, Granny. So, dry your eyes and stop feeling sorry for yourself.'

After first checking to make sure that her purse was still in the pocket of her work-dress and that the rest of her money had not also been lost, she started hurrying along the street towards Mr McGregor's wee newsagent and sweetie shop on the corner. With head bent, looking neither to left nor right, and intent on getting some of Granny's favourite soft peppermint-creams, she rushed along the deserted street. At this hour, and on such a cold winter's day, most people were indoors hugging their coal fires and making preparations for meals and the return of weary workers from shipyards, the Fruit Market or White's Chemical Works.

'Probably he's now sold my stuff all over again at Paddy's

Market. Honestly, I could kick myself. How could I have been so stupid, so trusting?'

However, when the door-bell pinged behind her, with poke of sweeties clutched in hand she left Mr McGregor's, she happened to glance down the side-street opposite to his shop, and there saw a loaded barrow, amazingly like the one which had earlier been at her own close-mouth.

With heart hammering in her breast, she crossed the cobbled street, pausing only to let the rag-and-bone man's horse and cart pass.

Then she walked down Glassford Street, all the while keeping her eyes firmly fixed on what she had by now decided in her own mind was an apparition. But when she was right beside the barrow, she reached out a hand and touched the satin of the ornate crib. On the point then of drawing it closer for a more detailed inspection, she heard an irate voice address her in broad Glasgow from the other side of the cart:

"Hey, Missus. Just you leave that stuff alone. Take your thieving hands off it."

She watched in fascination as a boy of about nine came round the cart towards her. Bootless, dressed in rags, and with a river of yellow slime coursing from his nose, he nevertheless had about him an air of authority. With the in-born insolence of his upbringing, he first of all looked her up and down, snorted up some of the overhang, and finished by scratching heartily at his nit-ridden locks.

"That stuff isnae yours. So just don't you touch it. It belongs to Auld-Shuggie, and he paid me good money for to watch it for him while he's in there."

This last comment was accompanied by a stern nod of the head towards the building behind her. Kate turned round and saw that she was standing in front of one of the local public-houses, of which there were all too many in the Candleriggs.

The filthy street urchin went on: "Aye, Auld Shuggie says to me: 'I've had a good day, son and I'm waiting for tae deliver this stuff to a wee woman round in Garth Street. But I'm dying for a wee refreshment. So, what say I give you a silver sixpence, Bonnie, will ye watch over my barrow?' That's what Auld Shuggie said. And I tell you, Missus, I've never had a whole sixpence in my hand in all my born days so I'll guard this barrow-load of stuff with my life – aye, to the death, if necessary."

Despite herself, Kate smiled. Then, more in admiration for the stand the urchin had taken than anything, she said: "Good for you, son. Listen, I've had a good day as well. In fact that stuff you've been guarding with your life, it's for me. And here's what I'll do, I'll –"

But she got no further, for at once the suspicion was back in the boy's eyes.

"Listen, Missus. You can say or do anything you like. But here I am and here I stay until Auld Shuggie comes back."

Kate shrugged her shoulders and said nothing in reply, as if accepting the inevitability of defeat. Then she reached into the pocket of her dress and withdrew her draw-string purse. She could feel the urchin's eyes following her every move and was aware of the tension between them mounting. Finally, between finger and thumb she extracted a silver threepenny-bit, which she then transferred to the palm of her left-hand. She held this inducement out to the boy.

"Look. This money is yours. All you have to do is go into the Hangman's Rest and ask Auld Shuggie to finish up his refreshment and come out here to speak to me. Now, that's not much to ask of you, is it? And at the end of it, the threepenny-bit will be yours when you bring Auld Shuggie out here to me."

That the boy was sorely tempted, Kate could read in his eyes. And from the conflicting emotions racing across his face, she knew the battle he was having with his conscience. Thus she was not surprised when, after biting at his lower lip in deliberation, he scowled.

"Missus, I'd like to earn that threepenny-bit, for between that and the sixpence I got from Auld Shuggie, my Mammy would think she was the Queen herself, But in my close, we cannae trust nobody. And I don't even know you. If you got rid of me into that pub, even for a minute, chances are you would take to your heels and run like the devil himself was after you – and run away with the barrow."

Far from being annoyed at his lack of trust in her, Kate could not prevent a slow smile spreading over her face at the mental picture conjured up of herself, a proud new Granny, running through the streets of Candleriggs with not only a stolen barrow, but a self-righteous, ragged urchin in hot pursuit. She was on the point of admitting defeat and resigning herself to a long wait outside the public-house. Given that Shuggie had entered its portals with a whole gold sovereign in his pocket, and also from the sounds of revelry now issuing from the depths of The Hangman's Rest, she realised with a sinking of the heart and a droop to her shoulders, that her wait could be a very long, drawn-out one indeed.

She shook her head in despair. With a reflective look on her face, she observed the boy, who was now standing, feet astride, and arms folded in front of his puny chest, with an air of complete authority and total security for his charge. With a deep sigh, Kate replaced the money in her purse, then without so much as another glance at the boy, she turned and set off at a slow pace back down the street. She had gone only a few paces when she thought she heard someone shout after her. Instead of turning round, she kept on walking, head bent against the sharp wind and convinced in her own mind that it had been some drunk who had called out to a woman alone in the deserted streets. But then she heard it again.

"Missus. Hey, Missus. Can you come back here for a wee minute? I've just had a great idea."

Kate turned her head and, seeing that it was the boy himself, she at once retraced her steps. Even if he had not mentioned his good idea, she would have known at once from the delighted expression on his face that he had gone some way to solving their problem. He had.

"Listen, Missus: I know fine well that a lady like you cannot go into a pub. And because I've been paid good money to stay here and guard the barrow, I can't go in either. So," and here he beckoned her closer, "this is what we do. We'll get Bugsie to go in with a message for Shuggie. Pure dead brilliant, eh?"

Without further ado, like a stage magician producing a rabbit from a hat, he whipped off the satin-edged blanket to reveal a sleeping toddler curled up inside the good, carriage-built pram.

For once in her life, Kate was lost for words and not least because the urchin had considered her to be a lady. And when the said Bugsie, having been rudely awakened by his brother, finally crawled out from his haven, she could see at once how the filthy child had come by his nickname. With his crumpled, torn rags which hung loosely on his thin body, his deeply-ingrained black bare feet, and his matted hair which was positively alive and moving with lice, he could be none other than Bugsie. As if hypnotised, it was all Kate could do to drag her eyes away from this apparition and over to a quick contemplation of the once-lovely and spotlessly-clean pram. She was sure that it was not a trick of the light; she had actually seen some of Bugsie's complement of fleas hopping over the white mattress and lace-edged pillow. There and then she decided in her own mind:

'First thing tonight – that's to say if I ever do get my precious pram home – then I'll disinfect it. Humph. Some bargain this has turned out to be. Jenny's wee Rosebud of a new-born baby will be having her first birthday before she ever sees her swanky pram.'

However, turning her attention to the problem in hand, she was suddenly aware that the guardian of the property was addressing her.

"Like I said, Missus, a lady like you cannot go into the Hangman's Rest. So, I'll stand guard out here with you. We'll send Bugsie in to do the needful. Just one thing – he's not exactly the full twenty-shillings to the pound – if you get my meaning."

Kate did get the full meaning – if anyone knew about someone being a wee bit daft in the head then she most certainly did. She nodded and waited for the urchin to outline his master plan.

She did not have long to wait. Placing a hand on top of Bugsie's seething head, the older boy explained the situation to him. Kate shuddered at the very thought of placing a hand on that moving mass of lice. In fact, auto-suggestion or not, she felt a compulsive urge to have a good scratch at her own top-knot. With a supreme effort, she managed concentrate instead on the detailed instructions being spelled out for wee Bugsie.

"Right. Now listen, son, I know you're a bit stupid – glaikit – like, and can't remember things too well. So here's what we do. Do you mind I took you round to see yon big building on fire? Right – so you know what fire looks like?"

Bugsie, his mouth agape, nodded.

"Good. Well, I'm going to push you into that pub. All you have to do is shout at your loudest, 'Hey, Shuggie, your barrow's on fire. Shuggie, your barrow's on fire.' Got that? That message will bring him out quick enough. Well, let me hear you saying it. One, two, three."

Thus suitably primed, the still half-asleep toddler was given a hearty shove into the Hangman's Rest where, presumably, he did his best to deliver his lines in true dramatic fashion, for in two minutes he was out again, but this time being held by the scruff of the neck by none other than a somewhat inebriated Auld Shuggie himself. The master plan had worked.

Chapter 26

The short winter day had already darkened and evening was closing in. Leerie with his pole was lighting the gas-lamps as Kate and Shuggie between them wheeled the barrow back round to Garth Street. True, the urchin, whose name she had since learnt was Archibald Strang, – otherwise known as Baldie – had offered to come with them and help unload the stuff at the other end. But when Kate considered that part of the deal would no doubt have included a free hurl in the already-bespoiled pram for Bugsie and his very active battalion of fleas and head-lice, she had declined with thanks, and suitable protestations of gratitude, his kind offer. At any rate, she reckoned if she carried the crib upstairs, even while befuddled with drink and still feeling no pain from the bucket or two of booze which he had so obviously imbibed, then Shuggie would surely manage to haul the pram up to her top-storey flat – even if it meant humping it up one step at a time.

Much to Kate's amazement, at last safely returned to her own close-mouth in Garth Street, Shuggie took one despairing look at his loaded barrow. Then, and with a pensive look on his face, after removing his flat tweed bunnet, he gave his balding head a thorough good scratch, as if in this way he could find the answer to whatever it was which was currently troubling him. At last, after an interval of several seconds, in the course of which he minutely examined whatever filth had accumulated in his black-rimmed finger-nails, he gave a long despairing sigh. If ever Kate had heard a sigh which prompted the immediate question of 'What's wrong?' it was that one.

"Something up, Shuggie? Don't tell me that with your track-record, you've actually got a hang-over. I thought you to be something more of a man, not to mention much more of a serious drinker than that."

Shuggie, on the same wavelength of pawky Glasgow humour with what – to the uninitiated – always came across as outrageous insults, grinned at her, threw back his head and gave a great belly laugh at her shaft of wit.

"Hangover, did ye say, Mistress Kinnon? Hangover be buggered. And if you weren't the respectable matron that you are, I'd soon show how you much of a man I am."

Together the oddly-assorted pair laughed in easy companionship. Then, as their laughter died away as clouds of vapour in the freezing night air, Shuggie's face became serious. Turning to his fully paid-up customer, he frowned towards the barrowload of goods.

"Well, I suppose in a manner of speaking, aye, there is a wee bit of a problem."

"Listen, Shuggie, don't you worry your head about nothing. Between the two of us we'll manage fine. I'll carry the wee crib and you can hump up the pram. It'll take us just a couple of minutes. Then you can get off and deliver the rest of the load to wherever it's bound. For time's getting on, you know."

These words were greeted in silence by the open-mouthed Shuggie and, if the look on his face was anything to go by, in something approaching stunned shock. Then, as if making a supreme effort to gather himself together, he shook his head slowly. But before he could say anything, Kate rushed to re-assure him.

"Don't worry, Shuggie," she patted his hand, not only to lend extra weight to her words but also to give him some measure of obviously sorely-needed comfort.

"There's no problem, Shuggie. Honestly. Nobody will touch the rest of your precious cargo. What we'll do is this, I'll go on up first and you stay here and keep a weather-eye on the load. Then, it'll be your turn to climb the stairs with the pram, while I act as guard. Now how does that wee ploy suit you?"

When Kate looked into his face and still could see no sign of ready agreement to her simple yet well thought-out plan, she felt a spurt of anger rising in her chest.

'*Either the man's uncommonly stupid or else he's even more drunk than I had imagined.*'

The old trader started to laugh and went on laughing heartily until his entire body shook with the effort of it. When at last it seemed that he was again in control and would be able to speak coherently, his words were lost to her in a fresh outburst of merriment.

All this while, Kate's Irish temper was struggling for expression in either angry words or perhaps even a hefty and no doubt satisfying thump across the stupid man's jaw. It was as well for both parties that, despite the fact that Kate had opened her mouth to speak, it was actually old Shuggie who got his word in first.

"Mistress Kinnon, do you still not realise? When you paid me that beautiful, golden sovereign – alas, now only of blessed memory – when you paid that, you bought not only the two items you've mentioned, but all the other bits and baubles on my barrow.

Kate drew in a sharp breath of utter amazement.

"What? Shuggie, I just don't believe this. You're drunk, you're making sport of me. It cannot be true."

The old trader, now with a delighted grin on his face, and invoking the testimony of all the Holy Angels above, affirmed that what he spoke was nothing short of God's Honest Truth. All the while that Shuggie had been crossing himself, appealing to the Angelic Holy Band above and even swearing on his dear-departed Mother's grave, Kate had been stock-taking, with delighted amazement, the contents of the barrow, of which bits and baubles she was now the sole and very proud owner. When she finally spoke, her voice was little more than a whisper, so emotionally drained was she at the shock of her sudden amazing good fortune.

"Shuggie. Oh, Shuggie. God bless you. You're a man in a million. Indeed that, you are. Here, let me give you a wee kiss."

Shuggie, now shuffling his feet in total embarrassment not only at the unexpected kiss planted on his withered cheek, but at the unlooked-for praise being heaped on his balding head, then did what he always did at such times of social unease. He withdrew from his trouser-pocket a red-spotted handkerchief, no doubt one of his own treasure-trove finds from Paddy's Market, gave a hefty trumpet into its crushed depths, and finished the face-saving operation by inspecting the resultant contents of the handkerchief.

Kate smiled and restrained a wild urge not only to bestow a further kiss on his bearded face, but also to give her kind-hearted saviour a hug. That she, in effect did neither, was due to her being afraid as to what an even more-embarrassed Shuggie might do for an encore to his nose-blowing efforts.

Instead, she again smiled at him.

"Just one thing, Shuggie. If all this lovely stuff now belongs to me, what exactly might be the wee problem you mentioned earlier?"

Shuggie sighed.

"Well, Mistress Kinnon, although I promised when we sealed our bargain with the sovereign that I would carry everything up to the top-flat for you, I had not the drink taken at that point, if you get my meaning. The thing is, you're such a decent wee body, paying me on the nose and all, the last thing I want to do is let you down."

Kate grinned with relief that this was the only problem on her immediate horizon. She grabbed the old man by his jacket.

"Listen, Shuggie. When all is said and done, you're not such a bad fellow yourself. Aye, you're a pretty decent wee body. So, worry not, my good old friend. Here's what we'll do. I'll run upstairs and have a wee word with Mistress Docherty and –"

"Mistress Docherty? Is that yon, wee shilpit, pardon-me-for-living woman with her own squad of Irish navvies – what is it, thirteen big strapping sons she has? God kens how she managed to bring in that Baker's Dozen of big bruisers into the world."

Kate grinned an impish smile, already feeling greatly daring and light-headed with the excitement of it all.

"I expect she managed it in exactly the same way as all we other poor, down-trodden wives. I don't suppose she had much choice in the matter – just had to get on with the job, whether she liked it or not."

Shuggie cackled in delighted appreciation, at the same time slapping his mole-skinned trouser-leg in his mirth.

"Aye, you're probably right there, Missus. Mind you, I don't mind telling you this; I thank God every night of my born-days that I wasn't born a woman. I don't think I could stomach all yon bloody carry-on."

"Shuggie, listen; I can't stand here chewing the fat with you all night, much as I'd like to, mind you. I'm off upstairs to have a wee word with Mrs Docherty. At least a couple of her sons should be back by now from work."

With that, a cheery wave to the patiently-waiting Shuggie and a muttered aside, '*The Docherty troops will soon lend us a hand. After all that's what neighbours are for,*' she was gone, and in her excitement and haste, and with all previous tiredness forgotten, she raced up the steps two at a time.

Chapter 27

Later still that same evening, when, with the help of many willing hands, all the goods had been transferred to Kate's best front room, there was a celebration to wet the baby's head such as put even the best Hogmanay shindigs in the shade. Instead of getting the promised fag and a cup of tea, Shuggie, who had instantly become the hero of the hour, was treated to a pipeful of best Virginia Dark from father Docherty's battered and well-used tobacco pouch; and perhaps even better and even more to his taste, several hefty measures from Granny's medicinal bottle of whisky. By the time good auld Shuggie, as he was now intimately and affectionately known to Kate's immediate neighbours, was leaving, he was in a fine old state of inebriation. So much so, he would have been hard put to say exactly what festivity it was he had been celebrating: Christmas, Easter, the riotous wake of a dear-departed friend, the safe birthing of a new-born heir or heiress, or even his own prowess as a canny man of business. As the party guests waved off his somewhat staggering departure down the many stairs to the close, several of the departing guests hung rather precariously over the spiral stairway and, with loud shouts of encouragement, monitored his progress. That done, and having seen he had safely negotiated the stairs and was now – albeit slowly – taking the breadth of the close in his stride, then making his way out into the gas-lit street beyond, some of the more responsible guests headed for Kate's front-room. From the great height and bird's-eye view of this eyrie, they could just make out the silhouette of man and now-empty barrow as together they negotiated a somewhat unsteady course for the

271

shadowed end of Garth Street and distant points Eastwards.

As Kate later saw off her other guests, the Docherty clan, she then turned to survey her best-front room, which now resembled nothing so much as an Aladdin's cave. She crossed her arms in front of her body, as if hugging to herself the many delights and surprises of the wonderful day. Apart from the disinfected satin-lined crib in which wee Rosebud was already sound asleep by her mother's side next door in Granny's cosy single-end, the rest of the treasure-trove lay in wait for the years ahead.

There was a high-chair, a baby's bath, a smart go-chair in addition to the carriage-built pram, a wicker-basket full of the most beautiful baby clothes, not least of which was a magnificent Christening Robe grand enough for a Royal Princess, and even a stout wooden-box crammed full of toys of every description.

Where or how Auld Shuggie had come by this assortment, Kate was not entirely sure. True, while in his cups, he had muttered something about a woman in a posh house in Monteith Row whose baby had been stillborn and who just could not bear to look a minute longer at the accoutrements of childhood. But the very mention of Monteith Row – far less the thought of its posh houses and their upper-class tenants – was enough to set Kate trembling, so that she did not pursue the matter further. Even at this distance in time the very name of those handsome houses, overlooking Glasgow Green, the scene of her shame and humiliation, was enough to upset her. With the drift of her thoughts to those long-ago events, she suddenly gave a start, remembering with a rush of guilt that it was some time since she had looked in on Pearce. She tip-toed through the darkened hallway and into the back kitchen, where, as she opened the door, she hoped against hope that for once it would not squeak in its usual fashion. But her hope was in vain. Hannah on the hurlie bed immediately stirred, opened her eyes and started crying. This in turn awoke Pearce who sat up in bed, rubbed his eyes and demanded to know: "What the hell is going on now? Is there no peace to be had?"

Kate sighed in frustration. However, she was determined that nothing and no-one on earth – and most certainly not her irascible husband – would spoil this memorable day nor even a fraction of the sheer delight which she felt at the birth of her first grandchild.

As she bustled around getting Pearce and Hannah a hot cup of tea with which to settle them yet again for the night, she smiled to herself at the turn her thoughts had taken.

'Bastard or not, that child is going to get the very best out of life. And I for one, as her Granny, will see that she does. She will never have to scrimp, save and work like a navvy in the way that I've had to do. I don't yet know how we're going to manage it. And yet look how things have turned out today. It's all been like a miracle. Yes, that wee darling's life is going to be a whole lot different from mine and from her own Mammy's. That wee pet will never have to be a sweeper in a mill. No, nor a kitchen skivvy neither.'

And with these thoughts still uppermost in her mind, Kate reached up on tiptoe, and turned down the gas to its night-time peep.

Chapter 28

On the last day of 1898 Kate made her way to Mrs Scott's. She hadn't seen the old lady since their pre-Christmas party on the twenty-third when Mrs Scott had given her the five guineas. Kate had some tasty bites for her and presents from both Hannah and Jenny. Although Mrs Scott had said not to bother coming to her until Kate's regular day on Monday January 2nd, 1899, Kate had decided she would pay her employer a visit to tell her about the baby's unexpected early arrival and Shuggie's barrow load of baby goods.

Kate tugged at the brass bell-pull on Mrs Scott's door. Despite having pulled the bell a number of times, there was still no answering call from her employer.

For good measure, she gave the brass lion's head a fierce tattoo. But when even this brought no response, laid her basket down carefully on the doormat, prised open the gleaming brass letter-box and put her mouth to the opening.

"Yoo-hoo. Mrs Scott. It's only me. Kate Kinnon. Only me. Take your time in getting to the door. No hurry."

When still she could hear neither movement nor reply from inside the flat, despite listening intently, Kate sighed wearily.

'*Ah, well. So much for that bright idea. Some day I'll learn to do what people tell me. Mistress Scott said not to bother coming till Monday. So, what do I do? Ignore her, go my own sweet way, as usual.*'

Kate stooped down to retrieve her basket from where it sat on the coarse-fibre door-mat. Then, hooking the basket over her left arm, she started making her way out of the close.

'*Perhaps Mrs Scott has gone to a relative to bring in the New Year tonight. After all, who wants to be alone on Hogmanay? It can be a sad enough occasion at the best of times. Or perhaps she's in visiting with a neighbour.*'

By now out again in the rain-drenched street, Kate stopped.

'*Mrs Scott, in visiting with a neighbour? Wait a minute. She hates the lot of them: stuck-up, self-important bitches, that's what she'd called hem. Not the same friendliness here as you have in your close, Kate. All right, so she's staying with a relative?*'

She wheeled round and started to run back to Mrs Scott's door.

'*Mrs Scott has no relatives. Oh, God. She must be there in the flat. Something's dreadfully wrong. I just know it.*'

This time she took the brass lion's head in both hands and gave it such a wallop that the door of the flat opposite opened, and a wizened prune of a woman peered out. With lips pursed and nostrils flared, as if getting the reek of stinking fish, this woman looked Kate up and down from head to toe. Then, just as Kate opened her mouth to speak, the woman took a step back into her own hallway and slammed the door with a clunk of finality.

'*Not much help to be had in that quarter,*' thought Kate grimly.

Again Kate shouted through the letter box, but this time instead of standing back to await admittance, she cocked her ear to the flap which she held open with her trembling fingers. As she strained to hear something, anything which might reassure her, she thought she detected a faint movement of some sort.

'*Yes. I was right. There it is again.*'

Only this time the faint beating sound was followed by the words: "Kate. Thank God. Let yourself in. The key's on a string behind the letter box."

Kate did. And once inside the flat, she was aware of an intense cold, as though there hadn't been a fire on for days. She looked first into the sitting-room, nobody. In the kitchen, it was the same story; neither fire nor any sign of Mrs Scott. It was at that point that she heard a weak voice calling from the bedroom.

"Kate. In here. Oh, Kate. You're a God-send. Come away in."

When Kate opened the bedroom door, she stopped in amazement at the sight which met her eyes. Mrs Scott was propped up in bed, her favourite pink bed-jacket draped round her shoulders, a filmy net on her head, while on the bedside table rested an enormous box of chocolates, a tumbler and a stack of books.

But, and this was what struck Kate as so utterly incongruous, everything, including Mrs Scott, was covered in a fine layer of soot. Automatically, Kate's eyes swivelled to the coal-fire on the other wall and at once she could see what had happened. Obviously there had been a fall of soot from the flat above – perhaps the result of a neighbour's over-zealous pre-Hogmanay cleaning. But Mrs Scott's own fire had gone out, the room itself was freezing cold, and every surface, including the beautiful marble mantelpiece, which was the old lady's pride and joy, was covered in an inky-black film. Kate blinked in amazement, especially when she took a closer look at her friend and employer. She opened her mouth and before she could stop herself, the words were out.

"God Almighty. Mistress Scott, you look like one of those black men we see coming off the boats."

The goggle-eyes looked back enquiringly, so Kate bent down to the dressing-table, lifted the soot-encased hand-mirror, and after wiping it with her fingers, she held it out to the old woman. Mrs Scott peered myopically into the mirror, then her shoulders started to heave with laughter. She went on laughing until the tears ran down her cheeks, leaving white funnels through the soot, thus further emphasising her ridiculous appearance. Kate joined in the gales of laughter, thinking to herself that this was the best way to diffuse what might otherwise have been a disastrous – if not fatal – situation, had she herself not arrived so timeously on the scene.

"Thank God you came today after all, Kate. Otherwise, I'd have been stuck here in my bed until you came next year. I fell yesterday evening. It didn't seem very bad at the time ... but ... my legs have all stiffened up lying in bed. The cold after the soot came down and my rheumatism hasn't helped. I did try to get up, but I couldn't. Could you help me to the toilet?"

Kate soon had the room clean. Mrs Scott washed and dressed up in a fresh nightie and mohair bed-cape and a pink ribbon in her hair, and soon there was even a bright fire blazing in the newly-scrubbed and polished hearth.

Kate rubbed her hands in satisfaction as she surveyed both the scene and her employer. They exchanged conspiratorial smiles as they each remembered not only what the situation had been but also what dire consequences might have resulted had the old woman been left alone to freeze for days on end in an unheated flat. Kate bent forward and adjusted Mrs Scott's pink hair ribbon to a more fetching angle.

"Mistress Scott. Sure and there's no need for you to be lonely this night. You'll be more than welcome at my fireside this Hogmanay night, or at any other time, for that matter."

For reply, Mrs Scott clutched on to Kate's hand, as if to a lifeline of which she would never let go.

"Kate, I want you to know, you're the best – in fact, the only – friend I have in the whole wide world. And believe me, I do appreciate your kind invitation – even though I'm now too old and too stiff to be going gallivanting; far less first-footing. But I thank you kindly. Now, did you say something about a cup of tea?"

As Kate bustled about the kitchen getting the tea-tray prepared, she stopped.

'If Mrs Scott can't come to my Hogmanay party tonight, we'll have one right now. The pair of us.'

So Kate looked out a much bigger tray which she set with a white crochet-edged cloth, on top of which she put all the dainty sweet-bites she had brought with her, and alongside them, the two home-made presents from Hannah and Jenny. When she bore the over-laden tray back in triumph into the bedroom, Mrs Scott's eyes widened in surprise and delight. After examining the contents of the tray she frowned and in a mock-serious tone said: "Oh, Kate. You've forgotten something."

Kate raised her eyebrows and cocked her head in an inquiring manner as she waited for the old woman to go on.

"You've forgotten two glasses and the medicinal bottle from the sideboard in the front room."

Kate needed no second bidding. She positioned the tray on Mrs Scott's knees and at once set off to forage for the requisite booze. Once back in the bedroom and with their glasses filled, Kate raised hers.

"Now, we know it's supposed to be bad luck to eat shortbread or toast in the New Year before the set-time. So here's what we'll do. This is not a Hogmanay party we're having. But what we're really doing is celebrating the birth of Jenny's baby; we're wetting the baby's head."

Mrs Scott smiled her agreement and delight at this arrangement, then paused with glass half way to her lips.

"Hold on a minute, Kate. Like I said, you're my only friend. So, if you're the baby's Granny ... I'd like to have the honour of being its Godmother. How would that be, Kate?"

At once, Kate's face was suffused with colour.

"Oh. Mistress Scott, I couldn't let you do that. You see ... well ... to tell you the truth ... the bairn ... wee Theresa ... she's ... er ... illegit–"

Mrs Scott waved aside Kate's words, refusing even to let her finish.

"Listen, Kate. If you're trying to tell me the baby's a bastard, forget it. I've already worked that out for myself. I'm not as green as I'm cabbagelike, you know. I'm an old woman and believe me, I've seen all that life has to offer."

Kate laughed. "Aye. but even so, Mistress Scott, I still think that –"

"Kate, if you're happy about the baby, so am I. And I'd count it a real blessing if you'd grant me the honour of being the bairn's Godmother."

Kate's eyes filled with tears.

"No problem. So, let's drink to both the new baby and her Godmother. Cheers. or as the wild Highlanders all say, sláinte mhath"

Mrs Scott took a gulp of the whisky, then she put down her glass.

"Right. Now we've got that settled; what about a wee present for my god-daughter? Do you think that one of those fancy, lace-trimmed cots would be suitable?"

Kate placed her glass on the tray and clapped her hands in delight at the co-incidence. She then told Mrs Scott the tale of Shuggie and his barrowload of goodies. When every facet of that memorable day had been related, Mrs Scott pursed her lips as if deep in thought. Then she smiled.

"Since it rather looks as if you yourself have more or less cornered the market in the range of baby wear, here's what I'll do. But first of all, tell me this, what is the baby's full name?"

The proud grandmother at once replied: "Theresa Rafferty Kinnon. But why do you ask, Mrs Scott?"

"I'll need to get the silver Christening-mug engraved, won't I ?"

Kate smiled in delight.

"A silver Christening-mug. Sure and 'tis only the gentry that have such things. Oh, the wonder of it ."

Without further ado, Kate rose to her feet and, coming over to the bedside, she enveloped her employer in a hug, much to the danger of the many items then wobbling about on the tea-tray. Mrs Scott laughed in delight. Then she extricated herself with some difficulty.

"Hold on a minute, girl. I haven't finished yet. Hear me out. I need the full name for another reason as well. I plan to open a bank account in the name of Theresa Rafferty Kinnon."

Pearce, despite his diatribes against the pregnant Jenny, now that the baby was born became very much the doting grandfather and, enfeebled as he now was, he spent hours talking to the baby and playing with it.

Chapter 29

As the last moments of 1899 ticked away, Kate paused and looked around her gleaming kitchen and at her family gathered there in anticipation of the delights to come. Already the over-heated room with its blazing coal fire and linen bedecked table groaning with shortbread, black bun, Madeira cake and slices of cluthie dumpling, was crowded. As ever, Granny was fussing with Hannah and tonight's game seemed to be that of retying, with a mock display of reluctance and much sighing and rolling of rheumy eyes, the girl's tartan hair-ribbon each time that Hannah managed to work it loose.

Jenny and the now ever-watchful Pearce could hardly take their eyes off the sleeping one-year-old baby Theresa. With this particular New Year being one of such importance, Pearce had decided that for once, he would stay and at least usher in the new century within the bosom of his family. The arrangement was that if later on he became too tired, or if the resulting ceilidh was too boisterous, then Jenny would help both her Dadda and wee Theresa into the quiet haven of Granny's single-end.

A silence stole on the group as, with every eye on the grandmother clock, they watched not only the old year, but the old century die away into the mists of time.

As the clock chimed out twelve times, Granny confirmed each stroke with a nod of her wizened face and balding head. On the last beat, the party was already awash with tears, especially when Kate rose to her feet and said: "Right. Time to let go of the old. And usher in the new century."

She crossed over to the sink, where, bending across the black steel cavern, she pushed up the kitchen window, at the same time reflecting that it was more than she could ever have done in her first home in Glasgow. It was more than a blast of cold air which entered, for a cacophony of vibrant sound: bells ringing, hooters blaring, excited voices shouting from the back-courts and the crowded, city streets beyond. Turning from the window, Kate, with tears glistening in her green Irish eyes, went over to her husband. She bent over him, threw her arms around him.

"Happy New Year, Pearce, my darling." Her voice choked with emotion. "Happy New Century."

Even as she said the set-words she knew what a hollow wish it was, for what possible happiness could lie ahead for the poor done old man that he had now become? But as he raised his head and patted her arm with a palsied hand, she fancied that, at least for a fleeting instant, she saw a glimpse of the young Pearce who, for all his faults, had nevertheless done his duty by her and stood beside her in trouble and in gladness – not that there had ever been much of the latter – throughout their many long years of marriage. Finally, it was the sound of Granny's cackle which caused her to turn aside from the deep wells of love, longing, sorrow and remembrance she could read in her husband's eyes.

At once she enveloped Granny in a hug. Then holding her old friend at arm's length, she saw the tears trickling down the life-lined face.

"Come on now, Granny. No time this, for tears. Happy New Year to you."

Granny tried to stem the flow of tears with the back of her hand.

"Kate. I'm only crying because I'm that happy. A new Century, begod. Never thought I'd live to see it."

"Well, you have. So, let's get this party under way. Come on, now Jenny, suppose you hand round the shortbread fingers? And I'll see that the glasses are filled to toast the year of our Lord nineteen hundred.

And listen, Jenny, best be quick, before the rest of the revellers start battering down the door."

No sooner was their somewhat subdued toast made and tossed back than there was indeed a thunderous tattoo at the door, accompanied by a strident ringing of the brass bell-pull.

Kate and Jenny both ran to the door, which they opened and threw wide to the wall. Into the narrow hallway erupted a jumble of singing, laughing, rioting humanity led by the dark-haired first-footer, Baldie McFarrel. Baldie, the local Primary School's martinet of a janitor, had obviously borrowed for this auspicious occasion the heavy brass hand-bell which normally summoned laggard children to school. Like a town crier, he clanged this bell, as all the while, he yelled: "Happy New Century to one and all. Happy Nineteen-Hundred."

As if all this were not enough excitement, Kate nearly lost her eyesight in amazement when she saw who was bringing up the rear of the party. It was none other than her old pal Shuggie, carrying a set of somewhat moth-eaten bagpipes which he was, even at that very moment, in the process of tuning-up. Kate gave a scream of delight and reaching out, dragged the would-be piper into the confines of her home.

"Shuggie. I just don't believe it. Oh, this is great. Great. I've never had a piper in my house before. I'm sure it's meant to be a lucky omen. What a way to celebrate the new Century. Come in, come in."

Auld Shuggie allowed himself to be drawn into the hall, which although dimly lit with borrowed light from the gas-lamp on the stairhead, was bright enough to reveal an amazing fact.

The bold Shuggie was dressed overall in full Highland dress regalia, right down to kiltie top-hose and silver-buckled brogues. Seeing this vision of splendour in her home, Kate clapped her hands in delight and then raced ahead to the kitchen where she announced to the waiting assembly:

"You'll never believe it: We've got a piper. Is that not the grand start to the new century?"

Scarcely were the words out of her mouth than Auld Shuggie came marching in, kilt swaying and pipes blaring. The volume of sound in the confines of the small, stuffy kitchen had to be heard to be believed and not a few of the guests winced in real pain as the noise physically assaulted their ear-drums. Shuggie chose to ignore this minor embarrassment and, with measured tread, dictated by his liberal intake of whisky, he paced to and fro in the tiny room, slapping down first one silver-buckled shoe, then the other, with all the while his bagpipes screaming at full pitch. At long, weary last, his ragged and ear-splitting rendition over, Shuggie lowered his bagpipes and gazed expectantly at his captive and by now nearly-deaf audience. But instead of the riotous applause which he so obviously expected, there was instead silence, a strained silence which could be felt. Whether people were too overcome by the emotion of the event, or were just plain stunned by the noise of it all, would have been hard to define.

There was a smattering of somewhat belated applause for the piper, who acknowledged their appreciation by hiking the front of his kilt waist high. This brought a roar of approval from the revellers, amid such ribald shouts as,

"Aye. No mystery noo"

"Good on you, Shuggie, lad. Mind you, there's no much there to do a song and dance about, is there?"

Shuggie took it all in good part, grinning from ear to ear.

"Well, sunshine, big or wee, there's one thing sure, at least it's livened up the party a bit. I was beginning to think I'd often been at a cheerier wake."

Strangely enough, the one member of his audience who appeared most of all to have enjoyed the medley of tunes was Hannah. Throughout Shuggie's recital, she had kept up a spirited rendition of her own by banging on the sides of her go-chair with a spoon, which had been thoughtfully provided by Granny for this express purpose. Hannah's face was still aglow with delight when the red-faced and perspiring piper staggered over to her. Between the exertion of his piping, the furnace heat of the small, crowded room and the streaming cold which he was hell-bent on sharing with everyone else in sight, it was clear that he was in urgent need of a handkerchief, and not just for his fevered brow. After a fruitless search through every pocket, in the course of which his half-bottle of cheap whisky was in danger of crashing to the floor, he finally gave up the unequal struggle. Tucking his bagpipes more firmly under his left armpit, he drew the arm of his sleeve across his dripping nose. That did it. One of the ornate silver buttons on the cuff somehow got jammed in his right nostril. In his befuddled, drunken state, and with a look of utter amazement on his vapid face, he chugged and chugged at the offending obstacle. If anything, this served only to lodge it more firmly. It was left to Kate, well-versed in such matters over many years of dealing with Hannah and her equally dramatic crises, to help get the luckless Shuggie out of his predicament. With one last tug from his rescuer and a screech of pain from the gallant piper, he was freed. The offending button dislodged itself not only from Shuggie's, by now, red-raw nostril, but also from his jumble-sale kiltie's jacket. As if released from a cannon, the button shot across the room, just missing Pearce's left eye by an inch. It was at this point that Hannah happened to look up and, finding herself eyeball to eyeball with the beady eyes of the indeterminate and flea-bitten animal whose life had been sacrificed to make a sporran for the Piper's full-dress regalia, she let out a scream of terror.

"Mammy, Mammy. Big monstra."

It took all of Kate's persuasion and Granny's offer of a sweet bite to reassure poor Hannah that it was not in fact a monster after her. Shuggie was having problems of his own, since he was being actively dissuaded from scrabbling about on the floor to hunt for his lost and suddenly precious 'silver' button. At last, Kate, with her most ingratiating hostess smile pinned to her face, managed to convince him that the sweeper-up would get it in the morning and later return his property to him. Thus re-assured, Shuggie, as was his due, seeing as he was the only one wearing a kilt, again adopted the mantle of Master of Ceremonies. He cast a bleary eye over the assemblage.

"Right then, you lot, this is supposed to be a party. And at a Scottish Ceilidh, everybody's supposed for to do their party-piece."

This announcement was met with a stunned silence. Then Stoorie Sanny, from the next close, recovered sufficiently to say: "Awa and bile yer heid, Shuggie. If you think I'm going to get up and dae a clog-dance or give a wee recitation, you're away with the fairies."

There was a murmur of assent from the other guests and reluctant performers. When it was clear that not one party-goer was willing to act the goat for the enjoyment of his fellows, Auld Shuggie frowned in perplexity. Then as his face brightened, he rubbed his hands before announcing his latest brain-wave.

"Right. If you're all going to be stick-in-the-muds, there's only one thing for it." Here he cast his eyes around the room, as though seeking something other than his precious silver button. At length, his eyes lit on an empty whisky bottle where it still rested by the side of the fireside kerb where an inebriated guest had laid it.

Shuggie crossed the room and, bending down, retrieved the bottle. Then holding it aloft, as if some hard-won trophy, he again addressed his captive audience.

"Now we're really in business, folks. So, here's what we do. It's quite easy and nobody needs to get themselves in a fankle about it: We spin the bottle on the floor and when it stops, if it's pointing to you, that means you've to do a turn. Fair, isn't it?"

Then without waiting for either agreement or denial, Shuggie bent down and gave the bottle a hefty spin. When it finally came to rest, it was pointing at Jenny. She blushed scarlet then, egged on by the prompting of the other guests who were only too relieved that it wasn't their turn, she mumbled her way through a half-forgotten poem, a relic from the dim and distant days of the Kinnon ceilidhs of blessed memory. This rendition was greeted with loud cheers and much back-slapping, so much so that the poor girl regained her seat in some confusion. Next to be chosen by the spin of the bottle was Donny McGinty. For some reason best known to himself and despite being in a fine state of intoxication, he chose of all things, *A Ballad of the Drunkard's Poor Wee Bairn*. This ran to several verses and was accompanied by much posturing, beating of breast and flinging wide of arms.

Over-acted it may well have been, yet this recital also received thunderous applause, in stark contrast to poor Shuggie's piper-playing efforts. Perhaps the guests were just so relieved that on this occasion, and for the moment at least, Auld Shuggie had not been chosen to perform. For the time being, their ear-drums were safe from further assault, and thankful they were for that no small mercy. So the bottle-spinning ceilidh went on far into the night and early morning. But the grande finale, and also the high spot of the recitations, surely had to be the monologue delivered by Mick McGarrigle. He took centre stage and, having adopted a grand theatrical pose, at once launched into his tale, one which, if the experience of previous years was anything to go by, would be a real tear-jerker. Throwing his arms wide to a scenario which only he could as yet see, he declaimed:

"The night was wild,

His heart was sore,

He was leaving the Homeland,

Would see his old Granny no more.

'Twas a cruel blow,

Fate dealt him thus,

But, to the far-flung

Wilds of Canada

Go, he must."

The harrowing tale of a poor young Irish lad, driven far from his Emerald Isle by poverty, the Potato Famine and the land-grabbing greed of the Irish landed gentry, went on for about twenty verses. By the time he had reached the thirteenth verse or so, the party was already awash in a flood of tears, whisky, and maudlin sentiment. The brave welcome for the new Century had by now lost all pretence at jolly Ceilidh and now resembled nothing so much as an Irish Wake in full-flight. Somewhere on or about the twenty-third verse, the orator reached a ringing climax, which drew tears from the hardest and most callous of hearts. From every corner of the room, low moans and keening sounds could be heard and in every hand, be it young or old, was clutched a twisted, damp handkerchief rag. The only thing now dry were the tumblers, drained of every drop of the comforting, golden water of life.

In the silence which followed the end of the epic, the only sounds to be heard were the ticking of the clock. and the snores of both Hannah and Pearce. But from the tense expression on every other face, it was obvious that, to a guest, they had tramped every weary mile of that Pioneer Trail right beside that poor heart-broken emigrant lad. With him, they had braved trial by Brown Bear and Red Indian; had endured not only pangs of hunger, but long, dark nights of longing for the Homeland; had triumphed over fiendish snow storms in the untamed Rocky Mountains. And for what? Had it all been in vain?

All that suffering, misery and endurance only to know at the end of it all that never again, in this world at least, would-he ever see his dear old Granny again, savour her potato-cakes or share with her the setting of the sun on dear old Galway Bay. It was enough to break the stoutest of hearts.

The first person to recover from the shared ordeal was none other than the intrepid piper himself, Auld Shuggie. Of course, it must have been many a long day since he had clapped eyes on his Granny, so perhaps it had not been such a harrowing experience for him. Whatever, it was still obvious to the rest of the revellers that he had to clear his throat a couple of times before he could trust himself to speak. At last, and making an almighty effort, he creaked his arthritic frame to its full height.

"Well, folks, now that we are all safely back from our trek to the Wild West of that heathen country of Canada, if I could just get a wee word in edge-ways.

Here he paused, and seeing that there were many in the group who were still mopping away at their red-rimmed eyes or even still letting the tear doon fall, he smiled round his bonhomie and encouragement.

"I'd just like to say a wee word of thanks for this wonderful experience and bountiful hospitality we've enjoyed here tonight."

There were murmurs of agreement and much nodding of heads. This was sufficient encouragement for the would be Toastmaster to expound, at length, the attributes of their gracious hostess Mistress Kate Kinnon, and finish his oration by giving a check-list of every delicious morsel which they'd had to eat and drink.

At last, this diatribe over, the party started breaking up and, amidst a welter of hand-shaking, back-slapping and cries of mutual goodwill, they gravitated to the hall.

Kate and Jenny, both of them by now almost asleep on their feet, ushered their staggering guests to the outer door, as all the while inebriated ones declared not only their undying friendship but also their sincere good wishes for the New Year.

The new century and the year of our Lord nineteen hundred had been well and truly christened and launched.

For the moment, Kate's most immediate future was to get Hannah and Pearce settled comfortably for the night and then tackle the clearing-up of the chaos left by her departing guests. As she surveyed the dishevelled state of her previously spotless and tidy kitchen, she sighed.

"Some things never change."

Chapter 30

The old Queen died on January 22nd 1901, and perhaps it was fitting that her loyal subject Pearce Claude Kinnon departed this life just a few days after his Monarch.

When it was obvious that Pearce lay dying, Kate, as had been her custom throughout his life, went out of her way to provide him with such material comforts as were to hand. On the third day of his crisis, when it was clear he was sinking fast, she bent over him.

"Listen, Pearce my darlin'. Is there anything at all you fancy to eat; a wee potato cake? A plate of Irish stovies? Anything at all, my dear, just you say it and I'll move heaven and earth to get it for you. That I will."

The only response to this was a slight shaking of his wizened head on the pillow, and even this weak action seemed to drain his strength. Seeing this, Kate leant over and stroked his damp, fevered brow.

"Well, if nothing special to eat, then is there anyone you would wish to see, Pearce?"

This remark caused a tremulous smile to flit over his death-mask face.

"The condemned man, eh, Kate?"

She gave a tut-tut of mock annoyance.

"Now then, Pearce, we're not having any defeatist talk like that. I simply thought, a visitor to your taste might perhaps cheer you up, give you a lift. Isn't there anyone you would like to see?'

From the conflicting emotions racing across his face it was clear Pearce was having an inner battle. Finally, after a bit more prompting:

"Yes, Kate, there is someone. But I would not wish to be seen like this, stuck here in the kitchen wall-bed."

Kate smiled gently.

"Pearce, my love. There would be no problem in getting you cosily established in the good front room. Jenny could give me a hand. Sure, there's not a pick of flesh on you, no weight on you whatever. Stoorie Sanny from the next close would very soon help you through there."

Pearce smiled weakly, then quickly frowned when Kate went onto say: "Only trouble is, I don't know where on earth to start looking for Daniel."

Pearce tried in vain to lift his weary head from the pillow. Then, summoning all his strength, he shook his head.

"'Twas not Daniel I had in mind as my favoured visitor."

Kate cocked her head on one side.

"Pearce, you've fair got me puzzled. For I know it certainly is not Granny Gorbals that you're desperate to see."

Pearce waved a trembling hand towards the battered wallet which lay on the bedside chair.

"In there. Her address is in the inner pocket."

Soon a note had been hand-delivered to one Mistress Josephine Delaney, now of Monteith Row, Glasgow Green, requesting her urgent presence at the death-bed of her old and valued friend Pearce Claude Kinnon.

A short time later, Josephine arrived in a flurry of furs, feathers and furbelows and was immediately ushered into the over-heated front room. What words passed between them, Kate would never know, for she observed Pearce's need for privacy at this solemn moment. When a weeping Josephine Delaney finally emerged from the room, she dabbed at her eyes with her dainty lace handkerchief and said in her refined Irish accent: "Pearce years ago mentioned a little red velvet jewel box he wished me to have as a memento, but today I could not catch where he said it was. When you find the box you can have it sent to me?"

Mrs Delaney had a strange faraway look in her eyes, and Kate wondered if she realised had she met Pearce in a different time and in a different place, then how altered everyone's lives might have been, with her the respected chatelaine of Laggan House, instead of merely the tolerated, paying lodger of an indigent gentlewoman in Glasgow Green, had not irresponsible youthful passions and lust dictated otherwise.

She replaced her handkerchief in her embroidered moiré reticule. That done, with ladylike elegance, she drew on her fine, long kid gloves and only then did she extend a hand towards her former landlady. She smiled bravely through her tears.

"Goodbye then, Mistress Kinnon. Thank you so much for having observed Pearces's last wishes in sending for me. I do appreciate that gesture more than you will ever know."

Kate, for once dumbstruck and struggling for words with which to reply, might just as well have saved herself the bother. For it was at once apparent that Mistress Josephine was determined to have the last word.

"I shall not be attending the funeral. I already have my own memories of our dear Pearce. And I prefer to remember him as he was in life. My only regret is that I never really knew him as a young man in the proper setting of Laggan House. Ah well."

She dabbed daintily at a tear trickling down her cheek.

"'Tis life, Mistress Kinnon, 'tis the way of things. So, this must needs be good-bye. You and I shall not meet again – at least not in this life. So, I bid you adieu and thank you again. You did exactly the right thing in sending for me. Goodbye. Goodbye."

And with a flurry of furs and trailing skirts, Josephine Delaney took her not-too-sad farewell of Kate Rafferty Kinnon.

As she always had done with her grand, ladylike ways and her inborn superior manner, she left Kate feeling like the not very bright kitchen skivvy. Kate shook her head sadly as she retraced her steps to her husband's bedside.

'*Yes, Kate, you were the one who bore his children, and put up with his temper tantrums. I'm damned if the already over-jewelled, spoiled, pampered bitch of a Delaney is going to get any red velvet jewellery box – if it exists.'*

She pursed her lips as she approached the inert, lifeless body of what had been Pearce Claude Kinnon. She gazed down at his waxen face through the mist of her tears.

'A fine state of affairs, this. Not only does Josephine think to inherit his worldly goods, she even has the last of his words spoken on this earth. There's nothing left for me now.'

She jumped in surprise when Pearce's hand moved, and he spoke so quietly that she had to bend over, her ear almost touching his lips, to hear.

"In my box ... the one I keep our documents in ... birth certificates, marriage lines ... the small key on my watch fob ..."

He stopped for so long Kate thought he was dead.

"... a red velvet box ... my grandmother's necklace ... given to me for my bride ... give it to ..."

'Death bed words or not, I'm damned if I'm going to give it to Mrs Delaney.'

"Make sure ... make sure ... my little Theresa gets it ... Katy girl."

Kate knelt at her husband's bedside. There would be much to arrange in the hours and days ahead, that she already knew. But for the time being, she knelt and prayed and, for that moment at least, Kate and her Pearce were together in death as they never had been in life.

"Mammy, are you all right, darlin'? I know this is a ... well ... a sad day for you. But I've never seen you look like this. Not even at the height of my problems. What is it, dear?'

Her daughter came and knelt beside her and stroked Kate's work-worn hand, as all the while she awaited her mother's reply. When it came, Jenny was startled.

"Oh, Jenny lass. I'm just sitting here thinking; the world is unevenly divided. Some with more money than they can ever use, and others with not two farthings to rub together."

Jenny frowned.

"'Tis a fact of life, Mammy. Sure and we all know that. Why, even the hymns tell us that."

Kate smiled sadly.

"I was just thinking, what a wasted life it had been for your poor Dadda, God rest his soul. And all my fault, of course, for having taken him away from the rich, good life at Laggan House. Now he's dead, I just feel so guilty."

Jenny rose to her feet and glanced at the wall-clock.

"Listen, Mammy, I'm going to make you a wee cup of tea. We've still got time. And it'll maybe stop all this havering. Can't think what's got into you this morning."

As Jenny turned away towards the sink, Kate reached out and caught hold of her daughter's hand.

"What little money he had in life he spent on us. Aye, and even on that ill-fated holiday for us, doon the watter."

Jenny looked down with compassion at her Mammy where she still sat at the kitchen table. She laid a comforting hand on her mother's cheek.

"Come on now, Mammy, we've important things to do. We've still to set the table for the funeral tea before we leave for the Necropolis. And you said it yourself, Granny Gorbals will be in any minute with some home-baking for the feast."

Jenny gave her mother a last, loving embrace, gently disengaged her hand and went over to the sink to fill the black kettle from the goose-necked tap. Once she had set the kettle on the hob of the blazing fire, she again turned to her mother.

"Tell you what, Mammy. You put out the mugs and I'll go in next door and help Granny through with the baking. Then we can all have a wee cup of tea together before we get dressed for the funeral. All right, dear? It might cheer you up a bit to have a wee blether with Granny."

By the time that Jenny and Granny Gorbals returned, both laden with plates piled high with pancakes, soda-bread, potato-cakes and even fingers of shortbread, Kate had still not stirred sufficiently to lay out the necessary three mugs. And the kettle on the hob was boiling furiously.

Jenny made no comment, but after laying the plates of sweet-bites on the table, she set about making a pot of tea.

Granny, her burden also deposited, came over and, throwing her arms wide, embraced her old friend and neighbour. The two women stayed locked in their silent embrace.

Once they were all seated round the table, Granny glanced over at the still-sleeping figure of Hannah.

"Aye. Just as well to let the poor girl sleep as long as possible. Once we've arranged the table for the funeral tea, time enough then to get her ready in her go-chair. Then Jenny can wheel both Hannah and wee Theresa in next door for me. I'll look after the pair of them while you and Jenny are at the funeral up at the Necropolis.

Kate shook her head sadly.

"Granny, Granny. What would I do without you?"

The old woman stretched over a hand which she laid on Kate's arm.

"Now, Kate. Don't go getting yourself worked up. You'll have enough upset before this day is through. That you will."

Kate gave a sad smile.

"You're right, Granny. I'll be glad when this day's work is over. And that's the truth. Mind you, poor Jenny has already had a time of it with me and my grieving."

"We had all better get a move on," Jenny said. "Or at this rate, poor old Dadda is going to be late for his own funeral."

The afternoon of Pearce's funeral, the whole street turned out, after having first drawn the blinds on every window, in the accepted and properly respectful manner. Not that any one of the neighbours had had much time for the cantankerous old man in life, yet in death it was a totally different matter. They came, not only out of a mark of respect to the universally liked Kate, but also out of a much more mundane reason. Knowing that the Kinnon household was locally famed as a guid meat-hoose the mourners were well aware that they'd be sure of a substantial funeral tea after the cemetery rites had been observed.

The day itself dawned dull with a grey, depressing drizzle and occasional sleet which dripped and whinged away throughout the morning, almost in the same way as Pearce himself had for so many years.

The local Episcopalian rector was persuaded to conduct the short interment service at the-graveside in Glasgow's vast Necropolis instead of the priest from the High Anglican Church Pearce had preferred.

The one bright spot in the day was when Kate, surrounded as she was on all sides by her daughter Jenny, her friends and neighbours, leant forward and laid a carefully hoarded pressed shamrock on the top of his coffin. At that very moment, as if right on cue, the sun broke forth from the grey, overcast sky and it was as if a searchlight beamed down on the tiny part of dear old Ireland which would go with Pearce to his grave. As the coffin was lowered into the depths of the earth, a lone piper played a haunting Scottish lament. This last touch had been Kate's own idea.

She remembered that the one happy time in their married life had been the one all-too-brief start of that long ago and ill-fated holiday doon the watter in Royal Rothesay. She could still recall the look of rare pleasure on her husband's face each time they had gone down to the pier, there to listen to the local band of pipers who often greeted the packed incoming boats of happy holidaymakers.

When she was making the myriad and essential arrangements for the funeral, the thought had come to her:

'I wasn't able to make him happy very often in life, so perhaps there's something I can do for him in death, to give him a good send-off.'

In the days that followed, she had racked her brains well into the wee small hours for what that special something might be. Then in a flash, one morning at dawn, it came to her.

'I know, I could use some of the money that Danny left with me, that Pearce would never let me spend, to pay a piper, to help him on his way to the Other Shore.'

She had actually seen a walking funeral while on the Island of Bute and the memory of it had stayed with her. Apparently, it had been some local dignitary and as his friends and mourners had bade him a sad farewell. At the harbour, the final, memorable mark of respect had been a haunting dirge played by a lone piper, resplendent in the regalia of full Highland dress.

As Kate relived the stirring memory of it, so strengthened her resolve to make sure that Pearce got the full and final respect due to him as the scion of the landed gentry. Throughout their life together, this respect for his exalted station in life had been all too sadly missing, as she knew to her cost in her dealings with the sad, embittered man he had become latterly. As his widow, it was up to her to ensure that her husband, materially poor as he had been throughout his life, and solely on account of his disastrous marriage to herself, would at least never have to lie in a pauper's grave.

So it was, as the haunting notes drifted in the air around them, Kate and Jenny bade their own farewell to Pearce Claude Kinnon.

Later that same day, at the funeral tea of cold boiled ham, eggs, tomatoes, soda-bread, pancakes, meringues, and even shortbread and a quivering jelly, all washed down with liberal helpings of whisky for the men and sherry for the women, Kate reflected that her life would never be the same again. True, she still had poor Hannah, Jenny, and the bairn, her wee job at the newsagents, and her cleaning jobs, but never again would she ever have to submit to a bitter husband's fierce rages, black moods of depression and dictatorial manner. No. No matter how she looked at it, life in the years ahead would take on an entirely different pattern and a new meaning for Kate Kinnon.

While Kate was thus sunk deep in her own thoughts, all around her the mood and noise level of the funeral tea was becoming more exuberant, as the good food and excellent whisky and sherry began to work its magic.

She was suddenly aware of a man's voice at her ear. Startled out of her reverie, she turned her head and found that she was staring into the glowing eyes of Auld Shuggie. He shook his head in mock annoyance.

"I said, and I don't think ye heard a word, I said, you've fair done Pearce proud this day, Kate."

Kate smiled and waved a dismissive hand towards the crumbs of the feast.

"Oh, 'twas Jenny and Granny to thank for such a spread."

But Shuggie, determined to compliment his hostess, would not be thwarted in his purpose.

"Aye, that's as maybe, Kate. But 'twas yourself, I'll be bound, who arranged for a piper, an Episcopalian Priest, and a layer of prime ground in the Necropolis. Aye, you've done him proud. Given him a grand send-off. As well as that, old Granny tells me you observed to the letter all the other important old customs. Stopping the clock and covering with a white napkin the mirror in the room where he breathed his last. Yes, altogether a grand send-off, Kate. I just hope I'll be as lucky when my time comes to cross to the land o' the Leal."

It was at this point that Kate's old friend, Big Betty Donovan, reached across and patted her hostess's hand.

"Shuggie's right, Kate. He couldn't have had a better send-off to the Other Shore, had he been Royalty himself."

With the sound of laughter, spirited discussion and maudlin sentiment raging all around her, Kate again retreated to the haven of her own thoughts and quiet introspection.

'Well, thank God the funeral has been such a success. Just a pity that the high-and-mighty Josephine Delaney, nor Lady Christabel herself could not have witnessed the triumph of it. Oh, well. Can't be helped. Anyway, there's one good thing. If the folks hereabouts remember nothing else, they'll at least know that my Pearce was a true Irish gentleman. And, God willing, they'll remember that he had

a burial, and a funeral tea, fully befitting his station in life. At least that's something.'

Shuggie's voice drew her back to awareness of the people round her.

"I hope ye dinnae mind, Kate, but I invited an auld friend of yours tae pay his respects."

From behind Shuggie, Terence stepped out.

"I only got back to Glasgow yesterday, Kate, and met with Shuggie this morning. I'm right sorry for your loss. Maybe we can talk again later like we used to?"

Kate smiled at him.

"I'll look forward to that, Terence."

Life, Fate, Destiny, call it what you will, was not yet finished with Kate Rafferty Kinnon.

She would survive.

The End

Also Available from BeWrite Books

Crime

The Knotted Cord	Alistair Kinnon
The Tangled Skein	Alistair Kinnon
Marks	Sam Smith
Porlock Counterpoint	Sam Smith
Scent of Crime	Linda Stone

Crime/Humour

Sweet Molly Maguire	Terry Houston

Horror

Chill	Terri Pine, Peter Lee, Andrew Müller

Fantasy/Humour

Zolin A Rockin' Good Wizard	Barry Ireland
The Hundredfold Problem	John Grant
Earthdoom!	David Langford & John Grant

Fantasy

The Far-Enough Window	John Grant
A Season of Strange Dreams	C. S. Thompson

Collections/ Short Stories

As the Crow Flies	Dave Hutchinson
The Loss of Innocence	Jay Mandal
Kaleidoscope	Various
Odie Dodie	Lad Moore
Tailwind	Lad Moore
The Miller Moth	Mike Broemmel
The Shadow Cast	Mike Broemmel

Humour

The Cuckoos of Batch Magna	Peter Maughan

Thriller

Deep Ice	Karl Kofoed
Blood Money	Azam Gill
Evil Angel	RD Larson
Disremembering Eddie	Anne Morgellyn
Flight to Pakistan	Azam Gill
Matabele Gold	Michael J Hunt
Removing Edith Mary	Anne Morgellyn
The African Journals of Petros Amm	Michael J Hunt

Historical Fiction

Ring of Stone	Hugh McCracken
Jahred and The Magi	Wilma Clark

Contemporary

The Care Vortex	Sam Smith
Someplace Like Home	Terrence Moore
Sick Ape	Sam Smith
A Tangle of Roots	David Hough
Whispers of Ghosts	Ron McLachlan

Young Adult

Rules of the Hunt	Hugh McCracken
The Time Drum	Hugh McCracken
Kitchen Sink Concert	Ishbel Moore
The Fat Moon Dance	Elizabeth Taylor
Grandfather and The Ghost	Hugh McCracken
Return from the Hunt	Hugh McCracken

Children's

The Secret Portal	Reno Charlton
The Vampire Returns	Reno Charlton

Autobiography/Biography

A Stranger and Afraid	Arthur Allwright
Vera & Eddy's War	Sam Smith

Poetry

A Moment for Me	Heather Grace
Shaken & Stirred	Various
Letters from Portugal	Jan Oskar Hansen
Routes	Twelve poets. A road less traveled.
Vinegar Moon	Donna Biffar

General

The Wounded Stone	Terry Houston
Magpies and Sunsets	Neil Alexander Marr
Redemption of Quapaw Mountain	Bertha Sutliff

Romance

A Different Kind of Love	Jay Mandal
The Dandelion Clock	Jay Mandal

Science Fiction

Gemini Turns	Anne Marie Duquette

Coming Soon

The Creature in the Rose	Various
And then the night	C.S. Thompson

All the above titles are available from

www.bewrite.net

Printed in the United Kingdom
by Lightning Source UK Ltd.
102094UKS00001B/91-153